Doctor Grimshawe's Secret

A Romance

by

Nathaniel Hawthorne

Doctor Grimshawe's Secret
A Romance
by Nathaniel Hawthorne

ISBN: 978-93-68097-47-1

Published by

DOUBLE 9 BOOKS

2/13-B, Ansari Road
Daryaganj, New Delhi – 110002
info@double9books.com
www.double9books.com
Tel. 011-40042856

ABOUT THE AUTHOR

Nathaniel Hawthorne (1804–1864) was an influential American novelist and short story writer known for his exploration of darker side of human nature. His works often delve into the complexities of the human soul, particularly the effects of Puritan morality on individual lives. His most famous work, The Scarlet Letter (1850), examines shame and social ostracism. Other significant works include The House of the Seven Gables (1851), a gothic tale of family curses and the past's haunting influence, and Young Goodman Brown (1835), a short story about the battle between good and evil. Doctor Grimshawe's Secret (1883), published posthumously, explores themes of mystery, identity, and the supernatural through the story of a reclusive doctor with a dark past.

Hawthorne's legacy as a master of psychological depth and moral complexity endures. His works continue to be studied for their insight into human nature, societal expectations, and the complexities of guilt and redemption.

CONTENTS

PREFACE

A preface generally begins with a truism; and I may set out with the admission that it is not always expedient to bring to light the posthumous work of great writers. A man generally contrives to publish, during his lifetime, quite as much as the public has time or inclination to read; and his surviving friends are apt to show more zeal than discretion in dragging forth from his closed desk such undeveloped offspring of his mind as he himself had left to silence. Literature has never been redundant with authors who sincerely undervalue their own productions; and the sagacious critics who maintain that what of his own an author condemns must be doubly damnable, are, to say the least of it, as often likely to be right as wrong.

Beyond these general remarks, however, it does not seem necessary to adopt an apologetic attitude. There is nothing in the present volume which any one possessed of brains and cultivation will not be thankful to read. The appreciation of Nathaniel Hawthorne's writings is more intelligent and wide-spread than it used to be; and the later development of our national literature has not, perhaps, so entirely exhausted our resources of admiration as to leave no welcome for even the less elaborate work of a contemporary of Dickens and Thackeray. As regards "Doctor Grimshawe's Secret," — the title which, for lack of a better, has been given to this Romance, — it can scarcely be pronounced deficient in either elaboration or profundity. Had Mr. Hawthorne written out the story in every part to its full dimensions, it could not have failed to rank among the greatest of his productions. He had looked forward to it as to the crowning achievement of his literary career. In the Preface to "Our Old Home" he alludes to it as a work into which he proposed to convey more of various modes of truth than he could have grasped by a direct effort. But circumstances prevented him from perfecting the design which had been before his mind for seven years, and upon the shaping of which he bestowed more thought and labor than upon anything else he had undertaken. The successive and consecutive series of notes or studies [Footnote: These studies, extracts from which will be published in one of our magazines, are hereafter to be added, in their complete form, to the Appendix of this volume.] which he wrote for this Romance would of themselves make a small volume, and one of autobiographical as well as literary interest. There is no other instance, that I happen to have met with, in which a writer's thought reflects itself upon paper so immediately and sensitively as in these studies. To read them is to look into the man's mind, and see its quality and action. The penetration, the subtlety, the tenacity; the stubborn gripe which he lays upon his subject, like that of Hercules upon the slippery Old Man of the Sea; the clear and cool common-sense, controlling the audacity of a rich and ardent imagination; the humorous gibes and strange expletives wherewith he ridicules, to himself, his own failure to reach his goal; the immense patience with which—again and again, and yet again—he "tries back," throwing the topic into fresh attitudes, and searching it to the marrow with a gaze so piercing as to be terrible;—all this gives an impression of power, of resource, of energy, of mastery, that exhilarates the reader. So many inspired prophets of Hawthorne have arisen of late, that the present writer, whose relation to the great Romancer is a filial one merely, may be excused for feeling some embarrassment in submitting his own uninstructed judgments to competition with theirs. It has occurred to him, however, that these undress rehearsals of the author of "The Scarlet Letter" might afford entertaining and even profitable reading to the later generation of writers whose pleasant fortune it is to charm one another and the public. It would appear that this author, in his preparatory work at least, has ventured in some manner to disregard the modern canons which debar writers from betraying towards their creations any warmer feeling than a cultured and critical indifference: nor was his interest in human nature such as to confine him to the dissection of the moral epidermis of shop-girls and hotel-boarders. On the contrary, we are presented with the spectacle of a Titan, baring his arms and plunging heart and soul into the arena, there to struggle for death or victory with the superb phantoms summoned to the conflict by his own genius. The men of new times and new conditions will achieve their triumphs in new ways; but it may still be worth while to consider the methods and materials of one who also, in his own fashion, won and wore the laurel of those who know and can portray the human heart.

But let us return to the Romance, in whose clear though shadowy atmosphere the thunders and throes of the preparatory struggle are inaudible and invisible, save as they are implied in the fineness of substance and beauty of form of the artistic structure. The story is divided into two parts, the scene of the first being laid in America; that of the second, in England. Internal evidence of various kinds goes to show that the second part was the first written; or, in other words, that the present first part is a rewriting of an original first part, afterwards discarded, and of which the existing second part is the continuation. The two parts overlap, and it shall be left to the ingenuity of critics to detect the precise point of junction. In rewriting the first part, the author made sundry minor alterations in the plot and characters of the story, which alterations were not carried into the second part. It results from this that the manuscript presents various apparent inconsistencies. In transcribing the work for the press, these inconsistent sentences and passages have been withdrawn from the text and inserted in the Appendix; or, in a few unimportant instances, omitted altogether. In other respects, the text is printed as the author left it, with the exception of the names of the characters. In the manuscript each personage figures in the course of the narrative under from three to six different names. This difficulty has been met by bestowing upon each of the *dramatis personæ* the name which last identified him to the author's mind, and keeping him to it throughout the volume.

The story, as a story, is complete as it stands; it has a beginning, a middle, and an end. There is no break in the narrative, and the legitimate conclusion is reached. To say that the story is complete as a work of art, would be quite another matter. It lacks balance and proportion. Some characters and incidents are portrayed with minute elaboration; others, perhaps not less important, are merely sketched in outline. Beyond a doubt it was the author's purpose to rewrite the entire work from the first page to the last, enlarging it, deepening it, adorning it with every kind of spiritual and physical beauty, and rounding out a moral worthy of the noble materials. But these last transfiguring touches to Aladdin's Tower were never to be given; and he has departed, taking with him his Wonderful Lamp. Nevertheless there is great splendor in the structure as we behold it. The character of old Doctor Grimshawe, and the picture of his surroundings, are hardly surpassed in vigor by anything their author has produced; and the dusky vision of the secret chamber, which sends a mysterious shiver through the tale, seems to be unique even in Hawthorne.

There have been included in this volume photographic reproductions of certain pages of the original manuscript of Doctor Grimshawe, selected at random, upon which those ingenious persons whose convictions are in advance of their instruction are cordially invited to try their teeth; for it has been maintained that Mr. Hawthorne's handwriting was singularly legible. The present writer possesses specimens of Mr. Hawthorne's chirography at various ages, from boyhood until a day or two before his death. Like the handwriting of most men, it was at its best between the twenty-fifth and the fortieth years of life; and in some instances it is a remarkably beautiful type of penmanship. But as time went on it deteriorated, and, while of course retaining its elementary characteristics, it became less and less easy to read, especially in those writings which were intended solely for his own perusal. As with other men of sensitive organization, the mood of the hour, a good or a bad pen, a ready or an obstructed flow of thought, would all be reflected in the formation of the written letters and words. In the manuscript of the fragmentary sketch which has just been published in a magazine, which is written in an ordinary commonplace-book, with ruled pages, and in which the author had not yet become possessed with the spirit of the story and characters, the handwriting is deliberate and clear. In the manuscript of "Doctor Grimshawe's Secret," on the other hand, which was written almost immediately after the other, but on unruled paper, and when the writer's imagination was warm and eager, the chirography is for the most part a compact mass of minute cramped hieroglyphics, hardly to be deciphered save by flashes of inspiration. The matter is not, in itself, of importance, and is alluded to here only as having been brought forward in connection with other insinuations, with the notice of which it seems unnecessary to soil these pages. Indeed, were I otherwise disposed, Doctor Grimshawe himself would take the words out of my mouth; his speech is far more poignant and eloquent than mine. In dismissing this episode, I will take the liberty to observe that it appears to indicate a spirit in our age less sceptical than is commonly supposed,—belief in miracles being still possible, provided only the miracle be a scandalous one.

It remains to tell how this Romance came to be published. It came into my possession (in the ordinary course of events) about eight years ago. I had at that time no intention of publishing it; and when, soon after, I left England to travel on the Continent, the manuscript, together with the bulk of my library, was packed and stored at a London repository, and was not again seen by me until last summer, when I unpacked it in this city. I then finished the perusal of it, and, finding it to be practically complete, I re-resolved to print it in connection with a biography of Mr. Hawthorne which I had in preparation. But upon further consideration it was decided to publish the Romance separately; and I herewith present it to the public, with my best wishes for their edification.

JULIAN HAWTHORNE

NEW YORK, November 21, 1882.

CHAPTER I

A long time ago, [Endnote: 1] in a town with which I used to be familiarly acquainted, there dwelt an elderly person of grim aspect, known by the name and title of Doctor Grimshawe,[Endnote: 2] whose household consisted of a remarkably pretty and vivacious boy, and a perfect rosebud of a girl, two or three years younger than he, and an old maid-of-all-work, of strangely mixed breed, crusty in temper and wonderfully sluttish in attire. [Endnote: 3] It might be partly owing to this handmaiden's characteristic lack of neatness (though primarily, no doubt, to the grim Doctor's antipathy to broom, brush, and dusting-cloths) that the house—at least in such portions of it as any casual visitor caught a glimpse of—was so overlaid with dust, that, in lack of a visiting card, you might write your name with your forefinger upon the tables; and so hung with cobwebs that they assumed the appearance of dusky upholstery.

It grieves me to add an additional touch or two to the reader's disagreeable impression of Doctor Grimshawe's residence, by confessing that it stood in a shabby by-street, and cornered on a graveyard, with which the house communicated by a back door; so that with a hop, skip, and jump from the threshold, across a flat tombstone, the two children [Endnote: 4] were in the daily habit of using the dismal cemetery as their playground. In their graver moods they spelled out the names and learned by heart doleful verses on the headstones; and in their merrier ones (which were much the more frequent) they chased butterflies and gathered dandelions, played hide-and-seek among the slate and marble, and tumbled laughing over the grassy mounds which were too eminent for the short legs to bestride. On the whole, they were the better for the graveyard, and its legitimate inmates slept none the worse for the two children's gambols and shrill merriment overhead. Here were old brick tombs with curious sculptures on them, and quaint gravestones, some of which bore puffy little cherubs, and one or two others the effigies of eminent Puritans, wrought out to a button, a fold of the ruff, and a wrinkle of the skull-cap; and these frowned upon the two children as if death had not made them a whit more genial than they were in life. But the children were of a temper to be more encouraged by the good-natured smiles of the puffy cherubs, than frightened or disturbed by the sour Puritans.

This graveyard (about which we shall say not a word more than may sooner or later be needful) was the most ancient in the town. The clay of the original settlers had been incorporated with the soil; those stalwart Englishmen of the Puritan epoch, whose immediate ancestors had been planted forth with succulent grass and daisies for the sustenance of the parson's cow, round the low-battlemented Norman church towers in the villages of the fatherland, had here contributed their rich Saxon mould to tame and Christianize the wild forest earth of the new world. In this point of view—as holding the bones and dust of the primeval ancestor—the cemetery was more English than anything else in the neighborhood, and might probably have nourished English oaks and English elms, and whatever else is of English growth, without that tendency to spindle upwards and lose their sturdy breadth, which is said to be the ordinary characteristic both of human and vegetable productions when transplanted hither. Here, at all events, used to be some specimens of common English garden flowers, which could not be accounted for,—unless, perhaps, they had sprung from some English maiden's heart, where the intense love of those homely things, and regret of them in the foreign land, had conspired together to keep their vivifying principle, and cause its growth after the poor girl was buried. Be that as it might, in this grave had been hidden from sight many a broad, bluff visage of husbandman, who had been taught to plough among the hereditary furrows that had been ameliorated by the crumble of ages: much had these sturdy laborers grumbled at the great roots that obstructed their toil in these fresh acres. Here, too, the sods had covered the faces of men known to history, and reverenced when not a piece of distinguishable dust remained of them; personages whom tradition told about; and here, mixed up with successive crops of native-born Americans, had been ministers, captains, matrons, virgins good and evil, tough and tender, turned up and battened down by the sexton's spade, over and over again; until every blade of grass had its relations with the human brotherhood of the old town. A hundred and fifty years was sufficient to do this; and so much time, at least, had elapsed since the first hole was dug among the difficult roots of the forest trees, and the first little hillock of all these green beds was piled up.

Thus rippled and surged, with its hundreds of little billows, the old graveyard about the house which cornered upon it; it made the street gloomy, so that people did not altogether like to pass along the high wooden fence that shut it in; and the old house itself, covering ground which else had been sown thickly with buried bodies, partook of its dreariness, because it seemed hardly possible that the dead people should not get up out of their graves and steal in to warm themselves at this convenient fireside. But I never heard that any of them did so; nor were the children ever startled by spectacles of dim horror in the night-time, but were as cheerful and fearless as if no grave had ever been dug. They were of that class of children whose material seems fresh, not taken at second hand, full of disease, conceits, whims, and weaknesses, that have already served many people's turns, and been moulded up, with some little change of combination, to serve the turn of some poor spirit that could not get a better case.

So far as ever came to the present writer's knowledge, there was no whisper of Doctor Grimshawe's house being haunted; a fact on which both writer and reader may congratulate themselves, the ghostly chord having been played upon in these days until it has become wearisome and nauseous as the familiar tune of a barrel-organ. The house itself, moreover, except for the convenience of its position close to the seldom-disturbed cemetery, was hardly worthy to be haunted. As I remember it, (and for aught I know it still exists in the same guise,) it did not appear to be an ancient structure, nor one that would ever have been the abode of a very wealthy or prominent family;—a three-story wooden house, perhaps a century old, low-studded, with a square front, standing right upon the street, and a small enclosed porch, containing the main entrance, affording a glimpse up and down the street through an oval window on each side, its characteristic was decent respectability, not sinking below the boundary of the genteel. It has often perplexed my mind to conjecture what sort of man he could have been who, having the means to build a pretty, spacious, and comfortable residence, should have chosen to lay its foundation on the brink of so many graves; each tenant of these narrow houses crying out, as it were, against the absurdity of bestowing much time or pains in preparing any earthly tabernacle save such as theirs. But deceased people see matters from an erroneous—at least too exclusive—point of view; a comfortable grave is an excellent possession for those who need it, but a comfortable house has likewise its merits and temporary advantages. [Endnote: 5.]

The founder of the house in question seemed sensible of this truth, and had therefore been careful to lay out a sufficient number of rooms and chambers, low, ill-lighted, ugly, but not unsusceptible of warmth and comfort; the sunniest and cheerfulest of which were on the side that looked into the graveyard. Of these, the one most spacious and convenient had been selected by Doctor Grimshawe as a study, and fitted up with bookshelves, and various machines and contrivances, electrical, chemical, and distillatory, wherewith he might pursue such researches as were wont to engage his attention. The great result of the grim Doctor's labors, so far as known to the public, was a certain preparation or extract of cobwebs, which, out of a great abundance of material, he was able to produce in any desirable quantity, and by the administration of which he professed to cure diseases of the inflammatory class, and to work very wonderful effects upon the human system. It is a great pity, for the good of mankind and the advantage of his own fortunes, that he did not put forth this medicine in pill-boxes or bottles, and then, as it were, by some captivating title, inveigle the public into his spider's web, and suck out its gold substance, and himself wax fat as he sat in the central intricacy.

But grim Doctor Grimshawe, though his aim in life might be no very exalted one, seemed singularly destitute of the impulse to better his fortunes by the exercise of his wits: it might even have been supposed, indeed, that he had a conscientious principle or religious scruple—only, he was by no means a religious man—against reaping profit from this particular nostrum which he was said to have invented. He never sold it; never prescribed it, unless in cases selected on some principle that nobody could detect or explain. The grim Doctor, it must be observed, was not generally acknowledged by the profession, with whom, in truth, he had never claimed a fellowship; nor had he ever assumed, of his own accord the medical title by which the public chose to know him. His professional practice seemed, in a sort, forced upon him; it grew pretty extensive, partly because it was understood to be a matter of favor and difficulty, dependent on a capricious will, to obtain his services at all. There was unquestionably an odor of quackery about him; but by no means of an ordinary kind. A sort of mystery—yet which, perhaps, need not have been a mystery, had any one thought it worth while to make systematic inquiry in reference to his previous life, his education, even his native land—assisted the impression which his peculiarities were calculated to make. He was evidently not a New-Englander, nor a native of any part of these Western shores. His speech was apt to be oddly and uncouthly idiomatic, and even when classical in its form was emitted with a strange, rough depth of utterance, that came from recesses of the lungs which we Yankees seldom put to any use. In person, he did not look like one of us; a broad, rather short personage, with a projecting forehead, a red, irregular face, and a squab nose; eyes that looked dull enough in their ordinary state, but had a faculty, in conjunction with the other features, which those who had ever seen it described as especially ugly and awful. As regarded dress, Doctor Grimshawe had a rough and careless exterior, and altogether a shaggy kind of aspect, the effect of which was much increased by a reddish beard, which, contrary to the usual custom of the day, he allowed to grow profusely; and the wiry perversity of which seemed to know as little of the comb as of the razor.

We began with calling the grim Doctor an elderly personage; but in so doing we looked at him through the eyes of the two children, who were his intimates, and who had not learnt to decipher the purport and value of his wrinkles and furrows and corrugations, whether as indicating age, or a different kind of wear and tear. Possibly—he seemed so aggressive and had such latent heat and force to throw out when occasion called—he might scarcely have seemed middle-aged; though here again we hesitate, finding him so stiffened in his own way, so little fluid, so encrusted with passions and humors, that he must have left his youth very far behind him; if indeed he ever had any.

The patients, or whatever other visitors were ever admitted into the Doctor's study, carried abroad strange accounts of the squalor of dust and cobwebs in which the learned and scientific person lived; and the dust, they averred, was all the more disagreeable, because it could not well be other than dead men's almost intangible atoms, resurrected from the adjoining graveyard. As for the cobwebs, they were no signs of housewifely neglect on the part of crusty Hannah, the handmaiden; but the Doctor's scientific material, carefully encouraged and preserved, each filmy thread more valuable to him than so much golden wire. Of all barbarous haunts in Christendom or elsewhere, this study was the one most overrun with spiders. They dangled from the ceiling, crept upon the tables, lurked in the corners, and wove the intricacy of their webs wherever they could hitch the end from point to point across the window-panes, and even across the upper part of the doorway, and in the chimney-place. It seemed impossible to move without breaking some of these mystic threads. Spiders crept familiarly towards you and walked leisurely across your hands: these were their precincts, and you only an intruder. If you had none about your person, yet you had an odious sense of one crawling up your spine, or spinning cobwebs in your brain,—so pervaded was the atmosphere of the place with spider-life. What they fed upon (for all the flies for miles about would not have sufficed them) was a secret known only to the Doctor. Whence they came was another riddle; though, from certain inquiries and transactions of Doctor Grimshawe's with some of the shipmasters of the port, who followed the East and West Indian, the African and the South American trade, it was supposed that this odd philosopher was in the habit of importing choice monstrosities in the spider kind from all those tropic regions. [Endnote: 6.]

All the above description, exaggerated as it may seem, is merely preliminary to the introduction of one single enormous spider, the biggest and ugliest ever seen, the pride of the grim Doctor's heart, his treasure, his glory, the pearl of his soul, and, as many people said, the demon to whom he had sold his salvation, on condition of possessing the web of the foul creature for a certain number of years. The grim Doctor, according to this theory, was but a great fly which this spider had subtly entangled in his web. But, in truth, naturalists are acquainted with this spider, though it is a rare one; the British Museum has a specimen, and, doubtless, so have many other scientific institutions. It is found in South America; its most hideous spread of legs covers a space nearly as large as a dinner-plate, and radiates from a body as big as a door-knob, which one conceives to be an agglomeration of sucked-up poison which the creature treasures through life; probably to expend it all, and life itself, on some worthy foe. Its colors, variegated in a sort of ugly and inauspicious splendor, were distributed over its vast bulb in great spots, some of which glistened like gems. It was a horror to think of this thing living; still more horrible to think of the foul catastrophe, the crushed-out and wasted poison, that would follow the casual setting foot upon it.

No doubt, the lapse of time since the Doctor and his spider lived has already been sufficient to cause a traditionary wonderment to gather over them both; and, especially, this image of the spider dangles down to us from the dusky ceiling of the Past, swollen into somewhat uglier and huger monstrosity than he actually possessed. Nevertheless, the creature had a real existence, and has left kindred like himself; but as for the Doctor, nothing could exceed the value which he seemed to put upon him, the sacrifices he made for the creature's convenience, or the readiness with which he adapted his whole mode of life, apparently, so that the spider might enjoy the conditions best suited to his tastes, habits, and health. And yet there were sometimes tokens that made people imagine that he hated the infernal creature as much as everybody else who caught a glimpse of him. [Endnote: 7.]

CHAPTER II

Considering that Doctor Grimshawe, when we first look upon him, had dwelt only a few years in the house by the graveyard, it is wonderful what an appearance he, and his furniture, and his cobwebs, and their unweariable spinners, and crusty old Hannah, all had of having permanently attached themselves to the locality. For a century, at least, it might be fancied that the study in particular had existed just as it was now; with those dusky festoons of spider-silk hanging along the walls, those book-cases with volumes turning their parchment or black-leather backs upon you, those machines and engines, that table, and at it the Doctor, in a very faded and shabby dressing-gown, smoking a long clay pipe, the powerful fumes of which dwelt continually in his reddish and grisly beard, and made him fragrant wherever he went. This sense of fixedness—stony intractability—seems to belong to people who, instead of hope, which exalts everything into an airy, gaseous exhilaration, have a fixed and dogged purpose, around which everything congeals and crystallizes. [Endnote: 1] Even the sunshine, dim through the dustiness of the two casements that looked upon the graveyard, and the smoke, as it came warm out of Doctor Grimshawe's mouth, seemed already stale. But if the two children, or either of them, happened to be in the study,—if they ran to open the door at the knock, if they came scampering and peeped down over the banisters,—the sordid and rusty gloom was apt to vanish quite away. The sunbeam itself looked like a golden rule, that had been flung down long ago, and had lain there till it was dusty and tarnished. They were cheery little imps, who sucked up fragrance and pleasantness out of their surroundings, dreary as these looked; even as a flower can find its proper perfume in any soil where its seed happens to fall. The great spider, hanging by his cordage over the Doctor's head, and waving slowly, like a pendulum, in a blast from the crack of the door, must have made millions and millions of precisely such vibrations as these; but the children were new, and made over every day, with yesterday's weariness left out.

The little girl, however, was the merrier of the two. It was quite unintelligible, in view of the little care that crusty Hannah took of her, and, moreover, since she was none of your prim, fastidious children, how daintily she kept herself amid all this dust; how the spider's webs never clung to her, and how, when—without being solicited—she clambered into the Doctor's arms and kissed him, she bore away no smoky reminiscences of the pipe that he kissed continually. She had a free, mellow, natural laughter, that seemed the ripened fruit of the smile that was generally on her little face, to be shaken off and scattered abroad by any breeze that came along. Little Elsie made playthings of everything, even of the grim Doctor, though against his will, and though, moreover, there were tokens now and then that the sight of this bright little creature was not a pleasure to him, but, on the contrary, a positive pain; a pain, nevertheless, indicating a profound interest, hardly less deep than though Elsie had been his daughter.

Elsie did not play with the great spider, but she moved among the whole brood of spiders as if she saw them not, and, being endowed with other senses than those allied to these things, might coexist with them and not be sensible of their presence. Yet the child, I suppose, had her crying fits, and her pouting fits, and naughtiness enough to entitle her to live on earth; at least crusty Hannah often said so, and often made grievous complaint of disobedience, mischief, or breakage, attributable to little Elsie; to which the grim Doctor seldom responded by anything more intelligible than a puff of tobacco-smoke, and, sometimes, an imprecation; which, however, hit crusty Hannah instead of the child. Where the child got the tenderness that a child needs to live upon, is a mystery to me; perhaps from some aged or dead mother, or in her dreams; perhaps from some small modicum of it, such as boys have, from the little boy; or perhaps it was from a Persian kitten, which had grown to be a cat in her arms, and slept in her little bed, and now assumed grave and protective airs towards her former playmate. [Endnote: 2.]

The boy, [Endnote: 3] as we have said, was two or three years Elsie's elder, and might now be about six years old. He was a healthy and cheerful child, yet of a graver mood than the little girl, appearing to lay a more forcible grasp on the circumstances about him, and to tread with a heavier footstep on the solid earth; yet perhaps not more so than was the necessary difference between a man-blossom, dimly conscious of coming things, and a mere baby, with whom there was neither past nor future. Ned, as he was named, was subject very early to fits of musing, the subject of which—if they had any definite subject, or were more than vague reveries—it was impossible to guess. They were of those states of mind, probably, which are beyond the sphere of human language, and would necessarily lose their essence in the attempt to communicate or record them. The little girl, perhaps, had some mode of sympathy with these unuttered thoughts or reveries, which grown people had ceased to have; at all events, she early learned to respect them, and, at other times as free and playful as her Persian kitten, she never in such circumstances ventured on any greater freedom than to sit down quietly beside him, and endeavor to look as thoughtful as the boy himself.

Once, slowly emerging from one of these waking reveries, little Ned gazed about him, and saw Elsie sitting with this pretty pretence of thoughtfulness and dreaminess in her little chair, close beside him; now and then peeping under her eyelashes to note what changes might come over his face. After looking at her a moment or two, he quietly took her willing and warm little hand in his own, and led her up to the Doctor.

The group, methinks, must have been a picturesque one, made up as it was of several apparently discordant elements, each of which happened to be so combined as to make a more effective whole. The beautiful grave boy, with a little sword by his side and a feather in his hat, of a brown complexion, slender, with his white brow and dark, thoughtful eyes, so earnest upon some mysterious theme; the prettier little girl, a blonde, round, rosy, so truly sympathetic with her companion's mood, yet unconsciously turning all to sport by her attempt to assume one similar;—these two standing at the grim Doctor's footstool; he meanwhile, black, wild-bearded, heavy-browed, red-eyed, wrapped in his faded dressing-gown, puffing out volumes of vapor from his long pipe, and making, just at that instant, application to a tumbler, which, we regret to say, was generally at his elbow, with some dark-colored potation in it that required to be frequently replenished from a neighboring black bottle. Half, at least, of the fluids in the grim Doctor's system must have been derived from that same black bottle, so constant was his familiarity with its contents; and yet his eyes were never redder at one time than another, nor his utterance thicker, nor his mood perceptibly the brighter or the duller for all his conviviality. It is true, when, once, the bottle happened to be empty for a whole day together, Doctor Grimshawe was observed by crusty Hannah and by the children to be considerably fiercer than usual: so that probably, by some maladjustment of consequences, his intemperance was only to be found in refraining from brandy.

Nor must we forget—in attempting to conceive the effect of these two beautiful children in such a sombre room, looking on the graveyard, and contrasted with the grim Doctor's aspect of heavy and smouldering fierceness—that over his head, at this very moment, dangled the portentous spider, who seemed to have come down from his web aloft for the purpose of hearing what the two young people could have to say to his patron, and what reference it might have to certain mysterious documents which the Doctor kept locked up in a secret cupboard behind the door.

"Grim Doctor," said Ned, after looking up into the Doctor's face, as a sensitive child inevitably does, to see whether the occasion was favorable, yet determined to proceed with his purpose whether so or not,—"Grim Doctor, I want you to answer me a question."

"Here's to your good health, Ned!" quoth the Doctor, eying the pair intently, as he often did, when they were unconscious. "So you want to ask me a question? As many as you please, my fine fellow; and I shall answer as many, and as much, and as truly, as may please myself!"

"Ah, grim Doctor!" said the little girl, now letting go of Ned's hand, and climbing upon the Doctor's knee, "'ou shall answer as many as Ned please to ask, because to please him and me!"

"Well, child," said Doctor Grimshawe, "little Ned will have his rights at least, at my hands, if not other people's rights likewise; and, if it be right, I shall answer his question. Only, let him ask it at once; for I want to be busy thinking about something else."

"Then, Doctor Grim," said little Ned, "tell me, in the first place, where I came from, and how you came to have me?"

The Doctor looked at the little man, so seriously and earnestly putting this demand, with a perplexed, and at first it might almost seem a startled aspect.

"That is a question, indeed, my friend Ned!" ejaculated he, putting forth a whiff of smoke and imbibing a nip from his tumbler before he spoke; and perhaps framing his answer, as many thoughtful and secret people do, in such a way as to let out his secret mood to the child, because knowing he could not understand it: "Whence did you come? Whence did any of us come? Out of the darkness and mystery; out of nothingness; out of a kingdom of shadows; out of dust, clay, mud, I think, and to return to it again. Out of a former state of being, whence we have brought a good many shadowy revelations, purporting that it was no very pleasant one. Out of a former life, of which the present one is the hell!—And why are you come? Faith, Ned, he must be a wiser man than Doctor Grim who can tell why you or any other mortal came hither; only one thing I am well aware of,—it was not to be happy. To toil and moil and hope and fear; and to love in a shadowy, doubtful sort of way, and to hate in bitter earnest,—that is what you came for!"

"Ah, Doctor Grim! this is very naughty," said little Elsie. "You are making fun of little Ned, when he is in earnest."

"Fun!" quoth Doctor Grim, bursting into a laugh peculiar to him, very loud and obstreperous. "I am glad you find it so, my little woman. Well, and so you bid me tell absolutely where he came from?"

Elsie nodded her bright little head.

"And you, friend Ned, insist upon knowing?"

"That I do, Doctor Grim!" answered Ned. His white, childish brow had gathered into a frown, such was the earnestness of his determination; and he stamped his foot on the floor, as if ready to follow up his demand by an appeal to the little tin sword which hung by his side. The Doctor looked at him with a kind of smile,—not a very pleasant one; for it was an unamiable characteristic of his temper that a display of spirit, even in a child, was apt to arouse his immense combativeness, and make him aim a blow without much consideration how heavily it might fall, or on how unequal an antagonist.

"If you insist upon an answer, Master Ned, you shall have it," replied he. "You were taken by me, boy, a foundling from an almshouse; and if ever hereafter you desire to know your kindred, you must take your chance of the first man you meet. He is as likely to be your father as another!"

The child's eyes flashed, and his brow grew as red as fire. It was but a momentary fierceness; the next instant he clasped his hands over his face, and wept in a violent convulsion of grief and shame. Little Elsie clasped her arms about him, kissing his brow and chin, which were all that her lips could touch, under his clasped hands; but Ned turned away uncomforted, and was blindly making his way towards the door.

"Ned, my little fellow, come back!" said Doctor Grim, who had very attentively watched the cruel effect of his communication.

As the boy did not reply, and was still tending towards the door, the grim Doctor vouchsafed to lay aside his pipe, get up from his arm-chair (a thing he seldom did between supper and bedtime), and shuffle after the two children in his slippers. He caught them on the threshold, brought little Ned back by main force,—for he was a rough man even in his tenderness,—and, sitting down again and taking him on his knee, pulled away his hands from before his face. Never was a more pitiful sight than that pale countenance, so infantile still, yet looking old and experienced already, with a sense of disgrace, with a feeling of loneliness; so beautiful, nevertheless, that it seemed to possess all the characteristics which fine hereditary traits and culture, or many forefathers, could do in refining a human stock. And this was a nameless weed, sprouting from some chance seed by the dusty wayside!

"Ned, my dear old boy," said Doctor Grim,—and he kissed that pale, tearful face,—the first and last time, to the best of my belief, that he was ever betrayed into that tenderness; "forget what I have said! Yes, remember, if you like, that you came from an almshouse; but remember, too,—what your friend Doctor Grim is ready to affirm and make oath of,—that he can trace your kindred and race through that sordid experience, and back, back, for a hundred and fifty years, into an old English line. Come, little Ned, and look at this picture."

He led the boy by the hand to a corner of the room, where hung upon the wall a portrait which Ned had often looked at. It seemed an old picture; but the Doctor had had it cleaned and varnished, so that it looked dim and dark, and yet it seemed to be the representation of a man of no mark; not at least of such mark as would naturally leave his features to be transmitted for the interest of another generation. For he was clad in a mean dress of old fashion,—a leather jerkin it appeared to be,—and round his neck, moreover, was a noose of rope, as if he might have been on the point of being hanged. But the face of the portrait, nevertheless, was beautiful, noble, though sad; with a great development of sensibility, a look of suffering and endurance amounting to triumph,—a peace through all.

"Look at this," continued the Doctor, "if you must go on dreaming about your race. Dream that you are of the blood of this being; for, mean as his station looks, he comes of an ancient and noble race, and was the noblest of them all! Let me alone, Ned, and I shall spin out the web that shall link you to that man. The grim Doctor can do it!"

The grim Doctor's face looked fierce with the earnestness with which he said these words. You would have said that he was taking an oath to overthrow and annihilate a race, rather than to build one up by bringing forward the infant heir out of obscurity, and making plain the links— the filaments—which cemented this feeble childish life, in a far country, with the great tide of a noble life, which had come down like a chain from antiquity, in old England.

Having said the words, however, the grim Doctor appeared ashamed both of the heat and of the tenderness into which he had been betrayed; for rude and rough as his nature was, there was a kind of decorum in it, too, that kept him within limits of his own. So he went back to his chair, his pipe, and his tumbler, and was gruffer and more taciturn than ever for the rest of the evening. And after the children went to bed, he leaned back in his chair and looked up at the vast tropic spider, who was particularly busy in adding to the intricacies of his web; until he fell asleep with his eyes fixed in that direction, and the extinguished pipe in one hand and the empty tumbler in the other.

CHAPTER III

Doctor Grimshawe, after the foregone scene, began a practice of conversing more with the children than formerly; directing his discourse chiefly to Ned, although Elsie's vivacity and more outspoken and demonstrative character made her take quite as large a share in the conversation as he.

The Doctor's communications referred chiefly to a village, or neighborhood, or locality in England, which he chose to call Newnham; although he told the children that this was not the real name, which, for reasons best known to himself, he wished to conceal. Whatever the name were, he seemed to know the place so intimately, that the children, as a matter of course, adopted the conclusion that it was his birthplace, and the spot where he had spent his schoolboy days, and had lived until some inscrutable reason had impelled him to quit its ivy-grown antiquity, and all the aged beauty and strength that he spoke of, and to cross the sea.

He used to tell of an old church, far unlike the brick and pine-built meeting-houses with which the children were familiar; a church, the stones of which were laid, every one of them, before the world knew of the country in which he was then speaking: and how it had a spire, the lower part of which was mantled with ivy, and up which, towards its very spire, the ivy was still creeping; and how there was a tradition, that, if the ivy ever reached the top, the spire would fall upon the roof of the old gray church, and crush it all down among its surrounding tombstones. [Endnote: 1] And so, as this misfortune would be so heavy a one, there seemed to be a miracle wrought from year to year, by which the ivy, though always flourishing, could never grow beyond a certain point; so that the spire and church had stood unharmed for thirty years; though the wise old people were constantly foretelling that the passing year must be the very last one that it could stand.

He told, too, of a place that made little Ned blush and cast down his eyes to hide the tears of anger and shame at he knew not what, which would irresistibly spring into them; for it reminded him of the almshouse where, as the cruel Doctor said, Ned himself had had his earliest home. And yet, after all, it had scarcely a feature of resemblance; and there was this great point of difference,—that whereas, in Ned's wretched abode (a large, unsightly brick house), there were many wretched infants like himself, as well as helpless people of all ages, widows, decayed drunkards, people of feeble wits, and all kinds of imbecility; it being a haven for those who could not contend in the hard, eager, pitiless struggle of life; in the place the Doctor spoke of, a noble, Gothic, mossy structure, there were none but aged men, who had drifted into this quiet harbor to end their days in a sort of humble yet stately ease and decorous abundance. And this shelter, the grim Doctor said, was the gift of a man who had died ages ago; and having been a great sinner in his lifetime, and having drawn lands, manors, and a great mass of wealth into his clutches, by violent and unfair means, had thought to get his pardon by founding this Hospital, as it was called, in which thirteen old men should always reside; and he hoped that they would spend their time in praying for the welfare of his soul. [Endnote: 2.]

Said little Elsie, "I am glad he did it, and I hope the poor old men never forgot to pray for him, and that it did good to the poor wicked man's soul."

"Well, child," said Doctor Grimshawe, with a scowl into vacancy, and a sort of wicked leer of merriment at the same time, as if he saw before him the face of the dead man of past centuries, "I happen to be no lover of this man's race, and I hate him for the sake of one of his descendants. I don't think he succeeded in bribing the Devil to let him go, or God to save him!"

"Doctor Grim, you are very naughty!" said Elsie, looking shocked.

"It is fair enough," said Ned, "to hate your enemies to the very brink of the grave, but then to leave him to get what mercy he can."

"After shoving him in!" quoth the Doctor; and made no further response to either of these criticisms, which seemed indeed to affect him very little—if he even listened to them. For he was a man of singularly imperfect moral culture; insomuch that nothing else was so remarkable about him as that—possessing a good deal of intellectual ability, made available by much reading and experience—he was so very dark on the moral side; as if he needed the natural perceptions that should have enabled him to acquire that better wisdom. Such a phenomenon often meets us in life; oftener than we recognize, because a certain tact and exterior decency generally hide the moral deficiency. But often there is a mind well polished, married to a conscience and natural impulses left as they were in childhood, except that they have sprouted up into evil and poisonous weeds, richly blossoming with strong-smelling flowers, or seeds which the plant scatters by a sort of impulse; even as the Doctor was now half-consciously throwing seeds of his evil passions into the minds of these children. He was himself a grown-up child, without tact, simplicity, and innocence, and with ripened evil, all the ranker for a native heat that was in him and still active, which might have nourished good things as well as evil. Indeed, it did cherish by chance a root or two of good, the fragrance of which was sometimes perceptible among all this rank growth of poisonous weeds. A grown-up child he was,—that was all.

The Doctor now went on to describe an old country-seat, which stood near this village and the ancient Hospital that he had been telling about, and which was formerly the residence of the wicked man (a knight and a brave one, well known in the Lancastrian wars) who had founded the latter. It was a venerable old mansion, which a Saxon Thane had begun to build more than a thousand years ago, the old English oak that he built into the frame being still visible in the ancient skeleton of its roof, sturdy and strong as if put up yesterday. And the descendants of the man who built it, through the French line (for a Norman baron wedded the daughter and heiress of the Saxon), dwelt there yet; and in each century they had done something for the old Hall,—building a tower, adding a suite of rooms, strengthening what was already built, putting in a painted window, making it more spacious and convenient,—till it seemed as if Time employed himself in thinking what could be done for the old house. As fast as any part decayed, it was renewed, with such simple art that the new completed, as it were, and fitted itself to the old. So that it seemed as if the house never had been finished, until just that thing was added. For many an age, the possessors had gone on adding strength to strength, digging out the moat to a greater depth, piercing the walls with holes for archers to shoot through, or building a turret to keep watch upon. But at last all necessity for these precautions passed away, and then they thought of convenience and comfort, adding something in every generation to these. And by and by they thought of beauty too; and in this time helped them with its weather-stains, and the ivy that grew over the walls, and the grassy depth of the dried-up moat, and the abundant shade that grew up everywhere, where naked strength would have been ugly.

"One curious thing in the house," said the Doctor, lowering his voice, but with a mysterious look of triumph, and that old scowl, too, at the children, "was that they built a secret chamber,—a very secret one!"

"A secret chamber!" cried little Ned; "who lived in it? A ghost?"

"There was often use for it," said Doctor Grim; "hiding people who had fought on the wrong side, or Catholic priests, or criminals, or perhaps— who knows?—enemies that they wanted put out of the way,—troublesome folks. Ah! it was often of use, that secret chamber: and is so still!"

Here the Doctor paused a long while, and leaned back in his chair, slowly puffing long whiffs from his pipe, looking up at the great spider-demon that hung over his head, and, as it seemed to the children by the expression of his face, looking into the dim secret chamber which he had spoken of, and which, by something in his mode of alluding to it, assumed such a weird, spectral aspect to their imaginations that they never wished to hear of it again. Coming back at length out of his reverie,—returning, perhaps, out of some weird, ghostly, secret chamber of his memory, whereof the one in the old house was but the less horrible emblem,—he resumed his tale. He said that, a long time ago, a war broke out in the old country between King and Parliament. At that period there were several brothers of the old family (which had adhered to the Catholic religion), and these chose the side of the King instead of that of the Puritan Parliament: all but one, whom the family hated because he took the Parliament side; and he became a soldier, and fought against his own brothers; and it was said among them that, so inveterate was he, he went on the scaffold, masked, and was the very man who struck off the King's head, and that his foot trod in the King's blood, and that always afterwards he made a bloody track wherever he went. And there was a legend that his brethren once caught the renegade and imprisoned him in his own birthplace—

"In the secret chamber?" interrupted Ned.

"No doubt!" said the Doctor, nodding, "though I never heard so."

They imprisoned him, but he made his escape and fled, and in the morning his prison-place, wherever it was, was empty. But on the threshold of the door of the old manor-house there was the print of a bloody footstep; and no trouble that the housemaids took, no rain of all the years that have since passed, no sunshine, has made it fade: nor have all the wear and tramp of feet passing over it since then availed to erase it.

"I have seen it myself," quoth the Doctor, "and know this to be true."

"Doctor Grim, now you are laughing at us," said Ned, trying to look grave. But Elsie hid her face on the Doctor's knee; there being something that affected the vivid little girl with peculiar horror in the idea of this red footstep always glistening on the doorstep, and wetting, as she fancied, every innocent foot of child or grown person that had since passed over it. [Endnote: 3.]

"It is true!" reiterated the grim Doctor; "for, man and boy, I have seen it a thousand times."

He continued the family history, or tradition, or fantastic legend, whichever it might be; telling his young auditors that the Puritan, the renegade son of the family, was afterwards, by the contrivances of his brethren, sent to Virginia and sold as a bond slave; and how he had vanished from that quarter and come to New England, where he was supposed to have left children. And by and by two elder brothers died, and this missing brother became the heir to the old estate and to a title. Then the family tried to track his bloody footstep, and sought it far and near, through green country paths, and old streets of London; but in vain. Then they sent messengers to see whether any traces of one stepping in blood could be found on the forest leaves of America; but still in vain. The idea nevertheless prevailed that he would come back, and it was said they kept a bedchamber ready for him yet in the old house. But much as they pretended to regret the loss of him and his children, it would make them curse their stars were a descendant of his to return now. For the child of a younger son was in possession of the old estate, and was doing as much evil as his forefathers did; and if the true heir were to appear on the threshold, he would (if he might but do it secretly) stain the whole doorstep as red as the Bloody Footstep had stained one little portion of it.

"Do you think he will ever come back?" asked little Ned.

"Stranger things have happened, my little man!" said Doctor Grimshawe, "than that the posterity of this man should come back and turn these usurpers out of his rightful inheritance. And sometimes, as I sit here smoking my pipe and drinking my glass, and looking up at the cunning plot that the spider is weaving yonder above my head, and thinking of this fine old family and some little matters that have been between them and me, I fancy that it may be so! We shall see! Stranger things have happened."

And Doctor Grimshawe drank off his tumbler, winking at little Ned in a strange way, that seemed to be a kind of playfulness, but which did not affect the children pleasantly; insomuch that little Elsie put both her hands on Doctor Grim's knees, and begged him not to do so any more. [Endnote: 4.]

CHAPTER IV

[Endnote: 1]

The children, after this conversation, often introduced the old English mansion into their dreams and little romances, which all imaginative children are continually mixing up with their lives, making the commonplace day of grown people a rich, misty, glancing orb of fairy-land to themselves. Ned, forgetting or not realizing the long lapse of time, used to fancy the true heir wandering all this while in America, and leaving a long track of bloody footsteps behind him; until the period when, his sins being expiated (whatever they might be), he should turn back upon his steps and return to his old native home. And sometimes the child used to look along the streets of the town where he dwelt, bending his thoughtful eyes on the ground, and think that perhaps some time he should see the bloody footsteps there, betraying that the wanderer had just gone that way.

As for little Elsie, it was her fancy that the hero of the legend still remained imprisoned in that dreadful secret chamber, which had made a most dread impression on her mind; and that there he was, forgotten all this time, waiting, like a naughty child shut up in a closet, until some one should come to unlock the door. In the pitifulness of her disposition, she once proposed to little Ned that, as soon as they grew big enough, they should set out in quest of the old house, and find their way into it, and find the secret chamber, and let the poor prisoner out. So they lived a good deal of the time in a half-waking dream, partly conscious of the fantastic nature of their ideas, yet with these ideas almost as real to them as the facts of the natural world, which, to children, are at first transparent and unsubstantial.

The Doctor appeared to have a pleasure, or a purpose, in keeping his legend forcibly in their memories; he often recurred to the subject of the old English family, and was continually giving new details about its history, the scenery in its neighborhood, the aspect of the mansion-house; indicating a very intense interest in the subject on his own part, of which this much talk seemed the involuntary overflowing.

There was, however, an affection mingled with this sentiment. It appeared to be his unfortunate necessity to let his thoughts dwell very constantly upon a subject that was hateful to him, with which this old

English estate and manor-house and family were somehow connected; and, moreover, had he spoken thus to older and more experienced auditors, they might have detected in the manner and matter of his talk, a certain hereditary reverence and awe, the growth of ages, mixed up with a newer hatred, impelling him to deface and destroy what, at the same time, it was his deepest impulse to bow before. The love belonged to his race; the hatred, to himself individually. It was the feeling of a man lowly born, when he contracts a hostility to his hereditary superior. In one way, being of a powerful, passionate nature, gifted with force and ability far superior to that of the aristocrat, he might scorn him and feel able to trample on him; in another, he had the same awe that a country boy feels of the magistrate who flings him a sixpence and shakes his horsewhip at him.

Had the grim Doctor been an American, he might have had the vast antipathy to rank, without the trace of awe that made it so much more malignant: it required a low-born Englishman to feel the two together. What made the hatred so fiendish was a something that, in the natural course of things, would have been loyalty, inherited affection, devoted self-sacrifice to a superior. Whatever it might be, it seemed at times (when his potations took deeper effect than ordinary) almost to drive the grim Doctor mad; for he would burst forth in wild diatribes and anathemas, having a strange, rough force of expression and a depth of utterance, as if his words came from a bottomless pit within himself, where burned an everlasting fire, and where the furies had their home; and plans of dire revenge were welded into shape as in the heat of a furnace. After the two poor children had been affrighted by paroxysms of this kind, the strange being would break out into one of his roars of laughter, that seemed to shake the house, and, at all events, caused the cobwebs and spiders suspended from the ceiling, to swing and vibrate with the motion of the volumes of reverberating breath which he thus expelled from his capacious lungs. Then, catching up little Elsie upon one knee and Ned upon the other, he would become gentler than in his usual moods, and, by the powerful magnetism of his character, cause them to think him as tender and sweet an old fellow as a child could desire for a playmate. Upon the whole, strange as it may appear, they loved the grim Doctor dearly; there was a loadstone within him that drew them close to him and kept them there, in spite of the horror of many things that he said and did. One thing that, slight as it seemed, wrought mightily towards their mutually petting each other, was that no amount of racket, hubbub, shouting, laughter, or noisy mischief which the two children could perpetrate, ever disturbed the Doctor's studies, meditations, or employments of whatever kind. He had a hardy set of nerves, not refined by careful treatment in himself or his ancestors, but probably accustomed from of old to be drummed on by harsh voices, rude sounds, and the clatter and clamor of household life among homely, uncultivated, strongly animal people.

As the two children grew apace, it behooved their strange guardian to take some thought for their instruction. So far as little Elsie was concerned, however, he seemed utterly indifferent to her having any cultivation: having imbibed no modern ideas respecting feminine capacities and privileges, but regarding woman, whether in the bud or in the blossom, as the plaything of man's idler moments, and the helpmeet—but in a humble capacity—of his daily life. He sometimes bade her go to the kitchen and take lessons of crusty Hannah in bread-making, sweeping, dusting, washing, the coarser needlework, and such other things as she would require to know when she came to be a woman; but carelessly allowed her to gather up the crumbs of such instruction as he bestowed on her playmate Ned, and thus learn to read, write, and cipher; which, to say the truth, was about as far in the way of scholarship as little Elsie cared to go.

But towards little Ned the grim Doctor adopted a far different system. No sooner had he reached the age when the soft and tender intellect of the child became capable of retaining impressions, than he took him vigorously in hand, assigning him such tasks as were fit for him, and curiously investigating what were the force and character of the powers with which the child grasped them. Not that the Doctor pressed him forward unduly; indeed, there was no need of it; for the boy manifested a remarkable docility for instruction, and a singular quickness in mastering the preliminary steps which lead to science: a subtle instinct, indeed, which it seemed wonderful a child should possess for anything as artificial as systems of grammar and arithmetic. A remarkable boy, in truth, he was, to have been found by chance in an almshouse; except that, such being his origin, we are at liberty to suppose for him whatever long cultivation and gentility we may think necessary, in his parentage of either side,—such as was indicated also by his graceful and refined beauty of person. He showed, indeed, even before he began to read at all, an instinctive attraction towards books, and a love for and interest in even the material form of knowledge,—the plates, the print, the binding of the Doctor's volumes, and even in a bookworm which he once found in an old volume, where it had eaten a circular furrow. But the little boy had too quick a spirit of life to be in danger of becoming a bookworm himself. He had this side of the intellect, but his impulse would be to mix with men, and catch something from their intercourse fresher than books could give him; though these would give him what they might.

In the grim Doctor, rough and uncultivated as he seemed, this budding intelligence found no inadequate instructor. Doctor Grimshawe proved himself a far more thorough scholar, in the classics and mathematics, than could easily have been found in our country. He himself must have had rigid and faithful instruction at an early period of life, though probably not in his boyhood. For, though the culture had been bestowed, his mind had been left in so singularly rough a state that it seemed as if the refinement of classical study could not have been begun very early. Or possibly the mind and nature were incapable of polish; or he may have had a coarse and sordid domestic life around him in his infancy and youth. He was a gem of coarse texture, just hewn out. An American with a like education would more likely have gained a certain fineness and grace, and it would have been difficult to distinguish him from one who had been born to culture and refinement. This sturdy Englishman, after all that had been done for his mind, and though it had been well done, was still but another ploughman, of a long race of such, with a few scratchings of refinement on his hard exterior. His son, if he left one, might be a little less of the ploughman; his grandson, provided the female element were well chosen, might approach to refinement; three generations—a century at least—would be required for the slow toil of hewing, chiselling, and polishing a gentleman out of this ponderous block, now rough from the quarry of human nature. But, in the mean time, he evidently possessed in an unusual degree the sort of learning that refines other minds,—the critical acquaintance with the great poets and historians of antiquity, and apparently an appreciation of their merits, and power to teach their beauty. So the boy had an able tutor, capable, it would seem, of showing him the way to the graces he did not himself possess; besides helping the growth of the strength without which refinement is but sickly and disgusting.

Another sort of culture, which it seemed odd that this rude man should undertake, was that of manners; but, in fact, rude as the grim Doctor's own manners were, he was one of the nicest and severest censors in that department that was ever known. It is difficult to account for this; although it is almost invariably found that persons in a low rank of life, such as servants and laborers, will detect the false pretender to the character of a gentleman, with at least as sure an instinct as the class into which they seek to thrust themselves. Perhaps they recognize something akin to their own vulgarity, rather than appreciate what is unlike themselves. The Doctor possessed a peculiar power of rich rough humor on this subject, and used to deliver lectures, as it were, to little Ned, illustrated with sketches of living individuals in the town where they dwelt; by an unscrupulous use of whom he sought to teach the boy what to avoid in manners, if he sought to be a gentleman. But it must be confessed he spared himself as little as other people, and often wound up with this compendious injunction, — "Be everything in your behavior that Doctor Grim is not!"

His pupil, very probably, profited somewhat by these instructions; for there are specialties and arbitrary rules of behavior which do not come by nature. But these are few; and beautiful, noble, and genial manners may almost be called a natural gift; and these, however he inherited them, soon proved to be an inherent possession of little Ned. He had a kind of natural refinement, which nothing could ever soil or offend; it seemed, by some magic or other, absolutely to keep him from the knowledge of much of the grim Doctor's rude and sordid exterior, and to render what was around him beautiful by a sort of affiliation, or reflection from that quality in himself, glancing its white light upon it. The Doctor himself was puzzled, and apparently both startled and delighted at the perception of these characteristics. Sometimes he would make a low, uncouth bow, after his fashion, to the little fellow, saying, "Allow me to kiss your hand, my lord!" and little Ned, not quite knowing what the grim Doctor meant, yet allowed the favor he asked, with a grave and gracious condescension that seemed much to delight the suitor. This refusal to recognize or to suspect that the Doctor might be laughing at him was a sure token, at any rate, of the lack of one vulgar characteristic in little Ned.

In order to afford little Ned every advantage to these natural gifts, Doctor Grim nevertheless failed not to provide the best attainable instructor for such positive points of a polite education as his own fierce criticism, being destructive rather than generative, would not suffice for. There was a Frenchman in the town—a M. Le Grand, secretly calling himself a Count—who taught the little people, and, indeed, some of their elders, the Parisian pronunciation of his own language; and likewise dancing (in which he was more of an adept and more successful than in the former branch) and fencing: in which, after looking at a lesson or two, the grim Doctor was satisfied of his skill. Under his instruction, with the stimulus of the Doctor's praise and criticism, Ned soon grew to be the pride of the Frenchman's school, in both the active departments; and the Doctor himself added a further gymnastic acquirement (not absolutely necessary, he said, to a gentleman's education, but very desirable to a man perfect at all points) by teaching him cudgel-playing and pugilism. In short, in everything that related to accomplishments, whether of mind or body, no pains were spared with little Ned; but of the utilitarian line of education, then almost exclusively adopted, and especially desirable for a fortuneless boy like Ned, dependent on a man not wealthy, there was little given.

At first, too, the Doctor paid little attention to the moral and religious culture of his pupil; nor did he ever make a system of it. But by and by, though with a singular reluctance and kind of bashfulness, he began to extend his care to these matters; being drawn into them unawares, and possibly perceiving and learning what he taught as he went along. One evening, I know not how, he was betrayed into speaking on this point, and a sort of inspiration seized him. A vista opened before him: handling an immortal spirit, he began to know its requisitions, in a degree far beyond what he had conceived them to be when his great task was undertaken. His voice grew deep, and had a strange, impressive pathos in it; his talk became eloquent with depth of meaning and feeling, as he told the boy of the moral dangers of the world, for which he was seeking to educate him; and which, he said, presented what looked like great triumphs, and yet were the greatest and saddest of defeats. He told him that many things that seemed nearest and dearest to the heart of man were destructive, eating and gnawing away and corroding what was best in him; and what a high, noble, re-creating triumph it was when these dark impulses were resisted and overthrown; and how, from that epoch, the soul took a new start. He denounced the selfish greed of gold, lawless passion, revenge,—and here the grim Doctor broke out into a strange passion and zeal of anathema against this deadly sin, making a dreadful picture of the ruin that it creates in the heart where it establishes itself, and how it makes a corrosive acid of those genial juices. Then he told the boy that the condition of all good was, in the first place, truth; then, courage; then, justice; then, mercy; out of which principles operating upon one another would come all brave, noble, high, unselfish actions, and the scorn of all mean ones; and how that from such a nature all hatred would fall away, and all good affections would be ennobled.

I know not at what point it was, precisely, in these ethical instructions that an insight seemed to strike the grim Doctor that something more—vastly more—was needed than all he had said; and he began, doubtfully, to speak of man's spiritual nature and its demands, and the emptiness of everything which a sense of these demands did not pervade, and condense, and weighten into realities. And going on in this strain, he soared out of himself and astonished the two children, who stood gazing at him, wondering whether it were the Doctor who was speaking thus; until some interrupting circumstance seemed to bring him back to himself, and he burst into one of his great roars of laughter. The inspiration, the strange light whereby he had been transfigured, passed out of his face; and there was the uncouth, wild-bearded, rough, earthy, passionate man, whom they called Doctor Grim, looking ashamed of himself, and trying to turn the whole matter into a jest. [Endnote: 2.]

It was a sad pity that he should have been interrupted, and brought into this mocking mood, just when he seemed to have broken away from the sinfulness of his hot, evil nature, and to have soared into a region where, with all his native characteristics transfigured, he seemed to have become an angel in his own likeness. Crusty Hannah, who had been drawn to the door of the study by the unusual tones of his voice,—a kind of piercing sweetness in it,—always averred that she saw the gigantic spider swooping round his head in great crafty circles, and clutching, as it were, at his brain with its great claws. But it was the old woman's absurd idea that this hideous insect was the Devil, in that ugly guise,—a superstition which deserves absolutely no countenance. Nevertheless, though this paroxysm of devotional feeling and insight returned no more to the grim Doctor, it was ever after a memorable occasion to the two children. It touched that religious chord, in both their hearts, which there was no mother to touch; but now it vibrated long, and never ceased to vibrate so long as they remained together,—nor, perhaps, after they were parted from each other and from the grim Doctor. And even then, in those after years, the strange music that had been awakened was continued, as it were the echo from harps on high. Now, at all events, they made little prayers for themselves, and said them at bedtime, generally in secret, sometimes in unison; and they read in an old dusty Bible which lay among the grim Doctor's books; and from little heathens, they became Christian children. Doctor Grimshawe was perhaps conscious of this result of his involuntary preachment, but he never directly noticed it, and did nothing either to efface or deepen the impression.

It was singular, however, that, in both the children's minds, this one gush of irresistible religious sentiment, breaking out of the grim Doctor's inner depths, like a sort of holy lava from a volcano that usually emitted quite other matter, (such as hot, melted wrath and hate,) quite threw out of sight, then and always afterwards, his darker characteristics. They remembered him, with faith and love, as a religious man, and forgot—what perhaps had made no impression on their innocent hearts—all the traits that other people might have called devilish. To them the grim Doctor was a saint, even during his lifetime and constant intercourse with them, and canonized forever afterwards. There is almost always, to be sure, this profound faith, with regard to those they love, in childhood; but perhaps, in this instance, the children really had a depth of insight that grown people lacked; a profound recognition of the bottom of this strange man's nature, which was of such stuff as martyrs and heroic saints might have been made of, though here it had been wrought miserably amiss. At any rate, his face with the holy awe upon it was what they saw and remembered, when they thought of their friend Doctor Grim.

One effect of his zealous and analytic instruction of the boy was very perceptible. Heretofore, though enduring him, and occasionally making a plaything of him, it may be doubted whether the grim Doctor had really any strong affection for the child: it rather seemed as if his strong will were forcing him to undertake, and carry sedulously forward, a self-imposed task. All that he had done—his redeeming the bright child from poverty and nameless degradation, ignorance, and a sordid life hopeless of better fortune, and opening to him the whole realm of mighty possibilities in an American life—did not imply any love for the little individual whom he thus benefited. It had some other motive.

But now, approaching the child in this close, intimate, and helpful way, it was very evident that his interest took a tenderer character. There was everything in the boy, that a boy could possess, to attract affection; he would have been a father's pride and joy. Doctor Grimshawe, indeed, was not his father; but to a person of his character this was perhaps no cause of lesser love than if there had been the whole of that holy claim of kindred between them. We speak of the natural force of blood; we speak of the paternal relation as if it were productive of more earnest affection than can exist between two persons, one of whom is protective, but unrelated. But there are wild, forcible, unrestricted characters, on whom the necessity and even duty of loving their own child is a sort of barrier to love. They perhaps do not love their own traits, which they recognize in their children; they shrink from their own features in the reflection presented by these little mirrors. A certain strangeness and unlikeness (such as gives poignancy to the love between the sexes) would excite a livelier affection. Be this as it may, it is not probable that Doctor Grimshawe would have loved a child of his own blood, with the coarse characteristics that he knew both in his race and himself, with nearly such fervor as this beautiful, slender, yet strenuous, intelligent, refined boy,—with such a high-bred air, handling common things with so refined a touch, yet grasping them so firmly; throwing a natural grace on all he did. Was he not his father,—he that took this fair blossom out of the sordid mud in which he must soon have withered and perished? Was not this beautiful strangeness, which he so wondered at, the result of his care?

And little Elsie? did the grim Doctor love her as well? Perhaps not, for, in the first place, there was a natural tie, though not the nearest, between her and Doctor Grimshawe, which made him feel that she was cast upon his love: a burden which he acknowledged himself bound to undertake. Then, too, there were unutterably painful reminiscences and thoughts, that made him gasp for breath, that turned his blood sour, that tormented his dreams with nightmares and hellish phantoms; all of which were connected with this innocent and happy child; so that, cheerful and pleasant as she was, there was to the grim Doctor a little fiend playing about his floor and throwing a lurid light on the wall, as the shadow of this sun-flickering child. It is certain that there was always a pain and horror mixed with his feelings towards Elsie; he had to forget himself, as it were, and all that was connected with the causes why she came to be, before he could love her. Amid his fondness, when he was caressing her upon his knee, pressing her to his rough bosom, as he never took the freedom to press Ned, came these hateful reminiscences, compelling him to set her down, and corrugating his heavy brows as with a pang of fiercely resented, strongly borne pain. Still, the child had no doubt contrived to make her way into the great gloomy cavern of the grim Doctor's heart, and stole constantly further and further in, carrying a ray of sunshine in her hand as a taper to light her way, and illuminate the rude dark pit into which she so fearlessly went.

CHAPTER V

Doctor Grim [Endnote: 1] had the English faith in open air and daily acquaintance with the weather, whatever it might be; and it was his habit, not only to send the two children to play, for lack of a better place, in the graveyard, but to take them himself on long rambles, of which the vicinity of the town afforded a rich variety. It may be that the Doctor's excursions had the wider scope, because both he and the children were objects of curiosity in the town, and very much the subject of its gossip: so that always, in its streets and lanes, the people turned to gaze, and came to their windows and to the doors of shops to see this grim, bearded figure, leading along the beautiful children each by a hand, with a surly aspect like a bulldog. Their remarks were possibly not intended to reach the ears of the party, but certainly were not so cautiously whispered but they occasionally did do so. The male remarks, indeed, generally died away in the throats that uttered them; a circumstance that doubtless saved the utterer from some very rough rejoinder at the hands of the Doctor, who had grown up in the habit of a very ready and free recourse to his fists, which had a way of doubling themselves up seemingly of their own accord. But the shrill feminine voices sometimes sent their observations from window to window without dread of any such repartee on the part of the subject of them.

"There he goes, the old Spider-witch!" quoth one shrill woman, "with those two poor babes that he has caught in his cobweb, and is going to feed upon, poor little tender things! The bloody Englishman makes free with the dead bodies of our friends and the living ones of our children!"

"How red his nose is!" quoth another; "he has pulled at the brandy-bottle pretty stoutly to-day, early as it is! Pretty habits those children will learn, between the Devil in the shape of a great spider, and this devilish fellow in his own shape! It were well that our townsmen tarred and feathered the old British wizard!"

And, as he got further off, two or three little blackguard barefoot boys shouted shrilly after him, —

"Doctor Grim, Doctor Grim,
The Devil wove a web for him!"

being a nonsensical couplet that had been made for the grim Doctor's benefit, and was hooted in the streets, and under his own windows. Hearing such remarks and insults, the Doctor would glare round at them with red eyes, especially if the brandy-bottle had happened to be much in request that day.

Indeed, poor Doctor Grim had met with a fortune which befalls many a man with less cause than drew the public attention on this odd humorist; for, dwelling in a town which was as yet but a larger village, where everybody knew everybody, and claimed the privilege to know and discuss their characters, and where there were few topics of public interest to take off their attention, a very considerable portion of town talk and criticism fell upon him. The old town had a certain provincialism, which is less the characteristic of towns in these days, when society circulates so freely, than then: besides, it was a very rude epoch, just when the country had come through the war of the Revolution, and while the surges of that commotion were still seething and swelling, and while the habits and morals of every individual in the community still felt its influence; and especially the contest was too recent for an Englishman to be in very good odor, unless he should cease to be English, and become more American than the Americans themselves in repudiating British prejudices or principles, habits, mode of thought, and everything that distinguishes Britons at home or abroad. As Doctor Grim did not see fit to do this, and as, moreover, he was a very doubtful, questionable, morose, unamiable old fellow, not seeking to make himself liked nor deserving to be so, he was a very unpopular person in the town where he had chosen to reside. Nobody thought very well of him; the respectable people had heard of his pipe and brandy-bottle; the religious community knew that he never showed himself at church or meeting; so that he had not that very desirable strength (in a society split up into many sects) of being able to rely upon the party sympathies of any one of them. The mob hated him with the blind sentiment that makes one surly cur hostile to another surly cur. He was the most isolated individual to be found anywhere; and, being so unsupported, everybody was his enemy.

The town, as it happened, had been pleased to interest itself much in this matter of Doctor Grim and the two children, insomuch as he never sent them to school, nor came with them to meeting of any kind, but was bringing them up ignorant heathen to all appearances, and, as many believed, was devoting them in some way to the great spider, to which he had bartered his own soul. It had been mooted among the selectmen, the fathers of the town, whether their duty did not require them to put the children under more suitable guardianship; a measure which, it may be, was chiefly hindered by the consideration that, in that case, the cost of supporting them would probably be transferred from the grim Doctor's shoulders to those of the community. Nevertheless, they did what they could. Maidenly ladies, prim and starched, in one or two instances called upon the Doctor—the two children meanwhile being in the graveyard at play—to give him Christian advice as to the management of his charge. But, to confess the truth, the Doctor's reception of these fair missionaries was not extremely courteous. They were, perhaps, partly instigated by a natural feminine desire to see the interior of a place about which they had heard much, with its spiders' webs, its strange machines and confusing tools; so, much contrary to crusty Hannah's advice, they persisted in entering. Crusty Hannah listened at the door; and it was curious to see the delighted smile which came over her dry old visage as the Doctor's growling, rough voice, after an abrupt question or two, and a reply in a thin voice on the part of the maiden ladies, grew louder and louder, till the door opened, and forth came the benevolent pair in great discomposure. Crusty Hannah averred that their caps were much rumpled; but this view of the thing was questioned; though it were certain that the Doctor called after them downstairs, that, had they been younger and prettier, they would have fared worse. A male emissary, who was admitted on the supposition of his being a patient, did fare worse; for (the grim Doctor having been particularly intimate with the black bottle that afternoon) there was, about ten minutes after the visitor's entrance, a sudden fierce upraising of the Doctor's growl; then a struggle that shook the house; and, finally, a terrible rumbling down the stairs, which proved to be caused by the precipitate descent of the hapless visitor; who, if he needed no assistance of the grim Doctor on his entrance, certainly would have been the better for a plaster or two after his departure.

Such were the terms on which Doctor Grimshawe now stood with his adopted townspeople; and if we consider the dull little town to be full of exaggerated stories about the Doctor's oddities, many of them forged, all retailed in an unfriendly spirit; misconceptions of a character which, in its best and most candidly interpreted aspects, was sufficiently amenable to censure; surmises taken for certainties; superstitions—the genuine hereditary offspring of the frame of public mind which produced the witchcraft delusion—all fermenting together; and all this evil and uncharitableness taking the delusive hue of benevolent interest in two helpless children;—we may partly judge what was the odium in which the grim Doctor dwelt, and amid which he walked. The horrid suspicion, too, countenanced by his abode in the corner of the graveyard, affording the terrible Doctor such facilities for making free, like a ghoul as he was, with the relics of mortality from the earliest progenitor to the man killed yesterday by the Doctor's own drugs, was not likely to improve his reputation.

He had heretofore contented himself with, at most, occasionally shaking his stick at his assailants; but this day the black bottle had imparted, it may be, a little more fire than ordinary to his blood; and besides, an unlucky urchin happened to take particularly good aim with a mud ball, which took effect right in the midst of the Doctor's bushy beard, and, being of a soft consistency, forthwith became incorporated with it. At this intolerable provocation the grim Doctor pursued the little villain, amid a shower of similar missiles from the boy's playmates, caught him as he was escaping into a back yard, dragged him into the middle of the street, and, with his stick, proceeded to give him his merited chastisement.

But, hereupon, it was astonishing how sudden commotion flashed up like gunpowder along the street, which, except for the petty shrieks and laughter of a few children, was just before so quiet. Forth out of every window in those dusky, mean wooden houses were thrust heads of women old and young; forth out of every door and other avenue, and as if they started up from the middle of the street, or out of the unpaved sidewalks, rushed fierce avenging forms, threatening at full yell to take vengeance on the grim Doctor; who still, with that fierce dark face of his,—his muddy beard all flying abroad, dirty and foul, his hat fallen off, his red eyes flashing fire,— was belaboring the poor hinder end of the unhappy urchin, paying off upon that one part of the boy's frame the whole score which he had to settle with the rude boys of the town; giving him at once the whole whipping which he had deserved every day of his life, and not a stroke of which he had yet received. Need enough there was, no doubt, that somebody should interfere with such grim and immitigable justice; and certainly the interference was prompt, and promised to be effectual.

"Down with the old tyrant! Thrash him! Hang him! Tar and feather the viper's fry! the wizard! the body-snatcher!" bellowed the mob, one member of which was raving with delirium tremens, and another was a madman just escaped from bedlam.

It is unaccountable where all this mischievous, bloodthirsty multitude came from,—how they were born into that quietness in such a moment of time! What had they been about heretofore? Were they waiting in readiness for this crisis, and keeping themselves free from other employment till it should come to pass? Had they been created for the moment, or were they fiends sent by Satan in the likeness of a blackguard population? There you might see the offscourings of the recently finished war,—old soldiers, rusty, wooden-legged: there, sailors, ripe for any kind of mischief; there, the drunken population of a neighboring grogshop, staggering helter-skelter to the scene, and tumbling over one another at the Doctor's feet. There came the father of the punished urchin, who had never shown heretofore any care for his street-bred progeny, but who now came pale with rage, armed with a pair of tongs; and with him the mother, flying like a fury, with her cap awry, and clutching a broomstick, as if she were a witch just alighted. Up they rushed from cellar doors, and dropped down from chamber windows; all rushing upon the Doctor, but overturning and thwarting themselves by their very multitude. For, as good Doctor Grim levelled the first that came within reach of his fist, two or three of the others tumbled over him and lay grovelling at his feet; the Doctor meanwhile having retreated into the angle between two houses. Little Ned, with a valor which did him the more credit inasmuch as it was exercised in spite of a good deal of childish trepidation, as his pale face indicated, brandished his fists by the Doctor's side; and little Elsie did what any woman may, — that is, screeched in Doctor Grim's behalf with full stretch of lungs. Meanwhile the street boys kept up a shower of mud balls, many of which hit the Doctor, while the rest were distributed upon his assailants, heightening their ferocity.

"Seize the old scoundrel! the villain! the Tory! the dastardly Englishman! Hang him in the web of his own devilish spider, — 't is long enough! Tar and feather him! tar and feather him!"

It was certainly one of those crises that show a man how few real friends he has, and the tendency of mankind to stand aside, at least, and let a poor devil fight his own troubles, if not assist them in their attack. Here you might have seen a brother physician of the grim Doctor's greatly tickled at his plight: or a decorous, powdered, ruffle-shirted dignitary, one of the weighty men of the town, standing at a neighbor's corner to see what would come of it.

"He is not a respectable man, I understand, this Grimshawe, — a quack, intemperate, always in these scuffles: let him get out as he may!"

And then comes a deacon of one of the churches, and several church-members, who, hearing a noise, set out gravely and decorously to see what was going forward in a Christian community.

"Ah! it is that irreligious and profane Grimshawe, who never goes to meeting. We wash our hands of him!"

And one of the selectmen said, —

"Surely this common brawler ought not to have the care of these nice, sweet children; something must be done about it; and when the man is sober, he must be talked to!"

Alas! it is a hard case with a man who lives upon his own bottom and responsibility, making himself no allies, sewing himself on to nobody's skirts, insulating himself,—hard, when his trouble comes; and so poor Doctor Grimshawe was like to find it.

He had succeeded by dint of good skill, and some previous practice at quarter-staff, in keeping his assailants at bay, though not without some danger on his own part; but their number, their fierceness, and the more skilled assault of some among them must almost immediately have been successful, when the Doctor's part was strengthened by an unexpected ally. This was a person [Endnote: 2] of tall, slight figure, who, without lifting his hands to take part in the conflict, thrust himself before the Doctor, and turned towards the assailants, crying,—

"Christian men, what would you do? Peace,—peace!"

His so well intended exhortation took effect, indeed, in a certain way, but not precisely as might have been wished: for a blow, aimed at Doctor Grim, took effect on the head of this man, who seemed to have no sort of skill or alacrity at defending himself, any more than at making an assault; for he never lifted his hands, but took the blow as unresistingly as if it had been kindly meant, and it levelled him senseless on the ground.

Had the mob really been enraged for any strenuous cause, this incident would have operated merely as a preliminary whet to stimulate them to further bloodshed. But, as they were mostly actuated only by a natural desire for mischief, they were about as well satisfied with what had been done as if the Doctor himself were the victim. And besides, the fathers and respectabilities of the town, who had seen this mishap from afar, now began to put forward, crying out, "Keep the peace! keep the peace! A riot! a riot!" and other such cries as suited the emergency; and the crowd vanished more speedily than it had congregated, leaving the Doctor and the two children alone beside the fallen victim of a quarrel not his own. Not to dwell too long on this incident, the Doctor, laying hold of the last of his enemies, after the rest had taken to their heels, ordered him sternly to stay and help him bear the man, whom he had helped to murder, to his house.

"It concerns you, friend; for, if he dies, you hang to a dead certainty!"

And this was done accordingly.

CHAPTER VI

About an hour thereafter there lay on a couch that had been hastily prepared in the study a person of singularly impressive presence: a thin, mild-looking man, with a peculiar look of delicacy and natural refinement about him, although he scarcely appeared to be technically and as to worldly position what we call a gentleman; plain in dress and simple in manner, not giving the idea of remarkable intellectual gifts, but with a kind of spiritual aspect, fair, clear complexion, gentle eyes, still somewhat clouded and obscured by the syncope into which a blow on the head had thrown him. He looked middle-aged, and yet there was a kind of childlike, simple expression, which, unless you looked at him with the very purpose of seeing the traces of time in his face, would make you suppose him much younger.

"And how do you find yourself now, my good fellow?" asked Doctor Grimshawe, putting forth his hand to grasp that of the stranger, and giving it a good, warm shake. "None the worse, I should hope?" [Endnote: 1.]

"Not much the worse," answered the stranger: "not at all, it may be. There is a pleasant dimness and uncertainty in my mode of being. I am taken off my feet, as it were, and float in air, with a faint delight in my sensations. The grossness, the roughness, the too great angularity of the actual, is removed from me. It is a state that I like well. It may be, this is the way that the dead feel when they awake in another state of being, with a dim pleasure, after passing through the brief darkness of death. It is very pleasant."

He answered dreamily, and sluggishly, reluctantly, as if there were a sense of repose in him which he disliked to break by putting any of his sensations into words. His voice had a remarkable sweetness and gentleness, though lacking in depth of melody.

"Here, take this," said the Doctor, who had been preparing some kind of potion in a teaspoon: it may have been a dose of his famous preparation of spider's web, for aught I know, the operation of which was said to be of a soothing influence, causing a delightful silkiness of sensation; but I know not whether it was considered good for concussions of the brain, such as it is to be supposed the present patient had undergone. "Take this: it will do you good; and here I drink your very good health in something that will do me good."

So saying, the grim Doctor quaffed off a tumbler of brandy and water.

"How sweet a contrast," murmured the stranger, "between that scene of violence and this great peace that has come over me! It is as when one can say, I have fought the good fight."

"You are right," said the Doctor, with what would have been one of his deep laughs, but which he modified in consideration of his patient's tenderness of brain. "We both of us fought a good fight; for though you struck no actual stroke, you took them as unflinchingly as ever I saw a man, and so turned the fortune of the battle better than if you smote with a sledge-hammer. Two things puzzle me in the affair. First, whence came my assailants, all in that moment of time, unless Satan let loose out of the infernal regions a synod of fiends, hoping thus to get a triumph over me. And secondly, whence came you, my preserver, unless you are an angel, and dropped down from the sky."

"No," answered the stranger, with quiet simplicity. "I was passing through the street to my little school, when I saw your peril, and felt it my duty to expostulate with the people."

"Well," said the grim Doctor, "come whence you will, you did an angel's office for me, and I shall do what an earthly man may to requite it. There, we will talk no more for the present."

He hushed up the children, who were already, of their own accord, walking on tiptoe and whispering, and he himself even went so far as to refrain from the usual incense of his pipe, having observed that the stranger, who seemed to be of a very delicate organization, had seemed sensible of the disagreeable effect on the atmosphere of the room. The restraint lasted, however, only till (in the course of the day) crusty Hannah had fitted up a little bedroom on the opposite side of the entry, to which she and the grim Doctor moved the stranger, who, though tall, they observed was of no great weight and substance,—the lightest man, the Doctor averred, for his size, that ever he had handled.

Every possible care was taken of him, and in a day or two he was able to walk into the study again, where he sat gazing at the sordidness and unneatness of the apartment, the strange festoons and drapery of spiders' webs, the gigantic spider himself, and at the grim Doctor, so shaggy, grizzly, and uncouth, in the midst of these surroundings, with a perceptible sense of something very strange in it all. His mild, gentle regard dwelt too on the two beautiful children, evidently with a sense of quiet wonder how they should be here, and altogether a sense of their unfitness; they, meanwhile, stood a little apart, looking at him, somewhat disturbed and awed, as children usually are, by a sense that the stranger was not perfectly well, that he had been injured, and so set apart from the rest of the world.

"Will you come to me, little one?" said he, holding out a delicate hand to Elsie.

Elsie came to his side without any hesitation, though without any of the rush that accompanied her advent to those whom she affected. "And you, my little man," added the stranger, quietly, and looking to Ned, who likewise willingly approached, and, shaking him by the offered hand, let it go again, but continued standing by his side.

"Do you know, my little friends," said the stranger, "that it is my business in life to instruct such little people as you?"

"Do they obey you well, sir?" asked Ned, perhaps conscious of a want of force in the person whom he addressed.

The stranger smiled faintly. "Not too well," said he. "That has been my difficulty; for I have moral and religious objections, and also a great horror, to the use of the rod, and I have not been gifted with a harsh voice and a stern brow; so that, after a while, my little people sometimes get the better of me. The present generation of men is too gross for gentle treatment."

"You are quite right," quoth Doctor Grimshawe, who had been observing this little scene, and trying to make out, from the mutual deportment of the stranger and the two children, what sort of man this fair, quiet stranger was, with his gentleness and weakness,—characteristics that were not attractive to himself, yet in which he acknowledged, as he saw them here, a certain charm; nor did he know, scarcely, whether to despise the one in whom he saw them, or to yield to a strange sense of reverence. So he watched the children, with an indistinct idea of being guided by them. "You are quite right: the world now—and always before, as far as I ever heard—requires a great deal of brute force, a great deal of animal food and brandy in the man that is to make an impression on it."

The convalescence of the stranger—he gave his name as Colcord— proceeded favorably; for the Doctor remarked that, delicate as his system was, it had a certain purity,—a simple healthfulness that did not run into disease as stronger constitutions might. It did not apparently require much to crush down such a being as this,—not much unkindly breath to blow out the taper of his life,—and yet, if not absolutely killed, there was a certain aptness to keep alive in him not readily to be overcome.

No sooner was he in a condition so to do, than he went forth to look after the little school that he had spoken of, but soon came back, announcing in a very quiet and undisturbed way that, during his withdrawal from duty, the scholars had been distributed to other instructors, and consequently he was without place or occupation [Endnotes: 2, 3, 4.]

"A hard case," said the Doctor, flinging a gruff curse at those who had so readily deserted the poor schoolmaster.

"Not so hard," replied Colcord. "These little fellows are an unruly set, born of parents who have led rough lives,—here in battle time, too, with the spirit of battle in them,—therefore rude and contentious beyond my power to cope with them. I have been taught, long ago," he added, with a peaceful smile, "that my business in life does not lie with grown-up and consolidated men and women; and so, not to be useless in my day, and to gain the little that my sustenance requires, I have thought to deal with children. But even for this I lack force."

"I dare say," said the Doctor, with a modified laugh. "Little devils they are, harder to deal with than men. Well, I am glad of your failure for one reason, and of your being thrown out of business; because we shall have the benefit of you the longer. Here is this boy to be instructed. I have made some attempts myself; but having no art of instructing, no skill, no temper I suppose, I make but an indifferent hand at it: and besides I have other business that occupies my thoughts. Take him in hand, if you like, and the girl for company. No matter whether you teach her anything, unless you happen to be acquainted with needlework."

"I will talk with the children," said Colcord, "and see if I am likely to do good with them. The lad, I see, has a singular spirit of aspiration and pride,—no ungentle pride,—but still hard to cope with. I will see. The little girl is a most comfortable child."

"You have read the boy as if you had his heart in your hand," said the Doctor, rather surprised. "I could not have done it better myself, though I have known him all but from the egg."

Accordingly, the stranger, who had been thrust so providentially into this odd and insulated little community, abode with them, without more words being spoken on the subject: for it seemed to all concerned a natural arrangement, although, on both parts, they were mutually sensible of something strange in the companionship thus brought about. To say the truth, it was not easy to imagine two persons apparently less adapted to each other's society than the rough, uncouth, animal Doctor, whose faith was in his own right arm, so full of the old Adam as he was, so sturdily a hater, so hotly impulsive, so deep, subtle, and crooked, so obstructed by his animal nature, so given to his pipe and black bottle, so wrathful and pugnacious and wicked, — and this mild spiritual creature, so milky, with so unforceful a grasp; and it was singular to see how they stood apart and eyed each other, each tacitly acknowledging a certain merit and kind of power, though not well able to appreciate its value. The grim Doctor's kindness, however, and gratitude, had been so thoroughly awakened, that he did not feel the disgust that he probably otherwise might at what seemed the mawkishness of Colcord's character; his want, morally speaking, of bone and muscle; his fastidiousness of character, the essence of which it seemed to be to bear no stain upon it; otherwise it must die.

On Colcord's part there was a good deal of evidence to be detected, by a nice observer, that he found it difficult to put up with the Doctor's coarse peculiarities, whether physical or moral. His animal indulgences of appetite struck him with wonder and horror; his coarse expressions, his free indulgence of wrath, his sordid and unclean habits; the dust, the cobwebs, the monster that dangled from the ceiling; his pipe, diffusing its fragrance through the house, and showing, by the plainest and simplest proof, how we all breathe one another's breath, nice and proud as we may be, kings and daintiest ladies breathing the air that has already served to inflate a beggar's lungs. He shrank, too, from the rude manhood of the Doctor's character, with its human warmth, — an element which he seemed not to possess in his own character. He was capable only of gentle and mild regard, — that was his warmest affection; and the warmest, too, that he was capable of exciting in others. So that he was doomed as much apparently as the Doctor himself to be a lonely creature, without any very deep companionship in the world, though not incapable, when he, by some rare chance, met a soul distantly akin, of holding a certain high spiritual communion. With the children, however, he succeeded in establishing some good and available relations; his simple and passionless character coincided with their simplicity, and their as yet unawakened passions: they appeared to understand him better than the Doctor ever succeeded in doing. He touched springs and elements in the nature of both that had never been touched till now, and that sometimes made a sweet, high music. But this was rarely; and as far as the general duties of an instructor went, they did not seem to be very successfully performed. Something was cultivated; the spiritual germ grew, it might be; but the children, and especially Ned, were intuitively conscious of a certain want of substance in the instructor, — a something of earthly bulk; a too etherealness. But his connection with our story does not lie in any excellence, or lack of excellence, that he showed as an instructor, and we merely mention these things as illustrating more or less his characteristics.

The grim Doctor's curiosity was somewhat piqued by what he could see of the schoolmaster's character, and he was desirous of finding out what sort of a life such a man could have led in a world which he himself had found so rough a one; through what difficulties he had reached middle age without absolutely vanishing away in his contact with more positive substances than himself; how the world had given him a subsistence, if indeed he recognized anything more dense than fragrance, like a certain people whom Pliny mentioned in Africa,—a point, in fact, which the grim Doctor denied, his performance at table being inappreciable, and confined, at least almost entirely, to a dish of boiled rice, which crusty Hannah set before him, preparing it, it might be, with a sympathy of her East Indian part towards him.

Well, Doctor Grimshawe easily got at what seemed to be all of the facts of Colcord's life; how that he was a New-Englander, the descendant of an ancient race of settlers, the last of them; for, once pretty numerous in their quarter of the country, they seemed to have been dying out,—exhaling from the earth, and passing to some other region.

"No wonder," said the Doctor bluffly. "You have been letting slip the vital principle, if you are a fair specimen of the race. You do not clothe yourself in substance. Your souls are not coated sufficiently. Beef and brandy would have saved you. You have exhaled for lack of them."

The schoolmaster shook his head, and probably thought his earthly salvation and sustenance not worth buying at such a cost. The remainder of his history was not tangible enough to afford a narrative. There seemed, from what he said, to have always been a certain kind of refinement in his race, a nicety of conscience, a nicety of habit, which either was in itself a want of force, or was necessarily connected with it, and which, the Doctor silently thought, had culminated in the person before him.

"It was always in us," continued Colcord, with a certain pride which people generally feel in their ancestral characteristics, be they good or evil. "We had a tradition among us of our first emigrant, and the causes that brought him to the New World; and it was said that he had suffered so much, before quitting his native shores, so painful had been his track, that always afterwards on the forest leaves of this land his foot left a print of blood wherever he trod." [Endnote: 5.]

CHAPTER VII

"A print of blood!" said the grim Doctor, breaking his pipe-stem by some sudden spasm in his gripe of it. "Pooh! the devil take the pipe! A very strange story that! Pray how was it?" [Endnote: 1.]

"Nay, it is but a very dim legend," answered the schoolmaster: "although there are old yellow papers and parchments, I remember, in my father's possession, that had some reference to this man, too, though there was nothing in them about the bloody footprints. But our family legend is, that this man was of a good race, in the time of Charles the First, originally Papists, but one of them—the second you, our legend says—was of a milder, sweeter cast than the rest, who were fierce and bloody men, of a hard, strong nature; but he partook most of his mother's character. This son had been one of the earliest Quakers, converted by George Fox; and moreover there had been love between him and a young lady of great beauty and an heiress, whom likewise the eldest son of the house had designed to make his wife. And these brothers, cruel men, caught their innocent brother and kept him in confinement long in his own native home—"

"How?" asked the Doctor. "Why did not he appeal to the laws?"

"Our legend says," replied the schoolmaster, "only that he was kept in a chamber that was forgotten." [Endnote: 2.]

"Very strange that!" quoth the Doctor. "He was sold by his brethren."

The schoolmaster went on to tell, with much shuddering, how a Jesuit priest had been mixed up with this wretched business, and there had been a scheme at once religious and political to wrest the estate and the lovely lady from the fortunate heir; and how this grim Italian priest had instigated them to use a certain kind of torture with the poor heir, and how he had suffered from this; but one night, when they left him senseless, he contrived to make his escape from that cruel home, bleeding as he went; and how, by some action of his imagination,—his sense of the cruelty and hideousness of such treatment at his brethren's hands, and in the holy name of his religion,—his foot, which had been crushed by their cruelty, bled as he went, and that blood had never been stanched. And thus he had come to America, and after many wanderings, and much track of blood along rough ways, to New England. [Endnote: 3.]

"And what became of his beloved?" asked the grim Doctor, who was puffing away at a fresh pipe with a very queer aspect.

"She died in England," replied the schoolmaster. "And before her death, by some means or other, they say that she found means to send him a child, the offspring of their marriage, and from that child our race descended. And they say, too, that she sent him a key to a coffin, in which was locked up a great treasure. But we have not the key. But he never went back to his own country; and being heart-broken, and sick and weary of the world and its pomps and vanities, he died here, after suffering much persecution likewise from the Puritans. For his peaceful religion was accepted nowhere."

"Of all legends, — all foolish legends," quoth the Doctor, wrathfully, with a face of a dark blood-red color, so much was his anger and contempt excited, "and of all absurd heroes of a legend, I never heard the like of this! Have you the key?"

"No; nor have I ever heard of it," answered the schoolmaster.

"But you have some papers?"

"They existed once: perhaps are still recoverable by search," said the schoolmaster. "My father knew of them."

"A foolish legend," reiterated the Doctor. "It is strange how human folly strings itself on to human folly, as a story originally false and foolish grows older."

He got up and walked about the room, with hasty and irregular strides and a prodigious swinging of his ragged dressing-gown, which swept away as many cobwebs as it would take a week to reproduce. After a few turns, as if to change the subject, the Doctor asked the schoolmaster if he had any taste for pictures, and drew his attention to the portrait which has been already mentioned, — the figure in antique sordid garb, with a halter round his neck, and the expression in his face which the Doctor and the two children had interpreted so differently. Colcord, who probably knew nothing about pictures, looked at it at first merely from the gentle and cool complaisance of his character; but becoming absorbed in the contemplation, stood long without speaking; until the Doctor, looking in his face, perceived his eyes were streaming with tears.

"What are you crying about?" said he, gruffly.

"I don't know," said the schoolmaster quietly. "But there is something in this picture that affects me inexpressibly; so that, not being a man passionate by nature, I have hardly ever been so moved as now!"

"Very foolish," muttered the Doctor, resuming his strides about the room. "I am ashamed of a grown man that can cry at a picture, and can't tell the reason why."

After a few more turns he resumed his easy-chair and his tumbler, and, looking upward, beckoned to his pet spider, which came dangling downward, great parti-colored monster that he was, and swung about his master's head in hideous conference as it seemed; a sight that so distressed the schoolmaster, or shocked his delicate taste, that he went out, and called the two children to take a walk with him, with the purpose of breathing air that was neither infected with spiders nor graves.

After his departure, Doctor Grimshawe seemed even more disturbed than during his presence: again he strode about the study; then sat down with his hands on his knees, looking straight into the fire, as if it imaged the seething element of his inner man, where burned hot projects, smoke, heat, blackness, ashes, a smouldering of old thoughts, a blazing up of new; casting in the gold of his mind, as Aaron did that of the Israelites, and waiting to see what sort of a thing would come out of the furnace. The children coming in from their play, he spoke harshly to them, and eyed little Ned with a sort of savageness, as if he meant to eat him up, or do some other dreadful deed: and when little Elsie came with her usual frankness to his knee, he repelled her in such a way that she shook her little hand at him, saying, "Naughty Doctor Grim, what has come to you?"

Through all that day, by some subtle means or other, the whole household knew that something was amiss; and nobody in it was comfortable. It was like a spell of weather; like the east wind; like an epidemic in the air, that would not let anything be comfortable or contented,—this pervading temper of the Doctor. Crusty Hannah knew it in the kitchen: even those who passed the house must have known it somehow or other, and have felt a chill, an irritation, an influence on the nerves, as they passed. The spiders knew it, and acted as they were wont to do in stormy weather. The schoolmaster, when he returned from his walk, seemed likewise to know it, and made himself secure and secret, keeping in his own room, except at dinner, when he ate his rice in silence, without looking towards the Doctor, and appeared before him no more till evening, when the grim Doctor summoned him into the study, after sending the two children to bed.

"Sir," began the Doctor, "you have spoken of some old documents in your possession relating to the English descent of your ancestors. I have a curiosity to see these documents. Where are they?" [Endnote: 4.]

"I have them about my person," said the schoolmaster; and he produced from his pocket a bundle of old yellow papers done up in a parchment cover, tied with a piece of white cord, and presented them to Doctor Grimshawe, who looked over them with interest. They seemed to consist of letters, genealogical lists, certified copies of entries in registers, things which must have been made out by somebody who knew more of business than this ethereal person in whose possession they now were. The Doctor looked at them with considerable attention, and at last did them hastily up in the bundle again, and returned them to the owner.

"Have you any idea what is now the condition of the family to whom these papers refer?" asked he.

"None whatever,—none for almost a hundred years," said the schoolmaster. "About that time ago, I have heard a vague story that one of my ancestors went to the old country and saw the place. But, you see, the change of name has effectually covered us from view; and I feel that our true name is that which my ancestor assumed when he was driven forth from the home of his fathers, and that I have nothing to do with any other. I have no views on the estate,—none whatever. I am not so foolish and dreamy."

"Very right," said the Doctor. "Nothing is more foolish than to follow up such a pursuit as this, against all the vested interests of two hundred years, which of themselves have built up an impenetrably strong allegation against you. They harden into stone, in England, these years, and become indestructible, instead of melting away as they do in this happy country."

"It is not a matter of interest with me," replied the schoolmaster.

"Very right,—very right!" repeated the grim Doctor.

But something was evidently amiss with him this evening. It was impossible to feel easy and comfortable in contact with him: if you looked in his face, there was the red, lurid glare of his eyes; meeting you fiercely and craftily as ever: sometimes he bit his lip and frowned in an awful manner. Once, he burst out into an awful fit of swearing, for no good reason, or any reason whatever that he explained, or that anybody could tell. Again, for no more suitable reason, he uplifted his stalwart arm, and smote a heavy blow with his fist upon the oak table, making the tumbler and black bottle leap up, and damaging, one would think, his own knuckles. Then he rose up, and resumed his strides about the room. He paused before the portrait before mentioned; then resumed his heavy, quick, irregular tread, swearing under his breath; and you would imagine, from what you heard, that all his thoughts and the movement of his mind were a blasphemy. Then again— but this was only once—he heaved a deep, ponderous sigh, that seemed to come up in spite of him, out of his depths, an exhalation of deep suffering, as if some convulsion had given it a passage to upper air, instead of its being hidden, as it generally was, by accumulated rubbish of later time heaped above it.

This latter sound appealed to something within the simple schoolmaster, who had been witnessing the demeanor of the Doctor, like a being looking from another sphere into the trouble of the mortal one; a being incapable of passion, observing the mute, hard struggle of one in its grasp.

"Friend," said he at length, "thou hast something on thy mind."

"Aye," said the grim Doctor, coming to a stand before his chair. "You see that? Can you see as well what it is?"

"Some stir and writhe of something in the past that troubles you, as if you had kept a snake for many years in your bosom, and stupefied it with brandy, and now it awakes again, and troubles you with bites and stings."

"What sort of a man do you think me?" asked the Doctor.

"I cannot tell," said the schoolmaster. "The sympathies of my nature are not those that should give me knowledge of such men."

"Am I, think you," continued the grim Doctor, "a man capable of great crime?"

"A great one, if any," said Colcord; "a great good, likewise, it might be."

"What would I be likely to do," asked Doctor Grim, "supposing I had a darling purpose, to the accomplishment of which I had given my soul,— yes, my soul,—my success in life, my days and nights of thought, my years of time, dwelling upon it, pledging myself to it, until at last I had grown to love the burden of it, and not to regret my own degradation? I, a man of strongest will. What would I do, if this were to be resisted?"

"I do not conceive of the force of will shaping out my ways," said the schoolmaster. "I walk gently along and take the path that opens before me."

"Ha! ha! ha!" shouted the grim Doctor, with one of his portentous laughs. "So do we all, in spite of ourselves; and sometimes the path comes to a sudden ending!" And he resumed his drinking.

The schoolmaster looked at him with wonder, and a kind of shuddering, at something so unlike himself; but probably he very imperfectly estimated the forces that were at work within this strange being, and how dangerous they made him. He imputed it, a great deal, to the brandy, which he had kept drinking in such inordinate quantities; whereas it is probable that this had a soothing, emollient effect, as far as it went, on the Doctor's emotions; a sort of like to like, that he instinctively felt to be a remedy, But in truth it was difficult to see these two human creatures together, without feeling their incompatibility; without having a sense that one must be hostile to the other. The schoolmaster, through his fine instincts, doubtless had a sense of this, and sat gazing at the lurid, wrathful figure of the Doctor, in a sort of trance and fascination: not able to stir; bewildered by the sight of the great spider and other surroundings; and this strange, uncouth fiend, who had always been abhorrent to him,—he had a kind of curiosity in it, waited to see what would come of it, but felt it to be an unnatural state to him. And again the grim Doctor came and stood before him, prepared to make another of those strange utterances with which he had already so perplexed him.

That night—that midnight—it was rumored through the town that one of the inhabitants, going home late along the street that led by the graveyard, saw the grim Doctor standing by the open window of the study behind the elm tree, in his old dressing-gown, chill as was the night, and flinging his arms abroad wildly into the darkness, and muttering like the growling of a tempest, with occasional vociferations that grew even shrill with passion. The listener, though affrighted, could not resist an impulse to pause, and attempt overhearing something that might let him into the secret counsels of this strange wild man, whom the town held in such awe and antipathy; to learn, perhaps, what was the great spider, and whether he were summoning the dead out of their graves. However, he could make nothing out of what he overheard, except it were fragmentary curses, of a dreadful character, which the Doctor brought up with might and main out of the depths of his soul, and flung them forth, burning hot, aimed at what, and why, and to what practical end, it was impossible to say; but as necessarily as a volcano, in a state of eruption, sends forth boiling lava, sparkling and scintillating stones, and a sulphurous atmosphere, indicative of its inward state. [Endnote: 5.]

Dreading lest some one of these ponderous anathemas should alight, reason or none, on his own head, the man crept away, and whispered the thing to his cronies, from whom it was communicated to the townspeople at large, and so became one of many stories circulating with reference to our grim hero, which, if not true to the fact, had undoubtedly a degree of appositeness to his character, of which they were the legitimate flowers and symbols. If the anathemas took no other effect, they seemed to have produced a very remarkable one on the unfortunate elm tree, through the naked branches of which the Doctor discharged this fiendish shot. For, the next spring, when April came, no tender leaves budded forth, no life awakened there; and never again, on that old elm, widely as its roots were imbedded among the dead of many years, was there rustling bough in the summer time, or the elm's early golden boughs in September; and after waiting till another spring to give it a fair chance of reviving, it was cut down and made into coffins, and burnt on the sexton's hearth. The general opinion was that the grim Doctor's awful profanity had blasted that tree, fostered, as it had been, on grave-mould of Puritans. In Lancashire they tell of a similar anathema. It had a very frightful effect, it must be owned, this idea of a man cherishing emotions in his breast of so horrible a nature that he could neither tell them to any human being, nor keep them in their plenitude and intensity within the breast where they had their germ, and so was forced to fling them forth upon the night, to pollute and put fear into the atmosphere, and that people should breathe-in somewhat of horror from an unknown source, and be affected with nightmare, and dreams in which they were startled at their own wickedness.

CHAPTER VIII

At the breakfast-table the next morning, however, appeared Doctor Grimshawe, wearing very much the same aspect of an uncombed, unshorn, unbrushed, odd sort of a pagan as at other times, and making no difference in his breakfast, except that he poured a pretty large dose of brandy into his cup of tea; a thing, however, by no means unexampled or very unusual in his history. There were also the two children, fresher than the morning itself, rosy creatures, with newly scrubbed cheeks, made over again for the new day, though the old one had left no dust upon them;[Endnote: 1] laughing with one another, flinging their little jokes about the table, and expecting that the Doctor might, as was often his wont, set some ponderous old English joke trundling round among the breakfast cups; eating the corn-cakes which crusty Hannah, with the aboriginal part of her, had a knack of making in a peculiar and exquisite fashion. But there was an empty chair at table; one cup, one little jug of milk, and another of pure water, with no guest to partake of them.

"Where is the schoolmaster?" said Ned, pausing as he was going to take his seat.

"Yes, Doctor Grim?" said little Elsie.

"He has overslept himself for once," quoth Doctor Grim gruffly; "a strange thing, too, for a man whose victuals and drink are so light as the schoolmaster's. The fiend take me if I thought he had mortal mould enough in him ever to go to sleep at all; though he is but a kind of dream-stuff in his widest-awake state. Hannah, you bronze jade, call the schoolmaster to come to breakfast."

Hannah departed on her errand, and was heard knocking at the door of the schoolmaster's chamber several times, till the Doctor shouted to her wrathfully to cease her clatter and open the door at once, which she appeared to do, and speedily came back.

"He no there, massa. Schoolmaster melted away!"

"Vanished like a bubble!" quoth the Doctor.

"The great spider caught him like a fly," quoth crusty Hannah, chuckling with a sense of mischief that seemed very pleasant to her strange combination.

"He has taken a morning walk," said little Ned; "don't you think so, Doctor Grim?"

"Yes," said the grim Doctor. "Go on with your breakfast, little monkey; the walk may be a long one, or he is so slight a weight that the wind may blow him overboard."

A very long walk it proved; or it might be that some wind, whether evil or good, had blown him, as the Doctor suggested, into parts unknown; for, from that time forth, the Yankee schoolmaster returned no more. It was a singular disappearance.

The bed did not appear to have been slept in; there was a bundle, in a clean handkerchief, containing two shirts, two pocket handkerchiefs, two pairs of cotton socks, a Testament, and that was all. Had he intended to go away, why did he not take this little luggage in his hand, being all he had, and of a kind not easily dispensed with? The Doctor made small question about it, however; he had seemed surprised, at first, yet gave certainly no energetic token of it; and when Ned, who began to have notions of things, proposed to advertise him in the newspapers, or send the town crier round, the Doctor ridiculed the idea unmercifully.

"Lost, a lank Yankee schoolmaster," quoth he, uplifting his voice after the manner of the town crier; "supposed to have been blown out of Doctor Grim's window, or perhaps have ridden off astride of a humble-bee."

"It is not pretty to laugh in that way, Doctor Grim," said little Elsie, looking into his face, with a grave shake of her head.

"And why not, you saucy little witch?" said the Doctor.

"It is not the way to laugh, Doctor Grim," persisted the child, but either could not or would not assign any reason for her disapprobation, although what she said appeared to produce a noticeable effect on Doctor Grimshawe, who lapsed into a rough, harsh manner, that seemed to satisfy Elsie better. Crusty Hannah, meanwhile, seemed to dance about the house with a certain singular alacrity, a wonderful friskiness, indeed, as if the diabolical result of the mixture in her nature was particularly pleased with something; so she went, with queer gesticulations, crossings, contortions, friskings, evidently in a very mirthful state; until, being asked by her master what was the matter, she replied, "Massa, me know what became of the schoolmaster. Great spider catch in his web and eat him!"

Whether that was the mode of his disappearance, or some other, certainly the schoolmaster was gone; and the children were left in great bewilderment at the sudden vacancy in his place. They had not contracted a very yearning affection for him, and yet his impression had been individual and real, and they felt that something was gone out of their lives, now that he was no longer there. Something strange in their circumstances made itself felt by them; they were more sensible of the grim Doctor's uncouthness, his strange, reprehensible habits, his dark, mysterious life,—in looking at these things, and the spiders, and the graveyard, and their insulation from the world, through the crystal medium of this stranger's character. In remembering him in connection with these things, a certain seemly beauty in him showed strikingly the unfitness, the sombre and tarnished color, the outréness, of the rest of their lot. Little Elsie perhaps felt the loss of him more than her playmate, although both had been interested by him. But now things returned pretty much to their old fashion; although, as is inevitably the case, whenever persons or things have been taken suddenly or unaccountably out of our sphere, without telling us whither and why they have disappeared, the children could not, for a long while, bring themselves to feel that he had really gone. Perhaps, in imitation of the custom in that old English house, of which the Doctor had told them, little Elsie insisted that his place should still be kept at the table; and so, whenever crusty Hannah neglected to do so, she herself would fetch a plate, and a little pitcher of water, and set it beside a vacant chair; and sometimes, so like a shadow had he been, this pale, slender creature, it almost might have been thought that he was sitting with them. But crusty Hannah shook her head, and grinned. "The spider know where he is. We never see him more!"

His abode in the house had been of only two or three weeks; and in the natural course of things, had he come and gone in an ordinary way, his recollection would have grown dim and faded out in two or three weeks more; but the speculations, the expectations, the watchings for his reappearance, served to cut and grave the recollection of him into the children's hearts, so that it remained a life-long thing with them,—a sense that he was something that had been lost out of their life too soon, and that was bound, sooner or later, to reappear, and finish what business he had with them. Sometimes they prattled around the Doctor's chair about him, and they could perceive sometimes that he appeared to be listening, and would chime in with some remark; but he never expressed either wonder or regret; only telling Ned, once, that he had no reason to be sorry for his disappearance.

"Why, Doctor Grim?" asked the boy.

The Doctor mused, and smoked his pipe, as if he himself were thinking why, and at last he answered, "He was a dangerous fellow, my old boy."

"Why?" said Ned again.

"He would have taken the beef out of you," said the Doctor.

I know not how long it was before any other visitor (except such as brought their shattered constitutions there in hopes that the Doctor would make the worn-out machinery as good as new) came to the lonely little household on the corner of the graveyard. The intercourse between themselves and the rest of the town remained as scanty as ever. Still, the grim, shaggy Doctor was seen setting doggedly forth, in all seasons and all weathers, at a certain hour of the day, with the two children, going for long walks on the sea-shore, or into the country, miles away, and coming back, hours afterwards, with plants and herbs that had perhaps virtue in them, or flowers that had certainly beauty; even, in their season, the fragrant magnolias, leaving a trail of fragrance after them, that grow only in spots, the seeds having been apparently dropped by some happy accident when those proper to the climate were distributed. Shells there were, also, in the baskets that they carried, minerals, rare things, that a magic touch seemed to have created out of the rude and common things that others find in a homely and ordinary region. The boy was growing tall, and had got out of the merely infantile age; agile he was, bright, but still with a remarkable thoughtfulness, or gravity, or I know not what to call it; but it was a shadow, no doubt, falling upon him from something sombre in his warp of life, which the impressibility of his age and nature so far acknowledged as to be a little pale and grave, without positive unhappiness; and when a playful moment came, as they often did to these two healthy children, it seemed all a mistake that you had ever thought either of them too grave for their age. But little Elsie was still the merrier. They were still children, although they quarrelled seldomer than of yore, and kissed seldomer, and had ceased altogether to complain of one another to the Doctor; perhaps the time when Nature saw these bickerings to be necessary to the growth of some of their faculties was nearly gone. When they did have a quarrel, the boy stood upon his dignity, and visited Elsie with a whole day, sometimes, of silent and stately displeasure, which she was accustomed to bear, sometimes with an assumption of cold indifference, sometimes with liveliness, mirth in double quantity, laughter almost as good as real,—little arts which showed themselves in her as naturally as the gift of tears and smiles. In fact, having no advantage of female intercourse, she could not well have learnt them unless from crusty Hannah, who was such an anomaly of a creature, with all her mixtures of race, that she struck you as having lost all sex as one result of it. Yet this little girl was truly feminine, and had all the manners and pre-eminently uncriticisable tenets proper to women at her early age.

She had made respectable advancement in study; that is, she had taught herself to write, with even greater mechanical facility than Ned; and other knowledge had fallen upon her, as it were, by a reflected light from him; or, to use another simile, had been spattered upon her by the full stream which the Doctor poured into the vessel of the boy's intellect. So that she had even some knowledge of the rudiments of Latin, and geometry, and algebra; inaccurate enough, but yet with such a briskness that she was sometimes able to assist Ned in studies in which he was far more deeply grounded than herself. All this, however, was more by sympathy than by any natural taste for such things; being kindly, and sympathetic, and impressible, she took the color of what was nearest to her, and especially when it came from a beloved object, so that it was difficult to discover that it was not really one of her native tastes. The only thing, perhaps, altogether suited to her idiosyncrasy (because it was truly feminine, calculated for dainty fingers, and a nice little subtlety) was that kind of embroidery, twisting, needle-work, on textile fabric, which, as we have before said, she learnt from crusty Hannah, and which was emblematic perhaps of that creature's strange mixture of races.

Elsie seemed not only to have caught this art in its original spirit, but to have improved upon it, creating strange, fanciful, and graceful devices, which grew beneath her finger as naturally as the variegated hues grow in a flower as it opens; so that the homeliest material assumed a grace and strangeness as she wove it, whether it were grass, twigs, shells, or what not. Never was anything seen, that so combined a wild, barbarian freedom with cultivated grace; and the grim Doctor himself, little open to the impressions of the beautiful, used to hold some of her productions in his hand, gazing at them with deep intentness, and at last, perhaps, breaking out into one of his deep roars of laughter; for it seemed to suggest thoughts to him that the children could not penetrate. This one feature of strangeness and wild faculty in the otherwise sweet and natural and homely character of Elsie had a singular effect; it was like a wreath of wild-flowers in her hair, like something that set her a little way apart from the rest of the world, and had an even more striking effect than if she were altogether strange.

Thus were the little family going on; the Doctor, I regret to say, growing more morose, self-involved, and unattainable since the disappearance of the schoolmaster than before; more given up to his one plaything, the great spider; less frequently even than before coming out of the grim seclusion of his moodiness, to play with the children, though they would often be sensible of his fierce eyes fixed upon them, and start and feel incommoded by the intensity of his regard;—thus things were going on, when one day there was really again a visitor, and not a dilapidated patient, to the grim Doctor's study. Crusty Hannah brought up his name as Mr. Hammond, and the Doctor—filling his everlasting pipe, meanwhile, and ordering Hannah to give him a coal (perhaps this was the circumstance that made people say he had imps to bring him coals from Tophet)—ordered him to be shown up. [Endnote: 2.]

A fresh-colored, rather young man [Endnote: 3] entered the study, a person of rather cold and ungraceful manners, yet genial-looking enough; at least, not repulsive. He was dressed in rather a rough, serviceable travelling-dress, and except for a nicely brushed hat, and unmistakably white linen, was rather careless in attire. You would have thought twice, perhaps, before deciding him to be a gentleman, but finally would have decided that he was; one great token being, that the singular aspect of the room into which he was ushered, the spider festoonery, and other strange accompaniments, the grim aspect of the Doctor himself, and the beauty and intelligence of his two companions, and even that horrific weaver, the great dangling spider,—neither one nor all of these called any expression of surprise to the stranger's face.

"Your name is Hammond?" begins the Doctor, with his usual sparseness of ornamental courtesy. [Endnote: 4.]

The stranger bowed.

"An Englishman, I perceive," continued the Doctor, but nowise intimating that the fact of being a countryman was any recommendation in his eyes.

"Yes, an Englishman," replied Hammond; "a briefless barrister, [Endnote: 5] in fact, of Lincoln's Inn, who, having little or nothing to detain him at home, has come to spend a few idle months in seeing the new republic which has been made out of English substance."

"And what," continued Doctor Grim, not a whit relaxing the repulsiveness of his manner, and scowling askance at the stranger,—"what may have drawn on me the good fortune of being compelled to make my time idle, because yours is so?"

The stranger's cheek flushed a little; but he smiled to himself, as if saying that here was a grim, rude kind of humorist, who had lost the sense of his own peculiarity, and had no idea that he was rude at all. "I came to America, as I told you," said he, "chiefly because I was idle, and wanted to turn my enforced idleness to what profit I could, in the way of seeing men, manners, governments, and problems, which I hope to have no time to study by and by. But I also had an errand intrusted to me, and of a singular nature; and making inquiry in this little town (where my mission must be performed, if at all), I have been directed to you, by your townspeople, as to a person not unlikely to be able to assist me in it."

"My townspeople, since you choose to call them so," answered the grim Doctor, "ought to know, by this time, that I am not the sort of man likely to assist any person, in any way."

"Yet this is so singular an affair," said the stranger, still with mild courtesy, "that at least it may excite your curiosity. I have come here to find a grave."

"To find a grave!" said Doctor Grim, giving way to a grim sense of humor, and relaxing just enough to let out a joke, the tameness of which was a little redeemed, to his taste, by its grimness. "I might help you there, to be sure, since it is all in the way of business. Like others of my profession, I have helped many people to find their graves, no doubt, and shall be happy to do the same for you. You have hit upon the one thing in which my services are ready."

"I thank you, my dear sir," said the young stranger, having tact enough to laugh at Dr. Grim's joke, and thereby mollifying him a little; "but as far as I am personally concerned, I prefer to wait a while before making the discovery of that little spot in Mother Earth which I am destined to occupy. It is a grave which has been occupied as such for at least a century and a half which I am in quest of; and it is as an antiquarian, a genealogist, a person who has had dealings with the dead of long ago, not as a professional man engaged in adding to their number, that I ask your aid."

"Ah, ahah!" said the Doctor, laying down his pipe, and looking earnestly at the stranger; not kindly nor genially, but rather with a lurid glance of suspicion out of those red eyes of his, but no longer with a desire to escape an intruder; rather as one who meant to clutch him. "Explain your meaning, sir, at once."

"Then here it is," said Mr. Hammond. "There is an old English family, one of the members of which, very long ago, emigrated to this part of America, then a wilderness, and long afterwards a British colony. He was on ill terms with his family. There is reason to believe that documents, deeds, titular proofs, or some other thing valuable to the family, were buried in the grave of this emigrant; and there have been various attempts, within a century, to find this grave, and if possible some living descendant of the man, or both, under the idea that either of these cases might influence the disputed descent of the property, and enable the family to prove its claims to an ancient title. Now, rather as a matter of curiosity, than with any real hope of success,—and being slightly connected with the family,—I have taken what seems to myself a wild-goose chase; making it merely incidental, you well understand, not by any means the main purpose of my voyage to America."

"What is the name of this family?" asked the Doctor, abruptly.

"The man whose grave I seek," said the stranger, "lived and died, in this country, under the assumed name of Colcord."

"How do you expect to succeed in this ridiculous quest?" asked the Doctor, "and what marks, signs, directions, have you to guide your search? And moreover, how have you come to any knowledge whatever about the matter, even that the emigrant ever assumed this name of Colcord, and that he was buried anywhere, and that his place of burial, after more than a century, is of the slightest importance?"

"All this was ascertained by a messenger on a similar errand with my own, only undertaken nearly a century ago, and more in earnest than I can pretend to be," replied the Englishman. "At that period, however, there was probably a desire to find nothing that might take the hereditary possessions of the family out of the branch which still held them; and there is strong reason to suspect that the information acquired was purposely kept secret by the person in England into whose hands it came. The thing is differently situated now; the possessor of the estate is recently dead; and the discovery of an American heir would not be unacceptable to many. At all events, any knowledge gained here would throw light on a somewhat doubtful matter."

"Where, as nearly as you can judge," said the Doctor, after a turn or two through the study, "was this man buried?"

"He spent the last years of his life, certainly, in this town," said Hammond, "and may be found, if at all, among the dead of that period."

"And they—their miserable dust, at least, which is all that still exists of them—were buried in the graveyard under these windows," said the Doctor. "What marks, I say,—for you might as well seek a vanished wave of the sea, as a grave that surged upward so long ago."

"On the gravestone," said Hammond, "a slate one, there was rudely sculptured the impress of a foot. What it signifies I cannot conjecture, except it had some reference to a certain legend of a bloody footstep, which is currently told, and some token of which yet remains on one of the thresholds of the ancient mansion-house."

Ned and Elsie had withdrawn themselves from the immediate vicinity of the fireside, and were playing at fox and geese in a corner near the window. But little Elsie, having very quick ears, and a faculty of attending to more affairs than one, now called out, "Doctor Grim, Ned and I know where that gravestone is."

"Hush, Elsie," whispered Ned, earnestly.

"Come forward here, both of you," said Doctor Grimshawe.

CHAPTER IX

The two children approached, and stood before the Doctor and his guest, the latter of whom had not hitherto taken particular notice of them. He now looked from one to the other, with the pleasant, genial expression of a person gifted with a natural liking for children, and the freemasonry requisite to bring him acquainted with them; and it lighted up his face with a pleasant surprise to see two such beautiful specimens of boyhood and girlhood in this dismal, spider-haunted house, and under the guardianship of such a savage lout as the grim Doctor. He seemed particularly struck by the intelligence and sensibility of Ned's face, and met his eyes with a glance that Ned long afterwards remembered; but yet he seemed quite as much interested by Elsie, and gazed at her face with a perplexed, inquiring glance.

"These are fine children," said he. "May I ask if they are your own?— Pardon me if I ask amiss," added he, seeing a frown on the Doctor's brow.

"Ask nothing about the brats," replied he grimly. "Thank Heaven, they are not my children; so your question is answered."

"I again ask pardon," said Mr. Hammond. "I am fond of children; and the boy has a singularly fine countenance; not in the least English. The true American face, no doubt. As to this sweet little girl, she impresses me with a vague resemblance to some person I have seen. Hers I should deem an English face."

"These children are not our topic," said the grim Doctor, with gruff impatience. "If they are to be so, our conversation is ended. Ned, what do you know of this gravestone with the bloody foot on it?"

"It is not a bloody foot, Doctor Grim," said Ned, "and I am not sure that it is a foot at all; only Elsie and I chose to fancy so, because of a story that we used to play at. But we were children then. The gravestone lies on the ground, within a little bit of a walk of our door; but this snow has covered it all over; else we might go out and see it."

"We will go out at any rate," said the Doctor, "and if the Englishman chooses to come to America, he must take our snows as he finds them. Take your shovel, Ned, and if necessary we will uncover the gravestone."

They accordingly muffled themselves in their warmest, and plunged forth through a back door into Ned and Elsie's playground, as the grim Doctor was wont to call it. The snow, except in one spot close at hand, lay deep, like cold oblivion, over the surging graves, and piled itself in drifted heaps against every stone that raised itself above the level; it filled enviously the letters of the inscriptions, enveloping all the dead in one great winding-sheet, whiter and colder than those which they had individually worn. The dreary space was pathless; not a footstep had tracked through the heavy snow; for it must be warm affection indeed that could so melt this wintry impression as to penetrate through the snow and frozen earth, and establish any warm thrills with the dead beneath: daisies, grass, genial earth, these allow of the magnetism of such sentiments; but winter sends them shivering back to the baffled heart.

"Well, Ned," said the Doctor, impatiently.

Ned looked about him somewhat bewildered, and then pointed to a spot within not more than ten paces of the threshold which they had just crossed; and there appeared, not a gravestone, but a new grave (if any grave could be called new in that often-dug soil, made up of old mortality), an open hole, with the freshly-dug earth piled up beside it. A little snow (for there had been a gust or two since morning) appeared, as they peeped over the edge, to have fallen into it; but not enough to prevent a coffin from finding fit room and accommodation in it. But it was evident that the grave had been dug that very day.

"The headstone, with the foot on it, was just here," said Ned, in much perplexity, "and, as far as I can judge, the old sunken grave exactly marked out the space of this new one." [Endnote: 1.]

"It is a shame," said Elsie, much shocked at the indecorum, "that the new person should be thrust in here; for the old one was a friend of ours."

"But what has become of the headstone!" exclaimed the young English stranger.

During their perplexity, a person had approached the group, wading through the snow from the gateway giving entrance from the street; a gaunt figure, with stooping shoulders, over one of which was a spade and some other tool fit for delving in the earth; and in his face there was the sort of keen, humorous twinkle that grave-diggers somehow seem to get, as if the dolorous character of their business necessitated something unlike itself by an inevitable reaction.

"Well, Doctor," said he, with a shrewd wink in his face, "are you looking for one of your patients? The man who is to be put to bed here was never caught in your spider's web."

"No," said Doctor Grimshawe; "when my patients have done with me, I leave them to you and the old Nick, and never trouble myself about them more. What I want to know is, why you have taken upon you to steal a man's grave, after he has had immemorial possession of it. By what right have you dug up this bed, undoing the work of a predecessor of yours, who has long since slept in one of his own furrows?"

"Why, Doctor," said the grave-digger, looking quietly into the cavernous pit which he had hollowed, "it is against common sense that a dead man should think to keep a grave to himself longer than till you can take up his substance in a shovel. It would be a strange thing enough, if, when living families are turned out of their homes twice or thrice in a generation, (as they are likely to be in our new government,) a dead man should think he must sleep in one spot till the day of judgment. No; turn about, I say, to these old fellows. As long as they can decently be called dead men, I let them lie; when they are nothing but dust, I just take leave to stir them on occasion. This is the way we do things under the republic, whatever your customs be in the old country."

"Matters are very much the same in any old English churchyard," said the English stranger. "But, my good friend, I have come three thousand miles, partly to find this grave, and am a little disappointed to find my labor lost."

"Ah! and you are the man my father was looking for," said the grave-digger, nodding his head at Mr. Hammond. "My father, who was a grave-digger afore me, died four and thirty years ago, when we were under the King; and says he, 'Ebenezer, do not you turn up a sod in this spot, till you have turned up every other in the ground.' And I have always obeyed him."

"And what was the reason of such a singular prohibition?" asked Hammond.

"My father knew," said the grave-digger, "and he told me the reason too; but since we are under the republic, we have given up remembering those old-world legends, as we used to. The newspapers keep us from talking in the chimney-corner; and so things go out of our minds. An old man, with his stories of what he has seen, and what his great-grandfather saw before him, is of little account since newspapers came up. Stop—I remember—no, I forget,—it was something about the grave holding a witness, who had been sought before and might be again."

"And that is all you know about it?" said Hammond.

"All,—every mite," said the old grave-digger. "But my father knew, and would have been glad to tell you the whole story. There was a great deal of wisdom and knowledge, about graves especially, buried out yonder where my old father was put away, before the Stamp Act was thought of. But it is no great matter, I suppose. People don't care about old graves in these times. They just live, and put the dead out of sight and out of mind."

"Well; but what have you done with the headstone?" said the Doctor. "You can't have eaten it up."

"No, no, Doctor," said the grave-digger, laughing; "it would crack better teeth than mine, old and crumbly as it is. And yet I meant to do something with it that is akin to eating; for my oven needs a new floor, and I thought to take this stone, which would stand the fire well. But here," continued he, scraping away the snow with his shovel, a task in which little Ned gave his assistance, — "here is the headstone, just as I have always seen it, and as my father saw it before me."

The ancient memorial, being cleared of snow, proved to be a slab of freestone, with some rude traces of carving in bas-relief around the border, now much effaced, and an impression, which seemed to be as much like a human foot as anything else, sunk into the slab; but this device was wrought in a much more clumsy way than the ornamented border, and evidently by an unskilful hand. Beneath was an inscription, over which the hard, flat lichens had grown, and done their best to obliterate it, although the following words might be written [Endnote: 2] or guessed: —

"Here lyeth the mortal part of Thomas Colcord, an upright man, of tender and devout soul, who departed this troublous life September ye nineteenth, 1667, aged 57 years and nine months. Happier in his death than in his lifetime. Let his bones be."

The name, Colcord, was somewhat defaced; it was impossible, in the general disintegration of the stone, to tell whether wantonly, or with a purpose of altering and correcting some error in the spelling, or, as occurred to Hammond, to change the name entirely.

"This is very unsatisfactory," said Hammond, "but very curious, too. But this certainly is the impress of what was meant for a human foot, and coincides strangely with the legend of the Bloody Footstep, — the mark of the foot that trod in the blessed King Charles's blood."

"For that matter," said the grave-digger, "it comes into my mind that my father used to call it the stamp of Satan's foot, because he claimed the dead man for his own. It is plain to see that there was a deep deft between two of the toes."

"There are two ways of telling that legend," remarked the Doctor. "But did you find nothing in the grave, Hewen?"

"O, yes,—a bone or two,—as much as could be expected after above a hundred years," said the grave-digger. "I tossed them aside; and if you are curious about them, you will find them when the snow melts. That was all; and it would have been unreasonable in old Colcord—especially in these republican times—to have wanted to keep his grave any longer, when there was so little of him left."

"I must drop the matter here, then," said Hammond, with a sigh. "Here, my friend, is a trifle for your trouble."

"No trouble," said the grave-digger, "and in these republican times we can't take anything for nothing, because it won't do for a poor man to take off his hat and say thank you."

Nevertheless, he did take the silver, and winked a sort of acknowledgment.

The Doctor, with unwonted hospitality, invited the English stranger to dine in his house; and though there was no pretence of cordiality in the invitation, Mr. Hammond accepted it, being probably influenced by curiosity to make out some definite idea of the strange household in which he found himself. Doctor Grimshawe having taken it upon him to be host,—for, up to this time, the stranger stood upon his own responsibility, and, having voluntarily presented himself to the Doctor, had only himself to thank for any scant courtesy he might meet,—but now the grim Doctor became genial after his own fashion. At dinner he produced a bottle of port, which made the young Englishman almost fancy himself on the other side of the water; and he entered into a conversation, which I fancy was the chief object which the grim Doctor had in view in showing himself in so amiable a light, [Endnote: 3] for in the course of it the stranger was insensibly led to disclose many things, as it were of his own accord, relating to the part of England whence he came, and especially to the estate and family which have been before mentioned,—the present state of that family, together with other things that he seemed to himself to pour out naturally,—for, at last, he drew himself up, and attempted an excuse.

"Your good wine," said he, "or the unexpected accident of meeting a countryman, has made me unusually talkative, and on subjects, I fear, which have not a particular interest for you."

"I have not quite succeeded in shaking off my country, as you see," said Doctor Grimshawe, "though I neither expect nor wish ever to see it again."

There was something rather ungracious in the grim Doctor's response, and as they now adjourned to his study, and the Doctor betook himself to his pipe and tumbler, the young Englishman sought to increase his acquaintance with the two children, both of whom showed themselves graciously inclined towards him; more warmly so than they had been to the schoolmaster, as he was the only other guest whom they had ever met.

"Would you like to see England, my little fellow?" he inquired of Ned.

"Oh, very much! more than anything else in the world," replied the boy, his eyes gleaming and his cheeks flushing with the earnestness of his response; for, indeed, the question stirred up all the dreams and reveries which the child had cherished, far back into the dim regions of his memory. After what the Doctor had told him of his origin, he had never felt any home feeling here; it seemed to him that he was wandering Ned, whom the wind had blown from afar. Somehow or other, from many circumstances which he put together and seethed in his own childish imagination, it seemed to him that he was to go back to that far old country, and there wander among the green, ivy-grown, venerable scenes; the older he grew, the more his mind took depth, the stronger was this fancy in him; though even to Elsie he had scarcely breathed it.

"So strong a desire," said the stranger, smiling at his earnestness, "will be sure to work out its own accomplishment. I shall meet you in England, my young friend, one day or another. And you, my little girl, are you as anxious to see England as your brother?"

"Ned is not my brother," said little Elsie.

The Doctor here interposed some remark on a different subject; for it was observable that he never liked to have the conversation turn on these children, their parentage, or relations to each other or himself.

The children were sent to bed; and the young Englishman, finding the conversation lag, and his host becoming gruffer and less communicative than he thought quite courteous, retired. But before he went, however, he could not refrain from making a remark on the gigantic spider, which was swinging like a pendulum above the Doctor's head.

"What a singular pet!" said he; for the nervous part of him had latterly been getting uppermost, so that it disturbed him; in fact, the spider above and the grim man below equally disturbed him. "Are you a naturalist? Have you noted his habits?"

"Yes," said the Doctor, "I have learned from his web how to weave a plot, and how to catch my victim and devour him!"

"Thank God," said the Englishman, as he issued forth into the cold gray night, "I have escaped the grim fellow's web, at all events. How strange a group,—those two sweet children, that grim old man!"

As regards this matter of the ancient grave, it remains to be recorded, that, when the snow melted, little Ned and Elsie went to look at the spot, where, by this time, there was a little hillock with the brown sods laid duly upon it, which the coming spring would make green. By the side of it they saw, with more curiosity than repugnance, a few fragments of crumbly bones, which they plausibly conjectured to have appertained to some part of the framework of the ancient Colcord, wherewith he had walked through the troublous life of which his gravestone spoke. And little Elsie, whose eyes were very sharp, and her observant qualities of the quickest, found something which Ned at first pronounced to be only a bit of old iron, incrusted with earth; but Elsie persisted to knock off some of the earth that seemed to have incrusted it, and discovered a key. The children ran with their prize to the grim Doctor, who took it between his thumb and finger, turned it over and over, and then proceeded to rub it with a chemical substance which soon made it bright. It proved to be a silver key, of antique and curious workmanship.

"Perhaps this is what Mr. Hammond was in search of," said Ned. "What a pity he is gone! Perhaps we can send it after him."

"Nonsense," said the gruff Doctor.

And attaching the key to a chain, which he took from a drawer, and which seemed to be gold, he hung it round Ned's neck.

"When you find a lock for this key," said he, "open it, and consider yourself heir of whatever treasure is revealed there!"

Ned continued that sad, fatal habit of growing out of childhood, as boys will, until he was now about ten years old, and little Elsie as much as six or seven. He looked healthy, but pale; something there was in the character and influences of his life that made him look as if he were growing up in a shadow, with less sunshine than he needed for a robust and exuberant development, though enough to make his intellectual growth tend towards a little luxuriance, in some directions. He was likely to turn out a fanciful, perhaps a poetic youth; young as he was, there had been already discoveries, on the grim Doctor's part, of certain blotted and clumsily scrawled scraps of paper, the chirography on which was arrayed in marshalled lines of unequal length, and each commanded by a capital letter and marching on from six to ten lame feet. Doctor Grim inspected these things curiously, and to say the truth most scornfully, before he took them to light his pipe withal; but they told him little as regarded this boy's internal state, being mere echoes, and very lugubrious ones, of poetic strains that were floating about in the atmosphere of that day, long before any now remembered bard had begun to sing. But there were the rudiments of a poetic and imaginative mind within the boy, if its subsequent culture should be such as the growth of that delicate flower requires; a brooding habit taking outward things into itself and imbuing them with its own essence until, after they had lain there awhile, they assumed a relation both to truth and to himself, and became mediums to affect other minds with the magnetism of his own. He lived far too much an inward life for healthfulness, at his age; the peculiarity of his situation, a child of mystery, with certain reaches and vistas that seemed to promise a bright solution of his mystery, keeping his imagination always awake and strong. That castle in the air,—so much more vivid than other castles, because it had perhaps a real substance of ancient, ivy-grown, hewn stone somewhere,—that visionary hall in England, with its surrounding woods and fine lawns, and the beckoning shadows at the ancient windows, and that fearful threshold, with the blood still glistening on it,—he dwelt and wandered so much there, that he had no real life in the sombre house on the corner of the graveyard; except that the loneliness of the latter, and the grim Doctor with his grotesque surroundings, and then the great ugly spider, and that odd, inhuman mixture of crusty Hannah, all served to remove him out of the influences of common life. Little Elsie was all that he had to keep life real, and substantial; and she, a child so much younger than he, was influenced by the same circumstances, and still more by himself, so that, as far as he could impart himself to her, he led her hand in hand through the same dream-scenery amid which he strayed himself. They knew not another child in town; the grim Doctor was their only friend. As for Ned, this seclusion had its customary and normal effect upon him; it had made him think ridiculously high of his own gifts, powers, attainments, and at the same time doubt whether they would pass with those of others; it made him despise all flesh, as if he were of a superior race, and yet have an idle and weak fear of coming in contact with them, from a dread of his incompetency to cope with them; so he at once depreciated and exalted, to an absurd degree, both himself and others.

"Ned," said the Doctor to him one day, in his gruffest tone, "you are not turning out to be the boy I looked for and meant to make. I have given you sturdy English instruction, and solidly grounded you in matters that the poor superficial people and time merely skim over; I looked to see the rudiments of a man in you, by this time; and you begin to mope and pule as if your babyhood were coming back on you. You seem to think more than a boy of your years should; and yet it is not manly thought, nor ever will be so. What do you mean, boy, by making all my care of you come to nothing, in this way?"

"I do my best, Doctor Grim," said Ned, with sullen dignity. "What you teach me, I learn. What more can I do?"

"I'll tell you what, my fine fellow," quoth Doctor Grim, getting rude, as was his habit. "You disappoint me, and I'll not bear it. I want you to be a man; and I'll have you a man or nothing. If I had foreboded such a fellow as you turn out to be, I never would have taken you from the place where, as I once told you, I found you, — the almshouse!"

"O, Doctor Grim, Doctor Grim!" cried little Elsie, in a tone of grief and bitter reproach.

Ned had risen slowly, as the Doctor uttered those last words, turning as white as a sheet, and stood gazing at him, with large eyes, in which there was a calm upbraiding; a strange dignity was in his childish aspect, which was no longer childish, but seemed to have grown older all in a moment.

"Sir," added the Doctor, incensed at the boy's aspect, "there is nonsense that ought to be whipt out of you."

"You have said enough, sir," said the boy. "Would to God you had left me where you found me![Endnote: 4] It was not my fault that you took me from the alms-house. But it will be my fault if I ever eat another bit of your bread, or stay under your roof an hour longer."

He was moving towards the door, but little Elsie sprung upon him and caught him round the neck, although he repelled her with severe dignity; and Doctor Grimshawe, after a look at the group in which a bitter sort of mirth and mischief struggled with a better and kindlier sentiment, at last flung his pipe into the chimney, hastily quaffed the remnant of a tumbler, and shuffled after Ned, kicking off his old slippers in his hurry. He caught the boy just by the door.

"Ned, Ned, my boy, I'm sorry for what I said," cried he. "I am a guzzling old blockhead, and don't know how to treat a gentleman when he honors me with his company. It is not in my blood nor breeding to have such knowledge. Ned, you will make a man, and I lied if I said otherwise. Come, I'm sorry, I'm sorry."

The boy was easily touched, at these years, as a boy ought to be; and though he had not yet forgiven the grim Doctor, the tears, to his especial shame, gushed out of his eyes in a torrent, and his whole frame shook with sobs. The Doctor caught him in his arms, and hugged him to his old tobacco-fragrant dressing-gown, hugged him like a bear, as he was; so that poor Ned hardly knew whether he was embracing him with his love, or squeezing him to death in his wrath.

"Ned," said he, "I'm not going to live a great while longer; I seem an eternal nuisance to you, I know; but it's not so, I'm mortal and I feel myself breaking up. Let us be friends while I live; for believe me, Ned, I've done as well by you as I knew, and care for nothing, love nothing, so much as you. Little Elsie here, yes. I love her too. But that's different. You are a boy, and will be a man; and a man whom I destine to do for me what it has been the object of my life to achieve. Let us be friends. We will—we must be friends; and when old Doctor Grim, worthless wretch that he is, sleeps in his grave, you shall not have the pang of having parted from him in unkindness. Forgive me, Ned; and not only that, but love me better than ever; for though I am a hasty old wretch, I am not altogether evil as regards you."

I know not whether the Doctor would have said all this, if the day had not been pretty well advanced, and if his potations had not been many; but, at any rate, he spoke no more than he felt, and his emotions thrilled through the sensitive system of the boy, and quite melted him down. He forgave Doctor Grim, and, as he asked, loved him better than ever; and so did Elsie. Then it was so sweet, so good, to have had this one outgush of affection,— he, poor child, who had no memory of mother's kisses, or of being cared for out of tenderness, and whose heart had been hungry, all his life, for some such thing; and probably Doctor Grim, in his way, had the same kind of enjoyment of this passionate crisis; so that though, the next day, they all three looked at one another a little ashamed, yet it had some remote analogy to that delicious embarrassment of two lovers, at their first meeting after they know all.

CHAPTER X

It is very remarkable that Ned had so much good in him as we find there; in the first place, born as he seemed to be of a wild, vagrant stock, a seedling sown by the breezes, and falling among the rocks and sands; the growing up without a mother to cultivate his tenderness with kisses and the inestimable, inevitable love of love breaking out on all little occasions, without reference to merit or demerit, unfailing whether or no; mother's faith in excellences, the buds which were yet invisible to all other eyes, but to which her warm faith was the genial sunshine necessary to their growth; mother's generous interpretation of all that was doubtful in him, and which might turn out good or bad, according as should be believed of it; mother's pride in whatever the boy accomplished, and unfailing excuses, explanations, apologies, so satisfactory, for all his failures; mother's deep intuitive insight, which should see the permanent good beneath all the appearance of temporary evil, being wiser through her love than the wisest sage could be,—the dullest, homeliest mother than the wisest sage. The Creator, apparently, has set a little of his own infinite wisdom and love (which are one) in a mother's heart, so that no child, in the common course of things, should grow up without some heavenly instruction. Instead of all this, and the vast deal more that mothers do for children, there had been only the gruff, passionate Doctor, without sense of religion, with only a fitful tenderness, with years' length between the fits, so fiercely critical, so wholly unradiant of hope, misanthropic, savagely morbid. Yes; there was little Elsie too; it must have been that she was the boy's preserver, being childhood, sisterhood, womanhood, all that there had been for him of human life, and enough—he being naturally of such good stuff—to keep him good. He had lost much, but not all: he was not nearly what he might have been under better auspices; flaws and imperfections there were, in abundance, great uncultivated wastes and wildernesses in his moral nature, tangled wilds where there might have been stately, venerable religious groves; but there was no rank growth of evil. That unknown mother, that had no opportunity to nurse her boy, must have had gentle and noblest qualities to endow him with; a noble father, too, a long, unstained descent, one would have thought. Was this an almshouse child?

Doctor Grim knew, very probably, that there was all this on the womanly side that was wanting to Ned's occasion; and very probably, too, being a man not without insight, he was aware that tender treatment, as a mother bestows it, tends likewise to foster strength, and manliness of character, as well as softer developments; but all this he could not have supplied, and now as little as ever. But there was something else which Ned ought to have, and might have; and this was intercourse with his kind, free circulation, free air, instead of the stived-up house, with the breeze from the graveyard blowing over it,—to be drawn out of himself, and made to share the life of many, to be introduced, at one remove, to the world with which he was to contend. To this end, shortly after the scene of passion and reconciliation above described, the Doctor took the resolution of sending Ned to an academy, famous in that day, and still extant. Accordingly they all three—the grim Doctor, Ned, and Elsie—set forth, one day of spring, leaving the house to crusty Hannah and the great spider, in a carryall, being the only excursion involving a night's absence that either of the two children remembered from the house by the graveyard, as at nightfall they saw the modest pine-built edifice, with its cupola and bell, where Ned was to be initiated into the schoolboy. The Doctor, remembering perhaps days spent in some gray, stately, legendary great school of England, instinct with the boyhood of men afterwards great, puffed forth a depreciating curse upon it; but nevertheless made all arrangements for Ned's behoof, and next morning prepared to leave him there.

"Ned, my son, good by," cried he, shaking the little fellow's hand as he stood tearful and wistful beside the chaise shivering at the loneliness which he felt settling around him,—a new loneliness to him,—the loneliness of a crowd. "Do not be cast down, my boy. Face the world; grasp the thistle strongly, and it will sting you the less. Have faith in your own fist! Fear no man! Have no secret plot! Never do what you think wrong! If hereafter you learn to know that Doctor Grim was a bad man, forgive him, and be a better one yourself. Good by, and if my blessing be good for anything, in God's name, I invoke it upon you heartily."

Little Elsie was sobbing, and flung her arms about Ned's neck, and he his about hers; so that they parted without a word. As they drove away, a singular sort of presentiment came over the boy, as he stood looking after them.

"It is all over,—all over," said he to himself: "Doctor Grim and little Elsie are gone out of my life. They leave me and will never come back,—not they to me, not I to them. O, how cold the world is! Would we three—the Doctor, and Elsie, and I—could have lain down in a row, in the old graveyard, close under the eaves of the house, and let the grass grow over us. The world is cold; and I am an alms-house child."

The house by the graveyard seemed dismal now, no doubt, to little Elsie, who, being of a cheerful nature herself, (common natures often having this delusion about a home,) had grown up with the idea that it was the most delightful spot in the world; the place fullest of pleasant play, and of household love (because her own love welled over out of her heart, like a spring in a barrel); the place where everybody was kind and good, the world beyond its threshold appearing perhaps strange and sombre; the spot where it was pleasantest to be, for its own mere sake; the dim old, homely place, so warm and cosey in winter, so cool in summer. Who else was fortunate enough to have such a home, — with that nice, kind, beautiful Ned, and that dear, kind, gentle, old Doctor Grim, with his sweet ways, so wise, so upright, so good, beyond all other men? O, happy girl that she was, to have grown up in such a home! Was there ever any other house with such cosey nooks in it? Such probably were the feelings of good little Elsie about this place, which has seemed to us so dismal; for the home feeling in the child's heart, her warm, cheerful, affectionate nature, was a magic, so far as she herself was concerned, and made all the house and its inmates over after her own fashion. But now that little Ned was gone, there came a change. She moped about the house, and, for the first time, suspected it was dismal.

As for the grim Doctor, there did not appear to be much alteration in that hard old character; perhaps he drank a little more, though that was doubtful, because it is difficult to see where he could find niches to stick in more frequent drinks. Nor did he more frequently breathe through the pipe. He fell into desuetude, however, of his daily walk, [Endnote: 1] and sent Elsie to play by herself in the graveyard (a dreary business enough for the poor child) instead of taking her to country or seaside himself. He was more savage and blasphemous, sometimes, than he had been heretofore known to be; but, on the other hand, he was sometimes softer, with a kind of weary consenting to circumstances, intervals of helpless resignation, when he no longer fought and struggled in his heart. He did not seem to be alive all the time; but, on the other hand, he was sometimes a good deal too much alive, and could not bear his potations as well as he used to do, and was overheard blaspheming at himself for being so weakly, and having a brain that could not bear a thimbleful, and growing to be a milksop like Colcord, as he said. This person, of whom the Doctor and his young people had had such a brief experience, appeared nevertheless to hang upon his remembrance in a singular way, — the more singular as there was little resemblance between them, or apparent possibility of sympathy. Little Elsie was startled to hear Doctor Grim sometimes call out, "Colcord! Colcord!" as if he were summoning a spirit from some secret place. He muttered, sitting by himself, long, indistinct masses of talk, in which this name was discernible, and other names. Going on mumbling, by the hour together, great masses of vague trouble, in which, if it only could have been unravelled and put in order, no doubt all the secrets of his life,—secrets of wrath, guilt, vengeance, love, hatred, all beaten up together, and the best quite spoiled by the worst, might have been found. His mind evidently wandered. Sometimes, he seemed to be holding conversation with unseen interlocutors, and almost invariably, so far as could be gathered, he was bitter, and then sat, immitigable, pouring out wrath and terror, denunciating, tyrannical, speaking as to something that lay at his feet, but which he would not spare. [Endnote: 2] Then suddenly, he would start, look round the dark old study, upward to the dangling spider overhead, and then at the quiet little girl, who, try as she might, could not keep her affrighted looks from his face, and always met his eyes with a loyal frankness and unyielded faith in him.

"Oh, you little jade, what have you been overhearing?"

"Nothing, Doctor Grim,—nothing that I could make out."

"Make out as much as you can," he said. "I am not afraid of you."

"Afraid of little Elsie, dear Doctor Grim!"

"Neither of you, nor of the Devil," murmured the Doctor,—"of nobody but little Ned and that milksop Colcord. If I have wronged anybody it is them. As for the rest, let the day of judgment come. Doctor Grim is ready to fling down his burden at the judgment seat and have it sorted there."

Then he would lie back in his chair and look up at the great spider, who (or else it was Elsie's fancy) seemed to be making great haste in those days, filling out his web as if he had less time than was desirable for such a piece of work.

One morning the Doctor arose as usual, and after breakfast (at which he ate nothing, and even after filling his coffee-cup half with brandy, half with coffee, left it untouched, save sipping a little out of a teaspoon) he went to the study (with a rather unsteady gait, chiefly remarkable because it was so early in the day), and there established himself with his pipe, as usual, and his medical books and machines, and his manuscript. But he seemed troubled, irresolute, weak, and at last he blew out a volley of oaths, with no apparent appropriateness, and then seemed to be communing with himself.

"It is of no use to carry this on any further," said he, fiercely, in a decided tone, as if he had taken a resolution. "Elsie, my girl, come and kiss me."

So Elsie kissed him, amid all the tobacco-smoke which was curling out of his mouth, as if there were a half-extinguished furnace in his inside.

"Elsie, my little girl, I mean to die to-day," said the old man.

"To die, dear Doctor Grim? O, no! O, no!"

"O, yes! Elsie," said the Doctor, in a very positive tone. "I have kept myself alive by main force these three weeks, and I find it hardly worth the trouble. It requires so much exercise of will;—and I am weary, weary. The pipe does not taste good, the brandy bewilders me. Ned is gone, too;—I have nothing else to do. I have wrought this many a year for an object, and now, taking all things into consideration, I don't know whether to execute it or no. Ned is gone; there is nobody but my little Elsie,—a good child, but not quite enough to live for. I will let myself die, therefore, before sunset."

"O, no! Doctor Grim. Let us send for Ned, and you will think it worth the trouble of living."

"No, Elsie, I want no one near my death-bed; when I have finished a little business, you must go out of the room, and I will turn my face to the wall, and say good-night. But first send crusty Hannah for Mr. Pickering."

He was a lawyer of the town, a man of classical and antiquarian tastes, as well as legal acquirement, and some of whose pursuits had brought him and Doctor Grim occasionally together. Besides calling this gentleman, crusty Hannah (of her own motion, but whether out of good will to the poor Doctor Grim, or from a tendency to mischief inherent in such unnatural mixtures as hers) summoned, likewise, in all haste, a medical man,—and, as it happened, the one who had taken a most decidedly hostile part to our Doctor,—and a clergyman, who had often devoted our poor friend to the infernal regions, almost by name, in his sermons; a kindness, to say the truth, which the Doctor had fully reciprocated in many anathemas against the clergyman. These two worthies, arriving simultaneously, and in great haste, were forthwith ushered to where the Doctor lay half reclining in his study; and upon showing their heads, the Doctor flew into an awful rage, threatening, in his customary improper way, when angry, to make them smell the infernal regions, and proceeding to put his threats into execution by flinging his odorous tobacco-pipe in the face of the medical man, and rebaptizing the clergyman with a half-emptied tumbler of brandy and water, and sending a terrible vociferation of oaths after them both, as they clattered hastily down the stairs. Really, that crusty Hannah must have been the Devil, for she stood grinning and chuckling at the foot of the stairs, curtseying grotesquely.

"He terrible man, our old Doctor Grim," quoth crusty Hannah. "He drive us all to the wicked place before him."

This, however, was the final outbreak of poor Doctor Grim. Indeed, he almost went off at once in the exhaustion that succeeded. The lawyer arrived shortly after, and was shut up with him for a considerable space; after which crusty Hannah was summoned, and desired to call two indifferent persons from the street, as witnesses to a will; and this document was duly executed, and given into the possession of the lawyer. This done, and the lawyer having taken his leave, the grim Doctor desired, and indeed commanded imperatively, that crusty Hannah should quit the room, having first—we are sorry to say—placed the brandy-bottle within reach of his hand, and leaving him propped up in his arm-chair, in which he leaned back, gazing up at the great spider, who was, dangling overhead. As the door closed behind crusty Hannah's grinning and yet strangely interested face, the Doctor caught a glimpse of little Elsie in the passage, bathed in tears, and lingering and looking earnestly into the chamber. [Endnote: 3.]

Seeing the poor little girl, the Doctor cried out to her, half wrathfully, half tenderly, "Don't cry, you little wretch! Come and kiss me once more." So Elsie, restraining her grief with a great effort, ran to him and gave him a last kiss.

"Tell Ned," said the Doctor solemnly, "to think no more of the old English hall, or of the bloody footstep, or of the silver key, or any of all that nonsense. Good by, my dear!" Then he said, with his thunderous and imperative tone, "Let no one come near me till to-morrow morning."

So that parting was over; but still the poor little desolate child hovered by the study door all day long, afraid to enter, afraid to disobey, but unable to go. Sometimes she heard the Doctor muttering, as was his wont; once she fancied he was praying, and dropping on her knees, she also prayed fervently, and perhaps acceptably; then, all at once, the Doctor called out, in a loud voice, "No, Ned, no. Drop it, drop it!"

And then there was an utter silence, unbroken forevermore by the lips that had uttered so many objectionable things.

And finally, after an interval which had been prescribed by the grim Doctor, a messenger was sent by the lawyer to our friend Ned, to inform him of this sad event, and to bring him back temporarily to town, for the purpose of hearing what were his prospects, and what disposition was now to be made of him. We shall not attempt to describe the grief, astonishment, and almost incredulity of Ned, on discovering that a person so mixed up with and built into his whole life as the stalwart Doctor Grimshawe had vanished out of it thus unexpectedly, like something thin as a vapor,—like a red flame, that one [instant] is very bright in its lurid ray, and then is nothing at all, amid the darkness. To the poor boy's still further grief and astonishment, he found, on reaching the spot that he called home, that little Elsie (as the lawyer gave him to understand, by the express orders of the

Doctor, and for reasons of great weight) had been conveyed away by a person under whose guardianship she was placed, and that Ned could not be informed of the place. Even crusty Hannah had been provided for and disposed of, and was no longer to be found. Mr. Pickering explained to Ned the dispositions in his favor which had been made by his deceased friend, who, out of a moderate property, had left him the means of obtaining as complete an education as the country would afford, and of supporting himself until his own exertions would be likely to give him the success which his abilities were calculated to win. The remainder of his property (a less sum than that thus disposed of) was given to little Elsie, with the exception of a small provision to crusty Hannah, with the recommendation from the Doctor that she should retire and spend the remainder of her life among her own people. There was likewise a certain sum left for the purpose of editing and printing (with a dedication to the Medical Society of the State) an account of the process of distilling balm from cobwebs; the bequest being worded in so singular a way that it was just as impossible as it had ever been to discover whether the grim Doctor was in earnest or no.

What disappointed the boy, in a greater degree than we shall try to express, was the lack of anything in reference to those dreams and castles of the air,—any explanation of his birth; so that he was left with no trace of it, except just so far as the alms-house whence the Doctor had taken him. There all traces of his name and descent vanished, just as if he had been made up of the air, as an aerolite seems to be before it tumbles on the earth with its mysterious iron.

The poor boy, in his bewilderment, had not yet come to feel what his grief was; it was not to be conceived, in a few days, that he was deprived of every person, thing, or thought that had hitherto kept his heart warm. He tried to make himself feel it, yearning for this grief as for his sole friend. Being, for the present, domiciled with the lawyer, he obtained the key of his former home, and went through the desolate house that he knew so well, and which now had such a silent, cold, familiar strangeness, with none in it, though the ghosts of the grim Doctor, of laughing little Elsie, of crusty Hannah,—dead and alive alike,—were all there, and his own ghost among them; for he himself was dead, that is, his former self, which he recognized as himself, had passed away, as they were. In the study everything looked as formerly, yet with a sort of unreality, as if it would dissolve and vanish on being touched; and, indeed, it partly proved so; for over the Doctor's chair seemed still to hang the great spider, but on looking closer at it, and finally touching it with the end of the Doctor's stick, Ned discovered that it was merely the skin, shell, apparition, of the real spider,[Endnote: 4] the reality of whom, it is to be supposed, had followed the grim Doctor, whithersoever he had gone.

A thought struck Ned while he was here; he remembered the secret niche in the wall, where he had once seen the Doctor deposit some papers. He looked, and there they were. Who was the heir of those papers, if not he? If there were anything wrong in appropriating them, it was not perceptible to him in the desolation, anxiety, bewilderment, and despair of that moment. He grasped the papers, and hurried from the room and down the stairs, afraid to look round, and half expecting to hear the gruff voice of Doctor Grim thundering after him to bring them back.

Then Ned went out of the back door, and found his way to the Doctor's new grave, which, as it happened, was dug close beside that one which occupied the place of the one which the stranger had come to seek; and, as if to spite the Doctor's professional antipathies, it lay beside a grave of an old physician and surgeon, one Doctor Summerton, who used to help diseases and kill patients above a hundred years ago. But Doctor Grim was undisturbed by these neighbors, and apparently not more by the grief of poor little Ned, who hid his face in the crumbly earth of the grave, and the sods that had not begun to grow, and wept as if his heart would break.

But the heart never breaks on the first grave; and, after many graves, it gets so obtuse that nothing can break it.

And now let the mists settle down over the trail of our story, hiding it utterly on its onward course, for a long way to come, until, after many years, they may disperse and discover something which, were it worth while to follow it through all that obscurity, would prove to be the very same track which that boy was treading when we last saw him,—though it may have lain over land and sea since then; but the footsteps that trod there are treading here.

CHAPTER XI

There is—or there was, now many years ago, and a few years also it was still extant—a chamber, which when I think of, it seems to me like entering a deep recess of my own consciousness, a deep cave of my nature; so much have I thought of it and its inmate, through a considerable period of my life. After I had seen it long in fancy, then I saw it in reality, with my waking eyes; and questioned with myself whether I was really awake.

Not that it was a picturesque or stately chamber; not in the least. It was dim, dim as a melancholy mood; so dim, to come to particulars, that, till you were accustomed to that twilight medium, the print of a book looked all blurred; a pin was an indistinguishable object; the face of your familiar friend, or your dearest beloved one, would be unrecognizable across it, and the figures, so warm and radiant with life and heart, would seem like the faint gray shadows of our thoughts, brooding in age over youthful images of joy and love. Nevertheless, the chamber, though so difficult to see across, was small. You detected that it was within very narrow boundaries, though you could not precisely see them; only you felt yourself shut in, compressed, impeded, in the deep centre of something; and you longed for a breath of fresh air. Some articles of furniture there seemed to be; but in this dim medium, to which we are unaccustomed, it is not well to try to make out what they were, or anything else—now at least—about the chamber. Only one thing; small as the light was, it was rather wonderful how there came to be any; for no windows were apparent; no communication with the outward day. [Endnote: 1.]

Looking into this chamber, in fancy it is some time before we who come out of the broad sunny daylight of the world discover that it has an inmate. Yes, there is some one within, but where? We know it; but do not precisely see him, only a presence is impressed upon us. It is in that corner; no, not there; only a heap of darkness and an old antique coffer, that, as we look closely at it, seems to be made of carved wood. Ah! he is in that other dim corner; and now that we steal close to him, we see him; a young man, pale, flung upon a sort of mattress-couch. He seems in alarm at something or other. He trembles, he listens, as if for voices. It must be a great peril, indeed, that can haunt him thus and make him feel afraid in such a seclusion as you feel this to be; but there he is, tremulous, and so pale that really his face is almost visible in the gloomy twilight. How came he here? Who is he? What does he tremble at? In this duskiness we cannot tell. Only that he is a young man, in a state of nervous excitement and alarm, looking about him, starting to his feet, sometimes standing and staring about him.

Has he been living here? Apparently not; for see, he has a pair of long riding-boots on, coming up to the knees; they are splashed with mud, as if he had ridden hastily through foul ways; the spurs are on the heel. A riding-dress upon him. Ha! is that blood upon the hand which he clasps to his forehead.

What more do you perceive? Nothing, the light is so dim; but only we wonder where is the door, and whence the light comes. There is a strange abundance of spiders, too, we perceive; spinning their webs here, as if they would entrammel something in them. A mouse has run across the floor, apparently, but it is too dim to detect him, or to detect anything beyond the limits of a very doubtful vagueness. We do not even know whether what we seem to have seen is really so; whether the man is young, or old, or what his surroundings are; and there is something so disagreeable in this seclusion, this stifled atmosphere, that we should be loath to remain here long enough to make ourselves certain of what was a mystery. Let us forth into the broad, genial daylight, for there is magic, there is a devilish, subtile influence, in this chamber; which, I have reason to believe, makes it dangerous to remain here. There is a spell on the threshold. Heaven keep us safe from it!

Hark! has a door unclosed? Is there another human being in the room? We have now become so accustomed to the dim medium that we distinguish a man of mean exterior, with a look of habitual subservence that seems like that of an English serving-man, or a person in some menial situation; decent, quiet, neat, softly-behaved, but yet with a certain hard and questionable presence, which we would not well like to have near us in the room.

"Am I safe?" asks the inmate of the prison-chamber.

"Sir, there has been a search."

"Leave the pistols," said the voice.

Again, [Endnote: 2] after this time, a long time extending to years, let us look back into that dim chamber, wherever in the world it was, into which we had a glimpse, and where we saw apparently a fugitive. How looks it now? Still dim,—perhaps as dim as ever,—but our eyes, or our imagination, have gained an acquaintance, a customariness, with the medium; so that we can discern things now a little more distinctly than of old. Possibly, there may have been something cleared away that obstructed the light; at any rate, we see now the whereabouts—better than we did. It is an oblong room, lofty but narrow, and some ten paces in length; its floor is heavily carpeted, so that the tread makes no sound; it is hung with old tapestry, or carpet, wrought with the hand long ago, and still retaining much of the ancient colors, where there was no sunshine to fade them; worked on them is some tapestried story, done by Catholic hands, of saints or devils, looking each equally grave and solemnly. The light, whence comes it? There is no window; but it seems to come through a stone, or something like it,—a dull gray medium, that makes noonday look like evening twilight. Though sometimes there is an effect as if something were striving to melt itself through this dull medium, and—never making a shadow—yet to produce the effect of a cloud gathering thickly over the sun. There is a chimney; yes, a little grate in which burns a coal fire, a dim smouldering fire, it might be an illumination, if that were desirable.

What is the furniture? An antique chair,—one chair, no more. A table, many-footed, of dark wood; it holds writing-materials, a book, too, on its face, with the dust gathered on its back. There is, moreover, a sort of antique box, or coffer, of some dark wood, that seems to have been wrought or carved with skill, wondrous skill, of some period when the art of carving wainscot with arms and devices was much practised; so that on this coffer— some six feet long it is, and two or three broad—most richly wrought, you see faces in relief of knight and dame, lords, heraldic animals; some story, very likely, told, almost revelling in Gothic sculpture of wood, like what we have seen on the marble sarcophagus of the old Greeks. It has, too, a lock, elaborately ornamented and inlaid with silver.

What else; only the spider's webs spinning strangely over everything; over that light which comes into the room through the stone; over everything. And now we see, in a corner, a strange great spider curiously variegated. The ugly, terrible, seemingly poisonous thing makes us shudder. [Endnote: 3.]

What, else? There are pistols; they lie on the coffer! There is a curiously shaped Italian dagger, of the kind which in a groove has poison that makes its wound mortal. On the old mantel-piece, over the fireplace, there is a vial in which are kept certain poisons. It would seem as if some one had meditated suicide; or else that the foul fiend had put all sorts of implements of self-destruction in his way; so that, in some frenzied moment, he might kill himself.

But the inmate! There he is; but the frenzied alarm in which we last saw him seems to have changed its character. No throb, now; no passion; no frenzy of fear or despair. He sits dull and motionless. See; his cheek is very pale; his hair long and dishevelled. His beard has grown, and curls round his face. He has on a sleeping-gown, a long robe as of one who abides within doors, and has nothing to do with outward elements; a pair of slippers. A dull, dreamy reverie seems to have possessed him. Hark! there is again a stealthy step on the floor, and the serving-man is here again. There is a peering, anxious curiosity in his face, as he struts towards him, a sort of enjoyment, one would say, in the way in which he looks at the strange case.

"I am here, you know," he says, at length, after feasting his eyes for some time on the spectacle.

"I hear you!" says the young man, in a dull, indifferent tone.

"Will not your honor walk out to-day?" says the man. "It is long now since your honor has taken the air."

"Very long," says the master, "but I will not go out to-day. What weather is it?"

"Sunny, bright, a summer day," says the man. "But you would never know it in these damp walls. The last winter's chill is here yet. Had not your honor better go forth?"

It might seem that there was a sort of sneer, deeply hidden under respect and obeisance, in the man's words and craftily respectful tone; deeply hidden, but conveying a more subtle power on that account. At all events, the master seemed aroused from his state of dull indifference, and writhed as with poignant anguish—an infused poison in his veins—as the man spoke.

"Have you procured me that new drug I spoke of?" asked the master.

"Here it is," said the man, putting a small package on the table.

"Is it effectual?"

"So said the apothecary," answered the man; "and I tried it on a dog. He sat quietly a quarter of an hour; then had a spasm or two, and was dead. But, your honor, the dead carcass swelled horribly."

"Hush, villain! Have there—have there been inquiries for me,—mention of me?"

"O, none, sir,—none, sir. Affairs go on bravely,—the new live. The world fills up. The gap is not vacant. There is no mention of you. Marry, at the alehouse I heard some idle topers talking of a murder that took place some few years since, and saying that Heaven's vengeance would come for it yet."

"Silence, villain, there is no such thing," said the young man; and, with a laugh that seemed like scorn, he relapsed into his state of sullen indifference; during which the servant stole away, after looking at him some time, as if to take all possible note of his aspect. The man did not seem so much to enjoy it himself, as he did to do these things in a kind of formal and matter-of-course way, as if he were performing a set duty; as if he were a subordinate fiend, and were doing the duty of a superior one, without any individual malice of his own, though a general satisfaction in doing what would accrue to the agglomeration of deadly mischief. He stole away, and the master was left to himself.

By and by, by what impulse or cause it is impossible to say, he started upon his feet in a sudden frenzy of rage and despair. It seemed as if a consciousness of some strange, wild miserable fate that had befallen him had come upon him all at once; how that he was a prisoner to a devilish influence, to some wizard might, that bound him hand and foot with spider's web. So he stamped; so he half shrieked, yet stopped himself in the midst, so that his cry was stifled and smothered. Then he snatched up the poisoned dagger and looked at it; the noose, and put it about his neck,—evil instrument of death,—but laid it down again. And then was a voice at the door: "Quietly, quietly you know, or they will hear you." And at that voice he sank into sullen indifference again.

CHAPTER XII

A traveller with a knapsack on his shoulders comes out of the duskiness of vague, unchronicled times, throwing his shadow before him in the morning sunshine along a well-trodden, though solitary path.

It was early summer, or perhaps latter spring, and the most genial weather that either spring or summer ever brought, possessing a character, indeed, as if both seasons had done their utmost to create an atmosphere and temperature most suitable for the enjoyment and exercise of life. To one accustomed to a climate where there is seldom a medium between heat too fierce and cold too deadly, it was a new development in the nature of weather. So genial it was, so full of all comfortable influences, and yet, somehow or other, void of the torrid characteristic that inevitably burns in our full sun-bursts. The traveller thought, in fact, that the sun was at less than his brightest glow; for though it was bright,—though the day seemed cloudless,—though it appeared to be the clear, transparent morning that precedes an unshadowed noon,—still there was a mild and softened character, not so perceptible when he directly sought to see it, but as if some veil were interposed between the earth and sun, absorbing all the passionate qualities out of the latter, and leaving only the kindly ones. Warmth was in abundance, and, yet, all through it, and strangely akin to it, there was a half-suspected coolness that gave the atmosphere its most thrilling and delicious charm. It was good for human life, as the traveller, felt throughout all his being; good, likewise, for vegetable life, as was seen in the depth and richness of verdure over the gently undulating landscape, and the luxuriance of foliage, wherever there was tree or shrub to put forth leaves.

The path along which the traveller was passing deserved at least a word or two of description: it was a well-trodden footpath, running just here along the edge of a field of grass, and bordered on one side by a hedge which contained materials within itself for varied and minute researches in natural history; so richly luxuriant was it with its diverse vegetable life, such a green intricacy did it form, so impenetrable and so beautiful, and such a Paradise it was for the birds that built their nests there in a labyrinth of little boughs and twigs, unseen and inaccessible, while close beside the human race to which they attach themselves, that they must have felt themselves as safe as when they sung to Eve. Homely flowers likewise grew in it, and many creeping and twining plants, that were an original part of the hedge, had come of their own accord and dwelt here, beautifying and enriching the verdant fence by way of repayment for the shelter and support which it afforded them. At intervals, trees of vast trunk and mighty spread of foliage, whether elms or oaks, grew in the line of the hedge, and the bark of those gigantic, age-long patriarchs was not gray and naked, like the trees which the traveller had been accustomed to see, but verdant with moss, or in many cases richly enwreathed with a network of creeping plants, and oftenest the ivy of old growth, clambering upward, and making its own twisted stem almost of one substance with the supporting tree. On one venerable oak there was a plant of mystic leaf, which the traveller knew by instinct, and plucked a bough of it with a certain reverence for the sake of the Druids and Christmas kisses and of the pasty in which it was rooted from of old.

The path in which he walked, rustic as it was and made merely by the feet that pressed it down, was one of the ancientest of ways; older than the oak that bore the mistletoe, older than the villages between which it passed, older perhaps than the common road which the traveller had crossed that morning; old as the times when people first debarred themselves from wandering freely and widely wherever a vagrant impulse led them. The footpath, therefore, still retains some of the characteristics of a woodland walk, taken at random, by a lover of nature not pressed for time nor restrained by artificial barriers; it sweeps and lingers along, and finds pretty little dells and nooks of delightful scenery, and picturesque glimpses of halls or cottages, in the same neighborhood where a highroad would disclose only a tiresome blank. They run into one another for miles and miles together, and traverse rigidly guarded parks and domains, not as a matter of favor, but as a right; so that the poorest man thus retains a kind of property and privilege in the oldest inheritance of the richest. The highroad sees only the outside; the footpath leads down into the heart of the country.

A pleasant feature of the footpath was the stile, between two fields; no frail and temporary structure, but betokening the permanence of this rustic way; the ancient solidity of the stone steps, worn into cavities by the hobnailed shoes that had pressed upon them: here not only the climbing foot had passed for ages, but here had sat the maiden with her milk-pail, the rustic on his way afield or homeward; here had been lover meetings, cheerful chance chats, song as natural as bird note, a thousand pretty scenes of rustic manners.

It was curious to see the traveller pause, to contemplate so simple a thing as this old stile of a few stone steps; antique as an old castle; simple and rustic as the gap in a rail fence; and while he sat on one of the steps, making himself pleasantly sensible of his whereabout, like one who should handle a dream and find it tangible and real, he heard a sound that bewitched him with still another dreamy delight. A bird rose out of the grassy field, and, still soaring aloft, made a cheery melody that was like a spire of audible flame,—rapturous music, as if the whole soul and substance of the winged creature had been distilled into this melody, as it vanished skyward.

"The lark! the lark!" exclaimed the traveller, recognizing the note (though never heard before) as if his childhood had known it.

A moment afterwards another bird was heard in the shadow of a neighboring wood, or some other inscrutable hiding-place, singing softly in a flute-like note, as if blown through an instrument of wood,—"Cuckoo! Cuckoo!"—only twice, and then a stillness.

"How familiar these rustic sounds!" he exclaimed. "Surely I was born here!"

The person who thus enjoyed these sounds, as if they were at once familiar and strange, was a young man, tall and rather slenderly built, and though we have called him young, there were the traces of thought, struggle, and even of experience in his marked brow and somewhat pale face; but the spirit within him was evidently still that of a youth, lithe and active, gazing out of his dark eyes and taking note of things about him, with an eager, centring interest, that seemed to be unusually awake at the present moment.

It could be but a few years since he first called himself a man; but they must have been thickly studded with events, turbulent with action, spent amidst circumstances that called for resources of energy not often so early developed; and thus his youth might have been kept in abeyance until now, when in this simple rural scene he grew almost a boy again. As for his station in life, his coarse gray suit and the knapsack on his shoulders did not indicate a very high one; yet it was such as a gentleman might wear of a morning, or on a pedestrian ramble, and was worn in a way that made it seem of a better fashion than it really was, as it enabled him to find a rare enjoyment, as we have seen, in by-path, hedge-row, rustic stile, lark, and cuckoo, and even the familiar grass and clover blossom. It was as if he had long been shut in a sick-chamber or a prison; or, at least, within the iron cage of busy life, that had given him but few glimpses of natural things through its bars; or else this was another kind of nature than he had heretofore known.

As he walked along (through a kind of dream, though he seemed so sensibly observant of trifling things around him,) he failed to notice that the path grew somewhat less distinctly marked, more infringed upon by grass, more shut in by shrubbery; he had deviated into a side track, and, in fact, a certain printed board nailed against a tree had escaped his notice, warning off intruders with inhospitable threats of prosecution. He began to suspect that he must have gone astray when the path led over plashy ground with a still fainter trail of preceding footsteps, and plunged into shrubbery, and seemed on the point of deserting him altogether, after having beguiled him thus far. The spot was an entanglement of boughs, and yet did not give one the impression of wildness; for it was the stranger's idea that everything in this long cultivated region had been touched and influenced by man's care, every oak, every bush, every sod,—that man knew them all, and that they knew him, and by that mutual knowledge had become far other than they were in the first freedom of growth, such as may be found in an American forest. Nay, the wildest denizens of this sylvan neighborhood were removed in the same degree from their primeval character; for hares sat on their hind legs to gaze at the approaching traveller, and hardly thought it worth their while to leap away among some ferns, as he drew near; two pheasants looked at him from a bough, a little inward among the shrubbery; and, to complete the wonder, he became aware of the antlers and brown muzzle of a deer protruding among the boughs, and though immediately there ensued a great rush and rustling of the herd, it seemed evidently to come from a certain lingering shyness, an instinct that had lost its purpose and object, and only mimicked a dread of man, whose neighborhood and familiarity had tamed the wild deer almost into a domestic creature. Remembering his experience of true woodland life, the traveller fancied that it might be possible to want freer air, less often used for human breath, than was to be found anywhere among these woods.

But then the sweet, calm sense of safety that was here: the certainty that with the wild element that centuries ago had passed out of this scene had gone all the perils of wild men and savage beasts, dwarfs, witches, leaving nature, not effete, but only disarmed of those rougher, deadlier characteristics, that cruel rawness, which make primeval Nature the deadly enemy even of her own children. Here was consolation, doubtless; so we sit down on the stone step of the last stile that he had crossed, and listen to the footsteps of the traveller, and the distant rustle among the shrubbery, as he goes deeper and deeper into the seclusion, having by this time lost the deceitful track. No matter if he go astray; even were it after nightfall instead of noontime, a will-o'-the-wisp, or Puck himself, would not lead him into worse harm than to delude him into some mossy pool, the depths of which the truant schoolboys had known for ages. Nevertheless, some little time after his disappearance, there was the report of a shot that echoed sharp and loud, startling the pheasants from their boughs, and sending the hares and deer a-scampering in good earnest.

We next find our friend, from whom we parted on the footpath, in a situation of which he then was but very imperfectly aware; for, indeed, he had been in a state of unconsciousness, lasting until it was now late towards the sunset of that same day. He was endeavoring to make out where he was, and how he came thither, or what had happened; or whether, indeed, anything had happened, unless to have fallen asleep, and to be still enveloped in the fragments of some vivid and almost tangible dream, the more confused because so vivid. His wits did not come so readily about him as usual; there may have been a slight delusion, which mingled itself with his sober perceptions, and by its leaven of extravagance made the whole substance of the scene untrue. Thus it happened that, as it were at the same instant, he fancied himself years back in life, thousands of miles away, in a gloomy cobwebbed room, looking out upon a graveyard, while yet, neither more nor less distinctly, he was conscious of being in a small chamber, panelled with oak, and furnished in an antique style. He was doubtful, too, whether or no there was a grim feudal figure, in a shabby dressing-gown and an old velvet cap, sitting in the dusk of the room, smoking a pipe that diffused a scent of tobacco,—quaffing a deep-hued liquor out of a tumbler,—looking upwards at a spider that hung above. "Was there, too, a child sitting in a little chair at his footstool?" In his earnestness to see this apparition more distinctly, he opened his eyes wider and stirred, and ceased to see it at all.

But though that other dusty, squalid, cobwebbed scene quite vanished, and along with it the two figures, old and young, grim and childish, of whose portraits it had been the framework, still there were features in the old, oaken-panelled chamber that seemed to belong rather to his dream. The panels were ornamented, here and there, with antique carving, representing over and over again an identical device, being a bare arm, holding the torn-off head of some savage beast, which the stranger could not know by species, any more than Agassiz himself could have assigned its type or kindred; because it was that kind of natural history of which heraldry alone keeps the menagerie. But it was just as familiar to his recollection as that of the cat which he had fondled in his childhood.

There was likewise a mantelpiece, heavily wrought of oak, quite black with smoke and age, in the centre of which, more prominent than elsewhere, was that same leopard's head that seemed to thrust itself everywhere into sight, as if typifying some great mystery which human nature would never be at rest till it had solved; and below, in a cavernous hollow, there was a smouldering fire of coals; for the genial day had suddenly grown chill, and a shower of rain spattered against the small window-panes, almost at the same time with the struggling sunshine. And over the mantelpiece, where the light of the declining day came strongest from the window, there was a larger and more highly relieved carving of this same device, and underneath it a legend, in Old English letters, which, though his eyes could not precisely trace it at that distance, he knew to be this:—

"*Hold hard the Head.*"

Otherwise the aspect of the room bewildered him by not being known, since these details were so familiar; a narrow precinct it was, with one window full of old-fashioned, diamond-shaped panes of glass, a small desk table, standing on clawed feet; two or three high-backed chairs, on the top of each of which was carved that same crest of the fabulous brute's head, which the carver's fancy seemed to have clutched so strongly that he could not let it go; in another part of the room a very old engraving, rude and strong, representing some ruffled personage, which the stranger only tried to make out with a sort of idle curiosity, because it was strange he should dream so distinctly.

Very soon it became intolerably irritating that these two dreams, both purposeless, should have mingled and entangled themselves in his mind. He made a nervous and petulant motion, intending to rouse himself fully; and immediately a sharp pang of physical pain took him by surprise, and made him groan aloud.

Immediately there was an almost noiseless step on the floor; and a figure emerged from a deep niche, that looked as if it might once have been an oratory, in ancient times; and the figure, too, might have been supposed to possess the devout and sanctified character of such as knelt in the oratories of ancient times. It was an elderly man, tall, thin, and pale, and wearing a long, dark tunic, and in a peculiar fashion, which—like almost everything else about him—the stranger seemed to have a confused remembrance of; this venerable person had a benign and pitiful aspect, and approached the bedside with such good will and evident desire to do the sufferer good, that the latter felt soothed, at least, by his very presence. He lay, a moment, gazing up at the old man's face, without being able to exert himself to say a word, but sensible, as it were, of a mild, soft influence from him, cooling the fever which seemed to burn in his veins.

"Do you suffer much pain?" asked the old man, gently.

"None at all," said the stranger; but again a slight motion caused him to feel a burning twinge in his shoulder. "Yes; there was a throb of strange anguish. Why should I feel pain? Where am I?"

"In safety, and with those who desire to be your friends," said the old man. "You have met with an accident; but do not inquire about it now. Quiet is what you need."

Still the traveller gazed at him; and the old man's figure seemed to enter into his dream, or delirium, whichever it might be, as if his peaceful presence were but a shadow, so quaint was his address, so unlike real life, in that dark robe, with a velvet skullcap on his head, beneath which his hair made a silvery border; and looking more closely, the stranger saw embroidered on the breast of the tunic that same device, the arm and the leopard's head, which was visible in the carving of the room. Yes; this must still be a dream, which, under the unknown laws which govern such psychical states, had brought out thus vividly figures, devices, words, forgotten since his boyish days. Though of an imaginative tendency, the stranger was nevertheless strongly tenacious of the actual, and had a natural horror at the idea of being seriously at odds, in beliefs, perceptions, conclusions, with the real world about him; so that a tremor ran through him, as if he felt the substance of the world shimmering before his eyes like a mere vaporous consistency.

"Are you real?" said he to the antique presence; "or a spirit? or a fantasy?"

The old man laid his thin, cool palm on the stranger's burning forehead, and smiled benignantly, keeping it there an instant.

"If flesh and blood are real, I am so," said he; "a spirit, too, I may claim to be, made thin by fantasy. Again, do not perplex yourself with such things. To-morrow you may find denser substance in me. Drink this composing draught, and close your eyes to those things that disturb you."

"Your features, too, and your voice," said the stranger, in a resigned tone, as if he were giving up a riddle, the solution of which he could not find, "have an image and echo somewhere in my memory. It is all an entanglement. I will drink, and shut my eyes."

He drank from a little old-fashioned silver cup, which his venerable guardian presented to his lips; but in so doing he was still perplexed and tremulously disturbed with seeing that same weary old device, the leopard's head, engraved on the side; and shut his eyes to escape it, for it irritated a certain portion of his brain with vague, fanciful, elusive ideas. So he sighed and spoke no more. The medicine, whatever it might be, had the merit, rare in doctor's stuff, of being pleasant to take, assuasive of thirst, and imbued with a hardly perceptible fragrance, that was so ethereal that it also seemed to enter into his dream and modify it. He kept his eyes closed, and fell into a misty state, in which he wondered whether this could be the panacea or medicament which old Doctor Grimshawe used to distil from cobwebs, and of which the fragrance seemed to breathe through all the waste of years since then. He wondered, too, who was this benign, saint-like old man, and where, in what former state of being, he could have known him; to have him thus, as no strange thing, and yet so strange, be attending at his bedside, with all this ancient garniture. But it was best to dismiss all things, he being so weak; to resign himself; all this had happened before, and had passed away, prosperously or unprosperously; it would pass away in this case, likewise; and in the morning whatever might be delusive would have disappeared.

CHAPTER XIII

The patient [Endnote: 1] had a favorable night, and awoke with a much clearer head, though still considerably feverish and in a state of great exhaustion from loss of blood, which kept down the fever. The events of the preceding day shimmered as it were and shifted illusively in his recollection; nor could he yet account for the situation in which he found himself, the antique chamber, the old man of mediæval garb, nor even for the wound which seemed to have been the occasion of bringing him thither. One moment, so far as he remembered, he had been straying along a solitary footpath, through rich shrubbery, with the antlered deer peeping at him, listening to the lark and the cuckoo; the next, he lay helpless in this oak-panelled chamber, surrounded with objects that appealed to some fantastic shadow of recollection, which could have had no reality. [Endnote: 2.]

To say the truth, the traveller perhaps wilfully kept hold of this strange illusiveness, and kept his thoughts from too harshly analyzing his situation, and solving the riddle in which he found himself involved. In his present weakness, his mind sympathizing with the sinking down of his physical powers, it was delightful to let all go; to relinquish all control, and let himself drift vaguely into whatever region of improbabilities there exists apart from the dull, common plane of life. Weak, stricken down, given over to influences which had taken possession of him during an interval of insensibility, he was no longer responsible; let these delusions, if they were such, linger as long as they would, and depart of their own accord at last. He, meanwhile, would willingly accept the idea that some spell had transported him out of an epoch in which he had led a brief, troubled existence of battle, mental strife, success, failure, all equally feverish and unsatisfactory, into some past century, where the business was to rest,—to drag on dreamy days, looking at things through half-shut eyes; into a limbo where things were put away, shows of what had once been, now somehow fainted, and still maintaining a sort of half-existence, a serious mockery; a state likely enough to exist just a little apart from the actual world, if we only know how to find our way into it. Scenes and events that had once stained themselves, in deep colors, on the curtain that Time hangs around us, to shut us in from eternity, cannot be quite effaced by the succeeding phantasmagoria, and sometimes, by a palimpsest, show more strongly than they. [Endnote: 3.]

In the course of the morning, however, he was a little too feelingly made sensible of realities by the visit of a surgeon, who proceeded to examine the wound in his shoulder, removing the bandages which he himself seemed to have put upon this mysterious hurt. The traveller closed his eyes, and submitted to the manipulations of the professional person, painful as they were, assisted by the gentle touch of the old palmer; and there was something in the way in which he resigned himself that met the approbation of the surgeon, in spite of a little fever, and slight delirium too, to judge by his eye.

"A very quiet and well-behaved patient," said he to the palmer. "Unless I greatly mistake, he has been under the surgeon's hand for a similar hurt ere now. He has learned under good discipline how to take such a thing easily. Yes, yes; just here is a mark where a bullet went in some time ago, — three or four years since, when he could have been little more than a boy. A wild fellow this, I doubt."

"It was an Indian bullet," said the patient, still fancying himself gone astray into the past, "shot at me in battle; 'twas three hundred years hereafter."

"Ah! he has served in the East Indies," said the surgeon. "I thought this sun-burned cheek had taken its hue elsewhere than in England."

The patient did not care to take the trouble which would have been involved in correcting the surgeon's surmise; so he let it pass, and patiently awaited the end of the examination, with only a moan or two, which seemed rather pleasing and desirable than otherwise to the surgeon's ear.

"He has vitality enough for his needs," said he, nodding to the palmer. "These groans betoken a good degree of pain; though the young fellow is evidently a self-contained sort of nature, and does not let us know all he feels. It promises well, however; keep him in bed and quiet, and within a day or two we shall see."

He wrote a recipe, or two or three, perhaps, (for in those days the medical fraternity had faith in their own art,) and took his leave.

The white-bearded palmer withdrew into the half concealment of the oratory which we have already mentioned, and then, putting on a pair of spectacles, betook himself to the perusal of an old folio volume, the leaves of which he turned over so gently that not the slightest sound could possibly disturb the patient. All his manifestations were gentle and soft, but of a simplicity most unlike the feline softness which we are apt to associate with a noiseless tread and movement in the male sex. The sunshine came through the ivy and glimmered upon his great book, however, with an effect which a little disturbed the patient's nerves; besides, he desired to have a fuller view of his benign guardian.

"Will you sit nearer the bedside?" said he. "I wish to look at you."

Weakness, the relaxation of nerves, and the state of dependence on another's care—very long unfelt—had made him betray what we must call childishness; and it was perceptible in the low half-complaining tone in which he spoke, indicating a consciousness of kindness in the other, a little plaintiveness in himself; of which, the next instant, weak and wandering as he was, he was ashamed, and essayed to express it. [Endnote: 4.]

"You must deem me very poor-spirited," said he, "not to bear this trifling hurt with a firmer mind. But perhaps it is not entirely that I am so weak, but I feel you to be so benign."

"Be weak, and be the stronger for it," said the old man, with a grave smile. "It is not in the pride of our strength that we are best or wisest. To be made anew, we even must be again a little child, and consent to be enwrapt quietly in the arms of Providence, as a child in its mother's arms."

"I never knew a mother's care," replied the traveller, in a low, regretful tone, being weak to the incoming of all soft feelings, in his present state. "Since my boyhood, I have lived among men,—a life of struggle and hard rivalry. It is good to find myself here in the long past, and in a sheltered harbor."

And here he smiled, by way of showing to this old palmer that he saw through the slight infirmity of mind that impelled him to say such things as the above; that he was not its dupe, though he had not strength, just now, to resist its impulse. After this he dozed off softly, and felt through all his sleep some twinges of his wound, bringing him back, as it were, to the conscious surface of the great deep of slumber, into which he might otherwise have sunk. At all such brief intervals, half unclosing his eyes, (like a child, when the mother sits by its bed and he fears that she will steal away if he falls quite asleep, and leave him in the dark solitude,) he still beheld the white-bearded, kindly old man, of saintly aspect, sitting near him, and turning over the pages of his folio volume so softly that not the faintest rustle did it make; the picture at length got so fully into his idea, that he seemed to see it even through his closed eyelids. After a while, however, the slumberous tendency left him more entirely, and, without having been consciously awake, he found himself contemplating the old man, with wide-open eyes. The venerable personage seemed soon to feel his gaze, and, ceasing to look at the folio, he turned his eyes with quiet inquiry to meet those of the stranger. [Endnote: 5.]

"What great volume is that?" asked the latter. [Endnote: 6.]

"It is a book of English chronicles," said the old man, "mostly relating to the part of the island where you now are, and to times previous to the Stuarts."

"Ah! it is to you, a contemporary, what reading the newspaper is to other men," said the stranger; then, with a smile of self-reproach, "I shall conquer this idle mood. I'm not so imbecile as you must think me. But there is something that strangely haunts me,—where, in what state of being, can I have seen your face before. There is nothing in it I distinctly remember; but some impression, some characteristic, some look, with which I have been long ago familiar haunts me and brings back all old scenes. Do you know me?"

The old man smiled. "I knew, long ago, a bright and impressible boy," said he.

"And his name?" said the stranger.

"It was Edward Redclyffe," said the old man.

"Ah, I see who you are," said the traveller, not too earnestly, but with a soft, gratified feeling, as the riddle thus far solved itself. "You are my old kindly instructor. You are Colcord! That is it. I remember you disappeared. You shall tell me, when I am quite myself, what was that mystery,—and whether it is your real self, or only a part of my dream, and going to vanish when I quite awake. Now I shall sleep and dream more of it."

One more waking interval he had that day, and again essayed to enter into conversation with the old man, who had thus strangely again become connected with his life, after having so long vanished from his path.

"Where am I?" asked Edward Redclyffe.

"In the home of misfortune," said Colcord.

"Ah! then I have a right to be here!" said he. "I was born in such a home. Do you remember it?"

"I know your story," said Colcord.

"Yes; from Doctor Grim," said Edward. "People whispered he had made away with you. I never believed it; but finding you here in this strange way, and myself having been shot, perhaps to death, it seems not so strange. Pooh! I wander again, and ought to sleep a little more. And this is the home of misfortune, but not like the squalid place of rage, idiocy, imbecility, drunkenness, where I was born. How many times I have blushed to remember that native home! But not of late! I have struggled; I have fought;

I have triumphed. The unknown boy has come to be no undistinguished man! His ancestry, should he ever reveal himself to them, need not blush for the poor foundling."

"Hush!" said the quiet watcher. "Your fever burns you. Take this draught, and sleep a little longer." [Endnote: 7.]

Another day or two found Edward Redclyffe almost a convalescent. The singular lack of impatience that characterized his present mood—the repose of spirit into which he had lapsed—had much to do with the favorable progress of his cure. After strife, anxiety, great mental exertion, and excitement of various kinds, which had harassed him ever since he grew to be a man, had come this opportunity of perfect rest;—this dream in the midst of which he lay, while its magic boundaries involved him, and kept far off the contact of actual life, so that its sounds and tumults seemed remote; its cares could not fret him; its ambitions, objects good or evil, were shut out from him; the electric wires that had connected him with the battery of life were broken for the time, and he did not feel the unquiet influence that kept everybody else in galvanic motion. So, under the benign influence of the old palmer, he lay in slumberous luxury, undisturbed save by some twinges of no intolerable pain; which, however, he almost was glad of, because it made him sensible that this deep luxury of quiet was essential to his cure, however idle it might seem. For the first time since he was a child, he resigned himself not to put a finger to the evolution of his fortune; he determined to accept all things that might happen, good or evil; he would not imagine an event beyond to-day, but would let one spontaneous and half-defined thought loiter after another, through his mind; listen to the spattering shower,—the puffs of shut-out wind; and look with half-shut eyes at the sunshine glimmering through the ivy-twigs, and illuminating those old devices on the wall; at the gathering twilight; at the dim lamp; at the creeping upward of another day, and with it the lark singing so far away that the thrill of its delicious song could not disturb him with an impulse to awake. Sweet as its carol was, he could almost have been content to miss the lark; sweet and clear, it was too like a fairy trumpet-call, summoning him to awake and struggle again with eager combatants for new victories, the best of which were not worth this deep repose.

The old palmer did his best to prolong a mood so beneficial to the wounded young man. The surgeon also nodded approval, and attributed this happy state of the patient's mind, and all the physical advantages growing out of it, to his own consummate skill; nor, indeed, was he undeserving of credit, not often to be awarded to medical men, for having done nothing to impede the good which kind Nature was willing to bring about. She was doing the patient more good, indeed, than either the surgeon or the palmer could fully estimate, in taking this opportunity to recreate a mind that had too early known stirring impulse, and that had been worked to a degree beyond what its organization (in some respects singularly delicate) ought to have borne. Once in a long while the weary actors in the headlong drama of life must have such repose or else go mad or die. When the machinery of human life has once been stopped by sickness or other impediment, it often needs an impulse to set it going again, even after it is nearly wound up.

But it could not last forever. The influx of new life into his being began to have a poignancy that would not let him lie so quietly, lapped in the past, in gone by centuries, and waited on by quiet Age, in the person of the old palmer; he began to feel again that he was young, and must live in the time when his lot was cast. He began to say to himself, that it was not well to be any longer passive, but that he must again take the troublesome burden of his own life on his own shoulders. He thought of this necessity, this duty, throughout one whole day, and determined that on the morrow he would make the first step towards terminating his inaction, which he now began to be half impatient of, at the same time that he clutched it still, for the sake of the deliciousness that it had had.

"To-morrow, I hope to be clothed and in my right mind," said he to the old palmer, "and very soon I must thank you, with my whole heart, for your kind care, and go. It is a shame that I burden the hospitality of this house so long."

"No shame whatever," replied the old man, "but, on the contrary, the fittest thing that could have chanced. You are dependent on no private benevolence, nor on the good offices of any man now living, or who has lived these last three hundred years. This ancient establishment is for the support of poverty, misfortune, and age, and, according to the word of the founder, it serves him:—he was indebted to the beneficiaries, not they to him, for, in return for his temporal bequests, he asked their prayers for his soul's welfare. He needed them, could they avail him; for this ponderous structure was built upon the founder's mortal transgressions, and even, I may say, out of the actual substance of them. Sir Edward Redclyffe was a fierce fighter in the Wars of the Roses, and amassed much wealth by spoil, rapine, confiscation, and all violent and evil ways that those disturbed times opened to him; and on his death-bed he founded this Hospital for twelve men, who should be able to prove kindred with his race, to dwell here with a stipend, and pray for him; and likewise provision for a sick stranger, until he should be able to go on his way again."

"I shall pray for him willingly," said Edward, moved by the pity which awaits any softened state of our natures to steal into our hearts. "Though no Catholic, I will pray for his soul. And that is his crest which you wear embroidered on his garment?"

"It is," said the old man. "You will see it carved, painted, embroidered, everywhere about the establishment; but let us give it the better and more reasonable interpretation;—not that he sought to proclaim his own pride of ancestry and race, but to acknowledge his sins the more manifestly, by stamping the emblem of his race on this structure of his penitence."

"And are you," said Redclyffe, impressed anew by the quiet dignity of the venerable speaker, "in authority in the establishment?"

"A simple beneficiary of the charity," said the palmer; "one of the twelve poor brethren and kinsmen of the founder. Slighter proofs of kindred are now of necessity received, since, in the natural course of things, the race has long been growing scarce. But I had it in my power to make out a sufficient claim."

"Singular," exclaimed Redclyffe, "you being an American!" [Endnote: 8.]

"You remember me, then," said the old man, quietly.

"From the first," said Edward, "although your image took the fantastic aspect of the bewilderment in which I then was; and now that I am in clearer state of mind, it seems yet stranger that you should be here. We two children thought you translated, and people, I remember, whispered dark hints about your fate."

"There was nothing wonderful in my disappearance," said the old man. "There were causes, an impulse, an intuition, that made me feel, one particular night, that I might meet harm, whether from myself or others, by remaining in a place with which I had the most casual connection. But I never, so long as I remained in America, quite lost sight of you; and Doctor Grimshawe, before his death, had knowledge of where I was, and gave me in charge a duty which I faithfully endeavored to perform. Singular man that he was! much evil, much good in him. Both, it may be, will live after him!"

Redclyffe, when the conversation had reached this point, felt a vast desire to reveal to the old man all that the grim Doctor had instilled into his childish mind, all that he himself, in subsequent years, had wrought more definitely out of it, all his accompanying doubts respecting the secret of his birth and some supposed claims which he might assert, and which, only half acknowledging the purpose, had availed to bring him, a republican, hither as to an ancestral centre. He even fancied that the benign old man seemed to expect and await such a confidence; but that very idea contributed to make it impossible for him to speak.

"Another time," he said to himself. "Perhaps never. It is a fantastic folly; and with what the workhouse foundling has since achieved, he would give up too many hopes to take the representation of a mouldy old English family."

"I find my head still very weak," said he, by way of cutting short the conversation. "I must try to sleep again."

CHAPTER XIV

The next day he called for his clothes, and, with the assistance of the pensioner, managed to be dressed, and awaited the arrival of the surgeon, sitting in a great easy-chair, with not much except his pale, thin cheeks, dark, thoughtful eyes, and his arm in a sling, to show the pain and danger through which he had passed. Soon after the departure of the professional gentleman, a step somewhat louder than ordinary was heard on the staircase, and in the corridor leading to the sick-chamber; the step (as Redclyffe's perceptions, nicely attempered by his weakness, assured him) of a man in perfect and robust health, and of station and authority. A moment afterwards, a gentleman of middle age, or a little beyond, appeared in the doorway, in a dress that seemed clerical, yet not very decidedly so; he had a frank, kindly, yet authoritative bearing, and a face that might almost be said to beam with geniality, when, as now, the benevolence of his nature was aroused and ready to express itself.

"My friend," said he, "Doctor Portingale tells me you are much better; and I am most happy to hear it."

There was something brusque and unceremonious in his manner, that a little jarred against Redclyffe's sensitiveness, which had become morbid in sympathy with his weakness. He felt that the new-comer had not probably the right idea as to his own position in life; he was addressing him most kindly, indeed, but as an inferior.

"I am much better, sir," he replied, gravely, and with reserve; "so nearly well, that I shall very soon be able to bid farewell to my kind nurse here, and to this ancient establishment, to which I owe so much."

The visitor seemed struck by Mr. Redclyffe's tone, and finely modulated voice, and glanced at his face, and then over his dress and figure, as if to gather from them some reliable data as to his station.

"I am the Warden of this Hospital," said he, with not less benignity than heretofore, and greater courtesy; "and, in that capacity, must consider you under my care,—as my guest, in fact,—although, owing to my casual absence, one of the brethren of the house has been the active instrument in attending you. I am most happy to find you so far recovered. Do you feel yourself in a condition to give any account of the accident which has befallen you?"

"It will be a very unsatisfactory one, at best," said Redclyffe, trying to discover some definite point in his misty reminiscences. "I am a stranger to this country, and was on a pedestrian tour with the purpose of making myself acquainted with the aspects of English scenery and life. I had turned into a footpath, being told that it would lead me within view of an old Hall, which, from certain early associations, I was very desirous of seeing. I think I went astray; at all events, the path became indistinct; and, so far as I can recollect, I had just turned to retrace my steps,—in fact, that is the last thing in my memory."

"You had almost fallen a sacrifice," said the Warden, "to the old preference which our English gentry have inherited from their Norman ancestry, of game to man. You had come unintentionally as an intruder into a rich preserve much haunted by poachers, and exposed yourself to the deadly mark of a spring-gun, which had not the wit to distinguish between a harmless traveller and a poacher. At least, such is our conclusion; for our old friend here, (who luckily for you is a great rambler in the woods,) when the report drew him to the spot, found you insensible, and the gun discharged."

"A gun has so little discretion," said Redclyffe, smiling, "that it seems a pity to trust entirely to its judgment, in a matter of life and death. But, to confess the truth, I had come this morning to the suspicion that there was a direct human agency in the matter; for I find missing a little pocket-book which I carried."

"Then," said the Warden, "that certainly gives a new aspect to the affair. Was it of value?"

"Of none whatever," said Redclyffe, "merely containing pencil memoranda, and notes of a traveller's little expenses. I had papers about me of far more value, and a moderate sum of money, a letter of credit, which have escaped. I do not, however, feel inclined, on such grounds, to transfer the guilt decidedly from the spring-gun to any more responsible criminal; for it is very possible that the pocket-book, being carelessly carried, might have been lost on the way. I had not used it since the preceding day."

"Much more probable, indeed," said the Warden. "The discharged gun is strong evidence against itself. Mr. Colcord," continued he, raising his voice, "how long was the interval between the discharge of the gun and your arrival on the spot."

"Five minutes, or less," said the old man, "for I was not far off, and made what haste I could, it being borne in on my spirit that mischief was abroad."

"Did you hear two reports?" asked the Warden.

"Only one," replied Colcord.

"It is a plain case against the spring-gun," said the Warden; "and, as you tell me you are a stranger, I trust you will not suppose that our peaceful English woods and parks are the haunt of banditti. We must try to give you a better idea of us. May I ask, are you an American, and recently come among us?"

"I believe a letter of credit is considered as decisive as most modes of introduction," said Redclyffe, feeling that the good Warden was desirous of knowing with some precision who and what he was, and that, in the circumstances, he had a right to such knowledge. "Here is mine, on a respectable house in London."

The Warden took it, and glanced it over with a slight apologetic bow; it was a credit for a handsome amount in favor of the Honorable Edward Redclyffe, a title that did not fail to impress the Englishman rather favorably towards his new acquaintance, although he happened to know something of their abundance, even so early in the republic, among the men branded sons of equality. But, at all events, it showed no ordinary ability and energy for so young a man to have held such position as this title denoted in the fiercely contested political struggles of the new democracy.

"Do you know, Mr. Redclyffe, that this name is familiar to us, hereabouts?" asked he, with a kindly bow and recognition, — "that it is in fact the principal name in this neighborhood, — that a family of your name still possesses Braithwaite Hall, and that this very Hospital, where you have happily found shelter, was founded by former representatives of your name? Perhaps you count yourself among their kindred."

"My countrymen are apt to advance claims to kinship with distinguished English families on such slight grounds as to make it ridiculous," said Redclyffe, coloring. "I should not choose to follow so absurd an example."

"Well, well, perhaps not," said the Warden, laughing frankly. "I have been amongst your republicans myself, a long while ago, and saw that your countrymen have no adequate idea of the sacredness of pedigrees, and heraldic distinctions, and would change their own names at pleasure, and vaunt kindred with an English duke on the strength of the assumed one. But I am happy to meet an American gentleman who looks upon this matter as Englishmen necessarily must. I met with great kindness in your country, Mr. Redclyffe, and shall be truly happy if you will allow me an opportunity of returning some small part of the obligation. You are now in a condition for removal to my own quarters, across the quadrangle. I will give orders to prepare an apartment, and you must transfer yourself there by dinnertime."

With this hospitable proposal, so decisively expressed, the Warden took his leave; and Edward Redclyffe had hardly yet recovered sufficient independent force to reject an invitation so put, even were he inclined; but, in truth, the proposal suited well with his wishes, such as they were, and was, moreover, backed, it is singular to say, by another of those dreamlike recognitions which had so perplexed him ever since he found himself in the Hospital. In some previous state of being, the Warden and he had talked together before.

"What is the Warden's name?" he inquired of the old pensioner.

"Hammond," said the old man; "he is a kinsman of the Redclyffe family himself, a man of fortune, and spends more than the income of his wardenship in beautifying and keeping up the glory of the establishment. He takes great pride in it."

"And he has been in America," said Redclyffe. "How strange! I knew him there. Never was anything so singular as the discovery of old acquaintants where I had reason to suppose myself unknowing and unknown. Unless dear Doctor Grim, or dear little Elsie, were to start up and greet me, I know not what may chance next."

Redclyffe took up his quarters in the Warden's house the next day, and was installed in an apartment that made a picture, such as he had not before seen, of English household comfort. He was thus established under the good Warden's roof, and, being very attractive of most people's sympathies, soon began to grow greatly in favor with that kindly personage.

When Edward Redclyffe removed from the old pensioner's narrow quarters to the far ampler accommodations of the Warden's house, the latter gentleman was taking his morning exercise on horseback. A servant, however, in a grave livery, ushered him to an apartment, where the new guest was surprised to see some luggage which two or three days before Edward had ordered from London, on finding that his stay in this part of the country was likely to be much longer than he had originally contemplated. The sight of these things—the sense which they conveyed that he was an expected and welcome guest—tended to raise the spirits of the solitary wanderer, and made him.... [Endnote: 1.]

The Warden's abode was an original part of the ancient establishment, being an entire side of the quadrangle which the whole edifice surrounded; and for the establishment of a bachelor (which was his new friend's condition), it seemed to Edward Redclyffe abundantly spacious and enviably comfortable. His own chamber had a grave, rich depth, as it were, of serene and time-long garniture, for purposes of repose, convenience, daily and nightly comfort, that it was soothing even to look at. Long accustomed, as Redclyffe had been, to the hardy and rude accommodations, if so they were to be called, of log huts and hasty, mud-built houses in the Western States of America, life, its daily habits, its passing accommodations, seemed to assume an importance, under these aspects, which it had not worn before; those deep downy beds, those antique chairs, the heavy carpet, the tester and curtains, the stateliness of the old room,—they had a charm as compared with the thin preparation of a forester's bedchamber, such as Redclyffe had chiefly known them, in the ruder parts of the country, that really seemed to give a more substantial value to life; so much pains had been taken with its modes and appliances, that it looked more solid than before. Nevertheless, there was something ghostly in that stately curtained bed, with the deep gloom within its drapery, so ancient as it was; and suggestive of slumberers there who had long since slumbered elsewhere.

The old servant, whose grave, circumspect courtesy was a matter quite beyond Redclyffe's experience, soon knocked at the chamber door, and suggested that the guest might desire to await the Warden's arrival in the library, which was the customary sitting-room. Redclyffe assenting, he was ushered into a spacious apartment, lighted by various Gothic windows, surrounded with old oaken cases, in which were ranged volumes, most or many of which seemed to be coeval with the foundation of the hospital; and opening one of them, Redclyffe saw for the first time in his life [Endnote: 2] a genuine book-worm, that ancient form of creature living upon literature; it had gnawed a circular hole, penetrating through perhaps a score of pages of the seldom opened volume, and was still at his musty feast. There was a fragrance of old learning in this ancient library; a soothing influence, as the American felt, of time-honored ideas, where the strife, novelties, uneasy agitating conflict, attrition of unsettled theories, fresh-springing thought, did not attain a foothold; a good place to spend a life which should not be agitated with the disturbing element; so quiet, so peaceful; how slowly, with how little wear, would the years pass here! How unlike what he had hitherto known, and was destined to know,—the quick, violent struggle of his mother country, which had traced lines in his young brow already. How much would be saved by taking his former existence, not as dealing with things yet malleable, but with fossils, things that had had their life, and now were unchangeable, and revered, here!

At one end of this large room there was a bowed window, the space near which was curtained off from the rest of the library, and, the window being filled with painted glass (most of which seemed old, though there were insertions evidently of modern and much inferior handiwork), there was a rich gloom of light, or you might call it a rich glow, according to your mood of mind. Redclyffe soon perceived that this curtained recess was the especial study of his friend, the Warden, and as such was provided with all that modern times had contrived for making an enjoyment out of the perusal of old books; a study table, with every convenience of multifarious devices, a great inkstand, pens; a luxurious study chair, where thought [Endnote: 3] upon. To say the truth, there was not, in this retired and thoughtful nook, anything that indicated to Redclyffe that the Warden had been recently engaged in consultation of learned authorities,—or in abstract labor, whether moral, metaphysical or historic; there was a volume of translations of Mother Goose's Melodies into Greek and Latin, printed for private circulation, and with the Warden's name on the title-page; a London newspaper of the preceding day; Lillebullero, Chevy Chase, and the old political ballads; and, what a little amused Redclyffe, the three volumes of a novel from a circulating library; so that Redclyffe came to the conclusion that the good Warden, like many educated men, whose early scholastic propensities are backed up by the best of opportunities, and all desirable facilities and surroundings, still contented himself with gathering a flower or two, instead of attempting the hard toil requisite to raise a crop.

It must not be omitted, that there was a fragrance in the room, which, unlike as the scene was, brought back, through so many years, to Redclyffe's mind a most vivid remembrance of poor old Doctor Grim's squalid chamber, with his wild, bearded presence in the midst of it, puffing his everlasting cloud; for here was the same smell of tobacco, and on the mantel-piece of a chimney lay a German pipe, and an old silver tobacco-box into which was wrought the leopard's head and the inscription in black letter. The Warden had evidently availed himself of one of the chief bachelor sources of comfort. Redclyffe, whose destiny had hitherto, and up to a very recent period, been to pass a feverishly active life, was greatly impressed by all these tokens of learned ease,—a degree of self-indulgence combined with duties enough to quiet an otherwise uneasy conscience,—by the consideration that this pensioner acted a good part in a world where no one is entitled to be an unprofitable laborer. He thought within himself, that his prospects in his own galvanized country, that seemed to him, a few years since, to offer such a career for an adventurous young man, conscious of motive power, had nothing so enticing as such a nook as this,—a quiet recess of unchangeable old time, around which the turbulent tide now eddied and rushed, but could not disturb it. Here, to be sure, hope, love, ambition, came not, progress came not; but here was what, just now, the early wearied American could appreciate better than aught else,—here was rest.

The fantasy took Edward to imitate the useful labors of the learned Warden, and to make trial whether his own classical condition—the results of Doctor Grim's tuition, and subsequently that of an American College— had utterly deserted him, by attempting a translation of a few verses of Yankee Doodle; and he was making hopeful progress when the Warden came in fresh and rosy from a morning's ride in a keen east wind. He shook hands heartily with his guest, and, though by no means frigid at their former interview, seemed to have developed at once into a kindlier man, now that he had suffered the stranger to cross his threshold, and had thus made himself responsible for his comfort.

"I shall take it greatly amiss," said he, "if you do not pick up fast under my roof, and gather a little English ruddiness, moreover, in the walks and rides that I mean to take you. Your countrymen, as I saw them, are a sallow set; but I think you must have English blood enough in your veins to eke out a ruddy tint, with the help of good English beef and ale, and daily draughts of wholesome light and air."

"My cheeks would not have been so very pale," said Edward, laughing, "if an English shot had not deprived me of a good deal of my American blood."

"Only follow my guidance," said the Warden, "and I assure you you shall have back whatever blood we have deprived you of, together with an addition. It is now luncheon-time, and we will begin the process of replenishing your veins."

So they went into a refectory, where were spread upon the board what might have seemed a goodly dinner to most Americans; though for this Englishman it was but a by-incident, a slight refreshment, to enable him to pass the midway stage of life. It is an excellent thing to see the faith of a hearty Englishman in his own stomach, and how well that kindly organ repays his trust; with what devout assimilation he takes to himself his kindred beef, loving it, believing in it, making a good use of it, and without any qualms of conscience or prescience as to the result. They surely eat twice as much as we; and probably because of their undoubted faith it never does them any harm. Dyspepsia is merely a superstition with us. If we could cease to believe in its existence, it would exist no more. Redclyffe, eating little himself, his wound compelling him to be cautious as to his diet, was secretly delighted to see what sweets the Warden found in a cold round of beef, in a pigeon pie, and a cut or two of Yorkshire ham; not that he was ravenous, but that his stomach was so healthy.

"You eat little, my friend," said the Warden, pouring out a glass of sherry for Redclyffe, and another for himself. "But you are right, in such a predicament as yours. Spare your stomach while you are weakly, and it will help you when you are strong This, now, is the most enjoyable meal of the day with me. You will not see me play such a knife and fork at dinner; though there too, especially if I have ridden out in the afternoon, I do pretty well. But, come now, if (like most of your countrymen, as I have heard) you are a lover of the weed, I can offer you some as delicate Latakia as you are likely to find in England."

"I lack that claim upon your kindness, I am sorry to say," replied Redclyffe. "I am not a good smoker, though I have occasionally taken a cigar at need."

"Well, when you find yourself growing old, and especially if you chance to be a bachelor, I advise you to cultivate the habit," said the Warden. "A wife is the only real obstacle or objection to a pipe; they can seldom be thoroughly reconciled, and therefore it is well for a man to consider, beforehand, which of the two he can best dispense with. I know not how it might have been once, had the conflicting claim of these two rivals ever been fairly presented to me; but I now should be at no loss to choose the pipe."

They returned to the study; and while the Warden took his pipe, Redclyffe, considering that, as the guest of this hospitable Englishman, he had no right to continue a stranger, thought it fit to make known to him who he was, and his condition, plans, and purposes. He represented himself as having been liberally educated, bred to the law, but (to his misfortune) having turned aside from that profession to engage in politics. In this pursuit, indeed, his success wore a flattering outside; for he had become distinguished, and, though so young, a leader, locally at least, in the party which he had adopted. He had been, for a biennial term, a member of Congress, after winning some distinction in the legislature of his native State; but some one of those fitful changes to which American politics are peculiarly liable had thrown him out, in his candidacy for his second term; and the virulence of party animosity, the abusiveness of the press, had acted so much upon a disposition naturally somewhat too sensitive for the career which he had undertaken, that he had resolved, being now freed from legislative cares, to seize the opportunity for a visit to England, whither he was drawn by feelings which every educated and impressible

American feels, in a degree scarcely conceivable by the English themselves. And being here (but he had already too much experience of English self-sufficiency to confess so much) he began to feel the deep yearning which a sensitive American—his mind full of English thoughts, his imagination of English poetry, his heart of English character and sentiment—cannot fail to be influenced by,—the yearning of the blood within his veins for that from which it has been estranged; the half-fanciful regret that he should ever have been separated from these woods, these fields, these natural features of scenery, to which his nature was moulded, from the men who are still so like himself, from these habits of life and thought which (though he may not have known them for two centuries) he still perceives to have remained in some mysterious way latent in the depths of his character, and soon to be reassumed, not as a foreigner would do it, but like habits native to him, and only suspended for a season.

This had been Redclyffe's state of feeling ever since he landed in England, and every day seemed to make him more at home; so that it seemed as if he were gradually awakening to a former reality.

CHAPTER XV

After lunch, the Warden showed a good degree of kind anxiety about his guest, and ensconced him in a most comfortable chair in his study, where he gave him his choice of books old and new, and was somewhat surprised, as well as amused, to see that Redclyffe seemed most attracted towards a department of the library filled with books of English antiquities, and genealogies, and heraldry; the two latter, indeed, having the preference over the others.

"This is very remarkable," said he, smiling. "By what right or reason, by what logic of character, can you, a democrat, renouncing all advantages of birth,—neither priding yourself on family, nor seeking to found one,— how therefore can you care for genealogies, or for this fantastic science of heraldry? Having no antiquities, being a people just made, how can you care for them?"

"My dear sir," said Redclyffe, "I doubt whether the most devoted antiquarian in England ever cares to search for an old thing merely because it is old, as any American just landed on your shores would do. Age is our novelty; therefore it attracts and absorbs us. And as for genealogies, I know not what necessary repulsion there may be between it and democracy. A line of respectable connections, being the harder to preserve where there is nothing in the laws to defend it, is therefore the more precious when we have it really to boast of."

"True," said the Warden, "when a race keeps itself distinguished among the grimy order of your commonalty, all with equal legal rights to place and eminence as itself, it must needs be because there is a force and efficacy in the blood. I doubt not," he said, looking with the free approval of an elder man at the young man's finely developed face and graceful form,—"I doubt not that you can look back upon a line of ancestry, always shining out from the surrounding obscurity of the mob."

Redclyffe, though ashamed of himself, could not but feel a paltry confusion and embarrassment, as he thought of his unknown origin, and his advent from the almshouse; coming out of that squalid darkness as if he were a thing that had had a spontaneous birth out of poverty, meanness, petty crime; and here in ancestral England, he felt more keenly than ever before what was his misfortune.

"I must not let you lie under this impression," said he manfully to the Warden. "I have no ancestry; at the very first step my origin is lost in impenetrable obscurity. I only know that but for the aid of a kind friend—on whose benevolence I seem to have had no claim whatever—my life would probably have been poor, mean, unenlightened."

"Well, well," said the kind Warden,—hardly quite feeling, however, the noble sentiment which he expressed,—"it is better to be the first noble illustrator of a name than even the worthy heir of a name that has been noble and famous for a thousand years. The highest pride of some of our peers, who have won their rank by their own force, has been to point to the cottage whence they sprung. Your posterity, at all events, will have the advantage of you,—they will know their ancestor."

Redclyffe sighed, for there was truly a great deal of the foolish yearning for a connection with the past about him; his imagination had taken this turn, and the very circumstances of his obscure birth gave it a field to exercise itself.

"I advise you," said the Warden, by way of changing the conversation, "to look over the excellent history of the county which you are now in. There is no reading better, to my mind, than these country histories; though doubtless a stranger would hardly feel so much interest in them as one whose progenitors, male or female, have strewn their dust over the whole field of which the history treats. This history is a fine specimen of the kind."

The work to which Redclyffe's attention was thus drawn was in two large folio volumes, published about thirty years before, bound in calf by some famous artist in that line, illustrated with portraits and views of ruined castles, churches, cathedrals, the seats of nobility and gentry; Roman, British, and Saxon remains, painted windows, oak carvings, and so forth.

And as for its contents the author ascended for the history of the county as far as into the pre-Roman ages, before Caesar had ever heard of Britain; and brought it down, an ever swelling and increasing tale, to his own days; inclusive of the separate histories, and pedigrees, and hereditary legends, and incidents, of all the principal families. In this latter branch of information, indeed, the work seemed particularly full, and contained every incident that would have worked well into historical romance.

"Aye, aye," said the Warden, laughing at some strange incident of this sort which Redclyffe read out to him. "My old friend Gibber, the learned author of this work, (he has been dead this score of years, so he will not mind my saying it,) had a little too much the habit of seeking his authorities in the cottage chimney-corners. I mean that an old woman's tale was just about as acceptable to him as a recorded fact; and to say the truth, they are really apt to have ten times the life in them."

Redclyffe saw in the volume a full account of the founding of the Hospital, its regulations and purposes, its edifices; all of which he reserved for future reading, being for the present more attracted by the mouldy gossip of family anecdotes which we have alluded to. Some of these, and not the least singular, referred to the ancient family which had founded the Hospital; and he was attracted by seeing a mention of a Bloody Footstep, which reminded him of the strange old story which good Doctor Grimshawe had related by his New England fireside, in those childish days when Edward dwelt with him by the graveyard, On reading it, however, he found that the English legend, if such it could be called, was far less full and explicit than that of New England. Indeed, it assigned various origins to the Bloody Footstep;— one being, that it was the stamp of the foot of the Saxon thane, who fought at his own threshold against the assault of the Norman baron, who seized his mansion at the Conquest; another, that it was the imprint of a fugitive who had sought shelter from the lady of the house during the Wars of the Roses, and was dragged out by her husband, and slain on the door-step; still another, that it was the footstep of a Protestant in Bloody Mary's days, who, being sent to prison by the squire of that epoch, had lifted his hands to Heaven, and stamped his foot, in appeal as against the unjust violence with which he was treated, and stamping his foot, it had left the bloody mark. It was hinted too, however, that another version, which out of delicacy to the family the author was reluctant to state, assigned the origin of the Bloody Footstep to so late a period as the wars of the Parliament. And, finally, there was an odious rumor that what was called the Bloody Footstep was nothing miraculous, after all, but most probably a natural reddish stain in the stone door-step; but against this heresy the excellent Dr. Gibber set his face most sturdily.

The original legend had made such an impression on Redclyffe's childish fancy, that he became strangely interested in thus discovering it, or something remotely like it, in England, and being brought by such unsought means to reside so near it. Curious about the family to which it had occurred, he proceeded to examine its records, as given in the County History. The name was Redclyffe. Like most English pedigrees, there was an obscurity about a good many of the earlier links; but the line was traced out with reasonable definiteness from the days of Coeur de Lion, and there was said to be a cross-legged ancestor in the village church, who (but the inscription was obliterated) was probably a Redclyffe, and had fought either under the Lion Heart or in the Crusades. It was, in subsequent ages, one of the most distinguished families, though there had been turbulent men in all those turbulent times, hard fighters. In one age, a barony of early creation seemed to have come into the family, and had been, as it were, playing bo-peep with the race for several centuries. Some of them had actually assumed the title; others had given it up for lack of sufficient proof; but still there was such a claim, and up to the time at which this County History was written, it had neither been made out, nor had the hope of doing so been relinquished.

"Have the family," asked Redclyffe of his host, "ever yet made out their claim to this title, which has so long been playing the will-of-the-wisp with them?"

"No, not yet," said the Warden, puffing out a volume of smoke from his meerschaum, and making it curl up to the ceiling. "Their claim has as little substance, in my belief, as yonder vanishing vapor from my pipe. But they still keep up their delusion. I had supposed that the claim would perish with the last squire, who was a childless man, — at least, without legitimate heirs; but this estate passed to one whom we can scarcely call an Englishman, he being a Catholic, the descendant of forefathers who have lived in Italy since the time of George II., and who is, moreover, a Catholic. We English would not willingly see an ancestral honor in the possession of such a man!"

"Is there, do you think, a prospect of his success?"

"I have heard so, but hardly believe it," replied the Warden. "I remember, some dozen or fifteen years ago, it was given out that some clue had been found to the only piece of evidence that was wanting. It had been said that there was an emigration to your own country, above a hundred years ago, and on account of some family feud; the true heir had gone thither and never returned. Now, the point was to prove the extinction of this branch of the family. But, excuse me, I must pay an official visit to my charge here. Will you accompany me, or continue to pore over the County History?"

Redclyffe felt enough of the elasticity of convalescence to be desirous of accompanying the Warden; and they accordingly crossed the enclosed quadrangle to the entrance of the Hospital portion of the large and intricate structure. It was a building of the early Elizabethan age, a plaster and timber structure, like many houses of that period and much earlier. [Endnote: 1] Around this court stood the building, with the date 1437 cut on the front. On each side, a row of gables looked upon the enclosed space, most venerable old gables, with heavy mullioned windows filled with little diamond panes of glass, and opening on lattices. On two sides there was a cloistered walk, under echoing arches, and in the midst a spacious lawn of the greenest and loveliest grass, such as England only can show, and which, there, is of perennial verdure and beauty. In the midst stood a stone statue of a venerable man, wrought in the best of mediæval sculpture, with robe and ruff, and tunic and venerable beard, resting on a staff, and holding what looked like a clasped book in his hand. The English atmosphere, together with the coal smoke, settling down in the space of centuries from the chimneys of the Hospital, had roughened and blackened this venerable piece of sculpture, enclosing it as it were in a superficies of decay; but still (and perhaps the more from these tokens of having stood so long among men) the statue had an aspect of venerable life, and of connection with human life, that made it strongly impressive.

"This is the effigy of Sir Edward Redclyffe, the founder of the Hospital," said the Warden. "He is a most peaceful and venerable old gentleman in his attire and aspect, as you see; but he was a fierce old fellow in his day, and is said to have founded the Hospital as a means of appeasing Heaven for some particular deed of blood, which he had imposed upon his conscience in the War of the Roses."

"Yes," said Redclyffe, "I have just read in the County History that the Bloody Footstep was said to have been imprinted in his time. But what is that thing which he holds in his hand?"

"It is a famous heirloom of the Redclyffes," said the Warden, "on the possession of which (as long as they did possess it) they prided themselves, it is said, more than on their ancient manor-house. It was a Saxon ornament, which a certain ancestor was said to have had from Harold, the old Saxon king; but if there ever was any such article, it has been missing from the family mansion for two or three hundred years. There is not known to be an antique relic of that description now in existence."

"I remember having seen such an article,—yes, precisely of that shape," observed Redclyffe, "in the possession of a very dear old friend of mine, when I was a boy."

"What, in America?" exclaimed the Warden. "That is very remarkable. The time of its being missed coincides well enough with that of the early settlement of New England. Some Puritan, before his departure, may have thought himself doing God service by filching the old golden gewgaw from the Cavalier; for it was said to be fine, ductile gold."

The circumstances struck Redclyffe with a pleasant wonder; for, indeed, the old statue held the closest possible imitation, in marble, of that strange old glitter of gold which he himself had so often played with in the Doctor's study; [Endnote: 2] so identical, that he could have fancied that he saw the very thing, changed from metal into stone, even with its bruises and other casual marks in it. As he looked at the old statue, his imagination played with it, and his naturally great impressibility half made him imagine that the old face looked at him with a keen, subtile, wary glance, as if acknowledging that it held some secret, but at the same time defying him to find it out. And then again came that visionary feeling that had so often swept over him since he had been an inmate of the Hospital.

All over the interior part of the building was carved in stone the leopard's head, with wearisome iteration; as if the founder were anxious to imprint his device so numerously, lest—when he produced this edifice as his remuneration to Eternal Justice for many sins—the Omniscient Eye should fail to be reminded that Sir Edward Redclyffe had done it. But, at all events, it seemed to Redclyffe that the ancient knight had purposed a good thing, and in a measurable degree had effected it; for here stood the venerable edifice securely founded, bearing the moss of four hundred years upon it; and though wars, and change of dynasties, and religious change, had swept around it, with seemingly destructive potency, yet here had the lodging, the food, the monastic privileges of the brethren been held secure, and were unchanged by all the altering mariners of the age. The old fellow, somehow or other, seemed to have struck upon an everlasting rock, and founded his pompous charity there.

They entered an arched door on the left of the quadrangle, and found themselves hi a dark old hall with oaken beams; to say the truth, it was a barn-like sort of enclosure, and was now used as a sort of rubbish-place for the Hospital, where they stored away old furniture, and where carpenter's work might be done. And yet, as the Warden assured Redclyffe, it was once a hall of state, hung with tapestry, carpeted, for aught he knew, with cloth of gold, and set with rich furniture, and a groaning board in the midst. Here, the hereditary patron of the Hospital had once entertained King James the First, who made a Latin speech on the occasion, a copy of which was still preserved in the archives. On the rafters of this old hall there were cobwebs in such abundance that Redclyffe could not but reflect on the joy which old Doctor Grimshawe would have had in seeing them, and the health to the human race which he would have hoped to collect and distil from them.

From this great, antique room they crossed the quadrangle and entered the kitchen of the establishment. A hospitable fire was burning there, and there seemed to be a great variety of messes cooking; and the Warden explained to Redclyffe that there was no general table in the Hospital; but the brethren, at their own will and pleasure, either formed themselves into companies or messes, of any convenient size, or enjoyed a solitary meal by themselves, each in their own apartments. There was a goodly choice of simple, but good and enjoyable food, and a sufficient supply of potent ale, brewed in the vats of the Hospital, which, among its other praiseworthy characteristics, was famous for this; having at some epoch presumed to vie with the famous ale of Trinity, in Cambridge, and the Archdeacon of Oxford,—these having come down to the hospital from a private receipt of Sir Edward's butler, which was now lost in the Redclyffe family; nor would the ungrateful Hospital give up its secret even out of loyalty to its founder.

"I would use my influence with the brewer," said the Warden, on communicating this little fact to Redclyffe; "but the present man—now owner of the estate—is not worthy to have good ale brewed in his house; having himself no taste for anything but Italian wines, wretched fellow that he is! He might make himself an Englishman if he would take heartily to our ale; and with that end in view, I should be glad to give it him."

The kitchen fire blazed warmly, as we have said, and roast and stewed and boiled were in process of cooking, producing a pleasant fume, while great heaps of wheaten loaves were smoking hot from the ovens, and the master cook and his subordinates were in fume and hiss, like beings that were of a fiery element, and, though irritable and scorching, yet were happier here than they could have been in any other situation. The Warden seemed to have an especial interest and delight in this department of the Hospital, and spoke apart to the head cook on the subject (as Redclyffe surmised from what he overheard) of some especial delicacy for his own table that day.

"This kitchen is a genial place," said he to Redclyffe, as they retired. "In the evening, after the cooks have done their work, the brethren have liberty to use it as a sort of common room, and to sit here over their ale till a reasonable bedtime. It would interest you much to make one at such a party; for they have had a varied experience in life, each one for himself, and it would be strange to hear the varied roads by which they have come hither."

"Yes," replied Redclyffe, "and, I presume, not one of them ever dreamed of coming hither when he started in life. The only one with whom I am acquainted could hardly have expected it, at all events."

"He is a remarkable man, more so than you may have had an opportunity of knowing," said the Warden. "I know not his history, for he is not communicative on that subject, and it was only necessary for him to make out his proofs of claim to the charity to the satisfaction of the Curators. But it has often struck me that there must have been strange and striking events in his life,—though how it could have been without his attracting attention and being known, I cannot say. I have myself often received good counsel from him in the conduct of the Hospital, and the present owner of the Hall seems to have taken him for his counsellor and confidant, being himself strange to English affairs and life."

"I should like to call on him, as a matter of course rather than courtesy," observed Redclyffe, "and thank him for his great kindness."

They accordingly ascended the dark oaken staircase with its black balustrade, and approached the old man's chamber, the door of which they found open, and in the blurred looking-glass which hung deep within the room Redclyffe was surprised to perceive the young face of a woman, who seemed to be arranging her head-gear, as women are always doing. It was but a moment, and then it vanished like a vision.

"I was not aware," he said, turning to the Warden, "that there was a feminine side to this establishment."

"Nor is there," said the old bachelor, "else it would not have held together so many ages as it has. The establishment has its own wise, monkish regulations; but we cannot prevent the fact, that some of the brethren may have had foolish relations with the other sex at some previous period of their lives. This seems to be the case with our wise old friend of whom we have been speaking, — whereby he doubtless became both wiser and sadder. If you have seen a female face here, it is that of a relative who resides out of the hospital, — an excellent young lady, I believe, who has charge of a school."

While he was speaking, the young lady in question passed out, greeting the Warden in a cheerful, respectful way, in which deference to him was well combined with a sense of what was due to herself.

"That," observed the Warden, who had returned her courtesy, with a kindly air betwixt that of gentlemanly courtesy and a superior's acknowledgment, — "that is the relative of our old friend; a young person — a gentlewoman, I may almost call her — who teaches a little school in the village here, and keeps her guardian's heart warm, no doubt, with her presence. An excellent young woman, I do believe, and very useful and faithful in her station."

CHAPTER XVI

On entering the old palmer's apartment, they found him looking over some ancient papers, yellow and crabbedly written, and on one of them a large old seal, all of which he did up in a bundle and enclosed in a parchment cover, so that, before they were well in the room, the documents were removed from view.

"Those papers and parchments have a fine old yellow tint, Colcord," said the Warden, "very satisfactory to an antiquary."

"There is nothing in them," said the old man, "of general interest. Some old papers they are, which came into my possession by inheritance, and some of them relating to the affairs of a friend of my youth;—a long past time, and a long past friend," added he, sighing.

"Here is a new friend, at all events," said the kindly Warden, wishing to cheer the old man, "who feels himself greatly indebted to you for your care." [Endnote: 1.]

There now ensued a conversation between the three, in the course of which reference was made to America, and the Warden's visit there.

"You are so mobile," he said, "you change so speedily, that I suppose there are few external things now that I should recognize. The face of your country changes like one of your own sheets of water, under the influence of sun, cloud, and wind; but I suppose there is a depth below that is seldom effectually stirred. It is a great fault of the country that its sons find it impossible to feel any patriotism for it."

"I do not by any means acknowledge that impossibility," responded Redclyffe, with a smile. "I certainly feel that sentiment very strongly in my own breast, more especially since I have left America three thousand miles behind me."

"Yes, it is only the feeling of self-assertion that rises against the self-complacency of the English," said the Warden. "Nothing else; for what else have you become the subject of this noble weakness of patriotism? You cannot love anything beyond the soil of your own estate; or in your case, if your heart is very large, you may possibly take in, in a quiet sort of way, the whole of New England. What more is possible? How can you feel a heart's love for a mere political arrangement, like your Union? How can you be loyal, where personal attachment—the lofty and noble and unselfish attachment of a subject to his prince—is out of the question? where your sovereign is felt to be a mere man like yourselves, whose petty struggles, whose ambition—mean before it grew to be audacious—you have watched, and know him to be just the same now as yesterday, and that to-morrow he will be walking unhonored amongst you again? Your system is too bare and meagre for human nature to love, or to endure it long. These stately degrees of society, that have so strong a hold upon us in England, are not to be done away with so lightly as you think. Your experiment is not yet a success by any means; and you will live to see it result otherwise than you think!"

"It is natural for you Englishmen to feel thus," said Redclyffe; "although, ever since I set my foot on your shores,—forgive me, but you set me the example of free speech,—I have had a feeling of coming change among all that you look upon as so permanent, so everlasting; and though your thoughts dwell fondly on things as they are and have been, there is a deep destruction somewhere in this country, that is inevitably impelling it in the path of my own. But I care not for this. I do aver that I love my country, that I am proud of its institutions, that I have a feeling unknown, probably, to any but a republican, but which is the proudest thing in me, that there is no man above me,—for my ruler is only myself, in the person of another, whose office I impose upon him,—nor any below me. If you would understand me, I would tell you of the shame I felt when first, on setting foot in this country, I heard a man speaking of his birth as giving him privileges; saw him looking down on laboring men, as of an inferior race. And what I can never understand, is the pride which you positively seem to feel in having men and classes of men above you, born to privileges which you can never hope to share. It may be a thing to be endured, but surely not one to be absolutely proud of. And yet an Englishman is so."

"Ah! I see we lack a ground to meet upon," said the Warden. "We can never truly understand each other. What you have last mentioned is one of our inner mysteries. It is not a thing to be reasoned about, but to be felt,—to be born within one; and I uphold it to be a generous sentiment, and good for the human heart."

"Forgive me, sir," said Redclyffe, "but I would rather be the poorest and lowest man in America than have that sentiment."

"But it might change your feeling, perhaps," suggested the Warden, "if you were one of the privileged class."

"I dare not say that it would not," said Redclyffe, "for I know I have a thousand weaknesses, and have doubtless as many more that I never suspected myself of. But it seems to me at this moment impossible that I should ever have such an ambition, because I have a sense of meanness in not starting fair, in beginning the world with advantages that my fellows have not."

"Really this is not wise," said the Warden, bluntly, "How can the start in life be fair for all? Providence arranges it otherwise. Did you yourself,—a gentleman evidently by birth and education,—did you start fair in the race of life?"

Redclyffe remembered what his birth, or rather what his first recollected place had been, and reddened.

"In birth, certainly, I had no advantages," said he, and would have explained further but was kept back by invincible reluctance; feeling that the bare fact of his origin in an almshouse would be accepted, while all the inward assurances and imaginations that had reconciled himself to the ugly fact would go for nothing. "But there were advantages, very early in life," added he, smiling, "which perhaps I ought to have been ashamed to avail myself of."

"An old cobwebby library,—an old dwelling by a graveyard,—an old Doctor, busied with his own fantasies, and entangled in his own cobwebs,—and a little girl for a playmate: these were things that you might lawfully avail yourself of," said Colcord, unheard by the Warden, who, thinking the conversation had lasted long enough, had paid a slight passing courtesy to the old man, and was now leaving the room. "Do you remain here long?" he added.

"If the Warden's hospitality holds out," said the American, "I shall be glad; for the place interests me greatly."

"No wonder," replied Colcord.

"And wherefore no wonder?" said Redclyffe, impressed with the idea that there was something peculiar in the tone of the old man's remark.

"Because," returned the other quietly, "it must be to you especially interesting to see an institution of this kind, whereby one man's benevolence or penitence is made to take the substance and durability of stone, and last for centuries; whereas, in America, the solemn decrees and resolutions of millions melt away like vapor, and everything shifts like the pomp of sunset clouds; though it may be as pompous as they. Heaven intended the past as a foundation for the present, to keep it from vibrating and being blown away with every breeze."

"But," said Redclyffe, "I would not see in my country what I see elsewhere,—the Past hanging like a mill-stone round a country's neck, or encrusted in stony layers over the living form; so that, to all intents and purposes, it is dead."

"Well," said Colcord, "we are only talking of the Hospital. You will find no more interesting place anywhere. Stay amongst us; this is the very heart of England, and if you wish to know the fatherland,—the place whence you sprung,—this is the very spot!"

Again Redclyffe was struck with the impression that there was something marked, something individually addressed to himself, in the old man's words; at any rate, it appealed to that primal imaginative vein in him which had so often, in his own country, allowed itself to dream over the possibilities of his birth. He knew that the feeling was a vague and idle one; but yet, just at this time, a convalescent, with a little play moment in what had heretofore been a turbulent life, he felt an inclination to follow out this dream, and let it sport with him, and by and by to awake to realities, refreshed by a season of unreality. At a firmer and stronger period of his life, though Redclyffe might have indulged his imagination with these dreams, yet he would not have let them interfere with his course of action; but having come hither in utter weariness of active life, it seemed just the thing for him to do,—just the fool's paradise for him to be in.

"Yes," repeated the old man, looking keenly in his face, "you will not leave us yet."

Redclyffe returned through the quadrangle to the Warden's house; and there were the brethren, sitting on benches, loitering in the sun, which, though warm for England, seemed scarcely enough to keep these old people warm, even with their cloth robes. They did not seem unhappy; nor yet happy; if they were so, it must be with the mere bliss of existence, a sleepy sense of comfort, and quiet dreaminess about things past, leaving out the things to come,—of which there was nothing, indeed, in their future, save one day after another, just like this, with loaf and ale, and such substantial comforts, and prayers, and idle days again, gathering by the great kitchen fire, and at last a day when they should not be there, but some other old men in their stead. And Redclyffe wondered whether, in the extremity of age, he himself would like to be one of the brethren of the Leopard's Head. The old men, he was sorry to see, did not seem very genial towards one another; in fact, there appeared to be a secret enjoyment of one another's infirmities, wherefore it was hard to tell, unless that each individual might fancy himself to possess an advantage over his fellow, which he mistook for a positive strength; and so there was sometimes a sardonic smile, when, on rising from his seat, the rheumatism was a little evident in an old fellow's joints; or when the palsy shook another's fingers so that he could barely fill his pipe; or when a cough, the gathered spasmodic trouble of thirty years, fairly convulsed another. Then, any two that happened to be sitting near one another looked into each other's cold eyes, and whispered, or suggested merely by a look (for they were bright to such perceptions), "The old fellow will not outlast another winter."

Methinks it is not good for old men to be much together. An old man is a beautiful object in his own place, in the midst of a circle of young people, going down in various gradations to infancy, and all looking up to the patriarch with filial reverence, keeping him warm by their own burning youth; giving him the freshness of their thought and feeling, with such natural influx that it seems as if it grew within his heart; while on them he reacts with an influence that sobers, tempers, keeps them down. His wisdom, very probably, is of no great account,—he cannot fit to any new state of things; but, nevertheless, it works its effect. In such a situation, the old man is kind and genial, mellow, more gentle and generous, and wider-minded than ever before. But if left to himself, or wholly to the society of his contemporaries, the ice gathers about his heart, his hope grows torpid, his love—having nothing of his own blood to develop it—grows cold; he becomes selfish, when he has nothing in the present or the future worth caring about in himself; so that, instead of a beautiful object, he is an ugly one, little, mean, and torpid. I suppose one chief reason to be, that unless he has his own race about him he doubts of anybody's love, he feels himself a stranger in the world, and so becomes unamiable.

A very few days in the Warden's hospitable mansion produced an excellent effect on Redclyffe's frame; his constitution being naturally excellent, and a flow of cheerful spirits contributing much to restore him to health, especially as the abode in this old place, which would probably have been intolerably dull to most young Englishmen, had for this young American a charm like the freshness of Paradise. In truth it had that charm, and besides it another intangible, evanescent, perplexing charm, full of an airy enjoyment, as if he had been here before. What could it be? It could be only the old, very deepest, inherent nature, which the Englishman, his progenitor, carried over the sea with him, nearly two hundred years before, and which had lain buried all that time under heaps of new things, new customs, new institutions, new snows of winter, new layers of forest leaves, until it seemed dead, and was altogether forgotten as if it had never been; but, now, his return had seemed to dissolve or dig away all this incrustation, and the old English nature awoke all fresh, so that he saw the green grass, the hedgerows, the old structures and old manners, the old clouds, the old raindrops, with a recognition, and yet a newness. Redclyffe had never been so quietly happy as now. He had, as it were, the quietude of the old man about him, and the freshness of his own still youthful years.

The Warden was evidently very favorably impressed with his Transatlantic guest, and he seemed to be in a constant state of surprise to find an American so agreeable a kind of person.

"You are just like an Englishman," he sometimes said. "Are you quite sure that you were not born on this side of the water?"

This is said to be the highest compliment that an Englishman can pay to an American; and doubtless he intends it as such. All the praise and good will that an Englishman ever awards to an American is so far gratifying to the recipient, that it is meant for him individually, and is not to be put down in the slightest degree to the score of any regard to his countrymen generally. So far from this, if an Englishman were to meet the whole thirty millions of Americans, and find each individual of them a pleasant, amiable, well-meaning, and well-mannered sort of fellow, he would acknowledge this honestly in each individual case, but still would speak of the whole nation as a disagreeable people.

As regards Redclyffe being precisely like an Englishman, we cannot but think that the good Warden was mistaken. No doubt, there was a common ground; the old progenitor (whose blood, moreover, was mixed with a hundred other streams equally English) was still there, under this young man's shape, but with a vast difference. Climate, sun, cold, heat, soil, institutions, had made a change in him before he was born, and all the life that he had lived since (so unlike any that he could have lived in England) had developed it more strikingly. In manners, I cannot but think that he was better than the generality of Englishmen, and different from the highest-mannered men, though most resembling them. His natural sensitiveness, a tincture of reserve, had been counteracted by the frank mixture with men which his political course had made necessary; he was quicker to feel what was right at the moment, than the Englishman; more alive; he had a finer grain; his look was more aristocratic than that of a thousand Englishmen of good birth and breeding; he had a faculty of assimilating himself to new manners, which, being his most un-English trait, was what perhaps chiefly made the Warden think him so like an Englishman. When an Englishman is a gentleman, to be sure, it is as deep in him as the marrow of his bones, and the deeper you know him, the more you are aware of it, and that generation after generation has contributed to develop and perfect these unpretending manners, which, at first, may have failed to impress you, under his plain, almost homely exterior. An American often gets as good a surface of manners, in his own progress from youth, through the wear and attrition of a successful life, to some high station in middle age; whereas a plebeian Englishman, who rises to eminent station, never does credit to it by his manners. Often you would not know the American ambassador from a duke. This is often merely external; but in Redclyffe, having delicate original traits in his character, it was something more; and, we are bold to say, when our countrymen are developed, or any one class of them, as they ought to be, they will show finer traits than have yet been seen. We have more delicate and quicker sensibilities; nerves more easily impressed; and these are surely requisites for perfect manners; and, moreover, the courtesy that proceeds on the ground of perfect equality is better than that which is a gracious and benignant condescension,—as is the case with the manners of the aristocracy of England.

An American, be it said, seldom turns his best side outermost abroad; and an observer, who has had much opportunity of seeing the figure which they make, in a foreign country, does not so much wonder that there should be severe criticism on their manners as a people. I know not exactly why, but all our imputed peculiarities—our nasal pronunciation, our ungraceful idioms, our forthputtingness, our uncouth lack of courtesy—do really seem to exist on a foreign shore; and even, perhaps, to be heightened of malice prepense. The cold, unbelieving eye of Englishmen, expectant of solecisms in manners, contributes to produce the result which it looks for. Then the feeling of hostility and defiance in the American must be allowed for; and partly, too, the real existence of a different code of manners, founded on, and arising from, different institutions; and also certain national peculiarities, which may be intrinsically as good as English peculiarities; but being different, and yet the whole result being just too nearly alike, and, moreover, the English manners having the prestige of long establishment, and furthermore our own manners being in a transition state between those of old monarchies and what is proper to a new republic,—it necessarily followed that the American, though really a man of refinement and delicacy, is not just the kind of gentleman that the English can fully appreciate. In cases where they do so, their standard being different from ours, they do not always select for their approbation the kind of man or manners whom we should judge the best; we are perhaps apt to be a little too fine, a little too sedulously polished, and of course too conscious of it,—a deadly social crime, certainly.

CHAPTER XVII

To return from this long discussion, the Warden took kindly, as we have said, to Redclyffe, and thought him a miraculously good fellow, to have come from the rude American republic. Hitherto, in the little time that he had been in England, Redclyffe had received civil and even kind treatment from the English with whom he had come casually in contact; but still—perhaps partly from our Yankee narrowness and reserve—he had felt, in the closest coming together, as if there were a naked sword between the Englishman and him, as between the Arabian prince in the tale and the princess whom he wedded; he felt as if that would be the case even if he should love an Englishwoman; to such a distance, into such an attitude of self-defence, does English self-complacency and belief in England's superiority throw the stranger. In fact, in a good-natured way, John Bull is always doubling his fist in a stranger's face, and though it be good-natured, it does not always produce the most amiable feeling.

The worthy Warden, being an Englishman, had doubtless the same kind of feeling; doubtless, too, he thought ours a poor, distracted country, perhaps prosperous for the moment, but as likely as not to be the scene of anarchy five minutes hence; but being of so genial a nature, when he came to see the amiableness of his young guest, and how deeply he was impressed with England, all prejudice died away, and he loved him like a treasure that he had found for himself, and valued him as if there were something of his own in him. And so the old Warden's residence had never before been so cheery as it was now; his bachelor life passed the more pleasantly with this quiet, vivacious, yet not troublesomely restless spirit beside him,—this eager, almost childish interest in everything English, and yet this capacity to take independent views of things, and sometimes, it might be, to throw a gleam of light even on things appertaining to England. And so, the better they came to know one another, the greater was their mutual liking.

"I fear I am getting too strong to burden you much longer," said Redclyffe, this morning. "I have no pretence to be a patient now."

"Pooh! nonsense!" ejaculated the Warden. "It will not be safe to leave you to yourself for at least a month to come. And I have half a dozen excursions in a neighborhood of twenty miles, in which I mean to show you what old England is, in a way that you would never find out for yourself. Do not speak of going. This day, if you find yourself strong enough, you shall go and look at an old village church."

"With all my heart," said Redclyffe.

They went, accordingly, walking slowly, in consequence of Redclyffe's yet imperfect strength, along the highroad, which was overshadowed with elms, that grew in beautiful shape and luxuriance in that part of England, not with the slender, drooping, picturesque grace of a New England elm, but more luxuriant, fuller of leaves, sturdier in limb. It was a day which the Warden called fine, and which Redclyffe, at home, would have thought to bode rain; though here he had learned that such weather might continue for weeks together, with only a few raindrops all the time. The road was in the finest condition, hard and dry.

They had not long emerged from the gateway of the Hospital,—at the venerable front and gables of which Redclyffe turned to look with a feeling as if it were his home,—when they heard the clatter of hoofs behind them, and a gentleman on horseback rode by, paying a courteous salute to the Warden as he passed. A groom in livery followed at a little distance, and both rode roundly towards the village, whither the Warden and his friend were going.

"Did you observe that man?" asked the Warden.

"Yes," said Redclyffe. "Is he an Englishman?"

"That is a pertinent question," replied the Warden, "but I scarcely know how to answer it."

In truth, Redclyffe's question had been suggested by the appearance of the mounted gentleman, who was a dark, thin man, with black hair, and a black moustache and pointed beard setting off his sallow face, in which the eyes had a certain pointed steeliness, which did not look English,—whose eyes, methinks, are usually not so hard as those of Americans or foreigners. Redclyffe, somehow or other, had fancied that these not very pleasant eyes had been fixed in a marked way on himself, a stranger, while at the same time his salute was evidently directed towards the Warden.

"An Englishman,—why, no," continued the latter. "If you observe, he does not even sit his horse like an Englishman, but in that absurd, stiff continental way, as if a poker should get on horseback. Neither has he an English face, English manners, nor English religion, nor an English heart; nor, to sum up the whole, had he English birth. Nevertheless, as fate would have it, he is the inheritor of a good old English name, a fine patrimonial estate, and a very probable claim to an old English title. This is Lord

Braithwaite of Braithwaite Hall, who if he can make his case good (and they say there is good prospect of it) will soon be Lord Hinchbrooke."

"I hardly know why, but I should be sorry for it," said Redclyffe. "He certainly is not English; and I have an odd sort of sympathy, which makes me unwilling that English honors should be enjoyed by foreigners. This, then, is the gentleman of Italian birth whom you have mentioned to me, and of whom there is a slight mention in the County History."

"Yes," said the Warden. "There have been three descents of this man's branch in Italy, and only one English mother in all that time. Positively, I do not see an English trait in his face, and as little in his manner. His civility is Italian, such as oftentimes, among his countrymen, has offered a cup of poison to a guest, or insinuated the stab of a stiletto into his heart."

"You are particularly bitter against this poor man," said Redclyffe, laughing at the Warden's vehemence. "His appearance—and yet he is a handsome man—is certainly not prepossessing; but unless it be countersigned by something in his actual life, I should hardly think it worth while to condemn him utterly."

"Well, well; you can forgive a little English prejudice," said the Warden, a little ashamed. "But, in good earnest, the man has few or no good traits, takes no interest in the country, dislikes our sky, our earth, our people, is close and inhospitable, a hard landlord, and whatever may be his good qualities, they are not such as flourish in this soil and climate, or can be appreciated here." [Endnote: 1.]

"Has he children?" asked Redclyffe.

"They say so,—a family by an Italian wife, whom some, on the other hand, pronounce to be no wife at all. His son is at a Catholic college in France; his daughter in a convent there."

In talk like this they were drawing near the little rustic village of Braithwaite, and saw, above a cloud of foliage, the small, low, battlemented tower, the gray stones of which had probably been laid a little after the Norman conquest. Approaching nearer, they passed a thatched cottage or two, very plain and simple edifices, though interesting to Redclyffe from their antique aspect, which denoted that they were probably older than the settlement of his own country, and might very likely have nursed children who had gone, more than two centuries ago, to found the commonwealth of which he was a citizen. If you considered them in one way, prosaically, they were ugly enough; but then there were the old latticed windows, and there the thatch, which was verdant with leek, and strange weeds, possessing a whole botanical growth. And birds flew in and out, as if they had their homes there. Then came a row of similar cottages, all joined on together, and each with a little garden before it divided from its neighbors by a hedge, now in full verdure. Redclyffe was glad to see some symptoms of natural love of beauty here, for there were plants of box, cut into queer shapes of birds, peacocks, etc., as if year after year had been spent in bringing these vegetable sculptures to perfection. In one of the gardens, moreover, the ingenious inhabitant had spent his leisure in building grotto-work, of which the English are rather ludicrously fond, on their little bits of lawn, and in building a miniature castle of oyster-shells, where were seen turrets, ramparts, a frowning arched gateway, and miniature cannon looking from the embrasures. A pleasanter and better adornment were the homely household flowers, and a pleasant sound, too, was the hum of bees, who had their home in several beehives, and were making their honey among the flowers of the garden, or come from afar, buzzing dreamily through the air, laden with honey that they had found elsewhere. Fruit trees stood erect, or, in some instances, were flattened out against the walls of cottages, looking somewhat like hawks nailed *in terrorem* against a barn door. The male members of this little community were probably afield, with the exception of one or two half-torpid great-grandsires, who [were] moving rheumatically about the gardens, and some children not yet in breeches, who stared with stolid eyes at the passers-by; but the good dames were busy within doors, where Redclyffe had glimpses of their interior with its pavement of stone flags. Altogether it seemed a comfortable settlement enough.

"Do you see that child yonder," observed the Warden, "creeping away from the door, and displaying a vista of his petticoats as he does so? That sturdy boy is the lineal heir of one of the oldest families in this part of England,—though now decayed and fallen, as you may judge. So, you see, with all our contrivances to keep up an aristocracy, there still is change forever going on."

"There is something not agreeable, and something otherwise, in the thought," replied Redclyffe. "What is the name of the old family, whose representative is in such a case?"

"Moseby," said the Warden. "Their family residence stood within three miles of Braithwaite Hall, but was taken down in the last century, and its place supplied by a grand show-place, built by a Birmingham manufacturer, who also originated here."

They kept onward from this outskirt of the village, and soon, passing over a little rising ground, and descending now into a hollow came to the new portion of it, clustered around its gray Norman church, one side of the tower of which was covered with ivy, that was carefully kept, the Warden said, from climbing to the battlements, on account of some old prophecy that foretold that the tower would fall, if ever the ivy mantled over its top. Certainly, however, there seemed little likelihood that the square, low mass would fall, unless by external violence, in less than as many ages as it had already stood.

Redclyffe looked at the old tower and little adjoining edifice with an interest that attached itself to every separate, moss-grown stone; but the Warden, like most Englishmen, was at once amazed and wearied with the American's enthusiasm for this spot, which to him was uninteresting for the very reason that made it most interesting to Redclyffe, because it had stood there such a weary while. It was too common an object to excite in his mind, as it did in Redclyffe's, visions of the long ago time when it was founded, when mass was first said there, and the glimmer of torches at the altar was seen through the vista of that broad-browed porch; and of all the procession of villagers that had since gone in and come out during nine hundred years, in their varying costume and fashion, but yet—and this was the strongest and most thrilling part of the idea—all, the very oldest of them, bearing a resemblance of feature, the kindred, the family likeness, to those who died yesterday,—to those who still went thither to worship; and that all the grassy and half-obliterated graves around had held those who bore the same traits.

In front of the church was a little green, on which stood a very ancient yew tree, [Endnote: 2] all the heart of which seemed to have been eaten away by time, so that a man could now creep into the trunk, through a wide opening, and, looking upward, see another opening to the sky.

"That tree," observed the Warden, "is well worth the notice of such an enthusiastic lover of old things; though I suppose aged trees may be the one antiquity that you do not value, having them by myriads in your primeval forests. But then the interest of this tree consists greatly in what your trees have not,—in its long connection with men and the goings of men. Some of its companions were made into bows for Harold's archers. This tree is of unreckonable antiquity; so old, that in a record of the time of Edward IV. it is styled the yew tree of Braithwaite Green. That carries it back to Norman times, truly. It was in comparatively modern times when it served as a gallows for one of James II.'s bloodthirsty judges to hang his victims on after Monmouth's rebellion."

On one side of this yew was a certain structure which Redclyffe did not recognize as anything that he had before seen, but soon guessed its purpose; though, from appearances, it seemed to have been very long since it had served that purpose. It was a ponderous old oaken framework, six or seven feet high, so contrived that a heavy cross-piece shut down over another, leaving two round holes; in short, it was a pair of stocks, in which, I suppose, hundreds of vagrants and petty criminals had sat of old, but which now appeared to be merely a matter of curiosity.

"This excellent old machine," said the Warden, "had been lying in a rubbish chamber of the church tower for at least a century; when the clerk, who is a little of an antiquarian, unearthed it, and I advised him to set it here, where it used to stand;—not with any idea of its being used (though there is as much need of it now as ever), but that the present age may see what comforts it has lost."

They sat down a few moments on the circular seat, and looked at the pretty scene of this quiet little village, clustered round the old church as a centre; a collection of houses, mostly thatched, though there were one or two, with rather more pretension, that had roofs of red tiles. Some of them were stone cottages, whitewashed, but the larger edifices had timber frames, filled in with brick and plaster, which seemed to have been renewed in patches, and to be a frailer and less durable material than the old oak of their skeletons. They were gabled, with lattice windows, and picturesquely set off with projecting stones, and many little patchwork additions, such as, in the course of generations, the inhabitants had found themselves to need. There was not much commerce, apparently, in this little village, there seeming to be only one shop, with some gingerbread, penny whistles, ballads, and such matters, displayed in the window; and there, too, across the little green, opposite the church, was the village alehouse, with its bench under the low projecting eaves, with a Teniers scene of two wayfaring yeomen drinking a pot of beer and smoking their pipes.

With Redclyffe's Yankee feelings, there was something sad to think how the generations had succeeded one another, over and over, in innumerable succession, in this little spot, being born here, living, dying, lying down among their fathers' dust, and forthwith getting up again, as it were, and recommencing the same meaningless round, and really bringing nothing to pass; for probably the generation of to-day, in so secluded and motionless a place as this, had few or no ideas in advance of their ancestors of five centuries ago. It seems not worth while that more than one generation of them should have existed. Even in dress, with their smock frocks and breeches, they were just like their fathers. The stirring blood of the new land,—where no man dwells in his father's house,—where no man thinks of dying in his birthplace,—awoke within him, and revolted at the thought; and, as connected with it, revolted at all the hereditary pretensions which, since his stay here, had exercised such an influence over the fanciful part of his nature. In another mood, the village might have seemed a picture of rural peace, which it would have been worth while to give up ambition to enjoy; now, as his warmer impulse stirred, it was a weariness to think of. The new American was stronger in him than the hereditary Englishman.

"I should go mad of it!" exclaimed he aloud.

He started up impulsively, to the amazement of his companion, who of course could not comprehend what seemed so to have stung his American friend. As they passed the tree, on the other side of its huge trunk, they saw a young woman, sitting on that side of it, and sketching, apparently, the church tower, with the old Elizabethan vicarage that stood near it, with a gate opening into the churchyard, and much embowered and ivy-hung.

"Ah, Miss Cheltenham," said the Warden. "I am glad to see that you have taken the old church in hand, for it is one of the prettiest rustic churches in England, and as well worthy as any to be engraved on a sheet of note-paper or put into a portfolio. Will you let my friend and me see your sketch?"

The Warden had made his request with rather more freedom than perhaps he would to a lady whom he considered on a level with himself, though with perfect respect, that being considered; and Redclyffe, looking at the person, saw that it was the same of whose face he had had a glimpse in the looking-glass, in the old palmer's chamber.

"No, Doctor Hammond," said the young lady, with a respectful sort of frankness, "you must excuse me. I am no good artist, and am but jotting down the old church because I like it."

"Well, well, as you please," said the Warden; and whispered aside to Redclyffe, "A girl's sketchbook is seldom worth looking at. But now, Miss Cheltenham, I am about to give my American friend here a lecture on gargoyles, and other peculiarities of sacred Gothic architecture; and if you will honor me with your attention, I should be glad to find my audience increased by one."

So the young lady arose, and Redclyffe, considering the Warden's allusion to him as a sort of partial introduction, bowed to her, and she responded with a cold, reserved, yet not unpleasant sort of courtesy. They went towards the church porch, and, looking in at the old stone bench on each side of the interior, the Warden showed them the hacks of the swords of the Roundheads, when they took it by storm. Redclyffe, mindful of the old graveyard on the edge of which he had spent his childhood, began to look at this far more antique receptacle, expecting to find there many ancient tombstones, perhaps of contemporaries or predecessors of the founders of his country. In this, however, he was disappointed, at least in a great measure; for the persons buried in the churchyard were probably, for the most part, of a humble rank in life, such as were not so ambitious as to desire a monument of any kind, but were content to let their low earth-mounds subside into the level, where their memory had waxed so faint that none among the survivors could point out the spot, or cared any longer about knowing it; while in other cases, where a monument of red freestone, or even of hewn granite, had been erected, the English climate had forthwith set to work to gnaw away the inscriptions; so that in fifty years—in a time that would have left an American tombstone as fresh as if just cut—it was quite impossible to make out the record. Their superiors, meanwhile, were sleeping less enviably in dismal mouldy and dusty vaults, instead of under the daisies. Thus Redclyffe really found less antiquity here, than in the graveyard which might almost be called his natal spot.

When he said something to this effect, the Warden nodded.

"Yes," said he, "and, in truth, we have not much need of inscriptions for these poor people. All good families—every one almost, with any pretensions to respectable station, has his family or individual recognition within the church, or upon its walls; or some of them you see on tombs on the outside. As for our poorer friends here, they are content, as they may well be, to swell and subside, like little billows of mortality, here on the outside."

"And for my part," said Redclyffe, "if there were anything particularly desirable on either side, I should like best to sleep under this lovely green turf, with the daisies strewn over me by Nature herself, and whatever other homely flowers any friend might choose to add."

"And, Doctor Hammond," said the young woman, "we see by this gravestone that sometimes a person of humble rank may happen to be commemorated, and that Nature—in this instance at least—seems to take especial pains and pleasure to preserve the record."

She indicated a flat gravestone, near the porch, which time had indeed beautified in a singular way, for there was cut deep into it a name and date, in old English characters, very deep it must originally have been; and as if in despair of obliterating it, Time had taken the kindlier method of filling up the letters with moss; so that now, high embossed in loveliest green, was seen the name "Richard Oglethorpe 1613";—green, and flourishing, and beautiful, like the memory of a good man. The inscription originally seemed to have contained some twenty lines, which might have been poetry, or perhaps a prose eulogy, or perhaps the simple record of the buried person's life; but all this, having been done in fainter and smaller letters, was now so far worn away as to be illegible; nor had they ever been deep enough to be made living in moss, like the rest of the inscription.

"How tantalizing," remarked Redclyffe, "to see the verdant shine of this name, impressed upon us as something remarkable—and nothing else. I cannot but think that there must be something worth remembering about a man thus distinguished. When two hundred years have taken all these natural pains to illustrate and emblazon 'Richard Oglethorpe 1613.' Ha! I surely recollect that name. It haunts me somehow, as if it had been familiar of old."

"And me," said the young lady.

"It was an old name, hereabouts," observed the Warden, "but has been long extinct,—a cottage name, not a gentleman's. I doubt not that Oglethorpes sleep in many of these undistinguished graves."

Redclyffe did not much attend to what his friend said, his attention being attracted to the tone—to something in the tone of the young lady, and also to her coincidence in his remark that the name appealed to some early recollection. He had been taxing his memory, to tell him when and how the name had become familiar to him; and he now remembered that it had occurred in the old Doctor's story of the Bloody Footstep, told to him and Elsie, so long ago. [Endnote: 3] To him and Elsie! It struck him— what if it were possible?—but he knew it was not—that the young lady had a remembrance also of the fact, and that she, after so many years, were mingling her thoughts with his. As this fancy recurred to him, he endeavored to get a glimpse of her face, and while he did so she turned it upon him. It was a quick, sensitive face, that did not seem altogether English; he would rather have imagined it American; but at all events he could not recognize it as one that he had seen before, and a thousand fantasies died within him as, in his momentary glance, he took in the volume of its contour.

CHAPTER XVIII

After the two friends had parted from the young lady, they passed through the village, and entered the park gate of Braithwaite Hall, pursuing a winding road through its beautiful scenery, which realized all that Redclyffe had read or dreamed about the perfect beauty of these sylvan creations, with the clumps of trees, or sylvan oaks, picturesquely disposed. To heighten the charm, they saw a herd of deer reposing, who, on their appearance, rose from their recumbent position, and began to gaze warily at the strangers; then, tossing their horns, they set off on a stampede, but only swept round, and settled down not far from where they were. Redclyffe looked with great interest at these deer, who were at once wild and civilized; retaining a kind of free forest citizenship, while yet they were in some sense subject to man. It seemed as if they were a link between wild nature and tame; as if they could look back, in their long recollections, through a vista, into the times when England's forests were as wild as those of America, though now they were but a degree more removed from domesticity than cattle, and took their food in winter from the hand of man, and in summer reposed upon his lawns. This seemed the last touch of that delightful conquered and regulated wildness, which English art has laid upon the whole growth of English nature, animal or vegetable.

"There is nothing really wild in your whole island," he observed to the Warden. "I have a sensation as if somebody knew, and had cultivated and fostered, and set out in its proper place, every tree that grows; as if somebody had patted the heads of your wildest animals and played with them. It is very delightful to me, for the present; and yet, I think, in the course of time, I should feel the need for something genuine, as it were,— something that had not the touch and breath of man upon it. I suppose even your skies are modified by the modes of human life that are going on beneath it. London skies, of course, are so; but the breath of a great people, to say nothing of its furnace vapors and hearth-smokes, make the sky other than it was a thousand years ago."

"I believe we English have a feeling like this occasionally," replied the Warden, "and it is from that, partly, that we must account for our adventurousness into other regions, especially for our interest in what is wild and new. In your own forests, now, and prairies, I fancy we find a charm that Americans do not. In the sea, too, and therefore we are yachters. For my part, however, I have grown to like Nature a little smoothed down, and enriched; less gaunt and wolfish than she would be if left to herself."

"Yes; I feel that charm too," said Redclyffe. "But yet life would be slow and heavy, methinks, to see nothing but English parks."

Continuing their course through the noble clumps of oaks, they by and by had a vista of the distant hall itself. It was one of the old English timber and plaster houses, many of which are of unknown antiquity; as was the case with a portion of this house, although other portions had been renewed, repaired, or added, within a century. It had, originally, the Warden said, stood all round an enclosed courtyard, like the great houses of the Continent; but now one side of the quadrangle had long been removed, and there was only a front, with two wings; the beams of old oak being picked out with black, and three or four gables in a line forming the front, while the wings seemed to be stone. It was the timber portion that was most ancient. A clock was on the midmost gable, and pointed now towards one o'clock. The whole scene impressed Redclyffe, not as striking, but as an abode of ancient peace, where generation after generation of the same family had lived, each making the most of life, because the life of each successive dweller there was eked out with the lives of all who had hitherto lived there, and had in it equally those lives which were to come afterwards; so that there was a rare and successful contrivance for giving length, fulness, body, substance, to this thin and frail matter of human life. And, as life was so rich in comprehensiveness, the dwellers there made the most of it for the present and future, each generation contriving what it could to add to the cosiness, the comfortableness, the grave, solid respectability, the sylvan beauty, of the house with which they seemed to be connected both before and after death. The family had its home there; not merely the individual. Ancient shapes, that had apparently gone to the family tomb, had yet a right by family hearth and in family hall; nor did they come thither cold and shivering, and diffusing dim ghostly terrors, and repulsive shrinkings, and death in life; but in warm, genial attributes, making this life now passing more dense as it were, by adding all the substance of their own to it. Redclyffe could not compare this abode, and the feelings that it aroused, to the houses of his own country; poor tents of a day, inns of a night, where nothing was certain, save that the family of him who built it would not dwell here, even if he himself should have the bliss to die under the roof, which, with absurdest anticipations, he had built for his posterity. Posterity! An American can have none.

"All this sort of thing is beautiful; the family institution was beautiful in its day," ejaculated he, aloud, to himself, not to his companion; "but it is a thing of the past. It is dying out in England; and as for ourselves, we never had it. Something better will come up; but as for this, it is past."

"That is a sad thing to say," observed the Warden, by no means comprehending what was passing in his friend's mind. "But if you wish to view the interior of the Hall, we will go thither; for, harshly as I have spoken of the owner, I suppose he has English feeling enough to give us lunch and show us the old house of his forefathers."

"Not at present, if you please," replied Redclyffe. "I am afraid of destroying my delightful visionary idea of the house by coming too near it. Before I leave this part of the country, I should be glad to ramble over the whole of it, but not just now."

While Redclyffe was still enjoying the frank hospitality of his new friend, a rather marked event occurred in his life; yet not so important in reality as it seemed to his English friend.

A large letter was delivered to him, bearing the official seal of the United States, and the indorsement of the State Department; a very important-looking document, which could not but add to the importance of the recipient in the eyes of any Englishman, accustomed as they are to bow down before any seal of government. Redclyffe opened it rather coolly, being rather loath to renew any of his political remembrances, now that he was in peace; or to think of the turmoil of modern and democratic politics, here in this quietude of gone-by ages and customs. The contents, however, took him by surprise; nor did he know whether to be pleased or not.

The official package, in short, contained an announcement that he had been appointed by the President, by and with the advice of the Senate, to one of the Continental missions, usually esteemed an object of considerable ambition to any young man in politics; so that, if consistent with his own pleasure, he was now one of the Diplomatic Corps, a Minister, and representative of his country. On first considering the matter, Redclyffe was inclined to doubt whether this honor had been obtained for him altogether by friendly aid, though it did happen to have much in it that might suit his half-formed purpose of remaining long abroad; but with an eye already rendered somewhat oblique by political practice, he suspected that a political rival—a rival, though of his own party—had been exerting himself to provide an inducement for Redclyffe to leave the local field to him; while he himself should take advantage of the vacant field, and his rival be thus insidiously, though honorably, laid on the shelf, whence if he should try to remove himself a few years hence the shifting influences of American politics would be likely enough to thwart him; so that, for the sake of being a few years nominally somebody, he might in fine come back to his own country and find himself permanently nobody. But Redclyffe had already sufficiently begun to suspect that he lacked some qualities that a politician ought to have, and without which a political life, whether successful or otherwise, is sure to be a most irksome one: some qualities he lacked, others he had, both almost equally an obstacle. When he communicated the offer, therefore, to his friend, the Warden, it was with the remark that he believed he should accept it.

"Accept it?" cried the Warden, opening his eyes. "I should think so, indeed! Why, it puts you above the level of the highest nobility of the Court to which you are accredited; simple republican as you are, it gives you rank with the old blood and birth of Europe. Accept it? By all means; and I will come and see you at your court."

"Nothing is more different between England and America," said Redclyffe, "than the different way in which the citizen of either country looks at official station. To an Englishman, a commission, of whatever kind, emanating from his sovereign, brings apparently a gratifying sense of honor; to an American, on the contrary, it offers really nothing of the kind. He ceases to be a sovereign,—an atom of sovereignty, at all events,—and stoops to be a servant. If I accept this mission, honorable as you think it, I assure you I shall not feel myself quite the man I have hitherto been; although there is no obstacle in the way of party obligations or connections to my taking it, if I please."

"I do not well understand this," quoth the good Warden. "It is one of the promises of Scripture to the wise man, that he shall stand before kings, and that this embassy will enable you to do. No man—no man of your country surely—is more worthy to do so; so pray accept."

"I think I shall," said Redclyffe.

Much as the Warden had seemed to affectionize Redclyffe hitherto, the latter could not but be sensible, thereafter, of a certain deference in his friend towards him, which he would fain have got rid of, had it been in his power. However, there was still the same heartiness under it all; and after a little he seemed, in some degree, to take Redclyffe's own view of the matter;—namely, that, being so temporary as these republican distinctions are, they really do not go skin deep, have no reality in them, and that the sterling quality of the man, be it higher or lower, is nowise altered by it;—an apothegm that is true even of an hereditary nobility, and still more so of our own Honorables and Excellencies. However, the good Warden was glad of his friend's dignity, and perhaps, too, a little glad that this high fortune had befallen one whom he chanced to be entertaining under his roof. As it happened, there was an opportunity which might be taken advantage of to celebrate the occasion; at least, to make it known to the English world so far as the extent of the county. [Endnote: 1.]

It was an hereditary custom for the warden of Braithwaite Hospital, once a year, to give a grand dinner to the nobility and gentry of the neighborhood; and to this end a bequest had been made by one of the former squires or lords of Braithwaite which would of itself suffice to feed forty or fifty Englishmen with reasonable sumptuousness. The present Warden, being a gentleman of private fortune, was accustomed to eke the limited income, devoted for this purpose, with such additions from his own resources as brought the rude and hearty hospitality contemplated by the first founder on a par with modern refinements of gourmandism. The banquet was annually given in the fine old hall where James II. had feasted; and on some of these occasions the Warden's table had been honored with illustrious guests; especially when any of them happened to be wanting an opportunity to come before the public in an after-dinner speech. Just at present there was no occasion of that sort; and the good Warden fancied that he might give considerable *éclat* to his hereditary feast by bringing forward the young American envoy, a distinguished and eloquent man, to speak on the well-worn topic of the necessity of friendly relations between England and America.

"You are eloquent, I doubt not, my young friend?" inquired he.

"Why, no," answered Redclyffe, modestly.

"Ah, yes, I know it," returned the Warden. "If one have all the natural prerequisites of eloquence; a quick sensibility, ready thought, apt expression, a good voice—and not making its way into the world through your nose either, as they say most of your countrymen's voices do. You shall make the crack speech at my dinner; and so strengthen the bonds of good fellowship between our two countries, that there shall be no question of war for at least six months to come."

Accordingly, the preparations for this stately banquet went on with great spirit; and the Warden exhorted Redclyffe to be thinking of some good topics for his international speech; but the young man laughed it off, and told his friend that he thought the inspiration of the moment, aided by the good old wine which the Warden had told him of, as among the treasures of the Hospital, would perhaps serve him better than any elaborate preparation.

Redclyffe, being not even yet strong, used to spend much time, when the day chanced to be pleasant, (which was oftener than his preconceptions of English weather led him to expect,) in the garden behind the Warden's house. It was an extensive one, and apparently as antique as the foundation of the establishment; and during all these years it had probably been growing richer and richer. Here were flowers of ancient race, and some that had been merely field or wayside flowers when first they came into the garden; but by long cultivation and hereditary care, instead of dying out, they had acquired a new richness and beauty, so that you would scarcely recognize the daisy or the violet. Roses too, there were, which Doctor Hammond said had been taken from those white and red rose-trees in the Temple Gardens, whence the partisans of York and Lancaster had plucked their fatal badges. With these, there were all the modern and far-fetched flowers from America, the East, and elsewhere; even the prairie flowers and the California blossoms were represented here; for one of the brethren had horticultural tastes, and was permitted freely to exercise them there. The antique character of the garden was preserved, likewise, by the alleys of box, a part of which had been suffered to remain, and was now grown to a great height and density, so as to make impervious green walls. There were also yew trees clipped into strange shapes of bird and beast, and uncouth heraldic figures, among which of course the leopard's head grinned triumphant; and as for fruit, the high garden wall was lined with pear trees, spread out flat against it, where they managed to produce a cold, flavorless fruit, a good deal akin to cucumbers.

Here, in these genial old arbors, Redclyffe used to recline in the sweet, mild summer weather, basking in the sun, which was seldom too warm to make its full embrace uncomfortable; and it seemed to him, with its fertility, with its marks everywhere of the quiet long-bestowed care of man, the sweetest and cosiest seclusion he had ever known; and two or three times a day, when he heard the screech of the railway train, rushing on towards distant London, it impressed him still more with a sense of safe repose here.

Not unfrequently he here met the white-bearded palmer in whose chamber he had found himself, as if conveyed thither by enchantment, when he first came to the Hospital. The old man was not by any means of the garrulous order; and yet he seemed full of thoughts, full of reminiscences, and not disinclined to the company of Redclyffe. In fact, the latter sometimes flattered himself that a tendency for his society was one of the motives that brought him to the garden; though the amount of their intercourse, after all, was not so great as to warrant the idea of any settled purpose in so doing. Nevertheless, they talked considerably; and Redclyffe could easily see that the old man had been an extensive traveller, and had perhaps occupied situations far different from his present one, and had perhaps been a struggler in troubled waters before he was drifted into the retirement where Redclyffe found him. He was fond of talking about the unsuspected relationship that must now be existing between many families in England and unknown consanguinity in the new world, where, perhaps, really the main stock of the family tree was now existing, and with a new spirit and life, which the representative growth here in England had lost by too long continuance in one air and one mode of life. For history and observation proved that all people—and the English people by no means less than others—needed to be transplanted, or somehow renewed, every few generations; so that, according to this ancient philosopher's theory, it would be good for the whole people of England now, if it could at once be transported to America, where its fatness, its sleepiness, its too great beefiness, its preponderant animal character, would be rectified by a different air and soil; and equally good, on the other hand, for the whole American people to be transplanted back to the original island, where their nervousness might be weighted with heavier influences, where their little women might grow bigger, where their thin, dry men might get a burden of flesh and good stomachs, where their children might, with the air, draw in a reverence for age, forms, and usage.

Redclyffe listened with complacency to these speculations, smiling at the thought of such an exodus as would take place, and the reciprocal dissatisfaction which would probably be the result. But he had greater pleasure in drawing out some of the old gentleman's legendary lore, some of which, whether true or not, was very curious. [Endnote: 2.]

As Redclyffe sat one day watching the old man in the garden, he could not help being struck by the scrupulous care with which he attended to the plants; it seemed to him that there was a sense of justice,—of desiring to do exactly what was right in the matter, not favoring one plant more than another, and doing all he could for each. His progress, in consequence, was so slow, that in an hour, while Redclyffe was off and on looking at him, he had scarcely done anything perceptible. Then he was so minute; and often, when he was on the point of leaving one thing to take up another, some small neglect that he saw or fancied called him back again, to spend other minutes on the same task. He was so full of scruples. It struck Redclyffe that this was conscience, morbid, sick, a despot in trifles, looking so closely into life that it permitted nothing to be done. The man might once have been strong and able, but by some unhealthy process of his life he had ceased to be so now. Nor did any happy or satisfactory result appear to come from these painfully wrought efforts; he still seemed to know that he had left something undone in doing too much in another direction. Here was a lily that had been neglected, while he paid too much attention to a rose; he had set his foot on a violet; he had grubbed up, in his haste, a little plant that he mistook for a weed, but that he now suspected was an herb of grace. Grieved by such reflections as these, he heaved a deep sigh, almost amounting to a groan, and sat down on the little stool that he carried with him in his weeding, resting his face in his hands.

Redclyffe deemed that he might be doing the old man a good service by interrupting his melancholy labors; so he emerged from the opposite door of the summer-house, and came along the adjoining walk with somewhat heavy footsteps, in order that the palmer might have warning of his approach without any grounds to suppose that he had been watched hitherto. Accordingly, when he turned into the other alley, he found the old man sitting erect on his stool, looking composed, but still sad, as was his general custom.

"After all your wanderings and experience," said he, "I observe that you come back to the original occupation of cultivating a garden,—the innocentest of all."

"Yes, so it would seem," said the old man; "but somehow or other I do not find peace in this."

"These plants and shrubs," returned Redclyffe, "seem at all events to recognize the goodness of your rule, so far as it has extended over them. See how joyfully they take the sun; how clear [they are] from all these vices that lie scattered round, in the shape of weeds. It is a lovely sight, and I could almost fancy a quiet enjoyment in the plants themselves, which they have no way of making us aware of, except by giving out a fragrance."

"Ah! how infinitely would that idea increase man's responsibility," said the old palmer, "if, besides man and beast, we should find it necessary to believe that there is also another set of beings dependent for their happiness on our doing, or leaving undone, what might have effect on them!"

"I question," said Redclyffe, smiling, "whether their pleasurable or painful experiences can be so keen, that we need trouble our consciences much with regard to what we do, merely as it affects them. So highly cultivated a conscience as that would be a nuisance to one's self and one's fellows."

"You say a terrible thing," rejoined the old man. "Can conscience be too much alive in us? is not everything however trifling it seems, an item in the great account, which it is of infinite importance therefore to have right? A terrible thing is that you have said."

"That may be," said Redclyffe; "but it is none the less certain to me, that the efficient actors—those who mould the world—are the persons in whom something else is developed more strongly than conscience. There must be an invincible determination to effect something; it may be set to work in the right direction, but after that it must go onward, trampling down small obstacles—small considerations of right and wrong—as a great rock, thundering down a hillside, crushes a thousand sweet flowers, and ploughs deep furrows in the innocent hillside."

As Redclyffe gave vent to this doctrine, which was not naturally his, but which had been the inculcation of a life, hitherto devoted to politics, he was surprised to find how strongly sensible he became of the ugliness and indefensibleness of what he said. He felt as if he were speaking under the eye of Omniscience, and as if every word he said were weighed, and its emptiness detected, by an unfailing intelligence. He had thought that he had volumes to say about the necessity of consenting not to do right in all matters minutely, for the sake of getting out an available and valuable right as the whole; but there was something that seemed to tie his tongue. Could it be the quiet gaze of this old man, so unpretending, so humble, so simple in aspect? He could not tell, only that he faltered, and finally left his speech in the midst.

But he was surprised to find how he had to struggle against a certain repulsion within himself to the old man. He seemed so nonsensical, interfering with everybody's right in the world; so mischievous, standing there and shutting out the possibility of action. It seemed well to trample him down; to put him out of the way—no matter how—somehow. It gave him, he thought, an inkling of the way in which this poor old man had made himself odious to his kind, by opposing himself, inevitably, to what was bad in man, chiding it by his very presence, accepting nothing false. You must either love him utterly, or hate him utterly; for he could not let you alone. Redclyffe, being a susceptible man, felt this influence in the strongest way; for it was as if there was a battle within him, one party pulling, wrenching him towards the old man, another wrenching him away, so that, by the agony of the contest, he felt disposed to end it by taking flight, and never seeing the strange individual again. He could well enough conceive how a brutal nature, if capable of receiving his influence at all, might find it so intolerable that it must needs get rid of him by violence,—by taking his blood if necessary.

All these feelings were but transitory, however; they swept across him like a wind, and then he looked again at the old man and saw only his simplicity, his unworldliness,—saw little more than the worn and feeble individual in the Hospital garb, leaning on his staff; and then turning again with a gentle sigh to weed in the garden. And then Redclyffe went away, in a state of disturbance for which he could not account to himself.

CHAPTER XIX

High up in the old carved roof, meanwhile, the spiders of centuries still hung their flaunting webs with a profusion that old Doctor Grimshawe would have been ravished to see; but even this was to be remedied, for one day, on looking in, Redclyffe found the great hall dim with floating dust, and down through it came great floating masses of cobweb, out of which the old Doctor would have undertaken to regenerate the world; and he saw, dimly aloft, men on ladders sweeping away these accumulations of years, and breaking up the haunts and residences of hereditary spiders.

The stately old hall had been in process of cleaning and adapting to the banquet purposes of the nineteenth century, which it was accustomed to subserve, in so proud a way, in the sixteenth. It was, in the first place, well swept and cleansed; the painted glass windows were cleansed from dust, and several panes, which had been unfortunately broken and filled with common glass, were filled in with colored panes, which the Warden had picked up somewhere in his antiquarian researches. They were not, to be sure, just what was wanted; a piece of a saint, from some cathedral window, supplying what was lacking of the gorgeous purple of a mediæval king; but the general effect was rich and good, whenever the misty English atmosphere supplied sunshine bright enough to pervade it. Tapestry, too, from antique looms, faded, but still gorgeous, was hung upon the walls. Some suits of armor, that hung beneath the festal gallery, were polished till the old battered helmets and pierced breastplates sent a gleam like that with which they had flashed across the battle-fields of old. [Endnote: 1.]

So now the great day of the Warden's dinner had arrived; and, as may be supposed, there were fiery times in the venerable old kitchen. The cook, according to ancient custom, concocted many antique dishes, such as used to be set before kings and nobles; dainties that might have called the dead out of their graves; combinations of ingredients that had ceased to be put together for centuries; historic dishes, which had long, long ceased to be in the list of revels. Then there was the stalwart English cheer of the sirloin, and the round; there were the vast plum-puddings, the juicy mutton, the venison; there was the game, now just in season,—the half-tame wild fowl of English covers, the half-domesticated wild deer of English parks, the heathcock from the far-off hills of Scotland, and one little prairie hen, and some canvas-back ducks—obtained, Heaven knows how, in compliment to Redclyffe—from his native shores. O, the old jolly kitchen! how rich the flavored smoke that went up its vast chimney! how inestimable the atmosphere of steam that was diffused through it! How did the old men peep into it, even venture across the threshold, braving the hot wrath of the cook and his assistants, for the sake of imbuing themselves with these rich and delicate flavors, receiving them in as it were spiritually; for, received through the breath and in the atmosphere, it was really a spiritual enjoyment. The ghosts of ancient epicures seemed, on that day and the few preceding ones, to haunt the dim passages, snuffing in with shadowy nostrils the rich vapors, assuming visibility in the congenial medium, almost becoming earthly again in the strength of their earthly longings for one other feast such as they used to enjoy.

Nor is it to be supposed that it was only these antique dainties that the Warden provided for his feast. No; if the cook, the cultured and recondite old cook, who had accumulated within himself all that his predecessors knew for centuries,—if he lacked anything of modern fashion and improvement, he had supplied his defect by temporary assistance from a London club; and the bill of fare was provided with dishes that Soyer would not have harshly criticised. The ethereal delicacy of modern taste, the nice adjustment of flowers, the French style of cookery, was richly attended to; and the list was long of dishes with fantastic names, fish, fowl, and flesh; and *entremets*, and "sweets," as the English call them, and sugared cates, too numerous to think of.

The wines we will not take upon ourselves to enumerate; but the juice, then destined to be quaffed, was in part the precious vintages that had been broached half a century ago, and had been ripening ever since; the rich and dry old port, so unlovely to the natural palate that it requires long English seasoning to get it down; the sherry, imported before these modern days of adulteration; some claret, the Warden said of rarest vintage; some Burgundy, of which it was the quality to warm the blood and genialize existence for three days after it was drunk. Then there was a rich liquid contributed to this department by Redclyffe himself; for, some weeks since, when the banquet first loomed in the distance, he had (anxious to evince his sense of the Warden's kindness) sent across the ocean for some famous Madeira which he had inherited from the Doctor, and never tasted yet. This, together with some of the Western wines of America, had arrived, and was ready to be broached.

The Warden tested these modern wines, and recognized a new flavor, but gave it only a moderate approbation; for, in truth, an elderly Englishman has not a wide appreciation of wines, nor loves new things in this kind more than in literature or life. But he tasted the Madeira, too, and underwent an ecstasy, which was only alleviated by the dread of gout, which he had an idea that this wine must bring on,—and truly, if it were so splendid a wine as he pronounced it, some pain ought to follow as the shadow of such a pleasure.

As it was a festival of antique date, the dinner hour had been fixed earlier than is usual at such stately banquets; namely, at six o'clock, which was long before the dusky hour at which Englishmen love best to dine. About that period, the carriages drove into the old courtyard of the Hospital in great abundance; blocking up, too, the ancient portal, and remaining in a line outside. Carriages they were with armorial bearings, family coaches in which came Englishmen in their black coats and white neckcloths, elderly, white-headed, fresh-colored, squat; not beautiful, certainly, nor particularly dignified, nor very well dressed, nor with much of an imposing air, but yet, somehow or other, producing an effect of force, respectability, reliableness, trust, which is probably deserved, since it is invariably experienced. Cold they were in deportment, and looked coldly on the stranger, who, on his part, drew himself up with an extra haughtiness and reserve, and felt himself in the midst of his enemies, and more as if he were going to do battle than to sit down to a friendly banquet. The Warden introduced him, as an American diplomatist, to one or two of the gentlemen, who regarded him forbiddingly, as Englishmen do before dinner.

Not long after Redclyffe had entered the reception-room, which was but shortly before the hour appointed for the dinner, there was another arrival betokened by the clatter of hoofs and grinding wheels in the courtyard; and then entered a gentleman of different mien from the bluff, ruddy, simple-minded, yet worldly Englishmen around him. He was a tall, dark man, with a black moustache and almost olive skin, a slender, lithe figure, a flexible face, quick, flashing, mobile. His deportment was graceful; his dress, though it seemed to differ in little or nothing from that of the gentlemen in the room, had yet a grace and picturesqueness in his mode of wearing it. He advanced to the Warden, who received him with distinction, and yet, Redclyffe fancied, not exactly with cordiality. It seemed to Redclyffe that the Warden looked round, as if with the purpose of presenting Redclyffe to this gentleman, but he himself, from some latent reluctance, had turned away and entered, into conversation with one of the other gentlemen, who said now, looking at the new-comer, "Are you acquainted with this last arrival?"

"Not at all," said Redclyffe. "I know Lord Braithwaite by sight, indeed, but have had no introduction. He is a man, certainly, of distinguished appearance."

"Why, pretty well," said the gentleman, "but un-English, as also are his manners. It is a pity to see an old English family represented by such a person. Neither he, his father, nor grandfather was born among us; he has far more Italian blood than enough to drown the slender stream of Anglo-Saxon and Norman. His modes of life, his prejudices, his estates, his religion, are unlike our own; and yet here he is in the position of an old English gentleman, possibly to be a peer. You, whose nationality embraces that of all the world, cannot, I suppose, understand this English feeling." [Endnote: 2.]

"Pardon me," said Redclyffe, "I can perfectly understand it. An American, in his feelings towards England, has all the jealousy and exclusiveness of Englishmen themselves,—perhaps, indeed, a little exaggerated."

"I beg your pardon," said the Englishman, incredulously, "I think you cannot possibly understand it!" [Endnote: 3.]

The guests were by this time all assembled, and at the Warden's bidding they moved from the reception-room to the dining-hall, in some order and precedence, of which Redclyffe could not exactly discover the principle, though he found that to himself—in his quality, doubtless, of Ambassador—there was assigned a pretty high place. A venerable dignitary of the Church—a dean, he seemed to be—having asked a blessing, the fair scene of the banquet now lay before the guests, presenting a splendid spectacle, in the high-walled, antique, tapestried hall, overhung with the dark, intricate oaken beams, with the high Gothic windows, through one of which the setting sunbeams streamed, and showed the figures of kings and warriors, and the old Braithwaites among them. Beneath and adown the hall extended the long line of the tables, covered with the snow of the damask tablecloth, on which glittered, gleamed, and shone a good quality of ancient ancestral plate, and an *épergne* of silver, extending down the middle; also the gleam of golden wine in the decanters; and truly Redclyffe thought that it was a noble spectacle, made so by old and stately associations, which made a noble banquet of what otherwise would be only a vulgar dinner. The English have this advantage and know how to make use of it. They bring—in these old, time-honored feasts—all the past to sit down and take the stately refreshment along with them, and they pledge the historic characters in their wine.

A printed bill of fare, in gold letters, lay by each plate, on which Redclyffe saw the company glancing with great interest. The first dish, of course, was turtle soup, of which—as the gentleman next him, the Mayor of a neighboring town, told Redclyffe—it was allowable to take twice. This was accompanied, according to one of those rules which one knows not whether they are arbitrary or founded on some deep reason, by a glass of punch. Then came the noble turbot, the salmon, the sole, and divers of fishes, and the dinner fairly set in. The genial Warden seemed to have given liberal orders to the attendants, for they spared not to offer hock, champagne, sherry, to the guests, and good bitter ale, foaming in the goblet; and so the stately banquet went on, with somewhat tedious magnificence; and yet with a fulness of effect and thoroughness of sombre life that made Redclyffe feel that, so much importance being assigned to it, — it being so much believed in, — it was indeed a feast. The cumbrous courses swept by, one after another; and Redclyffe, finding it heavy work, sat idle most of the time, regarding the hall, the old decaying beams, the armor hanging beneath the galleries, and these Englishmen feasting where their fathers had feasted for so many ages, the same occasion, the same men, probably, in appearance, though the black coat and the white neckcloth had taken the place of ruff, embroidered doublet, and the magnificence of other ages. After all, the English have not such good things to eat as we in America, and certainly do not know better how to make them palatable. [Endnote: 4.]

Well; but by and by the dinner came to a conclusion, as regarded the eating part; the cloth was withdrawn; a dessert of fruits, fresh and dried, pines, hothouse grapes, and all candied conserves of the Indies, was put on the long extent of polished mahogany. There was a tuning up of musicians, an interrogative drawing of fiddle-bows, and other musical twangs and puffs; the decanters opposite the Warden and his vice-president, — sherry, port, Redclyffe's Madeira, and claret, were put in motion along the table, and the guests filled their glasses for the toast which, at English dinner-tables, is of course the first to be honored, — the Queen. Then the band struck up the good old anthem, "God save the Queen," which the whole company rose to their feet to sing. It was a spectacle both interesting and a little ludicrous to Redclyffe, — being so apart from an American's sympathies, so unlike anything that he has in his life or possibilities, — this active and warm sentiment of loyalty, in which love of country centres, and assimilates, and transforms itself into a passionate affection for a person, in whom they love all their institutions. To say the truth, it seemed a happy notion; nor could the American — while he comforted himself in the pride of his democracy, and that he himself was a sovereign — could he help envying it a little, this childlike love and reverence for a person embodying all their country, their past, their earthly future. He felt that it might be delightful to have a sovereign, provided that sovereign were always a woman, — and perhaps a young and fine one. But, indeed, this is not the difficulty, methinks, in English institutions which the American finds it hardest to deal with. We could endure a born sovereign, especially if made such a mere pageant as the English make of theirs. What we find it hardest to conceive of is, the satisfaction with which Englishmen think of a race above them, with privileges that they cannot share, entitled to condescend to them, and to have gracious and beautiful manners at their expense; to be kind, simple, unpretending, because these qualities are more available than haughtiness; to be specimens of perfect manhood;—all these advantages in consequence of their position. If the peerage were a mere name, it would be nothing to envy; but it is so much more than a name; it enables men to be really so superior. The poor, the lower classes, might bear this well enough; but the classes that come next to the nobility,—the upper middle classes,—how they bear it so lovingly is what must puzzle the American. But probably the advantage of the peerage is the less perceptible the nearer it is looked at.

It must be confessed that Redclyffe, as he looked at this assembly of peers and gentlemen, thought with some self-gratulation of the probability that he had within his power as old a rank, as desirable a station, as the best of them; and that if he were restrained from taking it, it would probably only be by the democratic pride that made him feel that he could not, retaining all his manly sensibility, accept this gewgaw on which the ages—his own country especially—had passed judgment, while it had been suspended over his head. He felt himself, at any rate, in a higher position, having the option of taking this rank, and forbearing to do so, than if he took it. [Endnote: 5.]

After this ensued a ceremony which is of antique date in old English corporations and institutions, at their high festivals. It is called the Loving Cup. A sort of herald or toast-master behind the Warden's chair made proclamation, reciting the names of the principal guests, and announcing to them, "The Warden of the Braithwaite Hospital drinks to you in a Loving Cup"; of which cup, having sipped, or seemed to sip (for Redclyffe observed that the old drinkers were rather shy of it) a small quantity, he sent it down the table. Its progress was accompanied with a peculiar entanglement of ceremony, one guest standing up while another drinks, being pretty much as follows. First, each guest receiving it covered from the next above him, the same took from the silver cup its silver cover; the guest drank with a bow to the Warden and company, took the cover from the preceding guest, covered the cup, handed it to the next below him, then again removed the cover, replaced it after the guest had drunk, who, on his part, went through the same ceremony. And thus the cup went slowly on its way down the stately hall; these ceremonies being, it is said, originally precautions against the risk, in wild times, of being stabbed by the man who was drinking with you, or poisoned by one who should fail to be your taster. The cup was a fine, ancient piece of plate, massive, heavy, curiously wrought with armorial bearings, in which the leopard's head appeared. Its contents, so far as Redclyffe could analyze them by a moderate sip, appeared to be claret, sweetened, with spices, and, however suited to the peculiarity of antique palates, was not greatly to Redclyffe's taste. [Endnote: 6.]

Redclyffe's companion just below him, while the Loving Cup was beginning its march, had been explaining the origin of the custom as a defence of the drinker in times of deadly feud; when it had reached Lord Braithwaite, who drank and passed it to Redclyffe covered, and with the usual bow, Redclyffe looked into his Lordship's Italian eyes and dark face as he did so, and the thought struck him, that, if there could possibly be any use in keeping up this old custom, it might be so now; for, how intimated he could hardly tell, he was sensible in his deepest self of a deadly hostility in this dark, courteous, handsome face. He kept his eyes fixed on his Lordship as he received the cup, and felt that in his own glance there was an acknowledgment of the enmity that he perceived, and a defiance, expressed without visible sign, and felt in the bow with which they greeted one another. When they had both resumed their seats, Redclyffe chose to make this ceremonial intercourse the occasion of again addressing him.

"I know not whether your Lordship is more accustomed than myself to these stately ceremonials," said he.

"No," said Lord Braithwaite, whose English was very good. "But this is a good old ceremony, and an ingenious one; for does it not twine us into knotted links of love—this Loving Cup—like a wreath of Bacchanals whom I have seen surrounding an antique vase. Doubtless it has great efficacy in entwining a company of friendly guests into one affectionate society."

"Yes; it should seem so," replied Redclyffe, with a smile, and again meeting those black eyes, which smiled back on him. "It should seem so, but it appears that the origin of the custom was quite different, and that it was as a safeguard to a man when he drank with his enemy. What a peculiar flavor it must have given to the liquor, when the eyes of two deadly foes met over the brim of the Loving Cup, and the drinker knew that, if he withdrew it, a dagger would be in his heart, and the other watched him drink, to see if it was poison!"

"Ah!" responded his Lordship, "they had strange fashions in those rough old times. Nowadays, we neither stab, shoot, nor poison. I scarcely think we hate except as interest guides us, without malevolence."

This singular conversation was interrupted by a toast, and the rising of one of the guests to answer it. Several other toasts of routine succeeded; one of which, being to the honor of the old founder of the Hospital, Lord Braithwaite, as his representative, rose to reply,—which he did in good phrases, in a sort of eloquence unlike that of the Englishmen around him, and, sooth to say, comparatively unaccustomed as he must have been to the use of the language, much more handsomely than they. In truth, Redclyffe was struck and amused with the rudeness, the slovenliness, the inartistic quality of the English speakers, who rather seemed to avoid grace and neatness of set purpose, as if they would be ashamed of it. Nothing could be more ragged than these utterances which they called speeches; so patched, and darned; and yet, somehow or other—though dull and heavy as all which seemed to inspire them—they had a kind of force. Each man seemed to have the faculty of getting, after some rude fashion, at the sense and feeling that was in him; and without glibness, without smoothness, without form or comeliness, still the object with which each one rose to speak was accomplished,—and what was more remarkable, it seemed to be accomplished without the speaker's having any particular plan for doing it. He was surprised, too, to observe how loyally every man seemed to think himself bound to speak, and rose to do his best, however unfit his usual habits made him for the task. Observing this, and thinking how many an American would be taken aback and dumbfounded by being called on for a dinner speech, he could not but doubt the correctness of the general opinion, that Englishmen are naturally less facile of public speech than our countrymen.

"You surpass your countrymen," said Redclyffe, when his Lordship resumed his seat, amid rapping and loud applause.

"My countrymen? I scarcely know whether you mean the English or Italians," said Lord Braithwaite. "Like yourself, I am a hybrid, with really no country, and ready to take up with any."

"I have a country,—one which I am little inclined to deny," replied Redclyffe, gravely, while a flush (perhaps of conscientious shame) rose to his brow.

His Lordship bowed, with a dark Italian smile, but Redclyffe's attention was drawn away from the conversation by a toast which the Warden now rose to give, and in which he found himself mainly concerned. With a little preface of kind words (not particularly aptly applied) to the great and kindred country beyond the Atlantic, the worthy Warden proceeded to remark that his board was honored, on this high festival, with a guest from that new world; a gentleman yet young, but already distinguished in the councils of his country; the bearer, he remarked, of an honored English name, which might well claim to be remembered here, and on this occasion, although he had understood from his friend that the American bearers of this name did not count kindred with the English ones. This gentleman, he further observed, with considerable flourish and emphasis, had recently been called from his retirement and wanderings into the diplomatic service of his country, which he would say, from his knowledge, the gentleman was well calculated to honor. He drank the health of the Honorable Edward Redclyffe, Ambassador of the United States to the Court of Hohen-Linden.

Our English cousins received this toast with the kindest enthusiasm, as they always do any such allusion to our country; it being a festal feeling, not to be used except on holidays. They rose, with glass in hand, in honor of the Ambassador; the band struck up "Hail, Columbia"; and our hero marshalled his thoughts as well as he might for the necessary response; and when the tumult subsided he arose.

His quick apprehending had taught him something of the difference of taste between an English and an American audience at a dinner-table; he felt that there must be a certain looseness, and carelessness, and roughness, and yet a certain restraint; that he must not seem to aim at speaking well, although, for his own ambition, he was not content to speak ill; that, somehow or other, he must get a heartiness into his speech; that he must not polish, nor be too neat, and must come with a certain rudeness to his good points, as if he blundered on them, and were surprised into them. Above all, he must let the good wine and cheer, and all that he knew and really felt of English hospitality, as represented by the kind Warden, do its work upon his heart, and speak up to the extent of what he felt—and if a little more, then no great harm—about his own love for the father-land, and the broader grounds of the relations between the two countries. On this system, Redclyffe began to speak; and being naturally and habitually eloquent, and of mobile and ready sensibilities, he succeeded, between art and nature, in making a speech that absolutely delighted the company, who made the old hall echo, and the banners wave and tremble, and the board shake, and the glasses jingle, with their rapturous applause. What he said— or some shadow of it, and more than he quite liked to own—was reported in the county paper that gave a report of the dinner; but on glancing over it, it seems not worth while to produce this eloquent effort in our pages, the occasion and topics being of merely temporary interest.

Redclyffe sat down, and sipped his claret, feeling a little ashamed of himself, as people are apt to do after a display of this kind.

"You know the way to the English heart better than I do," remarked his Lordship, after a polite compliment to the speech. "Methinks these dull English are being improved in your atmosphere. The English need a change every few centuries,—either by immigration of new stock, or transportation of the old,—or else they grow too gross and earthly, with their beef, mutton, and ale. I think, now, it might benefit both countries, if your New England population were to be reciprocally exchanged with an equal number of Englishmen. Indeed, Italians might do as well."

"I should regret," said Redclyffe, "to change the English, heavy as they are."

"You are an admirable Englishman," said his Lordship. "For my part, I cannot say that the people are very much to my taste, any more than their skies and climate, in which I have shivered during the two years that I have spent here."

Here their conversation ceased; and Redclyffe listened to a long train of speechifying, in the course of which everybody, almost, was toasted; everybody present, at all events, and many absent. The Warden's old wine was not spared; the music rang and resounded from the gallery; and everybody seemed to consider it a model feast, although there were no very vivid signs of satisfaction, but a decorous, heavy enjoyment, a dull red heat of pleasure, without flame. Soda and seltzer-water, and coffee, by and by were circulated; and at a late hour the company began to retire.

Before taking his departure, Lord Braithwaite resumed his conversation with Redclyffe, and, as it appeared, with the purpose of making a hospitable proposition.

"I live very much alone," said he, "being insulated from my neighbors by many circumstances,—habits, religion, and everything else peculiarly English. If you are curious about old English modes of life, I can show you, at least, an English residence, little altered within a century past. Pray come and spend a week with me before you leave this part of the country. Besides, I know the court to which you are accredited, and can give you, perhaps, useful information about it."

Redclyffe looked at him in some surprise, and with a nameless hesitation; for he did not like his Lordship, and had fancied, in truth, that there was a reciprocal antipathy. Nor did he yet feel that he was mistaken in this respect; although his Lordship's invitation was given in a tone of frankness, and seemed to have no reserve, except that his eyes did not meet his like Anglo-Saxon eyes, and there seemed an Italian looking out from within the man. But Redclyffe had a sort of repulsion within himself; and he questioned whether it would be fair to his proposed host to accept his hospitality, while he had this secret feeling of hostility and repugnance,—which might be well enough accounted for by the knowledge that he secretly entertained hostile interests to their race, and half a purpose of putting them in force. And, besides this,—although Redclyffe was ashamed of the feeling,—he had a secret dread, a feeling that it was not just a safe thing to trust himself in this man's power; for he had a sense, sure as death, that he did not wish him well, and had a secret dread of the American. But he laughed within himself at this feeling, and drove it down. Yet it made him feel that there could be no disloyalty in accepting his Lordship's invitation, because it was given in as little friendship as it would be accepted.

"I had almost made my arrangements for quitting the neighborhood," said he, after a pause; "nor can I shorten the week longer which I had promised to spend with my very kind friend, the Warden. Yet your Lordship's kindness offers we a great temptation, and I would gladly spend the next ensuing week at Braithwaite Hall."

"I shall expect you, then," said Lord Braithwaite. "You will find me quite alone, except my chaplain,—a scholar, and a man of the world, whom you will not be sorry to know."

He bowed and took his leave, without shaking hands, as an American would have thought it natural to do, after such a hospitable agreement; nor did Redclyffe make any motion towards it, and was glad that his Lordship had omitted it. On the whole, there was a secret dissatisfaction with himself; a sense that he was not doing quite a frank and true thing in accepting this invitation, and he only made peace with himself on the consideration that Lord Braithwaite was as little cordial in asking the visit as he in acceding to it.

CHAPTER XX

The guests were now rapidly taking their departure, and the Warden and Redclyffe were soon left alone in the antique hall, which now, in its solitude, presented an aspect far different from the gay festivity of an hour before; the duskiness up in the carved oaken beams seemed to descend and fill the hall; and the remembrance of the feast was like one of those that had taken place centuries ago, with which this was now numbered, and growing ghostly, and faded, and sad, even as they had long been.

"Well, my dear friend," said the Warden, stretching himself and yawning, "it is over. Come into my study with me, and we will have a devilled turkey-bone and a pint of sherry in peace and comfort."

"I fear I can make no figure at such a supper," said Redclyffe. "But I admire your inexhaustibleness in being ready for midnight refreshment after such a feast."

"Not a glass of good liquor has moistened my lips to-night," said the Warden, "save and except such as was supplied by a decanter of water made brown with toast; and such a sip as I took to the health of the Queen, and another to that of the Ambassador to Hohen-Linden. It is the only way, when a man has this vast labor of speechifying to do; and indeed there is no possibility of keeping up a jolly countenance for such a length of time except on toast-water."

They accordingly adjourned to the Warden's sanctum, where that worthy dignitary seemed to enjoy himself over his sherry and cracked bones, in a degree that he probably had not heretofore; while Redclyffe, whose potations had been more liberal, and who was feverish and disturbed, tried the effect of a little brandy and soda-water. As often happens at such midnight symposiums, the two friends found themselves in a more kindly and confidential vein than had happened before, great as had been the kindness and confidence already grown up between them. Redclyffe told his friend of Lord Braithwaite's invitation, and of his own resolution to accept it.

"Why not? You will do well," said the Warden; "and you will find his Lordship an accustomed host, and the old house most interesting. If he knows the secrets of it himself, and will show them, they will be well worth the seeing."

"I have had a scruple in accepting this invitation," said Redclyffe.

"I cannot see why," said the Warden. "I advise it by all means, since I shall lose nothing by it myself, as it will not lop off any part of your visit to me."

"My dear friend," said Redclyffe, irresistibly impelled to a confidence which he had not meditated a moment before, "there is a foolish secret which I must tell you, if you will listen to it; and which I have only not revealed to you because it seemed to me foolish and dream-like; because, too, I am an American, and a democrat; because I am ashamed of myself and laugh at myself."

"Is it a long story?" asked the Warden.

"I can make it of any length, and almost any brevity," said Redclyffe.

"I will fill my pipe then," answered the Warden, "and listen at my ease; and if, as you intimate, there prove to be any folly in it, I will impute it all to the kindly freedom with which you have partaken of our English hospitality, and forget it before to-morrow morning."

He settled himself in his easy-chair, in a most luxurious posture; and Redclyffe, who felt a strange reluctance to reveal—for the first time in his life—the shadowy hopes, if hopes they were, and purposes, if such they could be called, with which he had amused himself so many years, begun the story from almost the earliest period that he could remember. He told even of his earliest recollection, with an old woman, in the almshouse, and how he had been found there by the Doctor, and educated by him, with all the hints and half-revelations that had been made to him. He described the singular character of the Doctor, his scientific pursuits, his evident accomplishments, his great abilities, his morbidness and melancholy, his moodiness, and finally his death, and the singular circumstances that accompanied it. The story took a considerable time to tell; and after its close, the Warden, who had only interrupted it by now and then a question to make it plainer, continued to smoke his pipe slowly and thoughtfully for a long while.

"This Doctor of yours was a singular character," said he. "Evidently, from what you tell me as to the accuracy of his local reminiscences, he must have been of this part of the country,—of this immediate neighborhood,—and such a man could not have grown up here without being known. I myself—for I am an old fellow now—might have known him if he lived to manhood hereabouts."

"He seemed old to me when I first knew him," said Redclyffe. "But children make no distinctions of age. He might have been forty-five then, as well as I can judge."

"You are now twenty-seven or eight," said the Warden, "and were four years old when you first knew him. He might now be sixty-five. Do you know, my friend, that I have something like a certainty that I know who your Doctor was?"

"How strange this seems!" exclaimed Redclyffe. "It has never struck me that I should be able to identify this singular personage with any surroundings or any friends."

The Warden, to requite his friend's story,—and without as yet saying a word, good or bad, on his ancestral claims,—proceeded to tell him some of the gossip of the neighborhood,—what had been gossip thirty or forty years ago, but was now forgotten, or, at all events, seldom spoken of, and only known to the old, at the present day. He himself remembered it only as a boy, and imperfectly. There had been a personage of that day, a man of poor estate, who had fallen deeply in love and been betrothed to a young lady of family; he was a young man of more than ordinary abilities, and of great promise, though small fortune. It was not well known how, but the match between him and the young lady was broken off, and his place was supplied by the then proprietor of Braithwaite Hall; as it was supposed, by the artifices of her mother. There had been circumstances of peculiar treachery in the matter, and Mr. Oglethorpe had taken it severely to heart; so severely, indeed, that he had left the country, after selling his ancestral property, and had only been occasionally heard of again. Now, from certain circumstances, it had struck the Warden that this might be the mysterious Doctor of whom Redclyffe spoke. [Endnote: 1.]

"But why," suggested Redclyffe, "should a man with these wrongs to avenge take such an interest in a descendant of his enemy's family?"

"That is a strong point in favor of my supposition," replied the Warden. "There is certainly, and has long been, a degree of probability that the true heir of this family exists in America. If Oglethorpe could discover him, he ousts his enemy from the estate and honors, and substitutes the person whom he has discovered and educated. Most certainly there is revenge in the thing. Should it happen now, however, the triumph would have lost its sweetness, even were Oglethorpe alive to partake of it; for his enemy is dead, leaving no heir, and this foreign branch has come in without Oglethorpe's aid."

The friends remained musing a considerable time, each in his own train of thought, till the Warden suddenly spoke.

"Do you mean to prosecute this apparent claim of yours?"

"I have not intended to do so," said Redclyffe.

"Of course," said the Warden, "that should depend upon the strength of your ground; and I understand you that there is some link wanting to establish it. Otherwise, I see not how you can hesitate. Is it a little thing to hold a claim to an old English estate and honors?"

"No; it is a very great thing, to an Englishman born, and who need give up no higher birthright to avail himself of it," answered Redclyffe. "You will laugh at me, my friend; but I cannot help feeling that I, a simple citizen of a republic, yet with none above me except those whom I help to place there,—and who are my servants, not my superiors,—must stoop to take these honors. I leave a set of institutions which are the noblest that the wit and civilization of man have yet conceived, to enlist myself in one that is based on a far lower conception of man, and which therefore lowers every one who shares in it. Besides," said the young man, his eyes kindling with the ambition which had been so active a principle in his life, "what prospects—what rewards for spirited exertion—what a career, only open to an American, would I give up, to become merely a rich and idle Englishman, belonging (as I should) nowhere, without a possibility of struggle, such as a strong man loves, with only a mockery of a title, which in these days really means nothing,—hardly more than one of our own Honorables. What has any success in English life to offer (even were it within my reach, which, as a stranger, it would not be) to balance the proud career of an American statesman?"

"True, you might be a President, I suppose," said the Warden, rather contemptuously,—"a four years' potentate. It seems to me an office about on a par with that of the Lord Mayor of London. For my part, I would rather be a baron of three or four hundred years' antiquity."

"We talk in vain," said Redclyffe, laughing. "We do not approach one another's ideas on this subject. But, waiving all speculations as to my attempting to avail myself of this claim, do you think I can fairly accept this invitation to visit Lord Braithwaite? There is certainly a possibility that I may arraign myself against his dearest interests. Conscious of this, can I accept his hospitality?"

The Warden paused. "You have not sought access to his house," he observed. "You have no designs, it seems, no settled designs at all events, against his Lordship,—nor is there a probability that they would be forwarded by your accepting this invitation, even if you had any. I do not see but you may go. The only danger is, that his Lordship's engaging qualities may seduce you into dropping your claims out of a chivalrous feeling, which I see is among your possibilities. To be sure, it would be more satisfactory if he knew your actual position, and should then renew his invitation."

"I am convinced," said Redclyffe, looking up from his musing posture, "that he does know them. You are surprised; but in all Lord Braithwaite's manner towards me there has been an undefinable something that makes me aware that he knows on what terms we stand towards each other. There is nothing inconceivable in this. The family have for generations been suspicious of an American line, and have more than once sent messengers to try to search out and put a stop to the apprehension. Why should it not have come to their knowledge that there was a person with such claims, and that he is now in England?"

"It certainly is possible," replied the Warden, "and if you are satisfied that his Lordship knows it, or even suspects it, you meet him on fair ground. But I fairly tell you, my good friend, that—his Lordship being a man of unknown principles of honor, outlandish, and an Italian in habit and moral sense—I scarcely like to trust you in his house, he being aware that your existence may be inimical to him. My humble board is the safer of the two."

"Pshaw!" said Redclyffe. "You Englishmen are so suspicious of anybody not regularly belonging to yourselves. Poison and the dagger haunt your conceptions of all others. In America you think we kill every third man with the bowie-knife. But, supposing there were any grounds for your suspicion, I would still encounter it. An American is no braver than an Englishman; but still he is not quite so chary of his life as the latter, who never risks it except on the most imminent necessity. We take such matters easy. In regard to this invitation, I feel that I can honorably accept it, and there are many idle and curious motives that impel me to it. I will go."

"Be it so; but you must come back to me for another week, after finishing your visit," said the Warden. "After all, it was an idle fancy in me that there could be any danger. His Lordship has good English blood in his veins, and it would take oceans and rivers of Italian treachery to wash out the sterling quality of it. And, my good friend, as to these claims of yours, I would not have you trust too much to what is probably a romantic dream; yet, were the dream to come true, I should think the British peerage honored by such an accession to its ranks. And now to bed; for we have heard the chimes of midnight, two hours agone."

They accordingly retired; and Redclyffe was surprised to find what a distinctness his ideas respecting his claim to the Braithwaite honors had assumed, now that he, after so many years, had imparted them to another. Heretofore, though his imagination had played with them so much, they seemed the veriest dreams; now, they had suddenly taken form and hardened into substance; and he became aware, in spite of all the lofty and patriotic sentiments which he had expressed to the Warden, that these prospects had really much importance in his mind.

Redclyffe, during the few days that he was to spend at the Hospital, previous to his visit to Braithwaite Hall, was conscious of a restlessness such as we have all felt on the eve of some interesting event. He wondered at himself at being so much wrought up by so simple a thing as he was about to do; but it seemed to him like a coming home after an absence of centuries. It was like an actual prospect of entrance into a castle in the air,— the shadowy threshold of which should assume substance enough to bear his foot, its thin, fantastic walls actually protect him from sun and rain, its hall echo with his footsteps, its hearth warm him. That delicious, thrilling uncertainty between reality and fancy, in which he had often been enwrapt since his arrival in this region, enveloped him more strongly than ever; and with it, too, there came a sort of apprehension, which sometimes shuddered through him like an icy draught, or the touch of cold steel to his heart. He was ashamed, too, to be conscious of anything like fear; yet he would not acknowledge it for fear; and indeed there was such an airy, exhilarating, thrilling pleasure bound up with it, that it could not really be so.

It was in this state of mind that, a day or two after the feast, he saw Colcord sitting on the bench, before the portal of the Hospital, in the sun, which—September though it was—still came warm and bright (for English sunshine) into that sheltered spot; a spot where many generations of old men had warmed their limbs, while they looked down into the life, the torpid life, of the old village that trailed its homely yet picturesque street along by the venerable buildings of the Hospital.

"My good friend," said Redclyffe, "I am about leaving you, for a time,— indeed, with the limited time at my disposal, it is possible that I may not be able to come back hither, except for a brief visit. Before I leave you, I would fain know something more about one whom I must ever consider my benefactor."

"Yes," said the old man, with his usual benignant quiet, "I saved your life. It is yet to be seen, perhaps, whether thereby I made myself your benefactor. I trust so."

"I feel it so, at least," answered Redclyffe, "and I assure you life has a new value for me since I came to this place; for I have a deeper hold upon it, as it were,—more hope from it, more trust in something good to come of it."

"This is a good change,—or should be so," quoth the old man.

"Do you know," continued Redclyffe, "how long you have been a figure in my life?"

"I know it," said Colcord, "though you might well have forgotten it."

"Not so," said Redclyffe. "I remember, as if it were this morning, that time in New England when I first saw you."

"The man with whom you then abode," said Colcord, "knew who I was."

"And he being dead, and finding you here now, by such a strange coincidence," said Redclyffe, "and being myself a man capable of taking your counsel, I would have you impart it to me: for I assure you that the current of my life runs darkly on, and I would be glad of any light on its future, or even its present phase."

"I am not one of those from whom the world waits for counsel," said the pensioner, "and I know not that mine would be advantageous to you, in the light which men usually prize. Yet if I were to give any, it would be that you should be gone hence."

"Gone hence!" repeated Redclyffe, surprised. "I tell you—what I have hardly hitherto told to myself—that all my dreams, all my wishes hitherto, have looked forward to precisely the juncture that seems now to be approaching. My dreaming childhood dreamt of this. If you know anything of me, you know how I sprung out of mystery, akin to none, a thing concocted out of the elements, without visible agency; how all through my boyhood I was alone; how I grew up without a root, yet continually longing for one,—longing to be connected with somebody, and never feeling myself so. Yet there was ever a looking forward to this time at which I now find myself. If my next step were death, yet while the path seemed to lead toward a certainty of establishing me in connection with my race, I would take it. I have tried to keep down this yearning, to stifle it, annihilate it, by making a position for myself, by being my own fact; but I cannot overcome the natural horror of being a creature floating in the air, attached to nothing; ever this feeling that there is no reality in the life and fortunes, good or bad, of a being so unconnected. There is not even a grave, not a heap of dry bones, not a pinch of dust, with which I can claim kindred, unless I find it here!"

"This is sad," said the old man,—"this strong yearning, and nothing to gratify it. Yet, I warn you, do not seek its gratification here. There are delusions, snares, pitfalls, in this life. I warn you, quit the search."

"No," said Redclyffe, "I will follow the mysterious clue that seems to lead me on; and, even now, it pulls me one step further."

"How is that?" asked the old man.

"It leads me onward even as far as the threshold—across the threshold—of yonder mansion," said Redclyffe.

"Step not across it; there is blood on that threshold!" exclaimed the pensioner. "A bloody footstep emerging. Take heed that there be not as bloody a one entering in!"

"Pshaw!" said Redclyffe, feeling the ridicule of the emotion into which he had been betrayed, as the old man's wildness of demeanor made him feel that he was talking with a monomaniac. "We are talking idly. I do but go, in the common intercourse of society, to see the old English residence which (such is the unhappy obscurity of my position) I fancy, among a thousand others, may have been that of my ancestors. Nothing is likely to come of it. My foot is not bloody, nor polluted with anything except the mud of the damp English soil."

"Yet go not in!" persisted the old man.

"Yes, I must go," said Redclyffe, determinedly, "and I will."

Ashamed to have been moved to such idle utterances by anything that the old man could say Redclyffe turned away, though he still heard the sad, half-uttered remonstrance of the old man, like a moan behind him, and wondered what strange fancy had taken possession of him.

The effect which this opposition had upon him made him the more aware how much his heart was set upon this visit to the Hall; how much he had counted upon being domiciliated there; what a wrench it would be to him to tear himself away without going into that mansion, and penetrating all the mysteries wherewith his imagination, exercising itself upon the theme since the days of the old Doctor's fireside talk, had invested it. In his agitation he wandered forth from the Hospital, and, passing through the village street, found himself in the park of Braithwaite Hall, where he wandered for a space, until his steps led him to a point whence the venerable Hall appeared, with its limes and its oaks around it; its look of peace, and aged repose, and loveliness; its stately domesticity, so ancient, so beautiful; its mild, sweet simplicity; it seemed the ideal of home. The thought thrilled his bosom, that this was his home,—the home of the wild Western wanderer, who had gone away centuries ago, and encountered strange chances, and almost forgotten his origin, but still kept a clue to bring him back; and had now come back, and found all the original emotions safe within him. It even seemed to him, that, by his kindred with those who had gone before,—by the line of sensitive blood linking him with that final emigrant,—he could remember all these objects;—that tree, hardly more venerable now than then; that clock-tower, still marking the elapsing time; that spire of the old church, raising itself beyond. He spread out his arms in a kind of rapture, and exclaimed:—

"O home, my home, my forefathers' home! I have come back to thee! The wanderer has come back!"

There was a slight stir near him; and on a mossy seat, that was arranged to take advantage of a remarkably good point of view of the old Hall, he saw Elsie sitting. She had her drawing-materials with her, and had probably been taking a sketch. Redclyffe was ashamed of having been overheard by any one giving way to such idle passion as he had been betrayed into; and yet, in another sense, he was glad,—glad, at least, that something of his feeling, as yet unspoken to human being, was shared, and shared by her with whom, alone of living beings, he had any sympathies of old date, and whom he often thought of with feelings that drew him irresistibly towards her.

"Elsie," said he, uttering for the first time the old name, "Providence makes you my confidant. We have recognized each other, though no word has passed between us. Let us speak now again with one another. How came you hither? What has brought us together again?—Away with this strangeness that lurks between us! Let us meet as those who began life together, and whose life-strings, being so early twisted in unison, cannot now be torn apart."

"You are not wise," said Elsie, in a faltering voice, "to break the restraint we have tacitly imposed upon ourselves. Do not let us speak further on this subject."

"How strangely everything evades me!" exclaimed Redclyffe. "I seem to be in a land of enchantment, where I can get hold of nothing that lends me a firm support. There is no medium in my life between the most vulgar realities and the most vaporous fiction, too thin to breathe. Tell me, Elsie, how came you here? Why do you not meet me frankly? What is there to keep you apart from the oldest friend, I am bold to say, you have on earth? Are you an English girl? Are you one of our own New England maidens, with her freedom, and her know-how, and her force, beyond anything that these demure and decorous damsels can know?"

"This is wild," said Elsie, straggling for composure, yet strongly moved by the recollections that he brought up. "It is best that we should meet as strangers, and so part."

"No," said Redclyffe; "the long past comes up, with its memories, and yet it is not so powerful as the powerful present. We have met again; our adventures have shown that Providence has designed a relation in my fate to yours. Elsie, are you lonely as I am?"

"No," she replied, "I have bonds, ties, a life, a duty. I must live that life and do that duty. You have, likewise, both. Do yours, lead your own life, like me."

"Do you know, Elsie," he said, "whither that life is now tending?"

"Whither?" said she, turning towards him.

"To yonder Hall," said he.

She started up, and clasped her hands about his arm.

"No, no!" she exclaimed, "go not thither! There is blood upon the threshold! Return: a dreadful fatality awaits you here."

"Come with me, then," said he, "and I yield my purpose."

"It cannot be," said Elsie.

"Then I, too, tell you it cannot be," returned Redclyffe. [Endnote: 2.]

The dialogue had reached this point, when there came a step along the wood-path; the branches rustled, and there was Lord Braithwaite, looking upon the pair with the ordinary slightly sarcastic glance with which he gazed upon the world.

"A fine morning, fair lady and fair sir," said he. "We have few such, except in Italy."

CHAPTER XXI

So Redclyffe left the Hospital, where he had spent many weeks of strange and not unhappy life, and went to accept the invitation of the lord of Braithwaite Hall. It was with a thrill of strange delight, poignant almost to pain, that he found himself driving up to the door of the Hall, and actually passing the threshold of the house. He looked, as he stept over it, for the Bloody Footstep, with which the house had so long been associated in his imagination; but could nowhere see it. The footman ushered him into a hall, which seemed to be in the centre of the building, and where, little as the autumn was advanced, a fire was nevertheless burning and glowing on the hearth; nor was its effect undesirable in the somewhat gloomy room. The servants had evidently received orders respecting the guest; for they ushered him at once to his chamber, which seemed not to be one of those bachelor's rooms, where, in an English mansion, young and single men are forced to be entertained with very bare and straitened accommodations; but a large, well, though antiquely and solemnly furnished room, with a curtained bed, and all manner of elaborate contrivances for repose; but the deep embrasures of the windows made it gloomy, with the little light that they admitted through their small panes. There must have been English attendance in this department of the household arrangements, at least; for nothing could exceed the exquisite nicety and finish of everything in the room, the cleanliness, the attention to comfort, amid antique aspects of furniture; the rich, deep preparations for repose.

The servant told Redclyffe that his master had ridden out, and, adding that luncheon would be on the table at two o'clock, left him; and Redclyffe sat some time trying to make out and distinguish the feelings with which he found himself here, and realizing a lifelong dream. He ran back over all the legends which the Doctor used to tell about this mansion, and wondered whether this old, rich chamber were the one where any of them had taken place; whether the shadows of the dead haunted here. But, indeed, if this were the case, the apartment must have been very much changed, antique though it looked, with the second, or third, or whatever other numbered arrangement, since those old days of tapestry hangings and rush-strewed floor. Otherwise this stately and gloomy chamber was as likely as any other to have been the one where his ancestor appeared for the last time in the paternal mansion; here he might have been the night before that mysterious Bloody Footstep was left on the threshold, whence had arisen so many wild legends, and since the impression of which nothing certain had ever been known respecting that ill-fated man,—nothing certain in England at least,— and whose story was left so ragged and questionable even by all that he could add.

Do what he could, Redclyffe still was not conscious of that deep home-feeling which he had imagined he should experience when, if ever, he should come back to the old ancestral place; there was strangeness, a struggle within himself to get hold of something that escaped him, an effort to impress on his mind the fact that he was, at last, established at his temporary home in the place that he had so long looked forward to, and that this was the moment which he would have thought more interesting than any other in his life. He was strangely cold and indifferent, frozen up as it were, and fancied that he would have cared little had he been to leave the mansion without so much as looking over the remaining part of it.

At last, he became weary of sitting and indulging this fantastic humor of indifference, and emerged from his chamber with the design of finding his way about the lower part of the house. The mansion had that delightful intricacy which can never be contrived; never be attained by design; but is the happy result of where many builders, many designs,—many ages, perhaps,—have concurred in a structure, each pursuing his own design. Thus it was a house that you could go astray in, as in a city, and come to unexpected places, but never, until after much accustomance, go where you wished; so Redclyffe, although the great staircase and wide corridor by which he had been led to his room seemed easy to find, yet soon discovered that he was involved in an unknown labyrinth, where strange little bits of staircases led up and down, and where passages promised much in letting him out, but performed nothing. To be sure, the old English mansion had not much of the stateliness of one of Mrs. Radcliffe's castles, with their suites of rooms opening one into another; but yet its very domesticity—its look as if long ago it had been lived in—made it only the more ghostly; and so Redclyffe felt the more as if he were wandering through a homely dream; sensible of the ludicrousness of his position, he once called aloud; but his voice echoed along the passages, sounding unwontedly to his ears, but arousing nobody. It did not seem to him as if he were going afar, but were bewildered round and round, within a very small compass; a predicament in which a man feels very foolish usually.

As he stood at an old window, stone-mullioned, at the end of a passage into which he had come twice over, a door near him opened, and a personage looked out whom he had not before seen. It was a face of great keenness and intelligence, and not unpleasant to look at, though dark and sallow. The dress had something which Redclyffe recognized as clerical, though not exactly pertaining to the Church of England,—a sort of arrangement of the vest and shirt-collar; and he had knee breeches of black. He did not seem like an English clerical personage, however; for even in this little glimpse of him Redclyffe saw a mildness, gentleness, softness, and asking-of-leave, in his manner, which he had not observed in persons so well assured of their position as the Church of England clergy.

He seemed at once to detect Redclyffe's predicament, and came forward with a pleasant smile, speaking in good English, though with a somewhat foreign accent.

"Ah, sir, you have lost your way. It is a labyrinthian house for its size, this old English Hall,—full of perplexity. Shall I show you to any point?"

"Indeed, sir," said Redclyffe, laughing, "I hardly know whither I want to go; being a stranger, and yet knowing nothing of the public places of the house. To the library, perhaps, if you will be good enough to direct me thither."

"Willingly, my dear sir," said the clerical personage; "the more easily too, as my own quarters are close adjacent; the library being my province. Do me the favor to enter here."

So saying, the priest ushered Redclyffe into an austère-looking yet exceedingly neat study, as it seemed, on one side of which was an oratory, with a crucifix and other accommodations for Catholic devotion. Behind a white curtain there were glimpses of a bed, which seemed arranged on a principle of conventual austerity in respect to limits and lack of softness; but still there was in the whole austerity of the premises a certain character of restraint, poise, principle, which Redclyffe liked. A table was covered with books, many of them folios in an antique binding of parchment, and others were small, thick-set volumes, into which antique lore was rammed and compressed. Through an open door, opposite to the one by which he had entered, there was a vista of a larger apartment, with alcoves, a rather dreary-looking room, though a little sunshine came through a window at the further end, distained with colored glass.

"Will you sit down in my little home?" said the courteous priest. "I hope we may be better acquainted; so allow me to introduce myself. I am Father Angelo, domestic chaplain to his Lordship. You, I know, are the American diplomatic gentleman, from whom his Lordship has been expecting a visit."

Redclyffe bowed.

"I am most happy to know you," continued the priest. "Ah; you have a happy country, most catholic, most recipient of all that is outcast on earth. Men of my religion must ever bless it."

"It certainly ought to be remembered to our credit," replied Redclyffe, "that we have shown no narrow spirit in this matter, and have not, like other Protestant countries, rejected the good that is found in any man on account of his religious faith. American statesmanship comprises Jew, Catholic, all."

After this pleasant little acknowledgment, there ensued a conversation having some reference to books; for though Redclyffe, of late years, had known little of what deserves to be called literature,—having found political life as much estranged from it as it is apt to be with politicians,—yet he had early snuffed the musty fragrance of the Doctor's books, and had learned to love its atmosphere. At the time he left college, he was just at the point where he might have been a scholar; but the active tendencies of American life had interfered with him, as with thousands of others, and drawn him away from pursuits which might have been better adapted to some of his characteristics than the one he had adopted. The priest gently felt and touched around his pursuits, and finding some remains of classic culture, he kept up a conversation on these points; showing him the possessions of the library in that department, where, indeed, were some treasures that he had discovered, and which seemed to have been collected at least a century ago.

"Generally, however," observed he, as they passed from one dark alcove to another, "the library is of little worth, except to show how much of living truth each generation contributes to the botheration of life, and what a public benefactor a bookworm is, after all. There, now! did you ever happen to see one? Here is one that I have watched at work, some time past, and have not thought it worth while to stop him."

Redclyffe looked at the learned little insect, who was eating a strange sort of circular trench into an old book of scholastic Latin, which probably only he had ever devoured,—at least ever found to his taste. The insect seemed in excellent condition, fat with learning, having doubtless got the essence of the book into himself. But Redclyffe was still more interested in observing in the corner a great spider, which really startled him,—not so much for its own terrible aspect, though that was monstrous, as because he seemed to see in it the very great spider which he had known in his boyhood; that same monster that had been the Doctor's familiar, and had been said to have had an influence in his death. He looked so startled that Father Angelo observed it.

"Do not be frightened," said he; "though I allow that a brave man may well be afraid of a spider, and that the bravest of the brave need not blush to shudder at this one. There is a great mystery about this spider. No one knows whence he came; nor how long he has been here. The library was very much shut up during the time of the last inheritor of the estate, and had not been thoroughly examined for some years when I opened it, and swept some of the dust away from its old alcoves. I myself was not aware of this monster until the lapse of some weeks, when I was startled at seeing him, one day, as I was reading an old book here. He dangled down from the ceiling, by the cordage of his web, and positively seemed to look into my face."

"He is of the species Condetas," said Redclyffe, — "a rare spider seldom seen out of the tropic regions."

"You are learned, then, in spiders," observed the priest, surprised.

"I could almost make oath, at least, that I have known this ugly specimen of his race," observed Redclyffe. "A very dear friend, now deceased, to whom I owed the highest obligations, was studious of spiders, and his chief treasure was one the very image of this."

"How strange!" said the priest. "There has always appeared to me to be something uncanny in spiders. I should be glad to talk further with you on this subject. Several times I have fancied a strange intelligence in this monster; but I have natural horror of him, and therefore refrain from interviews."

"You do wisely, sir," said Redclyffe. "His powers and purposes are questionably beneficent, at best."

In truth, the many-legged monster made the old library ghostly to him by the associations which it summoned up, and by the idea that it was really the identical one that had seemed so stuffed with poison, in the lifetime of the Doctor, and at that so distant spot. Yet, on reflection, it appeared not so strange; for the old Doctor's spider, as he had heard him say, was one of an ancestral race that he had brought from beyond the sea. They might have been preserved, for ages possibly, in this old library, whence the Doctor had perhaps taken his specimen, and possibly the one now before him was the sole survivor. It hardly, however, made the monster any the less hideous to suppose that this might be the case; and to fancy the poison of old times condensed into this animal, who might have sucked the diseases, moral and physical, of all this family into him, and to have made himself their demon. He questioned with himself whether it might not be well to crush him at once, and so perhaps do away with the evil of which he was the emblem.

"I felt a strange disposition to crush this monster at first," remarked the priest, as if he knew what Redclyffe was thinking of,—"a feeling that in so doing I should get rid of a mischief; but then he is such a curious monster. You cannot long look at him without coming to the conclusion that he is indestructible."

"Yes; and to think of crushing such a deep-bowelled monster!" said Redclyffe, shuddering. "It is too great a catastrophe."

During this conversation in which he was so deeply concerned, the spider withdrew himself, and hand over hand ascended to a remote and dusky corner, where was his hereditary abode.

"Shall I be likely to meet Lord Braithwaite here in the library?" asked Redclyffe, when the fiend had withdrawn himself. "I have not yet seen him since my arrival."

"I trust," said the priest, with great courtesy, "that you are aware of some peculiarities in his Lordship's habits, which imply nothing in detriment to the great respect which he pays all his few guests, and which, I know, he is especially desirous to pay to you. I think that we shall meet him at lunch, which, though an English institution, his Lordship has adopted very readily."

"I should hope," said Redclyffe, willing to know how far he might be expected to comply with the peculiarities—which might prove to be eccentricities—of his host, "that my presence here will not be too greatly at variance with his Lordship's habits, whatever they may be. I came hither, indeed, on the pledge that, as my host would not stand in my way, so neither would I in his."

"That is the true principle," said the priest, "and here comes his Lordship in person to begin the practice of it."

CHAPTER XXII

Lord Braithwaite came into the principal door of the library as the priest was speaking, and stood a moment just upon the threshold, looking keenly out of the stronger light into this dull and darksome apartment, as if unable to see perfectly what was within; or rather, as Redclyffe fancied, trying to discover what was passing between those two. And, indeed, as when a third person comes suddenly upon two who are talking of him, the two generally evince in their manner some consciousness of the fact; so it was in this case, with Redclyffe at least, although the priest seemed perfectly undisturbed, either through practice of concealment, or because he had nothing to conceal.

His Lordship, after a moment's pause, came forward, presenting his hand to Redclyffe, who shook it, and not without a certain cordiality; till he perceived that it was the left hand, when he probably intimated some surprise by a change of manner.

"I am an awkward person," said his Lordship. "The left hand, however, is nearest the heart; so be assured I mean no discourtesy."

"The Signor Ambassador and myself," observed the priest, "have had a most interesting conversation (to me at least) about books and bookworms, spiders, and other congruous matters; and I find his Excellency has heretofore made acquaintance with a great spider bearing strong resemblance to the hermit of our library."

"Indeed," said his Lordship. "I was not aware that America had yet enough of age and old misfortune, crime, sordidness, that accumulate with it, to have produced spiders like this. Had he sucked into himself all the noisomeness of your heat?"

Redclyffe made some slight answer, that the spider was a sort of pet of an old virtuoso to whom he owed many obligations in his boyhood; and the conversation turned from this subject to others suggested by topics of the day and place. His Lordship was affable, and Redclyffe could not, it must be confessed, see anything to justify the prejudices of the neighbors against him. Indeed, he was inclined to attribute them, in great measure, to the narrowness of the English view,—to those insular prejudices which have always prevented them from fully appreciating what differs from their own habits. At lunch, which was soon announced, the party of three became very pleasant and sociable, his Lordship drinking a light Italian red wine, and recommending it to Redclyffe; who, however, was English enough to prefer some bitter ale, while the priest contented himself with pure water,— which is, in truth, a less agreeable drink in chill, moist England than in any country we are acquainted with.

"You must make yourself quite at home here," said his Lordship, as they rose from table. "I am not a good host, nor a very genial man, I believe. I can do little to entertain you; but here is the house and the grounds at your disposal,—horses in the stable,—guns in the hall,—here is Father Angelo, good at chess. There is the library. Pray make the most of them all; and if I can contribute in any way to your pleasure, let me know."

All this certainly seemed cordial, and the manner in which it was said seemed in accordance with the spirit of the words; and yet, whether the fault was in anything of morbid suspicion in Redclyffe's nature, or whatever it was, it did not have the effect of making him feel welcome, which almost every Englishman has the natural faculty of producing on a guest, when once he has admitted him beneath his roof. It might be in great measure his face, so thin and refined, and intellectual without feeling; his voice which had melody, but not heartiness; his manners, which were not simple by nature, but by art;—whatever it was, Redclyffe found that Lord Braithwaite did not call for his own naturalness and simplicity, but his art, and felt that he was inevitably acting a part in his intercourse with him, that he was on his guard, playing a game; and yet he did not wish to do this. But there was a mobility, a subtleness in his nature, an unconscious tact,—which the mode of life and of mixing with men in America fosters and perfects,—that made this sort of finesse inevitable to him, with any but a natural character; with whom, on the other hand, Redclyffe could be as fresh and natural as any Englishman of them all.

Redclyffe spent the time between lunch and dinner in wandering about the grounds, from which he had hitherto felt himself debarred by motives of delicacy. It was a most interesting ramble to him, coming to trees which his ancestor, who went to America, might have climbed in his boyhood, might have sat beneath, with his lady-love, in his youth; deer there were, the descendants of those which he had seen; old stone stiles, which his foot had trodden. The sombre, clouded light of the day fell down upon this scene, which in its verdure, its luxuriance of vegetable life, was purely English, cultivated to the last extent without losing the nature out of a single thing. In the course of his walk he came to the spot where he had been so mysteriously wounded on his first arrival in this region; and, examining the spot, he was startled to see that there was a path leading to the other side of a hedge, and this path, which led to the house, had brought him here.

Musing upon this mysterious circumstance, and how it should have happened in so orderly a country as England, so tamed and subjected to civilization,—an incident to happen in an English park which seemed better suited to the Indian-haunted forests of the wilder parts of his own land,—and how no researches which the Warden had instituted had served in the smallest degree to develop the mystery,—he clambered over the hedge, and followed the footpath. It plunged into dells, and emerged from them, led through scenes which seemed those of old romances, and at last, by these devious ways, began to approach the old house, which, with its many gray gables, put on a new aspect from this point of view. Redclyffe admired its venerableness anew; the ivy that overran parts of it; the marks of age; and wondered at the firmness of the institutions which, through all the changes that come to man, could have kept this house the home of one lineal race for so many centuries; so many, that the absence of his own branch from it seemed but a temporary visit to foreign parts, from which he was now returned, to be again at home, by the old hearthstone.

"But what do I mean to do?" said he to himself, stopping short, and still looking at the old house. "Am I ready to give up all the actual life before me for the sake of taking up with what I feel to be a less developed state of human life? Would it not be better for me to depart now, to turn my back on this flattering prospect? I am not fit to be here,—I, so strongly susceptible of a newer, more stirring life than these men lead; I, who feel that, whatever the thought and cultivation of England may be, my own countrymen have gone forward a long, long march beyond them, not intellectually, but in a way that gives them a further start. If I come back hither, with the purpose to make myself an Englishman, especially an Englishman of rank and hereditary estate,—then for me America has been discovered in vain, and the great spirit that has been breathed into us is in vain; and I am false to it all!"

But again came silently swelling over him like a flood all that ancient peace, and quietude, and dignity, which looked so stately and beautiful as brooding round the old house; all that blessed order of ranks, that sweet superiority, and yet with no disclaimer of common brotherhood, that existed between the English gentleman and his inferiors; all that delightful intercourse, so sure of pleasure, so safe from rudeness, lowness, unpleasant rubs, that exists between gentleman and gentleman, where, in public affairs, all are essentially of one mind, or seem so to an American politician, accustomed to the fierce conflicts of our embittered parties; where life was made so enticing, so refined, and yet with a sort of homeliness that seemed to show that all its strength was left behind; that seeming taking in of all that was desirable in life, and all its grace and beauty, yet never giving life a hard enamel of over-refinement. What could there be in the wild, harsh, ill-conducted American approach to civilization, which could compare with this? What to compare with this juiciness and richness? What other men had ever got so much out of life as the polished and wealthy Englishmen of to-day? What higher part was to be acted, than seemed to lie before him, if he willed to accept it?

He resumed his walk, and, drawing near the manor-house, found that he was approaching another entrance than that which had at first admitted him; a very pleasant entrance it was, beneath a porch, of antique form, and ivy-clad, hospitable and inviting; and it being the approach from the grounds, it seemed to be more appropriate to the residents of the house than the other one. Drawing near, Redclyffe saw that a flight of steps ascended within the porch, old-looking, much worn; and nothing is more suggestive of long time than a flight of worn steps; it must have taken so many soles, through so many years, to make an impression. Judging from the make of the outside of the edifice, Redclyffe thought that he could make out the way from the porch to the hall and library; so he determined to enter this way.

There had been, as was not unusual, a little shower of rain during the afternoon; and as Redclyffe came close to the steps, they were glistening with the wet. The stones were whitish, like marble, and one of them bore on it a token that made him pause, while a thrill like terror ran through his system. For it was the mark of a footstep, very decidedly made out, and red, like blood,—the Bloody Footstep,—the mark of a foot, which seemed to have been slightly impressed into the rock, as if it had been a soft substance, at the same time sliding a little, and gushing with blood. The glistening moisture of which we have spoken made it appear as if it were just freshly stamped there; and it suggested to Redclyffe's fancy the idea, that, impressed more than two centuries ago, there was some charm connected with the mark which kept it still fresh, and would continue to do so to the end of time. It was well that there was no spectator there,—for the American would have blushed to have it known how much this old traditionary wonder had affected his imagination. But, indeed, it was as old as any bugbear of his mind—as any of those bugbears and private terrors which grow up with people, and make the dreams and nightmares of childhood, and the fever-images of mature years, till they haunt the deliriums of the dying bed, and after that possibly, are either realized or known no more. The Doctor's strange story vividly recurred to him, and all the horrors which he had since associated with this trace; and it seemed to him as if he had now struck upon a bloody track, and as if there were other tracks of this supernatural foot which he was bound to search out; removing the dust of ages that had settled on them, the moss and deep grass that had grown over them, the forest leaves that might have fallen on them in America—marking out the pathway, till the pedestrian lay down in his grave.

The foot was issuing from, not entering into, the house. Whoever had impressed it, or on whatever occasion, he had gone forth, and doubtless to return no more. Redclyffe was impelled to place his own foot on the track; and the action, as it were, suggested in itself strange ideas of what had been the state of mind of the man who planted it there; and he felt a strange, vague, yet strong surmise of some agony, some terror and horror, that had passed here, and would not fade out of the spot. While he was in these musings, he saw Lord Braithwaite looking at him through the glass of the porch, with fixed, curious eyes, and a smile on his face. On perceiving that Redclyffe was aware of his presence, he came forth without appearing in the least disturbed.

"What think you of the Bloody Footstep?" asked he.

"It seems to me, undoubtedly," said Redclyffe, stooping to examine it more closely, "a good thing to make a legend out of; and, like most legendary lore, not capable of bearing close examination. I should decidedly say that the Bloody Footstep is a natural reddish stain in the stone."

"Do you think so, indeed?" rejoined his Lordship. "It may be; but in that case, if not the record of an actual deed,—of a foot stamped down there in guilt and agony, and oozing out with unwipeupable blood,—we may consider it as prophetic;—as foreboding, from the time when the stone was squared and smoothed, and laid at this threshold, that a fatal footstep was really to be impressed here."

"It is an ingenious supposition," said Redclyffe. "But is there any sure knowledge that the prophecy you suppose has yet been fulfilled?"

"If not, it might yet be in the future," said Lord Braithwaite. "But I think there are enough in the records of this family to prove that there did one cross this threshold in a bloody agony, who has since returned no more. Great seekings, I have understood, have been had throughout the world for him, or for any sign of him, but nothing satisfactory has been heard."

"And it is now too late to expect it," observed the American.

"Perhaps not," replied the nobleman, with a glance that Redclyffe thought had peculiar meaning in it. "Ah! it is very curious to see what turnings up there are in this world of old circumstances that seem buried forever; how things come back, like echoes that have rolled away among the hills and been seemingly hushed forever. We cannot tell when a thing is really dead; it comes to life, perhaps in its old shape, perhaps in a new and unexpected one; so that nothing really vanishes out of the world. I wish it did."

The conversation now ceased, and Redclyffe entered the house, where he amused himself for some time in looking at the ancient hall, with its gallery, its armor, and its antique fireplace, on the hearth of which burned a genial fire. He wondered whether in that fire was the continuance of that custom which the Doctor's legend spoke of, and that the flame had been kept up there two hundred years, in expectation of the wanderer's return. It might be so, although the climate of England made it a natural custom enough, in a large and damp old room, into which many doors opened, both from the exterior and interior of the mansion; but it was pleasant to think the custom a traditionary one, and to fancy that a booted figure, enveloped in a cloak, might still arrive, and fling open the veiling cloak, throw off the sombre and drooping-brimmed hat, and show features that were similar to those seen in pictured faces on the walls. Was he himself—in another guise, as Lord Braithwaite had been saying—that long-expected one? Was his the echoing tread that had been heard so long through the ages—so far through the wide world—approaching the blood-stained threshold?

With such thoughts, or dreams (for they were hardly sincerely enough entertained to be called thoughts), Redclyffe spent the day; a strange, delicious day, in spite of the sombre shadows that enveloped it. He fancied himself strangely wonted, already, to the house; as if his every part and peculiarity had at once fitted into its nooks, and corners, and crannies; but, indeed, his mobile nature and active fancy were not entirely to be trusted in this matter; it was, perhaps, his American faculty of making himself at home anywhere, that he mistook for the feeling of being peculiarly at home here.

CHAPTER XXIII

Redclyffe was now established in the great house which had been so long and so singularly an object of interest with him. With his customary impressibility by the influences around him, he begun to take in the circumstances, and to understand them by more subtile tokens than he could well explain to himself. There was the steward, [Endnote: 1] or whatever was his precise office; so quiet, so subdued, so nervous, so strange! What had been this man's history? What was now the secret of his daily life? There he was, creeping stealthily up and down the staircases, and about the passages of the house; always as if he were afraid of meeting somebody. On seeing Redclyffe in the house, the latter fancied that the man expressed a kind of interest in his face; but whether pleasure or pain he could not well tell; only he sometimes found that he was contemplating him from a distance, or from the obscurity of the room in which he sat,—or from a corridor, while he smoked his cigar on the lawn. A great part, if not the whole of this, he imputed to his knowledge of Redclyffe's connections with the Doctor; but yet this hardly seemed sufficient to account for the pertinacity with which the old man haunted his footsteps,—the poor, nervous old thing,—always near him, or often unexpectedly so; and yet apparently not very willing to hold conversation with him, having nothing of importance to say.

"Mr. Omskirk," said Redclyffe to him, a day or two after the commencement of his visit, "how many years have you now been in this situation?"

"0, sir, ever since the Doctor's departure for America," said Omskirk, "now thirty and five years, five months, and three days."

"A long time," said Redclyffe, smiling, "and you seem to keep the account of it very accurately."

"A very long time, your honor," said Omskirk; "so long, that I seem to have lived one life before it began, and I cannot think of any life than just what I had. My life was broken off short in the midst; and what belonged to the earlier part of it was another man's life; this is mine."

"It might be a pleasant life enough, I should think, in this fine old Hall," said Redclyffe; "rather monotonous, however. Would you not like a relaxation of a few days, a pleasure trip, in all these thirty-five years? You old Englishmen are so sturdily faithful to one thing. You do not resemble my countrymen in that."

"0, none of them ever lived in an old mansion-house like this," replied Omskirk, "they do not know the sort of habits that a man gets here. They do not know my business either, nor any man's here."

"Is your master then, so difficult?" said Redclyffe.

"My master! Who was speaking of him?" said the old man, as if surprised. "Ah, I was thinking of Dr. Grimshawe. He was my master, you know."

And Redclyffe was again inconceivably struck with the strength of the impression that was made on the poor old man's mind by the character of the old Doctor; so that, after thirty years of other service, he still felt him to be the master, and could not in the least release himself from those earlier bonds. He remembered a story that the Doctor used to tell of his once recovering a hanged person, and more and more came to the conclusion that this was the man, and that, as the Doctor had said, this hold of a strong mind over a weak one, strengthened by the idea that he had made him, had subjected the man to him in a kind of slavery that embraced the soul.

And then, again, the lord of the estate interested him greatly, and not unpleasantly. He compared what he seemed to be now with what, according to all reports, he had been in the past, and could make nothing of it, nor reconcile the two characters in the least. It seemed as if the estate were possessed by a devil, — a foul and melancholy fiend, — who resented the attempted possession of others by subjecting them to himself. One had turned from quiet and sober habits to reckless dissipation; another had turned from the usual gayety of life to recluse habits, and both, apparently, by the same influence; at least, so it appeared to Redclyffe, as he insulated their story from all other circumstances, and looked at them by one light. He even thought that he felt a similar influence coming over himself, even in this little time that he had spent here; gradually, should this be his permanent residence, — and not so very gradually either, — there would come its own individual mode of change over him. That quick suggestive mind would gather the moss and lichens of decay. Palsy of its powers would probably be the form it would assume. He looked back through the vanished years to the time which he had spent with the old Doctor, and he felt unaccountably as if the mysterious old man were yet ruling him, as he did in his boyhood; as if his inscrutable, inevitable eye were upon him in all his movements; nay, as if he had guided every step that he took in coming hither, and were stalking mistily before him, leading him about. He sometimes would gladly have given up all these wild and enticing prospects, these dreams that had occupied him so long, if he could only have gone away and looked back upon the house, its inmates, and his own recollections no more; but there came a fate, and took the shape of the old Doctor's apparition, holding him back.

And then, too, the thought of Elsie had much influence in keeping him quietly here; her natural sunshine was the one thing that, just now, seemed to have a good influence upon the world. She, too, was evidently connected with this place, and with the fate, whatever it might be, that awaited him here. The Doctor, the ruler of his destiny, had provided her as well as all the rest; and from his grave, or wherever he was, he still seemed to bring them together.

So here, in this darkened dream, he waited for what should come to pass; and daily, when he sat down in the dark old library, it was with the thought that this day might bring to a close the doubt amid which he lived,—might give him the impetus to go forward. In such a state, no doubt, the witchcraft of the place was really to be recognized, the old witchcraft, too, of the Doctor, which he had escaped by the quick ebullition of youthful spirit, long ago, while the Doctor lived; but which had been stored up till now, till an influence that remained latent for years had worked out in active disease. He held himself open for intercourse with the lord of the mansion; and intercourse of a certain nature they certainly had, but not of the kind which Redclyffe desired. They talked together of politics, of the state of the relations between England and America, of the court to which Redclyffe was accredited; sometimes Redclyffe tried to lead the conversation to the family topics, nor, in truth, did Lord Braithwaite seem to decline his lead; although it was observable that very speedily the conversation would be found turned upon some other subject, to which it had swerved aside by subtle underhand movements. Yet Redclyffe was not the less determined, and at no distant period, to bring up the subject on which his mind dwelt so much, and have it fairly discussed between them.

He was sometimes a little frightened at the position and circumstances in which he found himself; a great disturbance there was in his being, the causes of which he could not trace. It had an influence on his dreams, through which the Doctor seemed to pass continually, and when he awoke it was often with the sensation that he had just the moment before been holding conversation with the old man, and that the latter—with that gesture of power that he remembered so well—had been impressing some command upon him; but what that command was, he could not possibly call to mind. He wandered among the dark passages of the house, and up its antique staircases, as if expecting at every turn to meet some one who would have the word of destiny to say to him. When he went forth into the park, it was as if to hold an appointment with one who had promised to meet him there; and he came slowly back, lingering and loitering, because this expected one had not yet made himself visible, yet plucked up a little alacrity as he drew near the house, because the communicant might have arrived in his absence, and be waiting for him in the dim library. It seemed as if he was under a spell; he could neither go away nor rest,—nothing but dreams, troubled dreams. He had ghostly fears, as if some one were near him whom he could not make out; stealing behind him, and starting away when he was impelled to turn round. A nervousness that his healthy temperament had never before permitted him to be the victim of, assailed him now. He could not help imputing it partly to the influence of the generations who had left a portion of their individual human nature in the house, which had become magnetic by them and could not rid itself of their presence in one sense, though, in another, they had borne it as far off as to where the gray tower of the village church rose above their remains.

Again, he was frightened to perceive what a hold the place was getting upon him; how the tendrils of the ivy seemed to hold him and would not let him go; how natural and homelike (grim and sombre as they were) the old doorways and apartments were becoming; how in no place that he had ever known had he had such a home-like feeling. To be sure, poor fellow, he had no earlier home except the almshouse, where his recollection of a fireside crowded by grim old women and pale, sickly children, of course never allowed him to have the reminiscences of a private, domestic home. But then there was the Doctor's home by the graveyard, and little Elsie, his constant playmate? No, even those recollections did not hold him like this heavy present circumstance. How should he ever draw himself away? No; the proud and vivid and active prospects that had heretofore spread themselves before him,—the striving to conquer, the struggle, the victory, the defeat, if such it was to be,—the experiences for good or ill,—the life, life, life,—all possibility of these was passing from him; all that hearty earnest contest or communion of man with man; and leaving him nothing but this great sombre shade, this brooding of the old family mansion, with its dreary ancestral hall, its mouldy dignity, its life of the past, its fettering honor, which to accept must bind him hand and foot, as respects all effort, such as he had trained himself for,—such as his own country offered. It was not any value for these,—as it seemed to Redclyffe,—but a witchcraft, an indefinable spell, a something that he could not define, that enthralled him, and was now doing a work on him analogous to, though different from, that which was wrought on Omskirk and all the other inhabitants, high and low, of this old mansion.

He felt greatly interested in the master of the mansion; although perhaps it was not from anything in his nature; but partly because he conceived that he himself had a controlling power over his fortunes, and likewise from the vague perception of this before-mentioned trouble in him. It seemed, whatever it might be, to have converted an ordinary superficial man of the world into a being that felt and suffered inwardly, had pangs, fears, a conscience, a sense of unseen things. It seemed as if underneath this manor-house were the entrance to the cave of Trophonius, one visit to which made a man sad forever after; and that Lord Braithwaite had been there once, or perhaps went nightly, or at any hour. Or the mansion itself was like dark-colored experience, the reality; the point of view where things were seen in their true lights; the true world, all outside of which was delusion, and here—dreamlike as its structures seemed—the absolute truth. All those that lived in it were getting to be a brotherhood; and he among them; and perhaps before the blood-stained threshold would grow up an impassable barrier, which would cause himself to sit down in dreary quiet, like the rest of them.

Redclyffe, as has been intimated, had an unavowed—unavowed to himself—suspicion that the master of the house cherished no kindly purpose towards him; he had an indistinct feeling of danger from him; he would not have been surprised to know that he was concocting a plot against his life; and yet he did not think that Lord Braithwaite had the slightest hostility towards him. It might make the thing more horrible, perhaps; but it has been often seen in those who poison for the sake of interest, without feelings of personal malevolence, that they do it as kindly as the nature of the thing will permit; they, possibly, may even have a certain degree of affection for their victims, enough to induce them to make the last hours of life sweet and pleasant; to wind up the fever of life with a double supply of enjoyable throbs; to sweeten and delicately flavor the cup of death that they offer to the lips of him whose life is inconsistent with some stated necessity of their own. "Dear friend," such a one might say to the friend whom he reluctantly condemned to death, "think not that there is any base malice, any desire of pain to thee, that actuates me in this thing. Heaven knows, I earnestly wish thy good. But I have well considered the matter,—more deeply than thou hast,—and have found that it is essential that one thing should be, and essential to that thing that thou, my friend, shouldst die. Is that a doom which even thou wouldst object to with such an end to be answered? Thou art innocent; thou art not a man of evil life; the worst thing that can come of it, so far as thou art concerned, would be a quiet, endless repose in yonder churchyard, among dust of thy ancestry, with the English violets growing over thee there, and the green, sweet grass, which thou wilt not scorn to associate with thy dissolving elements, remembering that thy forefather owed a debt, for his own birth and growth, to this English soil, and paid it not,—consigned himself to that rough soil of another clime, under the forest leaves. Pay it, dear friend, without repining, and leave me to battle a little longer with this troublesome world, and in a few years to rejoin thee, and talk quietly over this matter which we are now arranging. How slight a favor, then, for one friend to do another, will seem this that I seek of thee."

Redclyffe smiled to himself, as he thus gave expression to what he really half fancied were Lord Braithwaite's feelings and purposes towards him, and he felt them in the kindness and sweetness of his demeanor, and his evident wish to make him happy, combined with his own subtle suspicion of some design with which he had been invited here, or which had grown up since he came.

Whoever has read Italian history must have seen such instances of this poisoning without malice or personal ill-feeling.

His own pleasant, companionable, perhaps noble traits and qualities, may have made a favorable impression on Lord Braithwaite, and perhaps he regretted the necessity of acting as he was about to do, but could not therefore weakly relinquish his deliberately formed design. And, on his part, Redclyffe bore no malice towards Lord Braithwaite, but felt really a kindly interest in him, and could he have made him happy at any less cost than his own life, or dearest interests, would perhaps have been glad to do so. He sometimes felt inclined to remonstrate with him in a friendly way; to tell him that his intended course was not likely to lead to a good result; that they had better try to arrange the matter on some other basis, and perhaps he would not find the American so unreasonable as he supposed.

All this, it will be understood, were the mere dreamy suppositions of Redclyffe, in the idleness and languor of the old mansion, letting his mind run at will, and following it into dim caves, whither it tended. He did not actually believe anything of all this; unless it be a lawyer, or a policeman, or some very vulgar natural order of mind, no man really suspects another of crime. It is the hardest thing in the world for a noble nature—the hardest and the most shocking—to be convinced that a fellow-being is going to do a wrong thing, and the consciousness of one's own inviolability renders it still more difficult to believe that one's self is to be the object of the wrong. What he had been fancying looked to him like a romance. The strange part of the matter was, what suggested such a romance in regard to his kind and hospitable host, who seemed to exercise the hospitality of England with a kind of refinement and pleasant piquancy that came from his Italian mixture of blood? Was there no spiritual whisper here?

So the time wore on; and Redclyffe began to be sensible that he must soon decide upon the course that he was to take; for his diplomatic position waited for him, and he could not loiter many days more away in this half delicious, half painful reverie and quiet in the midst of his struggling life. He was yet as undetermined what to do as ever; or, if we may come down to the truth, he was perhaps loath to acknowledge to himself the determination that he had actually formed.

One day, at dinner, which now came on after candle-light, he and Lord Braithwaite sat together at table, as usual, while Omskirk waited at the sideboard. It was a wild, gusty night, in which an autumnal breeze of later autumn seemed to have gone astray, and come into September intrusively. The two friends—for such we may call them—had spent a pleasant day together, wandering in the grounds, looking at the old house at all points, going to the church, and examining the cross-legged stone statues; they had ridden, too, and taken a great deal of healthful exercise, and had now that pleasant sense of just weariness enough which it is the boon of the climate of England to incite and permit men to take. Redclyffe was in one of his most genial moods, and Lord Braithwaite seemed to be the same; so kindly they were both disposed to one another, that the American felt that he might not longer refrain from giving his friend some light upon the character in which he appeared, or in which, at least, he had it at his option to appear. Lord Braithwaite might or might not know it already; but at all events it was his duty to tell him, or to take his leave, having thus far neither gained nor sought anything from their connection which would tend to forward his pursuit—should he decide to undertake it.

When the cheerful fire, the rare wine, and the good fare had put them both into a good physical state, Redclyffe said to Lord Braithwaite,—

"There is a matter upon which I have been some time intending to speak to you."

Braithwaite nodded.

"A subject," continued he, "of interest to both of us. Has it ever occurred to you, from the identity of name, that I may be really, what we have jokingly assumed me to be,—a relation?"

"It has," said Lord Braithwaite, readily enough. "The family would be proud to acknowledge such a kinsman, whose abilities and political rank would add a public lustre that it has long wanted."

Redclyffe bowed and smiled.

"You know, I suppose, the annals of your house," he continued, "and have heard how, two centuries ago, or somewhat less, there was an ancestor who mysteriously disappeared. He was never seen again. There were tales of private murder, out of which a hundred legends have come down to these days, as I have myself found, though most of them in so strange a shape that I should hardly know them, had I not myself a clue."

"I have heard some of these legends," said Lord Braithwaite.

"But did you ever hear, among them," asked Redclyffe, "that the lost ancestor did not really die, — was not murdered, — but lived long, though in another hemisphere, — lived long, and left heirs behind him?"

"There is such a legend," said Lord Braithwaite.

"Left posterity," continued Redclyffe, — "a representative of whom is alive at this day."

"That I have not known, though I might conjecture something like it," said Braithwaite.

The coolness with which he took this perplexed Redclyffe. He resolved to make trial at once whether it were possible to move him.

"And I have reason to believe," he added, "that that representative is myself."

"Should that prove to be the case, you are welcome back to your own," said Lord Braithwaite, quietly. "It will be a very remarkable case, if the proofs for two hundred years, or thereabouts, can be so distinctly made out as to nullify the claim of one whose descent is undoubted. Yet it is certainly not impossible. I suppose it would hardly be fair in me to ask what are your proofs, and whether I may see them."

"The documents are in the hands of my agents in London," replied Redclyffe; "and seem to be ample, among them being a certified genealogy from the first emigrant downward, without a break. A declaration of two men of note among the first settlers, certifying that they knew the first emigrant, under a change of name, to be the eldest son of the house of Braithwaite; full proofs, at least on that head."

"You are a lawyer, I believe," said Braithwaite, "and know better than I what may be necessary to prove your claim. I will frankly own to you, that I have heard, long ago, — as long as when my connection with this hereditary property first began, — that there was supposed to be an heir extant for a long course of years, and that there, was no proof that that main line of the descent had ever become extinct. If these things had come fairly before me, and been represented to me with whatever force belongs to them, before my accession to the estate, — these and other facts which I have since become acquainted with, — I might have deliberated on the expediency of coming to such a doubtful possession. The property, I assure you, is not so desirable that, taking all things into consideration, it has much increased my happiness. But, now, here I am, having paid a price in a certain way,— which you will understand, if you ever come into the property,—a price of a nature that cannot possibly be refunded. It can hardly be presumed that I shall see your right a moment sooner than you make it manifest by law."

"I neither expect nor wish it," replied Redclyffe, "nor, to speak frankly, am I quite sure that you will ever have occasion to defend your title, or to question mine. When I came hither, to be your guest, it was almost with the settled purpose never to mention my proofs, nor to seek to make them manifest. That purpose is not, I may say, yet relinquished."

"Yet I am to infer from your words that it is shaken?" said Braithwaite. "You find the estate, then, so delightful,—this life of the old manor-house so exquisitely agreeable,—this air so cheering,—this moral atmosphere so invigorating,—that your scruples are about coming to an end. You think this life of an Englishman, this fair prospect of a title, so irresistibly enticing as to be worth more than your claim, in behalf of your American birthright, to a possible Presidency."

There was a sort of sneer in this, which Redclyffe did not well know how to understand; and there was a look on Braithwaite's face, as he said it, that made him think of a condemned soul, who should be dressed in magnificent robes, and surrounded with the mockery of state, splendor, and happiness, who, if he should be congratulated on his fortunate and blissful situation, would probably wear just such a look, and speak in just that tone. He looked a moment in Braithwaite's face.

"No," he replied. "I do not think that there is much happiness in it. A brighter, healthier, more useful, far more satisfactory, though tumultuous life would await me in my own country. But there is about this place a strange, deep, sad, brooding interest, which possesses me, and draws me to it, and will not let me go. I feel as if, in spite of myself and my most earnest efforts, I were fascinated by something in the spot, and must needs linger here, and make it my home if I can."

"You shall be welcome; the old hereditary chair will be filled at last," said Braithwaite, pointing to the vacant chair. "Come, we will drink to you in a cup of welcome. Take the old chair now."

In half-frolic Redclyffe took the chair.

He called to Omskirk to bring a bottle of a particularly exquisite Italian wine, known only to the most deeply skilled in the vintages of that country, and which, he said, was oftener heard of than seen,—oftener seen than tasted. Omskirk put it on the table in its original glass, and Braithwaite filled Redclyffe's glass and his own, and raised the latter to his lips, with a frank expression of his mobile countenance.

"May you have a secure possession of your estate," said he, "and live long in the midst of your possessions. To me, on the whole, it seems better than your American prospects."

Redclyffe thanked him, and drank off the glass of wine, which was not very much to his taste; as new varieties of wine are apt not to be. All the conversation that had passed had been in a free, careless sort of way, without apparently much earnestness in it; for they were both men who knew how to keep their more serious parts within them. But Redclyffe was glad that the explanation was over, and that he might now remain at Braithwaite's table, under his roof, without that uneasy feeling of treachery which, whether rightly or not, had haunted him hitherto. He felt joyous, and stretched his hand out for the bottle which Braithwaite kept near himself, instead of passing it.

"You do not yourself do justice to your own favorite wine," observed Redclyffe, seeing his host's full glass standing before him.

"I have filled again," said Braithwaite, carelessly; "but I know not that I shall venture to drink a second glass. It is a wine that does not bear mixture with other vintages, though of most genial and admirable qualities when taken by itself. Drink your own, however, for it will be a rare occasion indeed that would induce me to offer you another bottle of this rare stock."

Redclyffe sipped his second glass, endeavoring to find out what was this subtile and peculiar flavor that hid itself so, and yet seemed on the point of revealing itself. It had, he thought, a singular effect upon his faculties, quickening and making them active, and causing him to feel as if he were on the point of penetrating rare mysteries, such as men's thoughts are always hovering round, and always returning from. Some strange, vast, sombre, mysterious truth, which he seemed to have searched for long, appeared to be on the point of being revealed to him; a sense of something to come; something to happen that had been waiting long, long to happen; an opening of doors, a drawing away of veils; a lifting of heavy, magnificent curtains, whose dark folds hung before a spectacle of awe;—it was like the verge of the grave. Whether it was the exquisite wine of Braithwaite, or whatever it might be, the American felt a strange influence upon him, as if he were passing through the gates of eternity, and finding on the other side the revelation of some secret that had greatly perplexed him on this side. He thought that Braithwaite's face assumed a strange, subtile smile,—not malicious, yet crafty, triumphant, and at the same time terribly sad, and with that perception his senses, his life, welled away; and left him in the deep ancestral chair at the board of Braithwaite.

CHAPTER XXIV

When awake [Endnote: 1], or beginning to awake, he lay for some time in a maze; not a disagreeable one, but thoughts were running to and fro in his mind, all mixed and jumbled together. Reminiscences of early days, even those that were Preadamite; referring, we mean, to those times in the almshouse, which he could not at ordinary times remember at all; but now there seemed to be visions of old women and men, and pallid girls, and little dirty boys, which could only be referred to that epoch. Also, and most vividly, there was the old Doctor, with his sternness, his fierceness, his mystery; and all that happened since, playing phantasmagoria before his yet unclosed eyes; nor, so mysterious was his state, did he know, when he should unclose those lids, where he should find himself. He was content to let the world go on in this way, as long as it would, and therefore did not hurry, but rather kept back the proofs of awakening; willing to look at the scenes that were unrolling for his amusement, as it seemed; and willing, too, to keep it uncertain whether he were not back in America, and in his boyhood, and all other subsequent impressions a dream or a prophetic vision. But at length something stirring near him,—or whether it stirred, or whether he dreamed it, he could not quite tell,—but the uncertainty impelled him, at last, to open his eyes, and see whereabouts he was.

Even then he continued in as much uncertainty as he was before, and lay with marvellous quietude in it, trying sluggishly to make the mystery out. It was in a dim, twilight place, wherever it might be; a place of half-awakeness, where the outlines of things were not well defined; but it seemed to be a chamber, antique and vaulted, narrow and high, hung round with old tapestry. Whether it were morning or midday he could not tell, such was the character of the light, nor even where it came from; for there appeared to be no windows, and yet it was not apparently artificial light; nor light at all, indeed, but a gray dimness. It was so like his own half-awake state that he lay in it a longer time, not incited to finish his awaking, but in a languor, not disagreeable, yet hanging heavily, heavily upon him, like a dark pall. It was, in fact, as if he had been asleep for years, or centuries, or till the last day was dawning, and then was collecting his thoughts in such slow fashion as would then be likely.

Again that noise,—a little, low, quiet sound, as of one breathing somewhere near him. The whole thing was very much like that incident which introduced him to the Hospital, and his first coming to his senses there; and he almost fancied that some such accident must again have happened to him, and that when his sight cleared he should again behold the venerable figure of the pensioner. With this idea he let his head steady itself; and it seemed to him that its dizziness must needs be the result of very long and deep sleep. What if it were the sleep of a century? What if all things that were extant when he went to sleep had passed away, and he was waking now in another epoch of time? Where was America, and the republic in which he hoped for such great things? Where England? had she stood it better than the republic? Was the old Hospital still in being,—although the good Warden must long since have passed out of his warm and pleasant life? And himself, how came he to be preserved? In what musty old nook had he been put away, where Time neglected and Death forgot him, until now he was to get up friendless, helpless,—when new heirs had come to the estate he was on the point of laying claim to,—and go onward through what remained of life? Would it not have been better to have lived with his contemporaries, and to be now dead and dust with them? Poor, petty interests of a day, how slight!

Again the noise, a little stir, a sort of quiet moan, or something that he could not quite define; but it seemed, whenever he heard it, as if some fact thrust itself through the dream-work with which he was circumfused; something alien to his fantasies, yet not powerful enough to dispel them. It began to be irksome to him, this little sound of something near him; and he thought, in the space of another hundred years, if it continued, he should have to arouse himself and see what it was. But, indeed, there was something so cheering in this long repose,—this rest from all the troubles of earth, which it sometimes seems as if only a churchyard bed would give us,—that he wished the noise would let him alone. But his thoughts were gradually getting too busy for this slumberous state. He begun, perforce, to come nearer actuality. The strange question occurred to him, Had any time at all passed? Was he not still sitting at Lord Braithwaite's table, having just now quaffed a second glass of that rare and curious Italian wine? Was it not affecting his head very strangely,—so that he was put out of time as it were? He would rally himself, and try to set his head right with another glass. He must be still at table, for now he remembered he had not gone to bed at all. [Endnote: 2.]

Ah, the noise! He could not bear it, he would awake now, now!—silence it, and then to sleep again. In fact, he started up; started to his feet, in puzzle and perplexity, and stood gazing around him, with swimming brain. It was an antique room, which he did not at all recognize, and, indeed, in that dim twilight—which how it came he could not tell—he could scarcely discern what were its distinguishing marks. But he seemed to be sensible, that, in a high-backed chair, at a little distance from him, sat a figure in a long robe; a figure of a man with snow-white hair and a long beard, who seemed to be gazing at him, quietly, as if he had been gazing a hundred years. I know not what it was, but there was an influence as if this old man belonged to some other age and category of man than he was now amongst. He remembered the old family legend of the existence of an ancestor two or three centuries in age.

"It is the old family personified," thought he.

The old figure made no sign, but continued to sit gazing at him in so strangely still a manner that it made Redclyffe shiver with something that seemed like affright. There was an aspect of long, long time about him; as if he had never been young, or so long ago as when the world was young along with him. He might be the demon of this old house; the representative of all that happened in it, the grief, the long languor and weariness of life, the deaths, gathering them all into himself, and figuring them in furrows, wrinkles, and white hairs,—a being that might have been young, when those old Saxon timbers were put together, with the oaks that were saplings when Caesar landed, and was in his maturity when the Conqueror came, and was now lapsing into extreme age when the nineteenth century was elderly. His garb might have been of any time, that long, loose robe that enveloped him. Redclyffe remained in this way, gazing at this aged figure; at first without the least wonder, but calmly, as we feel in dreams, when, being in a land of enchantment, we take everything as if it were a matter of course, and feel, by the right of our own marvellous nature, on terms of equal kindred with all other marvels. So it was with him when he first became aware of the old man, sitting there with that age-long regard directed towards him.

But, by degrees, a sense of wonder had its will, and grew, slowly at first, in Redclyffe's mind; and almost twin-born with it, and growing piece by piece, there was a sense of awful fear, as his waking senses came slowly back to him. In the dreamy state, he had felt no fear; but, as a waking man, it was fearful to discover that the shadowy forms did not fly from his awaking eyes. He started at last to his feet from the low couch on which he had all this time been lying.

"What are you?" he exclaimed. "Where am I?"

The old figure made no answer; nor could Redclyffe be quite sure that his voice had any effect upon it, though he fancied that it was shaken a little, as if his voice came to it from afar. But it continued to gaze at him, or at least to have its aged face turned towards him in the dim light; and this strange composure, and unapproachableness, were very frightful. As his manhood gathered about his heart, however, the American endeavored to shake off this besetting fear, or awe, or whatever it was; and to bring himself to a sense of waking things,—to burst through the mist and delusive shows that bewildered him, and catch hold of a reality. He stamped upon the floor; it was solid stone, the pavement, or oak so old and stanch that it resembled it. There was one firm thing, therefore. But the contrast between this and the slipperiness, the unaccountableness, of the rest of his position, made him the more sensible of the latter. He made a step towards the old figure; another; another. He was face to face with him, within a yard of distance. He saw the faint movement of the old man's breath; he sought, through the twilight of the room, some glimmer of perception in his eyes.

"Are you a living man?" asked Redclyffe, faintly and doubtfully.

He mumbled, the old figure, some faint moaning sound, that, if it were language at all, had all the edges and angles worn off it by decay,— unintelligible, except that it seemed to signify a faint mournfulness and complainingness of mood; and then held his peace, continuing to gaze as before. Redclyffe could not bear the awe that filled him, while he kept at a distance, and, coming desperately forward, he stood close to the old figure; he touched his robe, to see if it were real; he laid his hand upon the withered hand that held the staff, in which he now recognized the very staff of the Doctor's legend. His fingers touched a real hand, though, bony and dry, as if it had been in the grave.

"Then you are real?" said Redclyffe doubtfully.

The old figure seemed to have exhausted itself—its energies, what there were of them—in the effort of making the unintelligible communication already vouchsafed. Then he seemed to lapse out of consciousness, and not to know what was passing, or to be sensible that any person was near him. But Redclyffe was now resuming his firmness and daylight consciousness even in the dimness. He ran over all that he had heard of the legend of the old house, rapidly considering whether there might not be something of fact in the legend of the undying old man; whether, as told or whispered in the chimney-corners, it might not be an instance of the mysterious, the half-spiritual mode, in which actual truths communicate themselves imperfectly through a medium that gives them the aspect of falsehood. Something in the atmosphere of the house made its inhabitants and neighbors dimly aware that there was a secret resident; it was by a language not audible, but of impression; there could not be such a secret in its recesses, without making itself sensible. This legend of the undying one translated it to vulgar apprehension. He remembered those early legends, told by the Doctor, in his childhood; he seemed imperfectly and doubtfully to see what was their true meaning, and how, taken aright, they had a reality, and were the craftily concealed history of his own wrongs, sufferings, and revenge. And this old man! who was he? He joined the Warden's account of the family to the Doctor's legends. He could not believe, or take thoroughly in, the strange surmise to which they led him; but, by an irresistible impulse, he acted on it.

"Sir Edward Redclyffe!" he exclaimed.

"Ha! who speaks to me?" exclaimed the old man, in a startled voice, like one who hears himself called at an unexpected moment.

"Sir Edward Redclyffe," repeated Redclyffe, "I bring you news of Norman Oglethorpe!" [Endnote: 3.]

"The villain! the tyrant! mercy! mercy! save me!" cried the old man, in most violent emotion of terror and rage intermixed, that shook his old frame as if it would be shaken asunder. He stood erect, the picture of ghastly horror, as if he saw before him that stern face that had thrown a blight over his life, and so fearfully avenged, from youth to age, the crime that he had committed. The effect, the passion, was too much, — the terror with which it smote, the rage that accompanied it, blazed up for a moment with a fierce flame, then flickered and went out. He stood tottering; Redclyffe put out his hand to support him; but he sank down in a heap on the floor, as if a thing of dry bones had been suddenly loosened at the joints, and fell in a rattling heap. [Endnote: 4.]

CHAPTER XXV

Redclyffe, apparently, had not communicated to his agent in London his change of address, when he left the Warden's residence to avail himself of the hospitality of Braithwaite Hall; for letters arrived for him, from his own country, both private and with the seal of state upon them; one among the rest that bore on the envelope the name of the President of the United States. The good Warden was impressed with great respect for so distinguished a signature, and, not knowing but that the welfare of the Republic (for which he had an Englishman's contemptuous interest) might be involved in its early delivery at its destination, he determined to ride over to Braithwaite Hall, call on his friend, and deliver it with his own hand. With this purpose, he mounted his horse, at the hour of his usual morning ride, and set forth; and, before reaching the village, saw a figure before him which he recognized as that of the pensioner. [Endnote: 1.]

"Soho! whither go you, old friend?" said the Warden, drawing his bridle as he came up with the old man.

"To Braithwaite Hall, sir," said the pensioner, who continued to walk diligently on; "and I am glad to see your honor (if it be so) on the same errand."

"Why so?" asked the Warden. "You seem much in earnest. Why should my visit to Braithwaite Hall be a special cause of rejoicing?"

"Nay," said the pensioner, "your honor is specially interested in this young American, who has gone thither to abide; and when one is in a strange country he needs some guidance. My mind is not easy about the young man."

"Well," said the Warden, smiling to himself at the old gentleman's idle and senile fears, "I commend your diligence on behalf of your friend."

He rode on as he spoke, and deep in one of the woodland paths he saw the flutter of a woman's garment, and, greatly to his surprise, overtook Elsie, who seemed to be walking along with great rapidity, and, startled by the approach of hoofs behind her, looked up at him, with a pale cheek.

"Good morning, Miss Elsie," said the Warden. "You are taking a long walk this morning. I regret to see that I have frightened you."

"Pray, whither are you going?" said she.

"To the Hall," said the Warden, wondering at the abrupt question.

"Ah, sir," exclaimed Elsie, "for Heaven's sake, pray insist on seeing Mr. Redclyffe,—take no excuse. There are reasons for it."

"Certainly, fair lady," responded the Warden, wondering more and more at this injunction from such a source. "And when I see this fascinating gentleman, pray what message am I to give him from Miss Elsie,—who, moreover, seems to be on the eve of visiting him in person?"

"See him! see him! Only see him!" said Elsie, with passionate earnestness, "and in haste! See him now!"

She waved him onward as she spoke; and the Warden, greatly commoted for the nonce, complied with the maiden's fantasy so far as to ride on at a quicker pace, uneasily marvelling at what could have aroused this usually shy and reserved girl's nervousness to such a pitch. The incident served at all events to titillate his English sluggishness; so that he approached the avenue of the old Hall with a vague expectation of something that had happened there, though he knew not of what nature it could possibly be. However, he rode round to the side entrance, by which horsemen generally entered the house, and, a groom approaching to take his bridle, he alighted and approached the door. I know not whether it were anything more than the glistening moisture common in an English autumnal morning; but so it was, that the trace of the Bloody Footstep seemed fresh, as if it had been that very night imprinted anew, and the crime made all over again, with fresh guilt upon somebody's soul.

When the footman came to the door, responsive to his ring, the Warden inquired for Mr. Redclyffe, the American gentleman.

"The American gentleman left for London, early this morning," replied the footman, in a matter-of-fact way.

"Gone!" exclaimed the Warden. "This is sudden; and strange that he should go without saying good by. Gone," and then he remembered the old pensioner's eagerness that the Warden should come here, and Elsie's strange injunction that he should insist on seeing Redclyffe. "Pray, is Lord Braithwaite at home?"

"I think, sir, he is in the library," said the servant, "but will see; pray, sir, walk in."

He returned in a moment, and ushered the Warden through passages with which he was familiar of old, to the library, where he found Lord

Braithwaite sitting with the London newspaper in his hand. He rose and welcomed his guest with great equanimity.

To the Warden's inquiries after Redclyffe, Lord Braithwaite replied that his guest had that morning left the house, being called to London by letters from America; but of what nature Lord Braithwaite was unable to say, except that they seemed to be of urgency and importance. The Warden's further inquiries, which he pushed as far as was decorous, elicited nothing more than this; and he was preparing to take his leave,—not seeing any reason for insisting (according to Elsie's desire) on the impossibility of seeing a man who was not there,—nor, indeed, any reason for so doing. And yet it seemed very strange that Redclyffe should have gone so unceremoniously; nor was he half satisfied, though he knew not why he should be otherwise.

"Do you happen to know Mr. Redclyffe's address in London," asked the Warden.

"Not at all," said Braithwaite. "But I presume there is courtesy enough in the American character to impel him to write to me, or both of us, within a day or two, telling us of his whereabouts and whatabouts. Should you know, I beg you will let me know; for I have really been pleased with this gentleman, and should have been glad could he have favored me with a somewhat longer visit."

There was nothing more to be said; and the Warden took his leave, and was about mounting his horse, when he beheld the pensioner approaching the house, and he remained standing until he should come up.

"You are too late," said he, as the old man drew near. "Our friend has taken French leave."

"Mr. Warden," said the old man solemnly, "let me pray you not to give him up so easily. Come with me into the presence of Lord Braithwaite."

The Warden made some objections; but the pensioner's manner was so earnest, that he soon consented; knowing that the strangeness of his sudden return might well enough be put upon the eccentricities of the pensioner, especially as he was so well known to Lord Braithwaite. He accordingly again rang at the door, which being opened by the same stolid footman, the Warden desired him to announce to Lord Braithwaite that the Warden and a pensioner desired to see him. He soon returned, with a request that they would walk in, and ushered them again to the library, where they found the master of the house in conversation with Omskirk at one end of the apartment,—a whispered conversation, which detained him a moment, after their arrival. The Warden fancied that he saw in old Omskirk's countenance a shade more of that mysterious horror which made him such a bugbear to children; but when Braithwaite turned from him and approached his visitor, there was no trace of any disturbance, beyond a natural surprise to see his good friend the Warden so soon after his taking leave. [Endnote: 2.]

"I see you are surprised," said the latter. "But you must lay the blame, if any, on our good old friend here, who, for some reason, best known to himself, insisted on having my company here."

Braithwaite looked to the old pensioner, with a questioning look, as if good-humoredly (yet not as if he cared much about it) asking for an explanation. As Omskirk was about leaving the room, having remained till this time, with that nervous look which distinguished him gazing towards the party, the pensioner made him a sign, which he obeyed as if compelled to do so.

"Well, my friend," said the Warden, somewhat impatient of the aspect in which he himself appeared, "I beg of you, explain at once to Lord Braithwaite why you have brought me back in this strange way."

"It is," said the pensioner quietly, "that in your presence I request him to allow me to see Mr. Redclyffe."

"Why, my friend," said Braithwaite, "how can I show you a man who has left my house, and whom in the chances of this life, I am not very likely to see again, though hospitably desirous of so doing?"

Here ensued a laughing sort of colloquy between the Warden and Braithwaite, in which the former jocosely excused himself for having yielded to the whim of the pensioner, and returned with him on an errand which he well knew to be futile.

"I have long been aware," he said apart, in a confidential way, "of something a little awry in our old friend's mental system. You will excuse him, and me for humoring him."

"Of course, of course," said Braithwaite, in the same tone. "I shall not be moved by anything the old fellow can say."

The old pensioner, meanwhile, had been as it were heating up, and gathering himself into a mood of energy which those who saw him had never before witnessed in his usually quiet person. He seemed somehow to grow taller and larger, more impressive. At length, fixing his eyes on Lord Braithwaite, he spoke again.

"Dark, murderous man," exclaimed he. "Your course has not been unwatched; the secrets of this mansion are not unknown. For two centuries back, they have been better known to them who dwell afar off than to those resident within the mansion. The foot that made the Bloody Footstep has returned from its long wanderings, and it passes on, straight as destiny, — sure as an avenging Providence, — to the punishment and destruction of those who incur retribution."

"Here is an odd kind of tragedy," said Lord Braithwaite, with a scornful smile. "Come, my old friend, lay aside this vein and talk sense."

"Not thus do you escape your penalty, hardened and crafty one!" exclaimed the pensioner. "I demand of you, before this worthy Warden, access to the secret ways of this mansion, of which thou dost unjustly retain possession. I shall disclose what for centuries has remained hidden, — the ghastly secrets that this house hides."

"Humor him," whispered the Warden, "and hereafter I will take care that the exuberance of our old friend shall be duly restrained. He shall not trouble you again."

Lord Braithwaite, to say the truth, appeared a little flabbergasted and disturbed by these latter expressions of the old gentleman. He hesitated, turned pale; but at last, recovering his momentary confusion and irresolution, he replied, with apparent carelessness: —

"Go wherever you will, old gentleman. The house is open to you for this time. If ever you have another opportunity to disturb it, the fault will be mine."

"Follow, sir," said the pensioner, turning to the Warden; "follow, maiden![Endnote: 3] Now shall a great mystery begin to be revealed."

So saying, he led the way before them, passing out of the hall, not by the doorway, but through one of the oaken panels of the wall, which admitted the party into a passage which seemed to pass through the thickness of the wall, and was lighted by interstices through which shone gleams of light. This led them into what looked like a little vestibule, or circular room, which the Warden, though deeming himself many years familiar with the old house, had never seen before, any more than the passage which led to it. To his surprise, this room was not vacant, for in it sat, in a large old chair, Omskirk, like a toad in its hole, like some wild, fearful creature in its den, and it was now partly understood how this man had the possibility of suddenly disappearing, so inscrutably, and so in a moment; and, when all quest for him was given up, of as suddenly appearing again.

"Ha!" said old Omskirk, slowly rising, as at the approach of some event that he had long expected. "Is he coming at last?"

"Poor victim of another's iniquity," said the pensioner. "Thy release approaches. Rejoice!"

The old man arose with a sort of trepidation and solemn joy intermixed in his manner, and bowed reverently, as if there were in what he heard more than other ears could understand in it.

"Yes; I have waited long," replied he. "Welcome; if my release is come."

"Well," said Lord Braithwaite, scornfully. "This secret retreat of my house is known to many. It was the priest's secret chamber when it was dangerous to be of the old and true religion, here in England. There is no longer any use in concealing this place; and the Warden, or any man, might have seen it, or any of the curiosities of the old hereditary house, if desirous so to do."

"Aha! son of Belial!" quoth the pensioner. "And this, too!"

He took three pieces from a certain point of the wall, which he seemed to know, and stooped to press upon the floor. The Warden looked at Lord Braithwaite, and saw that he had grown deadly pale. What his change of cheer might bode, he could not guess; but, at the pressure of the old pensioner's finger, the floor, or a segment of it, rose like the lid of a box, and discovered a small darksome pair of stairs, within which burned a lamp, lighting it downward, like the steps that descend into a sepulchre.

"Follow," said he, to those who looked on, wondering.

And he began to descend. Lord Braithwaite saw him disappear, then frantically followed, the Warden next, and old Omskirk took his place in the rear, like a man following his inevitable destiny. At the bottom of a winding descent, that seemed deep and remote, and far within, they came to a door, which the pensioner pressed with a spring; and, passing through the space that disclosed itself, the whole party followed, and found themselves in a small, gloomy room. On one side of it was a couch, on which sat Redclyffe; face to face with him was a white-haired figure in a chair.

"You are come!" said Redclyffe, solemnly. "But too late!"

"And yonder is the coffer," said the pensioner. "Open but that; and our quest is ended."

"That, if I mistake not, I can do," said Redclyffe.

He drew forth—what he had kept all this time, as something that might yet reveal to him the mystery of his birth—the silver key that had been found by the grave in far New England; and applying it to the lock, he slowly turned it on the hinges, that had not been turned for two hundred years. All—even Lord Braithwaite, guilty and shame-stricken as he felt— pressed forward to look upon what was about to be disclosed. What were the wondrous contents? The entire, mysterious coffer was full of golden ringlets, abundant, clustering through the whole coffer, and living with elasticity, so as immediately, as it were, to flow over the sides of the coffer, and rise in large abundance from the long compression. Into this—by a miracle of natural production which was known likewise in other cases— into this had been resolved the whole bodily substance of that fair and unfortunate being, known so long in the legends of the family as the Beauty of the Golden Locks. As the pensioner looked at this strange sight,—the lustre of the precious and miraculous hair gleaming and glistening, and seeming to add light to the gloomy room,—he took from his breast pocket another lock of hair, in a locket, and compared it, before their faces, with that which brimmed over from the coffer.

"It is the same!" said he.

"And who are you that know it?" asked Redclyffe, surprised.

"He whose ancestors taught him the secret,—who has had it handed down to him these two centuries, and now only with regret yields to the necessity of making it known."

"You are the heir!" said Redclyffe.

In that gloomy room, beside the dead old man, they looked at him, and saw a dignity beaming on him, covering his whole figure, that broke out like a lustre at the close of day.

APPENDIX

CHAP. I

Note 1. The MS. gives the following alternative openings: "Early in the present century"; "Soon after the Revolution"; "Many years ago."

Note 2. Throughout the first four pages of the MS. the Doctor is called "Ormskirk," and in an earlier draft of this portion of the romance, "Etheredge."

Note 3. Author's note.—"Crusty Hannah is a mixture of Indian and negro."

Note 4. Author's note.—"It is understood from the first that the children are not brother and sister.—Describe the children with really childish traits, quarrelling, being naughty, etc.—The Doctor should occasionally beat Ned in course of instruction."

Note 5. In order to show the manner in which Hawthorne would modify a passage, which was nevertheless to be left substantially the same, I subjoin here a description of this graveyard as it appears in the earlier draft: "The graveyard (we are sorry to have to treat of such a disagreeable piece of ground, but everybody's business centres there at one time or another) was the most ancient in the town. The dust of the original Englishmen had become incorporated with the soil; of those Englishmen whose immediate predecessors had been resolved into the earth about the country churches,—the little Norman, square, battlemented stone towers of the villages in the old land; so that in this point of view, as holding bones and dust of the first ancestors, this graveyard was more English than anything else in town. There had been hidden from sight many a broad, bluff visage of husbandmen that had ploughed the real English soil; there the faces of noted men, now known in history; there many a personage whom tradition told about, making wondrous qualities of strength and courage for him;—all these, mingled with succeeding generations, turned up and battened down again with the sexton's spade; until every blade of grass was human more than vegetable,—for an hundred and fifty years will do this, and so much time, at least, had elapsed since the first little mound was piled up in the virgin soil.

Old tombs there were too, with numerous sculptures on them; and quaint, mossy gravestones; although all kinds of monumental appendages were of a date more recent than the time of the first settlers, who had been content with wooden memorials, if any, the sculptor's art not having then reached New England. Thus rippled, surged, broke almost against the house, this dreary graveyard, which made the street gloomy, so that people did not like to pass the dark, high wooden fence, with its closed gate, that separated it from the street. And this old house was one that crowded upon it, and took up the ground that would otherwise have been sown as thickly with dead as the rest of the lot; so that it seemed hardly possible but that the dead people should get up out of their graves, and come in there to warm themselves. But in truth, I have never heard a whisper of its being haunted."

Note 6. *Author's note.*—"The spiders are affected by the weather and serve as barometers.—It shall always be a moot point whether the Doctor really believed in cobwebs, or was laughing at the credulous."

Note 7. *Author's note.*—"The townspeople are at war with the Doctor.— Introduce the Doctor early as a smoker, and describe.—The result of Crusty Hannah's strangely mixed breed should be shown in some strange way.— Give vivid pictures of the society of the day, symbolized in the street scenes."

CHAP. II

Note 1. *Author's note.*—"Read the whole paragraph before copying any of it."

Note 2. *Author's note.*—"Crusty Hannah teaches Elsie curious needlework, etc."

Note 3. These two children are described as follows in an early note of the author's: "The boy had all the qualities fitted to excite tenderness in those who had the care of him; in the first and most evident place, on account of his personal beauty, which was very remarkable,—the most intelligent and expressive face that can be conceived, changing in those early years like an April day, and beautiful in all its changes; dark, but of a soft expression, kindling, melting, glowing, laughing; a varied intelligence, which it was as good as a book to read. He was quick in all modes of mental exercise; quick and strong, too, in sensibility; proud, and gifted (probably by the circumstances in which he was placed) with an energy which the softness and impressibility of his nature needed.—As for the little girl, all the squalor of the abode served but to set off her lightsomeness and brightsomeness. She was a pale, large-eyed little thing, and it might have been supposed that the air of the house and the contiguity of the burial-place had a bad effect upon her health. Yet I hardly think this could have been the case, for she was of a very airy nature, dancing and sporting through the house as if melancholy had never been made. She took all kinds of childish liberties with the Doctor, and with his pipe, and with everything appertaining to him except his spiders and his cobwebs."—All of which goes to show that Hawthorne first conceived his characters in the mood of the "Twice-Told Tales," and then by meditation solidified them to the inimitable flesh-and-blood of "The House of the Seven Gables" and "The Blithedale Romance."

CHAP. III

Note 1. An English church spire, evidently the prototype of this, and concerning which the same legend is told, is mentioned in the author's "English Mote-Books."

Note 2. Leicester Hospital, in Warwick, described in "Our Old Home," is the original of this charity.

Note 3. Author's note.—"The children find a gravestone with something like a footprint on it."

Note 4. Author's note.—"Put into the Doctor's character a continual enmity against somebody, breaking out in curses of which nobody can understand the application."

CHAP. IV

Note 1. The Doctor's propensity for cobwebs is amplified in the following note for an earlier and somewhat milder version of the character: "According to him, all science was to be renewed and established on a sure ground by no other means than cobwebs. The cobweb was the magic clue by which mankind was to be rescued from all its errors, and guided safely back to the right. And so he cherished spiders above all things, and kept them spinning, spinning away; the only textile factory that existed at that epoch in New England. He distinguished the production of each of his ugly friends, and assigned peculiar qualities to each; and he had been for years engaged in writing a work on this new discovery, in reference to which he had already compiled a great deal of folio manuscript, and had unguessed at resources still to come. With this suggestive subject he interwove all imaginable learning, collected from his own library, rich in works that few others had read, and from that of his beloved University, crabbed with Greek, rich with Latin, drawing into itself, like a whirlpool, all that men had thought hitherto, and combining them anew in such a way that it had all the charm of a racy originality. Then he had projects for the cultivation of cobwebs, to which end, in the good Doctor's opinion, it seemed desirable to devote a certain part of the national income; and not content with this, all public-spirited citizens would probably be induced to devote as much of their time and means as they could to the same end. According to him, there was no such beautiful festoon and drapery for the halls of princes as the spinning of this heretofore despised and hated insect; and by due encouragement it might be hoped that they would flourish, and hang and dangle and wave triumphant in the breeze, to an extent as yet generally undreamed of. And he lamented much the destruction that has heretofore been wrought upon this precious fabric by the housemaid's broom, and insisted upon by foolish women who claimed to be good housewives. Indeed, it was the general opinion that the Doctor's celibacy was in great measure due to the impossibility of finding a woman who would pledge herself to co-operate with him in this great ambition of his life,—that of reducing the world to a cobweb factory; or who would bind herself to let her own drawing-room be ornamented with this kind of tapestry. But there never was a wife precisely fitted for our friend the Doctor, unless it had been Arachne herself, to whom, if she could again have been restored to her female shape, he would doubtless have lost no time in paying his addresses. It was doubtless the having dwelt too long among the musty and dusty clutter and litter of things gone by, that made the Doctor almost a monomaniac on this subject. There were cobwebs in his own brain, and so he saw nothing valuable but cobwebs in the world around him; and deemed that the march of created things, up to this time, had been calculated by foreknowledge to produce them."

Note 2. Author's note.—"Ned must learn something of the characteristics of the Catechism, and simple cottage devotion."

CHAP. V

Note 1. Author's note.—"Make the following scene emblematic of the world's treatment of a dissenter."

Note 2. Author's note.—"Yankee characteristics should be shown in the schoolmaster's manners."

CHAP. VI

Note 1. Author's note.—"He had a sort of horror of violence, and of the strangeness that it should be done to him; this affected him more than the blow."

Note 2. Author's note.—"Jokes occasionally about the schoolmaster's thinness and lightness,—how he might suspend himself from the spider's web and swing, etc."

Note 3. Author's note.—"The Doctor and the Schoolmaster should have much talk about England."

Note 4. Author's note.—"The children were at play in the churchyard."

Note 5. Author's note.—"He mentions that he was probably buried in the churchyard there."

CHAP. VII

Note 1. Author's note.—"Perhaps put this narratively, not as spoken."

Note 2. Author's note.—"He was privately married to the heiress, if she were an heiress. They meant to kill him in the wood, but, by contrivance, he was kidnapped."

Note 3. Author's note.—"They were privately married."

Note 4. Author's note.—"Old descriptive letters, referring to localities as they existed."

Note 5. Author's note.—"There should be symbols and tokens, hinting at the schoolmaster's disappearance, from the first opening of the scene."

CHAP. VIII

Note 1. Author's note.—"They had got up in remarkably good case that morning."

Note 2. Author's note.—"The stranger may be the future master of the Hospital.—Describe the winter day."

Note 3. Author's note.—"Describe him as clerical."

Note 4. Author's note.—"Represent him as a refined, agreeable, genial young man, of frank, kindly, gentlemanly manners."

Note 5. Alternative reading: "A clergyman."

CHAP. IX

Note 1. Author's note.—"Make the old grave-digger a *laudator temporis acti*,—especially as to burial customs."

Note 2. Instead of "written," as in the text, the author probably meant to write "read."

Note 3. The MS. has "delight," but "a light" is evidently intended.

Note 4. Author's note.—"He aims a blow, perhaps with his pipe, at the boy, which Ned wards off."

CHAP. X

Note 1. Author's note. — "No longer could play at quarter-staff with Ned."

Note 2. Author's note. — "Referring to places and people in England: the Bloody Footstep sometimes."

Note 3. In the original the following occurs, but marked to indicate that it was to be omitted: "And kissed his hand to her, and laughed feebly; and that was the last that she or anybody, the last glimpse they had of Doctor Grimshawe alive."

Note 4. Author's notes. — "A great deal must be made out of the spiders, and their gloomy, dusky, flaunting tapestry. A web across the orifice of his inkstand every morning; everywhere, indeed, except across the snout of his brandy-bottle. — Depict the Doctor in an old dressing-gown, and a strange sort of a cap, like a wizard's. — The two children are witnesses of many strange experiments in the study; they see his moods, too. — The Doctor is supposed to be writing a work on the Natural History of Spiders. Perhaps he used them as a blind for his real project, and used to bamboozle the learned with pretending to read them passages in which great learning seemed to be elaborately worked up, crabbed with Greek and Latin, as if the topic drew into itself, like a whirlpool, all that men thought and knew; plans to cultivate cobwebs on a large scale. Sometimes, after overwhelming them with astonishment in this way, he would burst into one of his laughs. Schemes to make the world a cobweb-factory, etc., etc. Cobwebs in his own brain. Crusty Hannah such a mixture of persons and races as could be found only at a seaport. There was a rumor that the Doctor had murdered a former maid, for having, with housewifely instinct, swept away the cobwebs; some said that he had her skeleton in a closet. Some said that he had strangled a wife with web of the great spider." — "Read the description of Bolton Hall, the garden, lawn, etc., Aug. 8, '53. — Bebbington church and churchyard, Aug. 29, '53. — The Doctor is able to love, — able to hate; two great and rare abilities nowadays. — Introduce two pine trees, ivy-grown, as at Lowwood Hotel, July 16, '58. — The family name might be Redclyffe. — Thatched cottage, June 22, '55. — Early introduce the mention of the cognizance of the family, — the Leopard's Head, for instance, in the first part of the romance; the Doctor may have possessed it engraved as coat of arms in a book. — The Doctor shall show Ned, perhaps, a drawing or engraving of the Hospital, with figures of the pensioners in the quadrangle, fitly dressed; and this picture and the figures shall impress themselves strongly on his memory."

The above dates and places refer to passages in the published "English Note-Books."

CHAP. XI

Note 1. *Author's note.*—"Compare it with Spenser's Cave of Despair. Put instruments of suicide there."

Note 2. *Author's note.*—"Once, in looking at the mansion, Redclyffe is struck by the appearance of a marble inserted into the wall, and kept clear of lichens."

Note 3. *Author's note.*—"Describe, in rich poetry, all shapes of deadly things."

CHAP. XII

Note 1. *Author's note.*—"Conferred their best qualities": an alternative phrase for "done their utmost."

Note 2. *Author's note.*—"Let the old man have a beard as part of the costume."

CHAP. XIII

Note 1. *Author's note.*—"Describe him as delirious, and the scene as adopted into his delirium."

Note 2. *Author's note.*—"Make the whole scene very dreamlike and feverish."

Note 3. *Author's note.*—"There should be a slight wildness in the patient's remark to the surgeon, which he cannot prevent, though he is conscious of it."

Note 4. *Author's note.*—"Notice the peculiar depth and intelligence of his eyes, on account of his pain and sickness."

Note 5. *Author's note.*—"Perhaps the recognition of the pensioner should not be so decided. Redclyffe thinks it is he, but thinks it as in a dream, without wonder or inquiry; and the pensioner does not quite acknowledge it."

Note 6. The following dialogue is marked to be omitted or modified in the original MS.; but it is retained here, in order that the thread of the narrative may not be broken.

Note 7. *Author's note.*—"The patient, as he gets better, listens to the feet of old people moving in corridors; to the ringing of a bell at stated periods; to old, tremulous voices talking in the quadrangle; etc., etc."

Note 8. At this point the modification indicated in Note 5 seems to have been made operative: and the recognition takes place in another way.

CHAP. XIV

Note 1. This paragraph is left incomplete in the original MS.

Note 2. The words "Rich old bindings" are interlined here, indicating, perhaps, a purpose to give a more detailed description of the library and its contents.

CHAP. XV

Note 1. Author's note.—"I think it shall be built of stone, however."

Note 2. This probably refers to some incident which the author intended to incorporate in the former portion of the romance, on a final revision.

CHAP. XVI

Note 1. Several passages, which are essentially reproductions of what had been previously treated, are omitted from this chapter. It belongs to an earlier version of the romance.

CHAP. XVII

Note 1. Author's note.—"Redclyffe shows how to find, under the surface of the village green, an old cross."

Note 2. Author's note.—"A circular seat around the tree."

Note 3. The reader now hears for the first time what Redclyffe recollected.

CHAP. XVIII

Note 1. Author's note.—"The dinner is given to the pensioners, as well as to the gentry, I think."

Note 2. Author's note.—"For example, a story of three brothers, who had a deadly quarrel among them more than two hundred years ago for the affections of a young lady, their cousin, who gave her reciprocal love to one of them, who immediately became the object of the deadly hatred of the two others. There seemed to be madness in their love; perhaps madness in the love of all three; for the result had been a plot to kidnap this unfortunate young man and convey him to America, where he was sold for a servant."

CHAP. XIX

Note 1. The following passage, though it seems to fit in here chronologically, is concerned with a side issue which was not followed up. The author was experimenting for a character to act as the accomplice of

Lord Braithwaite at the Hall; and he makes trial of the present personage, Mountford; of an Italian priest, Father Angelo; and finally of the steward, Omskirk, who is adopted. It will be noticed that Mountford is here endowed (for the moment) with the birthright of good Doctor Hammond, the Warden. He is represented as having made the journey to America in search of the grave. This alteration being inconsistent with the true thread of the story, and being, moreover, not continued, I have placed this passage in the Appendix, instead of in the text.

Redclyffe often, in the dim weather, when the prophetic intimations of rain were too strong to allow an American to walk abroad with peace of mind, was in the habit of pacing this noble hall, and watching the process of renewal and adornment; or, which suited him still better, of enjoying its great, deep solitude when the workmen were away. Parties of visitors, curious tourists, sometimes peeped in, took a cursory glimpse at the old hall, and went away; these were the only ordinary disturbances. But, one day, a person entered, looked carelessly round the hall, as if its antiquity had no great charm to him; then he seemed to approach Redclyffe, who stood far and dim in the remote distance of the great room. The echoing of feet on the stone pavement of the hall had always an impressive sound, and turning his head towards the visitant Edward stood as if there were an expectance for him in this approach. It was a middle-aged man—rather, a man towards fifty, with an alert, capable air; a man evidently with something to do in life, and not in the habit of throwing away his moments in looking at old halls; a gentlemanly man enough, too. He approached Redclyffe without hesitation, and, lifting his hat, addressed him in a way that made Edward wonder whether he could be an Englishman. If so, he must have known that Edward was an American, and have been trying to adapt his manners to those of a democratic freedom.

"Mr. Redclyffe, I believe," said he.

Redclyffe bowed, with the stiff caution of an Englishman; for, with American mobility, he had learned to be stiff.

"I think I have had the pleasure of knowing—at least of meeting—you very long ago," said the gentleman. "But I see you do not recollect me."

Redclyffe confessed that the stranger had the advantage of him in his recollection of a previous acquaintance.

"No wonder," said the other, "for, as I have already hinted, it was many years ago."

"In my own country then, of course," said Redclyffe.

"In your own country certainly," said the stranger, "and when it would have required a penetrating eye to see the distinguished Mr. Redclyffe. the representative of American democracy abroad, in the little pale-faced, intelligent boy, dwelling with an old humorist in the corner of a graveyard."

At these words Redclyffe sent back his recollections, and, though doubtfully, began to be aware that this must needs be the young Englishman who had come to his guardian on such a singular errand as to search an old grave. It must be he, for it could be nobody else; and, in truth, he had a sense of his identity,—which, however, did not express itself by anything that he could confidently remember in his looks, manner, or voice,—yet, if anything, it was most in the voice. But the image which, on searching, he found in his mind of a fresh-colored young Englishman, with light hair and a frank, pleasant face, was terribly realized for the worse in this somewhat heavy figure, and coarser face, and heavier eye. In fact, there is a terrible difference between the mature Englishman and the young man who is not yet quite out of his blossom. His hair, too, was getting streaked and sprinkled with gray; and, in short, there were evident marks of his having worked, and succeeded, and failed, and eaten and drunk, and being made largely of beef, ale, port, and sherry, and all the solidities of English life.

"I remember you now," said Redclyffe, extending his hand frankly; and yet Mountford took it in so cold a way that he was immediately sorry that he had done it, and called up an extra portion of reserve to freeze the rest of the interview. He continued, coolly enough, "I remember you, and something of your American errand,—which, indeed, has frequently been in my mind since. I hope you found the results of your voyage, in the way of discovery, sufficiently successful to justify so much trouble."

"You will remember," said Mountford, "that the grave proved quite unproductive. Yes, you will not have forgotten it; for I well recollect how eagerly you listened, with that queer little girl, to my talk with the old governor, and how disappointed you seemed when you found that the grave was not to be opened. And yet, it is very odd. I failed in that mission; and yet there are circumstances that have led me to think that I ought to have succeeded better,—that some other person has really succeeded better."

Redclyffe was silent; but he remembered the strange old silver key, and how he had kept it secret, and the doubts that had troubled his mind then and long afterwards, whether he ought not to have found means to convey it to the stranger, and ask whether that was what he sought. And now here was that same doubt and question coming up again, and he found himself quite as little able to solve it as he had been twenty years ago. Indeed, with the views that had come up since, it behooved him to be cautious, until he knew both the man and the circumstances.

"You are probably aware," continued Mountford,—"for I understand you have been some time in this neighborhood,—that there is a pretended claim, a contesting claim, to the present possession of the estate of Braithwaite, and a long dormant title. Possibly—who knows?—you yourself might have a claim to one or the other. Would not that be a singular coincidence? Have you ever had the curiosity to investigate your parentage with a view to this point?"

"The title," replied Redclyffe, "ought not to be a very strong consideration with an American. One of us would be ashamed, I verily believe, to assume any distinction, except such as may be supposed to indicate personal, not hereditary merit. We have in some measure, I think, lost the feeling of the past, and even of the future, as regards our own lines of descent; and even as to wealth, it seems to me that the idea of heaping up a pile of gold, or accumulating a broad estate for our children and remoter descendants, is dying out. We wish to enjoy the fulness of our success in life ourselves, and leave to those who descend from us the task of providing for themselves. This tendency is seen in our lavish expenditure, and the whole arrangement of our lives; and it is slowly—yet not very slowly, either—effecting a change in the whole economy of American life."

"Still," rejoined Mr. Mountford, with a smile that Redclyffe fancied was dark and subtle, "still, I should imagine that even an American might recall so much of hereditary prejudice as to be sensible of some earthly advantages in the possession of an ancient title and hereditary estate like this. Personal distinction may suit you better,—to be an Ambassador by your own talent; to have a future for yourself, involving the possibility of ranking (though it were only for four years) among the acknowledged sovereigns of the earth;—this is very good. But if the silver key would open the shut up secret to-day, it might be possible that you would relinquish these advantages."

Before Redclyffe could reply, (and, indeed, there seemed to be an allusion at the close of Mountford's speech which, whether intended or not, he knew not how to reply to,) a young lady entered the hall, whom he was at no loss, by the colored light of a painted window that fell upon her, translating her out of the common daylight, to recognize as the relative of the pensioner. She seemed to have come to give her fanciful superintendence to some of the decorations of the hall; such as required woman's taste, rather than the sturdy English judgment and antiquarian knowledge of the Warden. Slowly following after her came the pensioner himself, leaning on his staff and looking up at the old roof and around him with a benign composure, and himself a fitting figure by his antique and venerable appearance to walk in that old hall.

"Ah!" said Mountford, to Redclyffe's surprise, "here is an acquaintance—two acquaintances of mine."

He moved along the hall to accost them; and as he appeared to expect that Redclyffe would still keep him company, and as the latter had no reason for not doing so, they both advanced to the pensioner, who was now leaning on the young woman's arm. The incident, too, was not unacceptable to the American, as promising to bring him into a more available relation with her—whom he half fancied to be his old American acquaintance—than he had yet succeeded in obtaining.

"Well, my old friend," said Mountford, after bowing with a certain measured respect to the young woman, "how wears life with you? Rather, perhaps, it does not wear at all; you being so well suited to the life around you, you grow by it like a lichen on a wall. I could fancy now that you have walked here for three hundred years, and remember when King James of blessed memory was entertained in this hall, and could marshal out all the ceremonies just as they were then."

"An old man," said the pensioner, quietly, "grows dreamy as he wanes away; and I, too, am sometimes at a loss to know whether I am living in the past or the present, or whereabouts in time I am,—or whether there is any time at all. But I should think it hardly worth while to call up one of my shifting dreams more than another."

"I confess," said Redclyffe, "I shall find it impossible to call up this scene—any of these scenes—hereafter, without the venerable figure of this, whom I may truly call my benefactor, among them. I fancy him among them from the foundation,—young then, but keeping just the equal step with their age and decay,—and still doing good and hospitable deeds to those who need them."

The old man seemed not to like to hear these remarks and expressions of gratitude from Mountford and the American; at any rate, he moved away with his slow and light motion of infirmity, but then came uneasily back, displaying a certain quiet restlessness, which Redclyffe was sympathetic enough to perceive. Not so the sturdier, more heavily moulded Englishman, who continued to direct the conversation upon the pensioner, or at least to make him a part of it, thereby bringing out more of his strange characteristics. In truth, it is not quite easy for an Englishman to know how to adapt himself to the line feelings of those below him in point of station, whatever gentlemanly deference he may have for his equals or superiors.

"I should like now, father pensioner," said he, "to know how many steps you may have taken in life before your path led into this hole, and whence your course started."

"Do not let him speak thus to the old man," said the young woman, in a low, earnest tone, to Redclyffe. He was surprised and startled; it seemed like a voice that has spoken to his boyhood.

Note 2. Author's note.—"Redclyffe's place is next to that of the proprietor at table."

Note 3. Author's note.—"Dwell upon the antique liveried servants somewhat."

Note 4. Author's note.—"The rose-water must precede the toasts."

Note 5. Author's note.—"The jollity of the Warden at the feast to be noticed; and afterwards explain that he had drunk nothing."

Note 6. Author's note.—"Mention the old silver snuffbox which I saw at the Liverpool Mayor's dinner."

CHAP. XX

Note 1. This is not the version of the story as indicated in the earlier portion of the romance. It is there implied that Elsie is the Doctor's granddaughter, her mother having been the Doctor's daughter, who was ruined by the then possessor of the Braithwaite estates, and who died in consequence. That the Doctor's scheme of revenge was far deeper and more terrible than simply to oust the family from its possessions, will appear further on.

Note 2. The foregoing passage was evidently experimental, and the author expresses his estimate of its value in the following words,—"What unimaginable nonsense!" He then goes on to make the following memoranda as to the plot. It should be remembered, however, that all this part of the romance was written before the American part.

"Half of a secret is preserved in England; that is to say, in the particular part of the mansion in which an old coffer is hidden; the other part is carried to America. One key of an elaborate lock is retained in England, among some old curiosities of forgotten purpose; the other is the silver key that Redclyffe found beside the grave. A treasure of gold is what they expect; they find a treasure of golden locks. This lady, the beloved of the Bloody Footstep, had been murdered and hidden in the coffer on account of jealousy. Elsie must know the baselessness of Redclyffe's claims, and be loath to tell him, because she sees that he is so much interested in them. She has a paper of the old Doctor's revealing the whole plot,—a death-bed confession; Redclyffe having been absent at the time."

The reader will recollect that this latter suggestion was not adopted: there was no death-bed confession. As regards the coffer full of golden locks, it was suggested by an incident recorded in the "English Note-Books," 1854. "The grandmother of Mrs. O'Sullivan died fifty years ago, at the age of twenty-eight. She had great personal charms, and among them a head of beautiful chestnut hair. After her burial in a family tomb, the coffin of one of her children was laid on her own, so that the lid seems to have decayed, or been broken from this cause; at any rate, this was the case when the tomb was opened, about a year ago. The grandmother's coffin was then found to be filled with beautiful, glossy, living chestnut ringlets, into which her whole substance seems to have been transformed, for there was nothing else but these shining curls, the growth of half a century, in the tomb. An old man, with a ringlet of his youthful mistress treasured in his heart, might be supposed to witness this wonderful thing."

CHAP. XXIII

Note 1. In a study of the plot, too long to insert here, this new character of the steward is introduced and described. It must suffice to say, in this place, that he was intimately connected with Dr. Grimshawe, who had resuscitated him after he had been hanged, and had thus gained his gratitude and secured his implicit obedience to his wishes, even twenty years after his (Grimshawe's) death. The use the Doctor made of him was to establish him in Braithwaite Hall as the perpetual confidential servant of the owners thereof. Of course, the latter are not aware that the steward is acting in Grimshawe's interest, and therefore in deadly opposition to their own. Precisely what the steward's mission in life was, will appear here-after.

The study above alluded to, with others, amounting to about a hundred pages, will be published as a supplement to a future edition of this work.

CHAP. XXIV

Note 1. Author's note.—"Redclyffe lies in a dreamy state, thinking fantastically, as if he were one of the seven sleepers. He does not yet open his eyes, but lies there in a maze."

Note 2. Author's note.—"Redclyffe must look at the old man quietly and dreamily, and without surprise, for a long while."

Note 3. Presumably the true name of Doctor Grimshawe.

Note 4. This mysterious prisoner, Sir Edward Redclyffe, is not, of course, the Sir Edward who founded the Hospital, but a descendant of that man, who ruined Doctor Grimshawe's daughter, and is the father of Elsie. He had been confined in this chamber, by the Doctor's contrivance, ever since, Omskirk being his jailer, as is foreshadowed in Chapter XL He has been kept in the belief that he killed Grimshawe, in a struggle that took place between them; and that his confinement in the secret chamber is voluntary on his own part,—a measure of precaution to prevent arrest and execution for murder. In this miserable delusion he has cowered there for five and thirty years. This, and various other dusky points, are partly elucidated in the notes hereafter to be appended to this volume.

CHAP. XXV

Note 1. At this point, the author, for what reason I will not venture to surmise, chooses to append this gloss: "Bubble-and-Squeak!"

Note 2. Author's note.—"They found him in the hall, about to go out."

Note 3. Elsie appears to have joined the party.